Caroline Johnson

Also by Robert Clark

The Solace of Food

River of the West

In the Deep Midwinter

My Grandfather's House

Love Among the Ruins

Additional Praise for *Mr. White's Confession*

"Robert Clark has written a book that is instantly familiar and continually surprising, a meditation on memory, love, and loss, wrapped in the wrinkled suit of a classic American genre."

—James Lileks, *Star Tribune* (Minneapolis)

"A suspenseful page-turner and a surprisingly touching character study . . . [*Mr. White's Confession* is an] atmospheric rumination on good, evil, and the murky area in between."   —Steven Jenkins, *Detour*

"In Herbert White, Clark has both drawn a fascinating character and injected new ambiguity into a standard plot. . . . Clark gives this story the vividness of film, the immediacy of theater, and the depth that only a novel can achieve."   —David Bradley, *The News & Observer*

"You can almost feel the grit under your fingers as you turn the pages."

—Lois Blinkhorn, *Milwaukee Journal Sentinel*

"A gently, powerfully moving demonstration of the ways, as White concludes, that 'we are but a memory enfleshed by love.'"

—*Kirkus Reviews*

MR. WHITE'S CONFESSION

Robert Clark

PICADOR
NEW YORK

For Andrew Griggs Clark

ecce quantum spatiatus sum in memoria mea quaerens te domine et non te inveni extra eam ❧ neque enim aliquid de te invenio quod non meminissem ex quo didici te ❧ nam ex quo didici te, non sum oblitus tui ❧ ubi enim inveni veritatem ibi inveni deum meum ipsam veritatem quam ex quo didici non sum oblitus ❧ itaque ex quo te didici manes in memoria mea et illic te invenio cum reminiscor tui et delector in te ❧ hae sunt sanctae deliciae meae quas donasti mihi misericordia tua respiciens paupertatem meam

—Saint Augustine, *Confessions*, X:xxiv

PART I

CITY OF THE WORLD

THE FIRST TIME WESLEY HORNER SAW HIM WAS AT THE White Castle near Seven Corners, where Wesley was drinking coffee with his partner. He sat, balding and rotund, on his stool, like an egg in an eggcup, and ate three hamburgers, removing the pickle slices and stacking them on the saucer of his coffee cup. He ate slowly, delicately. His hands were fine but fleshy, the fingers arching as they took up the last hamburger, the coffee cup, and then the homburg from the counter. Then he rose, bobbing heavily, steadily upward, like wreckage surfacing on the sea, nodded to the waitress, and laid a quarter down, shyly waving away his change. He gathered up his parcels—a sack from the St. Paul Book & Stationery Company and a flat, rectangular Kodak-yellow box—and shambled to the door, his body moving as if in two unsynchronized halves, a donkey cart with mismatched wheels.

Wesley, on his stool, spun himself around to the big plate-glass window and watched him walk down the street toward the base of the hill on which the cathedral sat among the elms, their leaves amber and russet. Then Wesley looked over to his partner. O'Connor rolled his eyes and jerked his head slowly upward in a gesture of lugubrious disdain. "Sheesh," he said. "What a gimp!"

3

"Mighty peculiar," Wesley assented.

"Retard?"

"Maybe. Or a half-wit."

"Pansy?" O'Connor's eyes were big, amused, pressing Wesley for a conclusive judgment.

"Could be, Sergeant, could be," Wesley said wearily, refusing to be drawn. He tugged down on the brim of his fedora as though reckoning with a persistent itch. Then he and O'Connor sat in the window together, looking out, watching.

Wesley shook out the last cigarette from his pack, struck a match on the underside of the stool, and drew the flame to his face and the smoke into his chest. He pulled on his hat brim again, and the brim angled down in line with his long, fierce nose, his incredulous chin, the landslide of his face. Smoke spumed from his nostrils like water from a sluice.

He twisted the empty cigarette pack with his hands until it was taut, and then he threw it on the floor by his feet. He and O'Connor got up to leave, to go out and see what the street and the cooling air of dusk could tell them, and the cigarette pack lay on the oyster-tiled floor and even as they were leaving began to unknot itself with an imperceptible rustle of cellophane, green and writhing like a rupturing cocoon.

Friday, September 29, 1939

I am beginning a journal in this book today. I suppose that is self-evident, but this is how it happened, as best I can recall. After work (Mr. Wright said I could go, that the filing was all done, that there was nothing else for me today) I went to the stationery store to buy a new scrapbook, the same kind I always buy, the Ideal No. 51. The clerk told me they were out and they would be for some time. Needless to say, I was somewhat distraught, for this is the model of scrapbook I have been using since I was ten, since 1914, since the beginning of the Great War. It is no small matter, for this is how I know what has happened to me and to the world. It is my memory, so to speak, since I am not very good at remembering on my own.

In any event, I decided to make the best of a bad lot, and I told the clerk to show me what else they had. I ended up purchasing an Ideal No. 6, a larger model, with a spine strung with black cord and pages that can take nearly a whole newspaper broadsheet without folding. I was so pleased with this purchase that I had the clerk show me some writing books I had noticed, because I thought: Why should I not record a few thoughts and memories myself, rather than rely wholly on the newspaper and magazine clippings? Mr. Wright says I have a fine hand (the last of the copperplates, he calls me) and that I am well-spoken. It is only for myself, although I cannot but hope that as with the scrapbooks, someday what I record might perhaps be of some historical interest in its own small way, rather like the time capsule they have buried at the World's Fair in New York. Surely we are living in exciting times, on the verge of great things!

So I bought the Ideal No. 24, with cream pages ruled in green. The cover is like marble, black and white swirled together like thunderheads and milk, like the top of the washstand in my room at Nanna's. I am going to try to write every day. Nanna said I wrote like Ralph Waldo Emerson, whom we often used to read together. When she tried to enroll me at the Academy, they said I composed English as though it were Latin, which I would have thought a fine thing, since I knew no Latin and still know none. But I am not so sure that the masters at the Academy viewed it that way, or at least they suggested it might be best that I continue to be schooled at home.

After I bought the scrapbook and the writing book, I treated myself to supper at the White Castle. I had coffee and hamburgers, three of them, I think, for even now I am feeling well fed and content.

In the violet dawn light of Saturday morning, her red hair was deep as blue neon, and her skin was silvery white, except at the bottom of her body, where the blood had settled and colored her scarlet and brown and copper green. By the time the police came—alerted by a neighbor who heard the baying of the derelict who'd stumbled across her body in the weeds—a breeze had started up and the sun was full on the hillside. Her rayon dress was gathered up above her waist, and sometimes the hem brushed her neck and slithered in the wind. A garter stay, unsheathed from her stocking, luffed like a ship's pennant and slapped her leg.

Wesley and O'Connor came about ten o'clock, crunching through the dry grass and shattered leaves and blasted milkweed pods to the level spot where she lay. The coroner, Dr. Nash, was there with two patrolmen. He was kneeling on the ground and holding her chin, turning her face toward him and then away, regarding her neck intently. He stood up and brushed off his knees and looked at Wesley.

"Know anything yet?" Wesley asked. Nash sputtered out a long breath with his lips and wiped his forehead. O'Connor was crouching on his haunches two feet from her body, and he began to sift the dirt and the loose stones with his fingers.

"I don't think she's been here long," Nash said. "Hasn't been dead long, for that matter. Maybe only since early this morning."

"How?"

"How did she die? It looks like she was hit on the side of the head and then throttled." Nash knelt again and drew his finger over the crimson and lavender arc that ran around her neck.

"All done here, or someplace else?"

"I couldn't say. If it was done someplace else, it would have to be close by, given how recently the death must have occurred."

O'Connor stood, holding some rocks in his hand. He gestured up the slope. "You'd have to be pretty strong to carry a dead-weight into here."

"You'd have to be pretty strong to have strangled her in the first place," said Nash. Wesley nodded.

O'Connor held out his hand. "Fossils," he said. "In the rock. Little cylinder-type things with rings around them. And seashells and little horseshoe crab things no bigger than your thumbnail."

"Trilobites," said Nash, and he took one of the rocks from O'Connor's hand. "Caught in the limestone." He gestured around and out, down toward the flat and the river. "All this was under-water, at the bottom of the sea."

Wesley was still looking up to where the street was and to the head of a set of pedestrian steps leading down the hill to another street below. "So she could have been knocked out and strangled and then carried here. He must have used the steps and then cut over to here—too steep to have brought her straight down. And he'd have to be nuts to have carried her all the way *up.*"

"I'd think it goes without saying he was nuts," Nash inter-jected. "I'm assuming when we get her downtown we'll see signs of some kind of sexual violation, judging from the clothes and so forth."

Wesley was still looking out toward the steps, as though watch-ing for someone to descend. "He didn't have to be nuts. I'm not sure they're ever nuts; maybe just evil. In the bone." Wesley stopped for a moment. "Or this is just what they like to do, and it's all very planned and reasonable, like it's a job or a hobby—a pastime, like collecting stamps or something."

"That's an interesting view, Lieutenant Horner," said Nash with a bemused smile.

Wesley turned around to face him. "So we'll come see you around, say, four this afternoon, and you'll know a little more maybe?" Nash nodded.

"Okay," Wesley said, and then he called out to the two patrolmen. "You guys figure out how to get her downtown. I don't see you getting a gurney in here. Use some blankets or something. When she goes downtown with Dr. Nash, one of you stays here with Sergeant O'Connor. Start searching—all around here and up to the street and all along the steps. Maybe you'll find whatever he hit her with. Maybe a handbag, some clothing." Wesley looked down at her body. There was a cordon of tiny ants moving through her hair toward the wound above her ear. "Has she got shoes? No, she doesn't. Why hasn't she got any goddamned shoes? Maybe you'll find the shoes. Or maybe *he's* got the shoes. Anyway, now we know she didn't walk in here, don't we? He carried her. Or she walked in and then he killed her and he took the shoes with him, like a souvenir." He looked around at the patrolmen and at O'Connor and Dr. Nash. "One more thing. Nothing to the papers, not a word. Not until tonight, after the doctor's finished with her and maybe we know who she is."

Saturday, September 30, 1939

Today passed uneventfully although I varied my routine somewhat, leaving the house earlier than usual and walking down the Lawton Steps to catch the Grand Avenue streetcar instead of my regular route. Mr. Wright had me go to the post office and fill some envelopes with some papers. I had an egg salad sandwich for lunch, which I ate in the concourse at Union Station. In the afternoon, on my way home, I went to the camera store and bought some chemicals for the darkroom. It was a sunny, slightly windy day, and I decided to walk all the way home.

On the way, I had the notion to go into the cathedral. I am not a church member—particularly not of the Roman Church, which Nanna always insisted was nothing more than a cult of Irish laborers and superstitious ninnies. But I am always rather moved by the majesty of the building, and there is something of mystery—of perhaps the Orient—in the scent of the incense and the colored light and so forth. Anyway, I made a circuit of the passage running behind the main altar, where there are chapels dedicated to various saints, and on a whim I put a penny in a slot and lit one of those candles that sit in rows on a stand in little red glass jars. I don't really know why I did it, but I thought it could do no harm and perhaps might bring me luck in some form, or at least be a symbol of good intentions. I think my hands shook with some trepidation as I lit the candle, and I made a hasty exit, rather fearing that I might be accosted by one of the priests, who might object to my undertaking a practice reserved for members of the Roman faith or try to entice me into conversion. As I said, I told myself it was harmless at the very worst, and when I thought to myself about my candle, and of all the candles burning in the cathedral and in all the other churches around the world, I could not help but think that that is no small thing, all that light from those candles and the prayers and intentions or just whims that go with them.

I believe the particular chapel I stopped in was dedicated to Saint Anthony of Padua. It had a statue of that saint in it, a monk of some kind holding a child in his arms and, I suppose, of Italian origin. Nanna had an Italian gardener when I was small. I cannot say that he ever carried me in his arms, but I am sure he once pushed me around the garden in his wheelbarrow.

When I got home, I made myself a can of Hormel corned beef hash and another of Van Camp's lima beans, and then I worked in the darkroom on some prints from the rolls I took of Ruby from the Aragon Ballroom. Sometimes I notice that I feel very alone in the darkroom. It is quite dark, of course, and it is easy there to feel like a child shut in a closet, afraid of spooks. And of course when I look at a negative projected on the enlarger easel, with everything reversed, the people look like monsters and ghosts and it is not so hard to believe that I am looking at something real, at how things really are inside themselves, all ugly and inverted and just the opposite of how they normally seem. But then I become aware of my radio playing out in the hall, and I can hear the voices of the men, deep like Grandfather's, and the women, like birdsong, and I see the sliver of light under the doorway, and I know that I am inside my home and that what I see on the easel are only shadows—what things are before they are—and not how things truly are or ever shall be. For that comes about through the light of the enlarger onto the empty surface of the photographic paper and then in the tray where I watch the images become themselves like candles taking flame.

Afterward, I worked on my scrapbook and my collections, and now, before I go to my bed, I am writing this and thinking how really very fine and good everything is.

That afternoon Wesley went to see Dr. Nash at the morgue on Hill Street, down by the tracks by the river. Nash was sitting at a little oak desk in a room with green and black tile and tall frosted windows set above eye level. There were two steel tables, shallowly recessed, with a drain at either end, and on one of them there was a body, covered with a faded light-green sheet.

Wesley sat down at the desk and set his hat on the corner next to the telephone. "That her?" he asked Nash.

Nash said, "Yes. I'm done. Just waiting for you to come before I put her in the cooler."

"And?"

"Not so fast, Lieutenant." Nash took a pony of rye whiskey and two glasses from the desk drawer. "It's been a long day. Have a drink."

Wesley seemed to think for a minute. "Can I smoke?"

"I don't think anyone here's going to object."

"Okay, give me a drink. Can't drink without a smoke."

Wesley lit a cigarette and Nash poured two shots. They drank. Wesley exhaled. "So?" he said.

"She was a fine healthy girl. Probably not much over twenty-five. No other trauma than what we saw on the bluff. That surprised me."

"She hadn't been . . ."

"Violated? There was semen, yes. But no sign of force."

"But she was with someone close to the time of death?"

"Oh, yes. Quite fresh. Deposited at the entrance to the vagina, though, rather than well inside."

"So?" Wesley waved his cigarette and glanced around as though looking for an ashtray. "I can't put this on the floor. . . ."

"No, I wouldn't like that," Nash said, and pushed a kidney-shaped enamel dish across the desk toward him. "Anyway, the semen. The placement's consistent with rape, but there's no sign of force, as I said, no struggle, no fighting. So I'd guess it was just garden-variety premature ejaculation. That's Krafft-Ebing lingo for—"

"Johnny on the spot?"

"Exactly."

"So she had sex with him and then he killed her," Wesley said. "Unless she had sex with one guy and then met the killer after. Get any sense that she might be a hooker? Clap scars, stuff like that?"

"No. She wore a fair amount of makeup. But more in a theatrical way than anything cheap or lurid. She was a pretty girl, you know."

Wesley nodded. "So they do it, and then maybe they fight. But he doesn't slap her around. He just knocks her out and kills her. Cool as a cucumber."

"So you see it as premeditated."

"How else is there to see it?"

"Maybe it wasn't planned. Maybe he just did it. He makes love to her and then he feels sad. He feels remorse."

"So he kills her to cheer himself up?"

Nash looked annoyed. "No; because he can't bear what he's done."

"He screws a pretty, willing girl and he can't bear it?"

"Sometimes beauty is unbearable. It makes you sad. Sometimes people are sad after they make love," Nash said. "It's something poets have written about."

"This guy was no poet. Just a cold-blooded bastard."

"Well, I've given up trying to fathom the human heart. I've seen too many. I've seen too much."

"So how do you . . . bear this?" Wesley glanced around the

room. The ceiling was high, with transparent bulbs dangling from it on braided cords.

"Oh, this. This isn't unbearable."

"Takes a strong stomach, I'd guess."

Nash shrugged. "It's just life. Or what comes after. The residue. The footprints. That's why they call it pathology, my med school professor used to say. You're just following their path, trying to figure out which way they went, how they died." He unscrewed the pony and lapped what was left in it into their glasses. "That's how you lose your disgust, your fear of this. People think a body dead is really the same thing as a body alive, that it's still someone. But that's exactly what it lacks—being someone—and every second it's disintegrating, coming apart, being less and less, until it's nothing at all but some dust. So I can bear this. It makes me sad to think of the person a corpse used to be. Examining them, touching, I get intimations of who they were, or at least how they must have looked or maybe even moved, intimations of their beauty and their sufferings and all the rest that the body still carries."

Wesley shook his head and then he nodded. "I should go. We need an identification. Someone ought to be missing her by now."

Nash stood. "Do you want to see her? Before you go?"

"Okay."

Nash's shoes clicked and scuffed over the linoleum to the steel table, and he lifted the sheet and pulled it down. Wesley waved his hand as though fending off a blow. "You don't need to do that . . . ," he said.

"It's okay, Lieutenant. She's not anyone anymore. You can't embarrass her."

The girl's skin had grown darker, mottled as though the copper-green color was slowly wicking up through the rest of her body.

Her breasts were small and freckled, her fingers curled loosely, her lips gapped and a sliver apart. Nash touched her head. "Beautiful hair," he said.

But for the ring of purple around her neck and the wound above her ear, she might have been asleep, Wesley thought, but very, very cold. Her pallor was like a sheen of oil refracting a dozen shades of violet and indigo and green tending to orange as she darkened, as her body gave up the last of its heat. It was as if she were still dying and would be dying for a very long time, until she was dark and icy as a cinder. That was what Wesley saw, what he was watching happen. Every few moments he would find his eyes skittering uncontrolled down to her waist, drawn to the flame of her pubic hair, the lips that cleaved her mons, the well of sorrows and trouble that had brought her here. Wesley wanted to see her as a child, a frozen, drowned child, but his eyes wouldn't let him.

"You can cover her up," he said. Nash was standing absent-mindedly opposite Wesley, his fingers splayed like a pianist's on the table, next to the girl's shoulder. He looked down and then at Wesley with an expression like pity, not for the girl but in some way for Wesley himself. Then he drew the sheet up from the girl's feet and smoothed it with the flat of his hand over her head.

Nash expected Wesley would say something about the disposition of the body between now and the time when, presumably, somebody would step forward to identify and claim it. But instead he went back to Nash's desk and picked up his hat and turned and faced Nash, holding the hat in front of his waist, and said, "I had a daughter about her age. She'd be twenty-three now."

"I'm sorry. I didn't know. How long ago was it?" Nash said. "When she . . . ?"

"Oh, we don't know that she's dead. She just disappeared. Or left, or something . . ."

"Or something?"

"It was five years ago. She was supposed to have run off to Chicago with a man from the Hoover vacuum company. Or that was what her best friend thought. But we never heard anything from her, not a word. Never have. Never will, I suppose."

"I'm sorry. Sometimes not knowing seems worse than—"

"Worse than death? Well, it was the death of her mother. Got cancer a year after she'd gone, died a year after that."

"I knew about that. But I'm awfully—"

"You know what I don't understand—about my Louise or that one?" Wesley flung his arm out toward the table, and its shadow hung over the linoleum like a high, thin cloud. "Or any of them. I don't understand what gets into them or why they don't listen to their parents or their teachers or anybody with any sense. It just goes out the window, all for some lover boy or thinking they're going to go out to Hollywood or whatever. Breaking other people's hearts all along the way, without so much as a by-your-leave."

Nash looked as though he were standing very far away. Finally he said, "It's a terrible mystery, isn't it?" and Wesley saw he was still standing next to the girl, with his hand by her head.

Wesley hurried to excuse himself, pulling his hat on and tugging it down front and back with both hands. "Well, we'll let you know when there's an ID," he said, and he pushed through two sets of doors and into the long hallway, hung dimly with white, mushroom-shaped light globes down the center. It seemed to taper to an end in the far distance, and he could hear the echo of his own footsteps bouncing back to meet him, and his heart was a stone of dread he carried heavily before him. Because the truth was that here, in this empty, silent corridor, he could hear the winding down of the world, the guttering of its breath, feel the weight of its inexorable doom descending. It was what parents could not bring themselves to tell their children about. Perhaps if he'd told Louise, had he known then, she would have stayed. But then she could never have forgiven him for bringing her into such a place.

He thought of the girl in the morgue and of her body, and he imagined her alive and all the things women did that she must have done and that were incomprehensible to him; how she might have sat brushing her hair in indolent strokes or painting her toenails, bent like a bird to a nest of fledglings; how her voice, her fingers, her eyebrows, might inflect themselves in a hundred subtleties, faint as prayers; how her dress would hang on her hips, how it might brush the back of her calves. In all this he saw how her beauty in life might have been as unbearable as her beauty in death and that even reduced to a naked corpse, marbled with cold and congealing blood, prodded and assayed by coroners and detectives, she remained unknowable, as lost to his ken as Louise. And although it was not an answer to any of the things he had been thinking about, he found himself speaking to the dead girl, saying, "For your sake, I'll find the bastard that did this."

He was on the street and almost to his car when he was accosted by a man in a fedora and a suit with huge, pointed lapels. It was Farrell from the *Dispatch*, and Wesley did not want to deal with him, not now.

Farrell smiled narrowly at Wesley, as though he'd caught him in a fib. "I hear you guys have something down here, something you're sitting on."

"I can't say anything. Not now. Not yet."

"You ought to fess up," Farrell said, and he held his palm up and regarded it as though he could see the dead girl's face in it. "They say confession is good for the soul."

"I can't give you anything. There's things we don't know, people that have to be told. In the right way."

"I hear a capital crime's been committed. I'd say the public had a right to know."

"I can't help you, Farrell. I'm sorry."

Farrell frowned as though he'd been disappointed over what was a reasonable and inconsequential request. "Well, Lieutenant, I'm sorry. But I can't stop my editor from doing what he feels is right by the public, can I?"

Wesley exhaled tightly through his lips. "Look, Farrell. Give me until lunchtime tomorrow. Then I'll tell you everything we have."

"Me and everybody else, I suppose."

"Okay, okay. I'll hold the others off until five o'clock. It'll be all yours for the afternoon editions. That sound fair?"

"Fair enough. I'll see you at noon at your desk. Just the two of us."

Wesley nodded and watched Farrell stroll away with his hands in his pockets. Then Wesley slid into his car, bone weary. He lit a cigarette and sat with the windows rolled up, lost in the veils and palls of smoke.

Sunday, October 1, 1939

Today I went to the pictures at the Paramount. The show was *City of the World*, with Veronica Galvin, who is undoubtedly my favorite actress. The newsreel was about nothing but the new war in Europe and whether we shall be drawn into it, President Roosevelt's assurances to the contrary. But that was all as nothing once the picture began. I consumed an entire roll of Necco wafers without so much as a thought, so caught up was I in the picture and so enraptured by Miss Galvin. She is, of course, a splendid actress, but I think it is her hair—which I gather from the magazines is auburn—that I find most compelling, the way it drapes her face and swings when she whirls around and says something passionate or tips her head forward to hide her eyes.

I was going to stop and have an ice cream sundae at the fountain at the Rexall on the way home, but I felt compelled to rush back and record my thoughts here. It has occurred to me that I might kill two birds with one stone by writing directly to Miss Galvin—as I felt moved to do in any case—and composing the first draft here on these pages. I have written Miss Galvin before, and received a kind note and a signed photograph in reply. So here goes:

475 Laurel Avenue

Apartment B

St. Paul, Minnesota

Miss Veronica Galvin

Pantheon Pictures, Incorporated

Hollywood, California

Dear Miss Galvin,

I have written you before, so perhaps you will recall my name. In any case, I have just returned from seeing *City of the World* and was instantly moved to take up my pen and tell you how superb was your performance in the role of Kit O'Dea. It was not merely a matter of your acting or, of course, your beauty, but of the way you penetrated to the heart of the character and brought out the deeper, philosophical meaning of her lines. I am thinking particularly of the scene just before the climax of the picture, when you say to your costar—and I think I recall the lines accurately—"Don't you see, Johnny, that you can't go on running, running from the G-men, from me, from every good thing we could have together. Because I just want the things every decent girl wants. Johnny, please, just tell me you want them too." Then, when he looks over to the window to see if the G-men have found you yet, and he moves toward the door and you understand that he's leaving, you look up at him and then cast your eyes down and flip your hair and say, "Oh, Johnny, you're such a chump, and I . . . I've been such a fool."

I found this scene extremely moving and meaningful, perhaps because, rather like Kit and Johnny, I've had to find my own way in the world. I don't know if I mentioned this in my previous letter, but I was an orphan. My mother died giving birth to me, and when the war began, in 1914, my father signed up with a Canadian regiment and was killed in Europe. I myself suffer from a few maladies associated with my difficult birth, chiefly having to do with my memory and the coordination of my muscles. I think I am considered a little bit odd.

I mention this not to attract any sympathy but simply to say that I understand that we must make our own way in the world and that we must strive to see the good in it and in our lives and not resign ourselves to despair or cynicism or futility no matter what. When Johnny leaves you and goes up to the top of the peak and fights it out with the G-men who surround him and is gunned down (I must say, it seems to me that this is the fate of many of your leading men—I recall much the same denouement in *Salton Sea* and *Rio Negro*), it is because he does not understand this, unlike your character,

Kit. He seems to believe the world is divided into realms of light and darkness and that he has no choices in it and that love can accomplish nothing in it.

I think this is your finest performance since *To Marry and To Burn,* and I hope you will be acknowledged for it. It is certainly the equal of anything Miss Leigh did in *Gone With the Wind* earlier this year, a picture that I maintain does not speak nearly so well to our current concerns in the world. I hope you will be able to find a few moments to reply to me and perhaps give me your thoughts about these matters. I would be pleased to hear more of your personal philosophy of life, which I suspect may not be dissimilar to my own.

Assuring you of my devoted best wishes,

Yours sincerely,

Herbert W. White

I believe I should stop and copy this out onto letter paper immediately, while I remember to, and then go post it while it is still on my mind. It is a complicated business—I write things down in order to remember them, but then I must remember to read what I've written down. Fortunately, I don't have much of a problem with the things I am working on in the immediate moment or with the events of, say, the last week or so. And I can also recall the events of the distant past with great clarity. It is the middle distance that gives me difficulty—the things that have happened between the previous week and the previous year.

I suppose this failing of my mind would be disconcerting for anyone, but I must say it can also be rather amusing, if seen in the right light. For example, not long ago—I don't recall precisely when—a salesman from the Hoover vacuum cleaner company called on me at home and persuaded me to purchase one of their new upright models, a brown one with a dust bag in fabric rather like Harris tweed. I thought he looked familiar, but I suppose I was carried off by his "sales patter" and general conviviality. He told me that when he returned home to Chicago, he would toast me and my purchase in the bar at the Palmer House Hotel.

After he left, I thought I would put the new vacuum cleaner away in the hall closet. Well, imagine my surprise when I opened the door and beheld an identical vacuum cleaner already there, one I had presumably purchased sometime earlier and forgotten about. I assume that is why the salesman looked familiar. He must be a scoundrel, unless, perhaps, he has the same sort of memory difficulties as me. But if that were the case, I rather doubt he would be able to perform a salesman's duties.

Needless to say, this sort of thing happens with some frequency. Just yesterday I went to the selfsame closet, and when I opened it I found a pair of rather pretty women's shoes there, thrown in the back. I have no idea where they came from—presumably one of the girls I've had over for photography, Ruby or Clare or Gwendolyn. I think perhaps they get lost in their beauty just as I do, and then, like me, forget things.

Farrell leaned his insolent, stilt-skinny ass on Wesley's desk. "So?" he said.

Wesley had a headache, and he was determined to give Farrell the absolute minimum, just enough to make him go away. "I'm afraid we still haven't got much," Wesley said, and put his hands out in front of him, palms up and open.

"Oh, a little goes a long way, Lieutenant Horner."

"We got a missing person report last night. Girl says her roommate's gone missing since two days ago, which fits our case."

"And who's the girl?"

"If we knew, I still couldn't tell you until we'd notified the next of kin."

"Couldn't—or wouldn't?"

Wesley stopped to light a cigarette, paused to hold the smoke in his lungs for a while. He exhaled slowly, like a punctured tire. "Both. Because those are the rules and because I'm not a jerk."

"A cop with a heart. How touching. How rare." Farrell bent down and began to fiddle with his shoelace. "But you could still tell me the name of the roommate, couldn't you? That would be the very least you could do for me, considering what you promised."

"I didn't promise to turn you reptiles loose on this girl. She just went down to ID her friend's body two hours ago, for Christ's sake."

Farrell lifted his foot up next to him on the desk and began to retie his shoe. "Just help me fill in the gaps, and maybe I can leave her out of it."

"Get your slimy Florsheims off my desk."

"Ask nice, Lieutenant."

Wesley looked away, toward the window. He said quietly, "She was a dancer at the Aragon on Wabasha. She had red hair." He looked back at Farrell. "Any dope ought to be able to run her to ground with that much."

Farrell uncoiled his leg and stood up. "It's been a pleasure, Lieutenant."

Wesley stayed in his chair. "Why is it," he said, "that you act like you've got something on me, when I know damn well you don't?"

"Because I could, Lieutenant. It wouldn't take me five minutes. Because, like the book says, none of us is without stain."

"Keep away from the roommate, Farrell. Keep away from the family."

Farrell tugged at the knot of his tie and fanned his hand across the bottom of his double-breasted jacket and the seat of his pants as though brushing away something distasteful. "Much obliged, Lieutenant. For the assistance."

Monday, October 2, 1939

After work—I walked all the way home; it was a fine sunny afternoon with a nip in the air—I updated my scrapbook and I ate a tin of beef stew and three slices of bread. I had fallen two days behind on the scrapbook—there is so much news these days, mainly from Europe and none of it cheering. But despite Poland and France and all the rest, I cannot but continue to believe that the whole world is on the verge of great things. Perhaps it is simply that Europe, as is her wont, must throw herself into one last struggle before the future that is so close is finally in our grasp.

After I ate, I mixed chemicals for the darkroom in the kitchen sink in order to print the last roll I took of Ruby from the Aragon. I opened a fresh box of Velox and set to work, with the radio in the hall tuned to NBC Blue. Working with the lights off—or rather with only the red safe light on—is a strange sensation, like what I imagine being deep under water must be like. And I must say I have imagined that perhaps this is what death might be like, or the passage into death, a kind of blind trudge into the dark.

That is not to say that all my thoughts in the darkroom are so morbid. Sometimes, as I think I have said before, when I see the faces projected in negatives on the enlarger easel, I think they look like ghosts or what I fancy demons might look like or simply the faces of the dead, but that is not the main thing I feel about the darkroom. For it is really about beauty. Tonight I worked on Ruby from the Aragon, and she is undoubtedly a pretty girl with a pretty face, but I am not sure that that is the source of her beauty. I think it is more in her particulars—in all the small things that are commingled in her—than in any one feature or thing that she might possess. For when I was photographing her and now, in the darkroom even more, I see beauty emanating from a hundred tiny places on her body—the crook of her arm where the softest, whitest flesh of the inside of her forearm and upper arm touch; the taper of the back of her thigh where it rises out of the concavity behind her knee; the place above and behind her ear where her hair sweeps around, where the ear nestles; the curl of her toes encased in the curl of her fingers, with her whole body arched over her knees in a whorl, like a nautilus shell.

Those are the places, I believe, where beauty makes its home, and in the darkroom I am shining a light into them. When I am making a print, when I am dodging or burning an exposure, I am gilding them, illuminating them, or protecting the tenderest places from the scald of light, burnishing them with shadow. It is as close as I ever come to touching them, but I am helping them be—or rather become, for a photograph is only a moment of becoming. What finally emerges in the developing tray—and what happens there is itself a kind of becoming—is the face and the body as it never was before and as it never shall be again. I am standing there in the dark, and the chemicals smell of lemon and vinegar and what I imagine the sea smells like (for I have never been to the ocean), and the paper is slippery and shiny in my hands like what I imagine kelp feels like, and the image comes of a sudden, as of a flutter of wings.

Perhaps everything is a little like that. For surely our lives and everything else in creation is mere becoming—we age and the world erodes, and nothing is ever the same for more than a blink of the eye, yielding up one shape and receiving another. And if that is the case, perhaps my memory impairment— which I have always been told and always believed has barred me from so much of life—is not of much consequence. For if we are never fixed—never one thing but a succession of things— what is the loss in being unable to recall one instance of all that becoming? Not so very much, I would venture.

Maybe there is some connection between that and beauty. Because it seems to me that beauty is always a surprise—that we delight in its being unexpected, in its always seeming new—and yet there is always an ache, an apprehension of loss, because we know it is passing, becoming something else even as we behold it. So perhaps in beauty the nature of things—both what they are and what they do—is most apparent to us. And for that, I think the creator, whoever or whatever he may be, must be good. I fancy he made beauty to please himself and for our sake also.

I had stopped writing just now and had gotten up to put my scrapbook upon the shelf and to stack up the newspapers. I saw in tonight's paper that a girl has been killed here in the city. It rather leaves one with a hollow feeling.

Still, I cannot help but think that what I just wrote above must be so, and of course it gives one great hope for the future and also fondness for the past and trust in the present—for per-haps things are, for all their mystery, already as they should be. But right now—from the World's Fair to events in Europe—we are so full of the future. Nothing is; instead everything is immi-nent. It is as though we are on the verge of moving permanently into the future, like moving to a new house. We shall just vacate the present and its wars and diseases and crises and slumps entirely. People talk as if they can simply open the door and step into it. I suppose that would be a very fine thing for me, for if we truly lived in the future, memory would be just a memory and that would be the end of my affliction.

But I wonder if it would be an entirely good thing. For if we cast off this ceaseless becoming and loss and memory and everything that goes with it, perhaps we would lose beauty too. Maybe the future the world is wishing for is a rather dangerous time, and that is part of the hollowness one feels.

Farrell had let the cat out of the bag in last night's paper, albeit without the girl's name. Wesley assumed he had found that out too but was withholding it for a day or two—not out of the goodness of his heart but to produce an additional, separate scoop with which to best his rival reporters. And now what had been an unexplained tragedy, a happenstance without a story, became Wesley's public burden to bear, his responsibility to fix, to untangle, almost as though he were the guilty party. Of course, he wouldn't be a hero if he found the killer, he'd be only a civic functionary about the business of his function; but if he didn't find the killer, he would be a villain or at least a failure.

Wesley sat at his desk thinking these things, or rather letting them settle onto him like a coat he was accustomed to wear, and he arched his fingers and tapped them on the desk as though preparing to set to work, to deal a deck of cards he'd just shuffled.

What he had, in fact, was paper: Nash's report, more tentative than anything he'd told Wesley at the morgue; statements taken yesterday by O'Connor from girls who worked at the Aragon and the guy who ran it; stuff they'd taken from the girl's apartment—

an address book, a photo album, a fat novel, apparently unread, by Thomas Wolfe the girl had used as a sort of accordion file for letters and cards and notes. He leafed through the scrapbook, from the baby pictures at the front to the cheesecake-style things at the back—the roommate had said she'd worked as a model as well as a taxi dancer—and it seemed her eyes were following him, the diaphanous gaze he'd seen at the morgue now sharp, piercing, focused on him.

Wesley hooked his index finger on a page toward the front and put his thumb under the last page and flipped back and forth between them. The earlier photograph was some sort of first communion or confirmation portrait, the girl in a white, lacy dress, maybe twelve years old, her teeth still a little too big for her smile, the smile trying to contain itself for the occasion. In the second, clearly taken quite recently, she sat lengthwise on a fussy, pig-legged Victorian couch, her knees bent, encircled by her arms, her head tilted down, her glance directed to something at the far left side of the picture. She was wearing a long-sleeved, tight-fitting sweater of some kind, a pair of abbreviated shorts, and incongruous high-heeled sandals. Her hair was as it was the morning Wesley found her on the hillside, her lips were painted dark, in a pensive expression whose severity suggested it did not come to her by nature.

Wesley flipped back and forth, and he could have said to himself, "This is what you came to, from this to that and then to Nash's table on Hill Street." But he merely flipped back and forth as though humming little rhymes or rounds to himself: seven/snake eyes, eleven/boxcars, red and black, night and day, dark and light, here and gone, far and away, God and the devil, the girl and—in the dawn on the hill—who?

O'Connor came in, his tie askew and his hat on his head and

his face fixed in a smug grin like a pelt pinned on a wall. "Got a phone call off the *Dispatch* story. Lady who lives at the bottom of the steps says she saw a suspicious character that morning. Early."

"And?"

"And I sent over a patrolman to get the description."

"You don't send anybody anywhere without telling me first," Wesley said. "Fix your tie. Take off your goddamn hat."

"I figured we'd better jump at it. I'm sorry, okay?"

Wesley nodded.

"Anyhow, this isn't your average passerby. She said he was big, kind of chubby, wore a bowler hat or something. And moved funny, like with a limp."

"Christ, another reader. They get this crap out of mystery books. 'The killer had a limp,' for Christ's sake. Go away, Sergeant. I've got a murderer to find."

"No, no. She's for real. She just said he moved funny. Could be a gimpy leg, gimpy back, gimpy arm, any of that stuff."

Wesley was looking at O'Connor's hat, which the sergeant held penitently over his crotch. "And a bowler?"

"Something *like* a bowler."

"And big. Rotund. Like a ball. Like Humpty-Dumpty." Wesley was almost whispering, and his eyes glided toward the ceiling as if he thought it might rain. And then he felt it come down—not rain but a sensation like prickly heat or a shiver, his notion of grace. "I got something," he said, and O'Connor smiled as though he already knew.

Wesley went on deliberately, intently, as though circuiting a billiard table, slowly sinking one shot after the next. "Remember the weird guy in the Seven Corners White Castle? Maybe a week ago?" O'Connor nodded. "Let's find him. Just for fun maybe, but let's find him. See if he's a regular there. And see if he ever hung around the Aragon." Then he waved O'Connor away. "Go. Do it. No, wait." O'Connor spun around, and Wesley pulled the last photograph free from the gummed corners that held it in the dead girl's album. He handed it to O'Connor, and O'Connor began a whistle, which, catching himself, he managed to stifle into something like a plaintive sigh. "See those shoes?" said Wesley. "Go to her place again. See if you can find them there." Then he sent O'Connor away with a flip of his palm.

Wesley was tingling inside, thrumming like high-tension wires. He went back to the papers. He thought he would call Farrell at the *Dispatch* and dole out a little more of what he had, let him feel like a big guy with his hooks into the lead cop on a murder investigation. Then shake the tree a little, see what else the public knew, maybe show Farrell who had who on the line.

Tuesday, October 3, 1939
  Caught up with scrapbook. I do not feel like writing tonight.

"Got him," said O'Connor that evening, almost bashful in his pride. "Goes to White Castle every week at least—has done since they opened. The name is White, Herbert White. Works as a clerk and dogsbody at Griggs-Cooper. I talked to his boss, guy named Wright. Says he's an odd nut—not simpleminded but sort of goofy, absentminded. Same thing with the body. It's like he was born and the mold never quite jelled."

Wesley nodded impatiently, urging O'Connor on with his fingertips.

"Anyhow, he's worked there since he left school. The job was sort of a favor to his family, although they're all passed away. Lives alone in an apartment on Laurel. Got the address right here," said O'Connor, and he patted his breast pocket.

Wesley felt short of breath, as if a little bird was pounding its wings in the back of his throat. "And the Aragon?"

O'Connor grinned. "A guy who looks just like him goes in there regular. But not to dance. Here's the good part: to take pictures. He likes to talk to the girls and take their pictures. I don't know which girls. I have to go back later tonight."

"So he snaps their pictures in the club, with a Brownie or something?" Wesley could scarcely get the words out, hoping he was wrong.

"No. See, he gets them to come to his place. He's got a sort of studio or something, darkroom and all."

"Christ on a crutch," Wesley said. His fingers whirled, fumbling with his cigarette pack. "So you went to the girl's apartment and . . ."

"And those shoes, *they're not there.*" O'Connor chanted the words triumphantly.

Wesley had dug out a cigarette. He struck the match, and the match head caught flame and parted the air with a sound like the opening of a furnace door. "I think maybe after you make a few more inquiries with the ladies at the Aragon, we ought to call on Mr. White. Tomorrow, after he gets home from work. He wouldn't skip town, would he?"

"His boss says he's regular as a clock. Never goes anywhere. Same routine, two suit coats, two hats, goes to the pictures every Sunday like it was church. Creature of habit."

"Still, I don't want to lose him. You check, make sure he's at his place tonight. Same thing in the morning. Then we follow him home from work."

"The captain's got a raid on Shacktown set up tonight. All hands required."

"Christ. Of all the penny-ante malarkey . . ."

"Welshinger's in charge."

"Oh my aching back," muttered Wesley.

Wesley and O'Connor ate supper, coffee and hamburgers, across the street from the Public Safety Building, and then they drove over to the Aragon. Wesley waited in the car while O'Connor went in. He came back a minute later. "The one we need—the one who knows him for sure—isn't here tonight. Name's Ruby Fahey. She'll be back tomorrow."

"What about the others, other girls in there that might know him?"

O'Connor shook his head. "The Jew who runs it says he doesn't know who else knows him for sure. I can go back in and ask around. . . ."

"No. You'd just stir 'em up, cause alarm where we don't want none." Wesley drew on his cigarette and read his watch dial by the glow of the coal. "Time for Welshinger's little jamboree anyway." He jerked his head sideways toward the steering wheel, for O'Connor to get in and drive.

They parked under the trestle a block below Shacktown, as they always did, and waited. After five minutes, a squad car and two other sedans sidled up next to them and parked silently, save for the ratcheting of parking brakes and the dull slams of their doors. Welshinger appeared at O'Connor's window, his face illuminated from below by his flashlight, the cusps of his nostrils glowing a dull translucent crimson. "Well, crimestoppers, ready to clear up some unsolved incidents?" he asked in what he took to be the tone of a radio announcer. An express roared overhead, its headlight corkscrewing through the dark, and left the air singing like a plucked metal string. After the noise died away, he opened O'Connor's door officiously and said, "Please, gentlemen, join us."

Wesley and O'Connor got out, Wesley with a show of evident weariness. They followed Welshinger and five others out from under the trestle and off to the right where the road along the railroad tracks sloped up to the hobo camp and squatters' village they called Shacktown. The frost was settling into the road with the deepening nightfall, and the gravel rang like broken glass under their feet. Welshinger and his partner, Trent, from Vice led the way, their flashlights extinguished. Then came Gundersen and Tyler from Robbery/Burglary and Strunsky and Mills, patrolmen normally assigned to Traffic.

They or some similar assortment of men came here every two or three weeks, usually when the moon was ebbing, always in the dark, laboring up the hill, carrying their truncheons and pipes like hoes to a field. They could see shapes in the distance, fires amid ribbons and shoals of smoke, and smell the piercing odor of sour garbage underlaid by blunt chords of creosote and tar and stale urine. The barren earth, furrowed and torn but devoid of vegetation, was studded with junked railway wheels, springs, bogies, boilers, rods and axles and steam tubes, pallets and crates, capsized flatcars and boxcars, mounds of ash and cinders that fulminated like panting, exhausted beasts in the black night.

Such sounds as there were came dull and echoed from far away: the tolling of hammer blows in the wheelwright's foundry, the clunk and shudder of cars as they coupled and uncoupled in the yards. Welshinger stopped and tilted his head up into the air, as though to smell the cold, and then he began walking again, into the heart of the encampment, speaking and gesticulating as he strolled among the trash and junk. He said to the others, "Let's be quick about this. I've got the Black Maria coming in ten minutes. It'll hold eight, ten in a pinch." He pointed toward a fire next to a boxcar one hundred yards up the slope. "You, Strunsky and Mills, roust that bunch. And let's show some pep here, some craftsmanship, not just a bunch of vagrancies. We've got backlogs to clear. Get me some burglars. I've got burglaries like a faggot's got piles."

Welshinger stopped at an inverted crate with a tiny, smoking fire of green limbs huddled next to it. He turned on his flashlight and aimed it inside. "Well, speak of the devil," he said, and kicked the side of the crate. "You two, out." A ragged, grimy man of indeterminate age slithered out feetfirst, sliding his bottom on the ground and clutching a half-pint bottle of peach brandy. Another man, trying to smile at Welshinger with a mouth full of ruined teeth, crawled out on all fours. Both shivered and blinked, rubbing their eyes as though stunned by the flashlight, by the gleam of Welshinger's black shoes.

"Had your hands in each other's BVDs, didn't you?" Welshinger said, and he spat into the little fire.

The one holding the bottle began, "We wasn't doing nothing, we was just sleeping—"

"Don't tell me what I didn't see, what I saw with my own goddamn eyes," Welshinger bellowed, and the other man began to push his hand nervously through his filthy hair. "Playing with each other's private parts, that's sodomy. You faggots know what that is?"

Both shook their heads. "Well, you do now. That and sucking each other's dicks and cornholing and all that stuff. It's a serious vice charge."

The first man said, "We wasn't doing nothing. We . . . we was just passing this bottle," and the other began to blubber softly.

"I told you not to tell me what I saw," Welshinger said quietly, and plucked the bottle from the man's hand. "I don't need some faggot tramp to learn me the law. I learn *you* the law." He kicked at an empty tin can next to the fire. "This is littering. And this fire is a public nuisance within city limits. And this"—he nudged a rusting coffeepot at the edge of the fire—"is operating a kitchen without proper health and fire permits." Welshinger held the bottle in his palm and regarded the label. "And this, for Christ's sake, is an open container in the furtherance of public drunkenness," and he grasped the bottle by its neck and swung into the first man's temple.

The man fell to the earth with a wail, and Welshinger snapped his black shoe into the man's side. "Now I'm learning you the law, aren't I?" The man whimpered, and the other man began to shake and shuffle his feet. Welshinger regarded him with a narrow smile. "Quit fidgeting, or I'll have you for operating a dance hall without a license." He turned to Trent and Wesley and O'Connor, who had been silently watching. "Gentlemen, I need to have a confidential interrogation of these suspects. Why don't you see what you can round up while I deal with that?"

Trent nodded, and the three ambled away, Trent's hands in his pockets. He moved toward a boxcar that lay on its side some distance away, and O'Connor and Wesley followed him. There was another fire and a man and a woman and a boy sitting next to it. The woman was stirring a pot, and the boy prodded the fire with a length of metal. The man hunkered, rolling a cigarette. Trent stood over them and tipped his hat. "Evening, folks," he said. "I wonder if you'd be so kind as to show me your camping permit."

The woman looked up from her pot. "Didn't know anything

34

about a camping permit, did we, Frank?" she said, and looked at the man. The man said, "Nope. Didn't know about any such thing."

"Well, you do now," Trent said.

"And where do you get one of these things?" the man asked.

"Oh, downtown, I suspect," said Trent. "Of course, until you get one, you'll have to vacate these . . . premises."

"Ain't got noplace to go," the woman said wearily.

"Well, I'm sorry about that, but I don't make the rules." Trent paused. "Of course, I suppose I could issue one myself, here and now. It's a bit irregular, but I could see my way to doing it, under the circumstances."

"What's this permit cost?" the man asked.

"Oh, a buck or so would about get you there."

"We ain't got but six bits."

Trent put his index finger to his lips and bit the tip. "So you're two bits short, aren't you?" He lifted his shoe to the rim of the pot the woman was tending and let it hover there, as though he were going to scrape the sole on it, and then he lowered it and rocked the pot on the coals. "I bet you could borrow it." He looked around the encampment. "Maybe from one of your friends here." Gundersen and Tyler led three men in handcuffs past the fire. Trent said, "Wes . . ."

The woman began, "We don't know—"

"Don't interrupt me in the course of my duties, ma'am," Trent said. "Wes, I wonder if Officer O'Connor could assist Gundersen and Tyler with those suspects there?" Wesley nodded to O'Connor.

Trent returned his gaze to the man and the woman at the fire. "Now, I'm just trying to lend you a hand here, bend the rules a little bit. But I can only do so much. . . ." He shook his head, and then his eyes lighted on the boy, moved over the boy's shoulder to a bicycle that lay behind, an old Schwinn whose red paint had moldered to a muddy oxblood. "That's a fine bicycle there. That yours, son?"

"Yes, sir."

"Where'd you get it?"

"My daddy," the boy said, and glanced over to the man. "My daddy got it for me."

"How much did he pay for that bicycle, son?"

"I don't know, sir."

"A fine bicycle like that would cost at least five dollars, I'd reckon. But your daddy just told me—"

The man broke in. "He don't know—"

"You shut up while I conduct this interrogation. You got plenty of trouble already." Trent turned back to the boy. "But your daddy says he hasn't got but six bits. So where would he get five dollars to buy you a bicycle, son?"

"I don't know, sir," the boy said.

"Neither do I," said Trent. "I'm worried about that." He shifted his attention back to the man and said nothing for a moment. Wesley looked away into the distance, toward the little fire where Welshinger was with the two hoboes. He seemed to see Welshinger in silhouette, his back to Wesley, his legs apart as though tensed, his hands on his hips. Wesley could just make out the figure of one of the men pressed up close against Welshinger, on his knees.

Trent was talking to the boy's father. "You got a job?"

"Nope."

"Why not?"

The man looked at Trent incredulously. "There ain't no jobs for a guy like me."

"What kind of guy is that? Shiftless? No-count? You ought to think more positive. The slump's done. The future's here for them that wants it."

The man said nothing, and Trent looked over to the boy. "Your daddy ought to get a job, raise you right."

The woman had been digging around in a carpetbag, and now she extended her palm to Trent. There were four quarters, and she emptied them out into Trent's hand as though she were ladling water. "Now you can leave us alone, can't you?" she said.

"Well, ma'am, I'm glad we could clear up this little matter of the permit. I hate to bother folks about . . . red tape." Trent paused and looked at the man and the boy. "But we've still got this little problem of the bicycle."

The man's voice was tight. "I got it at a junkyard. In Minneapolis. Paid two bits for it."

"Two bits for a fine bicycle like that—with the tires and the chrome handlebars?" said Trent. "You got a receipt, I suppose."

The man shook his head. Gundersen, Tyler, and O'Connor had returned from the Black Maria and stood watching Trent. Strunsky and Mills trudged by in the opposite direction, prodding a man forward with their truncheons. Trent said, "I'm afraid I have to take you in on suspicion of burglary." He stooped down and looked intently at the boy. "I'm sorry to do this, son, but I have to take this bicycle into evidence. There's been a bunch of thefts out of garages over in Crocus Hill. Tires, tools, bicycles just like this one." He stood up. "You fellows escort this suspect to the wagon while Lieutenant Horner and I take a little more of a look-see around." The woman was crying, gulping down drafts of air; the boy had sat down next to the bicycle and was spinning the rear wheel, letting the spokes tinkle against his fingernails.

Trent and Wesley walked up the slope toward the tracks, and

Wesley thought to say something to him. He wasn't sure about the bicycle—it probably was, in fact, stolen—but Trent was out of line on the shakedown. Still, it was only a buck, and they'd lied about having the money, hadn't they? Wesley just wanted to go home, out of the smoke and the filth, to his empty little house near the brewery.

They were walking by a long metal cylinder, like a big culvert but made of steel plate and rivets, evidently the boiler of an old locomotive. Trent stopped and raised his finger to his lips. They heard a sound like breathing inside, and then a moan. Trent smiled a scrunched-up little grin and took out his flashlight and went around to the open end of the cylinder. Strands of copper tubing hung limply from the ceiling, sweating with moisture, and the breathing echoed down toward them. Trent stepped inside and aimed his light up to the far end. A man's buttocks thrust and drove between two legs, and a girl's voice called out. The man, his breeches pulled down and gathered around his knees, pulled away and spun around, a thread of ejaculate dangling from his penis like a cobweb. "What the hell?" he yelled angrily. "Get the hell out of here!"

Trent took a further step inside the cylinder and hunched over, perhaps twelve feet from the man and the girl. "Top of the evening," he said. "My partner, Lieutenant Horner, and I were just walking our beat through your pleasant little neighborhood here. Heard some noise in here and thought we ought to investigate." While Trent talked, he played the beam of his flashlight over the man and the girl. The man was on his knees, buttoning his trousers. The girl, her face now revealed, was tugging down her dress, and she kept pulling on it, as though it were longer than it really was. She began to snuffle, and the corners of her eyes shone pink as the inside of a mouse's ear. She looked fifteen years old.

Trent bent down and moved closer. "Oh, dear," he said. "Was this gentleman bothering you, miss? I kind of suspect he might have been." He did not wait for the girl, now sobbing, to reply. He thrust his flashlight violently at the man and held it under his chin, stabbing at his sweaty, beard-stubbled throat, at his quaking, globular Adam's apple. "I'd say we're looking at rape here, sonny, statutory rape anyhow."

The man began to stammer. "Weren't no rape. She's—"

Trent drove the flashlight into the vault of his chin. "You shut up, speak when you're spoken to." He looked at the girl. "Now, how old are you, honey?"

The girl hesitated. "Eighteen," she said, her voice quavering upward, as though it were more a question than a statement.

"I don't think so, honey. Let's try again. How old are you?"

The girl was silent. Finally she said, "I don't know."

"You don't know?" Trent said. "That's a good answer, I suppose. I'm going to help you out. I'd say you were fourteen at the outside. And I'd say this fellow raped you and I'd say he's going to rot in prison for it and his soul's going to burn in hell."

The man yelped. "God damn it, Maggie. Help me. Say—"

Trent threw the fist of his free hand into the man's solar plexus and held him there, pressing in and up, as though the man were hooked and suspended off the floor. The girl wailed. "He's—he's my sweetheart. We come up from Moline together. He's been looking after me."

"Oh, I can see that," Trent said, and pulled his fist from the man's gut like a cork from a bottle. "Taking you to all the best places and such." Trent wagged his head, weighing the situation, and said, "I'm going to take your friend downtown and see that he gets his due. I ought to take you too, get you sent over to the county home. But my hands are pretty full. If Lieutenant Horner would be so kind, I'm going to leave you in his custody. Maybe he can give you some good advice."

Trent grabbed the man's wrist and bent it behind his waist and prodded him forward. "Let's go," he said, and then he winked at Wesley. "You enjoy yourself chaperoning the young lady here, Lieutenant."

Wesley nodded, and then he heard Trent's and the man's footsteps echo waterily down the cylinder, like oars striking the battens of a rowboat. He realized that he and the girl were now in the dark, and he flicked on his flashlight. She still cowered there, on a filthy pallet, clutching her knees.

"You'd better tell me your name," Wesley said.

"Margaret. They call me Maggie."

"Who's 'they'?"

"Folks. People at home. Billy calls me that too."

"Billy's your friend here?"

The girl nodded. She looked up and pushed her bangs out of her eyes. Her hair was dark, thin and straight, fettered by barrettes on either side. "What are they going to do to him?"

"Question him. Then maybe book him. Maybe let him off with a warning. It's not my division. All depends. Rape is a serious charge."

"Wasn't any rape. I'll say so."

"Your being so young, your say-so doesn't mean anything. And me and Lieutenant Trent saw what you kids were doing, plain as day."

The girl stared at him, and then she looked down and picked

at the tops of the ankle socks she wore. "So it don't matter what really happened or what anybody says about it 'cept you."

"We see what we see. And what I saw was you doing something you shouldn't."

Wesley tucked the flashlight under his armpit and got a cigarette from his pocket. He lit it, and the match flared toward the copper tubing draped from the ceiling.

The girl unclasped her knees and pulled her feet under her, sitting up erect on them. She looked at Wesley deeply. "Couldn't you do something for Billy, so they'd let him go? Couldn't you, if you really wanted to?"

Wesley was looking at her face, at her lips, a child's swelling, magenta lips, and her ragged, harried fingernails, and the down on her arms. She twisted her torso so her little breasts shifted under her dress like a shadow under water. Wesley spoke. "It's not my division—"

The girl broke in. "Because if you could, if you could do something, I could . . ." Her voice trailed off and she looked down and then she feathered her fingertips across her waist. She looked up at Wesley and began afresh, as though she were explaining something. "Once when Billy and I got in a jam with some railway police, I let one of them—"

"I don't want to know about it," Wesley said, and he thought to himself that he sounded not firm but plaintive. He cleared his throat. "Get up off of there. Let's go outside." He led the way down the cylinder and out into the night. At the entrance, he stopped and waited for her, and when she came out he could see her breath condensing in the cold and the gooseflesh rising on her arms where the rayon dress left off. "You haven't got a coat?" he said.

41

She nodded back into the cylinder. "I got a blanket in there."

"Never you mind." He took off his jacket and draped it over her shoulders, and the dress and her body were shrouded in it, lost in the bulk of the lapels and sleeves. "I'll get you something else in a minute, out of the squad car," he said.

"What are you going to do with me?"

"I can't leave you here, can I?"

"I can fend for myself. Or me and Billy can, if you could just see your way clear to . . ."

"By rights you ought to be in the county home. And he ought to be on the work farm for leading young girls astray."

"Billy didn't lead me nowhere. I was fixing to go."

"You think that, but you don't know—don't know how the world pulls you away from your family, from the people that love you, into what's filthy and evil—"

"No one's ever loved me but Billy."

Wesley didn't say anything. And then he sighed. "I'm not going to argue with you. If that's what you want to believe, you go right ahead." He could hear the clanging in the yards in the distance, and then the Black Maria started up and reversed, and its headlights swung onto the ground below where he and the girl stood, and it seemed to smolder with smoke and steam. "You go right ahead and think that," Wesley said. "But I got a girl like you lying in the icebox down at the morgue who found out different."

"She got killed or something?"

"Murdered. Maybe by some guy she thought was sweet on her. Working as a taxi dancer, all Max Factored up. Probably thought she knew better than everybody else, probably nobody could talk sense to her either." Wesley stopped. "Maggie, you ought to go home to Moline or wherever the hell you come from, before you end up the same."

"Maybe if Billy gets off we will."

Wesley spat and threw his cigarette on the ground. "Christ, this Billy's probably the root of all your troubles."

"He's all I got, family or friends. You don't know. You don't know nothing about it."

Wesley started, "Once I had—" And then he stopped himself. She was right: he didn't know anything about it. He only knew that he had no one at all, not even someone like Billy.

He aimed the flashlight beam down the slope and cocked his head in the direction of his car, where he saw O'Connor leaning, smoking a cigarette, looking up as though he were searching for the moon. Wesley started to walk, and the girl followed, and he looked back and said, "I'll talk to Trent about your boyfriend. I think he might see his way to letting him off, provided he leaves town. But you have to promise me you'll go home."

The girl looked at him, and her eyes began to well. "But I told you, I ain't—"

Wesley looked at her hard. "You have to promise me, promise me like you really mean it."

She stopped, standing near the fire where Welshinger had apprehended the hoboes, and smoke blew sideways across her legs, over the cracked and mottled leather of her shoes. She looked at Wesley, frightened, dwarfed in his huge coat, and she said, "Okay. I promise."

"I have to *believe* you, Maggie."

She began again, slowly, deliberately. "I promise. With all my heart. On Jesus and Mary and the saints."

"That's good, Maggie. That's good."

Wednesday, October 4, 1939

It is an odd sensation, but I think I am being watched.

Yesterday morning a man came to the office and spoke to Mr. Wright. They stood at the end of the hall of the file room, and it was as if they were looking at me and talking about me, the strange man in particular. All day I wondered about this, and I must say the feeling of eeriness was furthered by the papers being full of news about the unsolved brutal murder that, it turns out, took place not four or five blocks from here. By the time Mr. Wright sent me home, about four o'clock, I felt I must flee, that something was after me. I rode the streetcar, and when it went through the tunnel someone came and sat down next to me and was trying to read what the *Dispatch* said about the murdered girl. There in the streetcar, with the dim lights flashing by in the tunnel, I became so unnerved that I got off before my stop, just after the cathedral, and I wasn't so sure that the person who had sat down next to me hadn't also gotten off, so I went into the cathedral, not in the big open part, but behind the altar, where the little chapels are, where I had lighted the candle to Saint Anthony. I thought I would stop there and light a candle, and I felt in my vest pocket for a piece of change, and then I heard footsteps, the clopping kind that new leather makes, and I must have felt a little like Veronica Galvin in *Grand Central Terminal* when she's being chased along the train platforms by her boyfriend's nemesis. In any event, I dropped the coin in the slot without lighting the candle and hastened as quickly as I felt I could around to the far side of the altar. The steps kept coming, and there was a row of doors—like closet doors—and I darted in one and stood stock-still. A little hatch slid open, and a voice said something in a foreign language, and I think I probably cried out, and certainly I shuddered.

Then the voice said, "Have you come to make your confession, my child?" and the voice rather reminded me of Mr.

Feeney, who used to drive and run errands for Nanna. I said no, no I hadn't, and I was very sorry to intrude, but I'd become unnerved and thus ducked into his closet. The voice asked what had frightened me, and I told him. He asked me if I had done anything which would cause anyone to follow me for any evil end, and I said no, I didn't think I had. Then, he said, perhaps it is nothing, or perhaps it is something holy, because Jesus and his mother, Mary, and the saints are in the world, and sometimes they loom over us, they follow our hearts. I asked him if they'd want to cause one such a fright as I'd had. He said they probably would not, but that sometimes the holy is dreadful to our apprehension. Then he asked me if I knew the prayer called the "Hail Mary," and I said I did not. He asked me if I knew the one called the "Our Father," and I told him that if that was the one Nanna called "The Lord's Prayer," then I did. Then he told me I should say it a half-dozen times but to leave off the part that comes after "but deliver us from evil," for that was extraneous, and he said not to be afraid.

I went back out onto the street and walked down Selby Avenue, and as I did so, I said the prayer to myself, probably several more times than I was supposed to. In any case, by the time I got home, I did indeed feel better, if only for a little while, and I was still too distracted to do anything but paste clippings in the scrapbook.

I thought I would have forgotten all about the dread of the previous day, but in the morning, as I went out to go to work, there was a car parked across the street and a man in it, smoking, and it seemed to be the same man that visited Mr. Wright yesterday, and with all due respect to the priest in the closet, I do not think he resembled Jesus or his mother or any of the saints in the least. I went straight downtown and to the office, without stopping for so much as a doughnut, and tried to lose myself in work. But when I came out in the afternoon, I bought the *Dispatch,* and there was more about the murdered girl, and it seems that she worked at the Aragon Ballroom and had posed for artists and photographers, and I am not so very sure

He seemed larger than Wesley remembered, big as a bull in the doorway but with a face bland and soft and round like a biscuit. He had watery blue eyes behind tiny round wire-framed spectacles, and he seemed to squint even in the dim light of the apartment-house hallway.

"Are you Herbert White?" Wesley asked.

"Oh, yes. You must excuse me. I was just writing—"

"Police, Mr. White. I wonder if we could come in and ask a few questions."

Herbert looked to either side of him as though clearing the matter with unseen associates. "Oh, I suppose. My home is very modest . . . ," he said, and wandered off down the hall to the right, reaching out to close a closet door that was slightly ajar. He entered the parlor and stood by the fireplace and formed a tent with his hands. "Please sit down." There were two easy chairs with faded yellow upholstery and a sofa with a yard-high pile of newspapers perched on one end.

"We'll stand," Wesley said.

Herbert squinted and bobbed his head. He looked around. "Oh, the radio," he said. "I suppose I should turn it off."

"It's okay," Wesley said.

Herbert eased himself backward down onto the sofa as though he were being pushed. Then he started to rise again. "I wonder if I should get you something to drink. I have tea and Sanka and Ovaltine. Milk also."

"That's okay, Mr. White."

"Oh, good. So which would you like? I rather prefer some Ovaltine—"

"No, it's okay. We'll pass, go without."

Herbert paused and screwed up his eyes and then smiled weakly. "Oh, I see," he said. "So we're all squared away, then, aren't we?" Wesley nodded, and Herbert sat back down.

Wesley took an envelope from under his arm and held it in front of him like something he was going to read from. "Mr. White, do you know a woman named Charlene Mortensen?"

"Oh, goodness, I hope not—I mean, I'm sure I don't," Herbert blurted.

"She also used the name Carla Marie LaBreque. She sold dances at the Aragon on Wabasha. Also posed for photographers."

Herbert looked at his feet, and then he seemed to be scanning the carpet on the parlor floor. His doughy hands were gripping his knees, and the knuckles were blanching.

"Do you know her, Mr. White? We understand that you've patronized the Aragon, that you've taken some pictures of the girls there."

"That's true. I've just finished some studies of Ruby, Ruby Fahey. Do you know her? She's very lovely."

O'Connor nodded deeply. "Yeah, she's a looker."

"Hair like cornsilk," Herbert said softly.

"Who *we* know isn't pertinent, Mr. White," Wesley interrupted. "I'm asking if you know Charlene Mortensen."

"I don't know that I do. Of course, I could. It's possible."

"You don't seem very sure of yourself, Mr. White."

"Well, you see, my memory is not all it could be. Of course, I want to cooperate with the authorities, as any good citizen does. But I want to be correct too." Herbert smiled at Wesley as though he were sharing a wistful memory. "Once, Ruby introduced me to several of the other girls and we sat down in a booth together and I bought them all cocktails, exotic things with colored liqueurs and crushed ice and foam and so forth." He held an index finger up in the air. "So you see I could have met her. Was she pretty?"

"She had red hair," said O'Connor.

"Oh, my. Red hair, like Veronica Galvin, the cinema actress. I should think I would remember that. But you see, I have this impairment and really don't remember much of anything except what's just happened and what happened long ago. That's why I have these." Herbert slapped the pile of newspapers and then waved his arm at the bookcase and around the perimeter of the room. Wesley saw the bookcase was full of identical scrapbooks and the floor was piled with stacks of newspapers and magazines.

"Well, maybe we can help you out," Wesley said, and opened the envelope he was holding. He moved toward Herbert and handed him a photograph. "I wonder if you know this girl."

Herbert pulled the photograph close to his face, like a jeweler examining a stone with a loupe. "Is this Carla Marie LaBreque? Who is also Charlene Mortensen?" He looked up. "You see, I'm not so bad with things I've just heard."

"That's her."

"She's lovely. Shapely"—Herbert paused for air—"calves. Pity you can only see her in profile. Still, not a bad study. I'd have dodged around the . . . bust . . . here, but—"

"Did you take it?"

"Who? Me? I should think not," Herbert said. "Mind you, I could have. But I don't think I did. I haven't got a couch like that. My grandmother did. She called it a fainting couch. Though I never saw anyone faint on it, or even near it."

"So you don't think you knew the girl and you don't think you took the photo, but you're telling us you don't know so."

"Well, yes, that's about the best I can do. It's about the best I can ever do."

"And you'd like us to believe that."

"Well, Officer—"

"Lieutenant."

"Very sorry. No rudeness intended. Lieutenant, as I was saying, every man must believe as he sees fit."

"What I'm asking is if you're telling us the truth."

"It's what I believe to be the truth."

Wesley's voice went taut. "Just yes or no: Do you know this girl? Did you take this photograph?"

"I don't think so."

"Yes or no, Mr. White?"

Herbert looked at Wesley imploringly and rubbed at the corner of his eye as if composing himself. He began slowly: "But that's just what I can't do. I've tried to explain. I could have met the girl. And the photograph—well, I don't recognize that room and I don't recognize the girl, even if she is very pretty and I should very much like to recognize her. And I suppose I could have taken the photograph—I should like to have taken the photograph, though I don't much care for this kind of profile—although I doubt I printed it." Herbert stopped and let his hands hang at his sides. "So there you are."

"Yes or no, Mr. White?"

"I suppose no."

"You suppose?"

"All right, then. No."

"So your answer is that you do not know Charlene Mortensen and you did not take this photograph?"

"I don't think so," Herbert said.

"Don't ask me to repeat myself, Mr. White. Yes or no?"

"If you insist, then no."

"Your answer is no."

Herbert nodded.

"All right. I think that will do it for now. We might need to talk to you again—probably will need to talk to you again. But in the meanwhile I want you to think about something. Do you know what perjury is?" Wesley didn't stop. "I bet you do, a well-spoken gent like yourself. Because you know you can spend a good number of years rotting inside Stillwater for perjury. See if you can remember that for me. Until next time."

Herbert swung his head from side to side, facing down like a browsing animal, and then Wesley turned toward the hall and Herbert began to lead them out of the parlor. In the hall, as he passed the closet door, his hand reached out and touched the doorknob absentmindedly, involuntarily, as though for good luck.

Wesley saw Herbert's hand from the corner of his eye, and he remembered his touching it earlier, when they'd walked in, and a clarity fell on him, a sense of good fortune and breathlessness. He stopped and said, "What's in there?" and Herbert whirled around like a top out of kilter and said, "In there?"

"Yeah, in there. That closet or whatever."

"Oh, that's . . . my coat, my hats, things I use. . . ."

"Mind if we have a look?"

Herbert's scarlet face began to pale, and he said, "It's nothing—"

O'Connor had flicked the door open and chuckled. "Hey, you got two Hoovers. Guess you like to keep the place real clean."

"It's a mistake . . ." Herbert was saying, and even then Wesley's eyes fluttered and fixed and lit like two black crows on the floor in the back, on the shoes.

that I might not have known her. But that is beside the point now, because just as I was writing that, there was a knock at the door, and the police had come to talk to me. There were two of them, the smaller, impetuous one, and the bigger one, who I gather is in charge and who is a very grim individual indeed. He kept asking me if I knew a certain woman from the Aragon Ballroom or if I had taken a photograph of her that he had with him. Although he never said as much, I assumed she was the girl found dead near the Lawton Steps.

I tried to be cooperative and honest and attempted to explain about my impairment, but he would not be satisfied until I would say definitely "yes" or "no" to his questions, which I tried to explain to him would be a lie in either case, as my memory will not permit me to definitely assent to either position with accuracy: the truth being that I don't know, rather than "yes" or "no." But he would not have it. He has a rather angular face, like the prow of a ship, and he plowed on, and everything must be either this way or that, with no deviation. And when I gave him the sort of answer he required, that didn't please him either—he suggested it must be a lie and that I could go to the penitentiary for lying to him.

But the worst thing happened just now, as they were leaving. I don't know what possessed him, but the big, grim one demanded that I open the hall closet for him—presumably on some whim—and when he saw the shoes I discovered there the other day, he became all flushed and his eyes seemed almost to burn, like those of the prophets in the Old Testament. And I could see he was scarcely breathing, and he asked me where the shoes had come from and I told him the truth—that I didn't know—and this produced much the same reaction as before. To explain, to placate him, I suppose, I told him the story about the two vacuums. I thought it might even amuse him, but instead he became visibly angry, and he wanted to know all about the Hoover salesman from Chicago, although I couldn't see what it had to do with the girl from the Aragon. Then he calmed down and just looked like he had before, like he was burdened with all the weight of the world. He took the shoes with him.

At the door, he told me not to leave town, just as they do in the movies. Now I am terribly afraid he must think I had something to do with the death of this girl. And the truth is, I cannot say that I did not. But he was silly to tell me not to leave town. This is my home and I don't know a soul in the world, and for all that I do not say that I am lonely in the world. But just now the things that I take pleasure and solace in do not afford me much comfort—the radio has been on all this time and I hadn't even noticed—and I feel very alone indeed.

For a long time, Wesley and O'Connor sat in their car outside Herbert White's apartment house and Wesley smoked, deeply and deliberately. Then he hooked his hands together by the fingertips and tugged, and exhaled as if his whole soul were smoke going up a chimney. He turned to O'Connor and said, "Well, Sergeant?"

O'Connor grinned. "I'd say you had all your ducks in a row: witness placing him at the scene, acquaintance of the victim, physical evidence tying him to the victim and the scene. And he doesn't even really want to deny it." He turned the key and revved the engine lightly. "Sheesh, what a chump."

Wesley rolled down his window and flung his cigarette into the gutter. Then he nodded for O'Connor to drive on. "What about motive?"

"Being a goddamned weirdie, that's his motive."

Wesley shook his head. "I want to do better than that. 'Weirdie' doesn't cut it. I figure all of them have got their own particular mark or stain or whatever—their own evil. I just need to find his, name it, and take the whole package to the prosecutor." Wesley took out his watch. It was nine o'clock. "Go ahead and drop me off at home."

O'Connor nodded and turned down the hill, and they could see the electric sign above the brewery near Wesley's house. They drove for a little while without speaking, and then O'Connor said, "So what's his evil?"

"Oh, probably a sex thing. Which is a woman thing. Which is a love thing that's become a hate thing."

"Hip bone's connected to the leg bone, eh?" O'Connor snickered and then squelched himself as Wesley remained silent, staring out the window at the bare trees and the dimly lit windows of the houses of his neighborhood.

Finally, as they were pulling up to his dark little house, the tiny yard full of unraked leaves, Wesley said, "You know what clinches it? That he never asked us what we were investigating. Never said, 'Hey, what's this about?' He already knew what it was about, like he knew we'd be coming for him."

"He could have just assumed, could have just known about it like anybody would," O'Connor said. "He had enough goddamned newspapers."

"But anybody else would have said, 'Hey, what's this about?' Or they'd say, 'If this is about that girl, I didn't kill any girl.' But he didn't even deny knowing her, taking her picture. It just all went without saying—that he knew and we knew, and he was just waiting for us to come see him. You see, that's why this stuff isn't just weirdness, Sergeant. They got this thing, this evil, and they know they've got it, like they've got a dog or lumbago. So they trip up on that—on it being second nature to them—and they don't even think to ask, 'Hey, what's this about?' Because they're living with it all the time."

"So what's next?"

"I just want to talk to that other girl at the Aragon—the one he admits to knowing. Then we bring him in. I bet he fesses up by suppertime. He's a softy, a mama's boy but with no mama." Wesley seized the door handle and pulled himself wearily out onto the sidewalk.

O'Connor said, "So I come by at eight tomorrow?"

"Sure, that's fine. It's going to be a good day," Wesley said, and he pushed the door shut. O'Connor drove away, the smoke coiling from the tailpipe like a serpent formed of fog.

On the step, Wesley found his key, a little brass one with a round head that said "Yale" on it, and opened his door. He had lived in this house for nineteen years, since he and Rose had moved here with Louise when she was four years old. Rose made the curtain, now yellow, almost amber, that hung behind the glass of the front door. She made the curtains and the valances and the cloths for tables and the coverlets draped on the arms of the sofa that lay against the far wall like a dying elephant, made them all on the black Singer machine that sat on the little table under the window in the dining room.

Without turning on the lights, Wesley walked through the living room to the dining room table, square, with four chairs and a round doily in the middle, and he put down his hat and the envelope with Charlene Mortensen's picture inside it. He pulled out a chair and sat down and laid his arms on the table and his head on his arms and listened to the silence of his house.

After a time, it was not so quiet. He could hear a radio playing somewhere down the street and a breeze beating against the trees, knocking down the coloring leaves. Then the icebox clicked on with a sound like pigeons chortling and settled into a pulsing drone of rheumy, brittle metal. He was looking out the window over the top of the sewing machine all this time, and for an instant he thought he heard it too, the catching of the belt and then the whir and the whir's withering away when Rose stopped to shunt the cloth in a different direction with her fingertips, with the butt of her palm.

Wesley got up, and he shuffled into the kitchen and pulled the chain on the light in the center of the room, which hung over the oilcloth-covered table. He found a glass above the white sink and took a bottle from the shelf next to it and poured himself a shot, and the whiskey sat dark on the white drain board like a caramel in a girl's gloved hand.

He drank half of it, but he couldn't relax enough to sit down, so he wandered the house. There were two bedrooms, Louise's at the front, his and Rose's at the back, and together with the living room and the little dining room and the even littler kitchen, that was all there was to it. He had bought the house when he was still a patrolman, and as the years passed, he had wished they'd had something bigger, although when the crash came and other people couldn't meet their mortgages, he was glad of his small house. But it was for Louise that he wanted it, and still more for Rose. He kept up with the modern devices for her sake: the icebox and the Singer, the phonograph and the washing machine with the electric wringer, and the big radio with a facade that looked like the society people's Presbyterian church on Summit Avenue.

He had always told Rose that they would move someday, but he could never bring himself to do anything about it. He was gripped by an unshakable notion about another house, that it would bring them down, and the world with it. And 1929 had proved him right. But after that, when he saw they would be all right, even if the world would not be, he still could not countenance it. Then, after Louise had gone and Rose had gotten sick, he asked Rose if she'd like to move and he promised her he would look into it the very next day. And she raised her bony, mottled arm from their black iron bed and moved her hand in a broad stroke, as if she were sketching the horizon line, and said, "What would be the point, Wes? With just the two of us here now?"

He was sitting on Louise's bed in Louise's room, thinking about that, and this room seemed to be the emptiest room in an emptied-out world, no photographs or keepsakes, just the stale bone-yellow pillowcases and the tabletop and the windowsill and the floor furred with dust. And now his pettiness, his lack of faith, had won him his just reward, and the house was not too small, but too big. He should live in an apartment, like White, the murderer, the pariah, who could not even bring himself to lie on behalf of his evil.

Wesley took the last of the whiskey and set the glass down on the floor and let his arm hang there, fingering the fringe of Louise's bedspread. He dozed and then pulled himself awake with a shudder, went back out into the hall and the living room and the dining room and the kitchen, and he turned out the light. Then he walked back to his room, to Rose's room, and stripped down to his shorts and lay on the bed. The clock glowed Palmolive green on the nightstand, and once a minute, the big hand thunked ahead.

Wesley was thinking of how he was going to collar Herbert White the next morning, not so much with pleasure but as one might anticipate a good solid hot lunch: macaroni and cheese and lima beans, say, but no gravy. Then he pushed the covers down, arcing his body above them, and inserted his feet and settled into the linen. He smelled the scent of Fels Naptha and of autumn damp, and as he fell asleep, he thought he could hear the simmer of Rose's iron on his shirt and the ringing of Louise's jacks as they fell on the sidewalk, the scrape of her shoe leather, the hollow plop of her ball at the end of its descent.

Thursday, October 5, 1939

I came home after lunch, having told Mr. Wright I did not feel well. Now I am waiting for them to come, the big one with the grim face, the avenging angel, and I am writing in this book— not in the evening, as is my wont, but in the afternoon, and it makes everything seem a bit out of kilter, like I am doing something I should not be doing or I am in some place I should not be. The afternoon light pours down blue and cold like rain, and it is as though I am a shut-in, kept inside while the rest of the world attends a party and I am the only one not there. But really I am waiting. I am wondering what they will do with me, what they will make of me.

The Jew who ran the Aragon had offered them a drink, and although it was one o'clock in the afternoon, Wesley had shot O'Connor a look to indicate there was no possibility of accepting. The Jew kept getting up, circling the table, emptying ashtrays, bringing over bowls of pretzels. "I don't know where she is. She's a reliable girl. I mean, they all are, but her especially. But this business with Carla Marie's got them all shook up," and Wesley pulled out a cigarette and the Jew leaned over with his lighter and said, "Let me get that for you," and then brought his hands together and let them fall away from each other like a peacock opening its fan. "But what can I say? This is a decent place. Not like some I'm sure you fellows are familiar with. A gentleman can come here, dance with a pretty girl, enjoy her conversation. This is not a strip joint, this is not a cathouse. It's really a social club. That's how I think of it, and I think we have a discerning clientele. What some of the customers do in their private lives, I don't know—I don't want to know. But if one of them had something to do with Carla Marie's . . . misfortune, well, that's going to frighten the girls, and that is something I don't want, not that I want the papers coming around either. I don't need that. Which is to say I hope you fellows are planning to clear this business up—as of course I'm sure you are."

Wesley nodded, and the Jew sat down, and then there was some noise on the stair and he got up again and left the room and a moment later returned with a girl. She was a little out of breath, button-nosed, brunette, pretty, but at this moment florid-faced. The Jew introduced her with a suggestion of a bow. "This is Ruby, Ruby Fahey," and the girl said, "Pleased to meet you," and Wesley motioned for her to sit. The Jew sat down next to her and folded his hands and began, "Ruby's one of our top girls, been here two years—"

"I'm saving up to go to California, to act," the girl broke in.

"—one of the customers' favorites," the Jew continued.

Wesley nodded, raking his memory for the Jew's name, and at last said, "Mr. Stein, I think now that Miss Fahey has arrived, it would be best if we talked to her privately."

"Oh, as you wish. But if there's anything, anything at all . . ."

Stein withdrew like a tide, backward, unwilling, bending and slightly off balance, as though he were being pulled by the back of his belt.

Ruby smiled at O'Connor and at Wesley. "Hyman likes to look after us, after everyone, really." She smiled again. "He's a sweetie."

Wesley nodded and then looked at his watch. "I'm sure he does. Miss Fahey, we need to ask you a few questions about Charlene Mortensen."

"About Char? I called her Char. I told Sergeant O'Connor everything I could think of."

"Yes, I know that. But I just want to go into a few details, okay?"

"Sure."

"You told Sergeant O'Connor that Miss Mortensen didn't have any regulars that you knew of—that right?"

"She's only been here a little while, only worked a couple of nights a week," the girl said. "Not that many of us have regulars. Most of the customers are just passing through town. I mean, if they lived here, they'd probably have a sweetheart or a date or wives or something, wouldn't they?"

"I suppose so. Now, did Miss Mortensen have a sweetheart herself, a boyfriend, somebody who took her out?"

"Not that she ever mentioned."

"Did she ever talk about having her picture taken?"

"Not that I recall. But most of us have had our portraits done, what with so many of us wanting to go on the stage or into pictures. Sometimes Hyman puts them in the window."

"Do you know a man named Herbert White?"

Ruby smiled as though recalling an amusing story. "Oh, sure. He's been taking my picture, matter of fact."

"Do you know if he might have also taken Miss Mortensen's picture?"

"Not that I heard. Never even met her. And I think I would have heard. He did Clare and Gwendolyn once or twice, but mostly he's been doing me. He calls them 'studies.' He's kind of sweet on me, I think." She laughed.

Wesley's eyes narrowed, and he leaned closer to the girl. "Has he ever done anything untoward?"

"You mean has he got fresh with me?" She smiled.

"Yes, or maybe shown unusual . . . inclinations."

"Oh, no. Herbert's a sweetie. He's never so much as patted me on the fanny. Doesn't even want to dance. Just talks. Actually, doesn't even really talk. He just listens and buys you drinks and watches you with this big dreamy smile on his face, like you're the prettiest thing he's ever seen. He's a sweetie," the girl said, and then she giggled.

"What about the photographs. What sort of pictures are they?"

"Oh, nothing naughty. Not even cheesecake really. More the glamour type of thing. Or just what you might have in a family scrapbook, only nicer. More dressed up."

"More dressed up?"

"Like in certain clothes he thought were pretty or smart or whatever. Scarves. Shoes."

"Shoes. What kind of shoes?"

"I think he kind of likes open-toed ones, kind of sandal style, so he can still see your feet."

"And he'd get these for you to wear?"

"No. I'd just bring things from home, or from here. Sometimes Hyman gets us things, all identical. Like shoes. Actually, I left a pair at Herbert's that Hyman had gotten for all the girls. Have to get them back."

"Were they the sandal style you mentioned?"

The girl nodded. "Those were the ones. I think Herbert thought maybe they were a little common."

"So Miss Mortensen would have had a pair too?"

"I imagine so. Of course, she had little feet compared to me. I'm an eight and a half. I bet she was scarcely a six. Char had pretty feet, that and the beautiful hair."

Wesley nodded aimlessly, not in distraction but as the hope ebbed out of him, as his heart sank. He rose from his chair and said, "Well, Miss Fahey, I think that's all we need from you." O'Connor stood and added, "Much obliged."

Ruby dipped her head and smiled. "Charmed, I'm sure," she said, and clattered away on her heels toward the bar.

On the way downstairs, Wesley said, "You still got the shoes in the car?"

"In the trunk," O'Connor said.

"Let's check 'em."

Out on Wabasha Street, Wesley stood on the sidewalk and lit a cigarette, while O'Connor opened the trunk and fiddled among the objects in it. He looked up at Wesley over the lid. "Sorry," he said. "Eight and a half."

"Christ," Wesley hissed. "Christ, Christ, Christ."

He and O'Connor drove to the Public Safety Building in silence, and when they parked the car and got out, he said, "So what's left, Sergeant?"

"Still got the old lady who saw him on the steps."

"Yeah, but not much else—no shoes, nobody who says they knew each other, no evidence that he took the picture."

"We could search his place, look for negatives, other stuff that might connect him."

"But the room in the photo isn't even in his place."

"So he got a hotel room, set up his gear, and had the girl come up."

"Too far-fetched. I mean, it's clear he's done all the other girls at home."

"Just trying to be helpful."

"I know, I know. You go get some coffee or whatever. I'll let you know what we're going to do." O'Connor nodded and wandered off, sliding his hands into his pockets. The air was bright and hollow, and Wesley thought he could hear O'Connor whistling "Where or When" as he walked away.

In his office, Wesley sat at his desk and laid out three Luckies in front of him and smoked the first one. The Charlene Mortensen file sat by his left arm, tawdry and disconsolate, mocking him. While he was picking up the second cigarette, Welshinger came in and sat down across from him. "I hear you lost your collar on the Mortensen girl," he said.

Wesley nodded. "Yeah, this weird photography gimp. Thought I had him, but I couldn't quite tie him in. It was so goddamned close. It felt so right."

"You sound like you got a broken heart, like you lost your girl." Welshinger snorted.

Wesley ignored the gibe. "I was doing it for the girl, the girl the creep killed."

"And now you got nothing?"

"Next to nothing. Except the feeling that this guy did it, that he could have done it. Which he doesn't deny."

"He doesn't deny it?"

Wesley shuffled the Lucky from one hand to the other. "Says he's got something wrong with his memory."

"Handy for him."

"Don't I know it. And now there's no physical evidence."

Welshinger took out a box of matches and struck one, and Wesley put the cigarette to his lips. Welshinger brought the flame up to Wesley's face. "You know what I say, Wes? I say when you got lemons, make lemonade." Wesley drew on the cigarette, and Welshinger pinched the match out with his thumb and forefinger. "So if the guy isn't denying it, it's like his memory's a blank canvas, and we just help him out. Bring him downtown, maybe kind of late, when things are quiet, and discombobulate him a little. I bet we could help him recollect a few things. Hell, I bet we could make him goddamned nostalgic." Welshinger chortled.

"I still wouldn't have anything physical. And the guy doesn't seem like a murderer. I don't know that anyone would believe him if he *did* confess. Gotta have something physical."

"Physical, shmysical. You know what the Hindus say about the physical world? I read this in a magazine. They say it's a bunch of hooey, a bunch of illusion. There's this story: three blind men feeling an elephant, and each of them thinks it's something different and they can't agree and none of them really knows for true what it is. It might be Kate Smith's ass, for all they know. So there you are. But if you want something physical, we'll get you something physical. I mean, I like you, Wes. I'm your friend. And I've seen what you've gone through the last couple of years. So I want to do something for you."

"I appreciate it. But it's got to be real."

"Don't worry," said Welshinger. "Here's what we do. The guy's a shutterbug, I hear. Shoots cheesecake. So Trent and I search his place, looking for dirty pictures. We got a legitimate tip, so we go in."

"What he does is supposed to be pretty tame stuff."

"Do I know that? All I know is I've had a tip that there's pornography on the premises. And Wes, you know there will be. Even if it's not his."

"It's got to be real."

"Don't worry. It will be. Trust me. So anyway, now your suspect is at the center of a pornography ring with girls from the Aragon. That puts the circumstantial stuff in a different light. It's a whole new ball game. Now he's scared. Now maybe he remembers something different, remembers it better."

"I can see it, Welshinger, but I don't know. Let me think about it. I'll let you know, okay? I mean, don't you and Trent get all excited."

"Sure. Just here to help out any way we can."

"Good. So I'm going to think this through." Wesley snuffed out the cigarette, and Welshinger stood. "One more thing," Wesley said. "Trent brought in these two from Shacktown the other night—boy and girl, maybe fifteen, we caught screwing. I was hoping Trent would see his way to cutting them some slack. I asked him as a favor."

"Yeah; don't worry. We turned the girl loose right out the door here. The guy we softened up a little around the kidneys—just to get him religion, make an impression—and Trent dumped him down on the tracks by the stockyards. Told him to find himself a ride home."

"So the girl didn't go to the county home?"

"No; she's just wandering around, living by her wits. It beats jail. Beats being dead too."

Wesley said, "They grow up fast these days, so much faster than they used to."

Welshinger nodded. "And business is booming in my store."

He chuckled. "Hell, in the future—hell, now for all I know—they'll just be born grown up. It'll save time."

Wesley said, "Hope I die before I see that," and he took up the third cigarette and said, "So I'll let you know. By the end of the day."

Very late, Thursday, October 5, 1939

They came in the night, finally, when I was already asleep. Not the grim one and his short partner but two others, whom I didn't know. They were lean and nervous and scowling. The one who seemed to be in charge had a mouth like a slit that went in two directions, a smirk at one end, a grimace at the other. I answered the door in my bathrobe, and they pushed in without saying anything I can recall.

I asked if they had come to ask me more about the girl from the Aragon Ballroom, and the one with the odd mouth said no, he didn't know anything about that; that they were vice officers and they had a tip there was pornography on the premises and they had come to search it and I could make it easy on myself or hard. While he was telling me this, the other had already gone to the bookcase in my sitting room and was flipping through my scrapbooks, and he looked down the hall at me and asked, How many of these things you got here? And I told him at least thirty, perhaps even forty; that there was at least one volume for each of the last twenty-five years. And he said, That's real interesting, and he opened his hands like a magician making something disappear and let a scrapbook just fall on the floor. The binding split and clippings went this way and that, and I said he must be careful. The one in charge said, This is a police investigation, and I wasn't to tell them how to conduct it.

Then he called down the hall to the other one and said, Hank, quit monkeying with that stuff, and he turned back to me and asked if I was running a photographic studio on the premises.

I said, No, not in the strict sense of the word, but that photography was certainly my dearest avocation, and I had my own darkroom, and he said, Suppose you show us that. I led the way and opened the door, and the one in charge clicked the light switch on and the safe light went on. The other one went inside and asked didn't I have a proper light in there and I showed him where it was. Then he started to pick things up and put them back down, always in someplace other than where he'd found it, and then he opened a fresh envelope of Velox and slid out the black interior envelope and then opened it and withdrew a couple of blank sheets. And I said, no doubt with some impatience, Please, that is unexposed photographic paper, and now it's ruined. The one in charge said I should not make him repeat himself—that this was a police investigation and I wasn't to tell them what to do. He picked up a new print I'd enlarged two days ago of Ruby from the Aragon and asked, Was this the sort of thing I liked? Was this how I liked to see a woman looking? I told him I didn't know exactly what he meant, but that yes, I was rather pleased with the photograph, and he looked at the other one and shrugged his shoulders and said, To each his own, and tossed the print into the sink.

I wanted to object to this, but before I could, he went back out into the hall, and I didn't know whether I should be watching him or keeping an eye on the other, who was now rifling through all the boxes and envelopes in the darkroom and was exposing every sheet of paper in it to the light. But the one in charge asked me where I kept all my finished prints and negatives, and I told him they were in my bedroom, and he sent the other one down the hall. I started to follow, and the one in charge said where the h*** did I think I was going, and that I ought to quit interfering or they'd take me downtown for obstructing police business. I said I had no idea that this was the manner the police conducted their business and that as a citizen I was shocked and affronted.

He moved a step closer to me and put his face very close to mine. He was as tall as I am, which is unusual, and I thought he was going to hit me or try to knock me down, but he merely opened his mouth and then began to roar with laughter, almost to bray like a horse, the kind of big horse that pulled the milk wagon that always came to Nanna's house when I was little. Then he said, Herb—he had been calling me that for several minutes—if you're a citizen, I'm the Pope's a**wipe, and he said I was scum, that I was a pervert, and I was lucky he and his partner didn't drop me down the nearest sewer hole, where I could float like the g**d*** *Queen Mary* among the turds and the balled-up monthlies rags of the nigger and Jew women.

I told him as politely as I could that I thought this was a bit overstated, that he could see for himself that my photography was in the art and glamour mode. I was now hearing a fair amount of noise from my bedroom and kept looking down the hall in that direction, and I imagine my face must have conveyed no small degree of alarm. He said, Herb, don't you mind about that, Lieutenant Trent is a highly trained police officer, and then he called down the hall, Hank, take your time—me and Herb got some business to attend to.

The one in charge gripped me by the shoulder, hard, with his fingertips digging under my collarbone, and steered me toward the kitchen and into the pantry, and then he pulled the pantry door shut and said, Herb, I got a little project for you to concentrate on while we're finishing up here. Then he reached into his coat and took out a pistol, and he said, Herb, this is my sidearm, my revolver. Maybe you want to touch it, but I don't think you'd better, and then he raised it up and laid the barrel against the side of my head and stroked the hair above my ear with it. But then there was a voice calling out in the hall, and he said, G** d*** it, and put the gun away and left me standing there in the pantry.

After half a minute, I went out into the hall myself, and I saw him talking to the man who had been here last night, the grim-faced one, who was now clearly quite agitated. The grim-faced one was gesticulating and saying, G** d*** it, this is bull****. And the other kept saying, Sorry, Wes, this was the captain's decision, his orders. And the grim-faced one said, You get off my patch, away from my g**d*** suspect. I came down the hall and asked what the matter was, and they both turned toward me, and the grim-faced one said why didn't I take a g**d*** powder off the High Bridge so he could get some peace. Then the one who had been in my bedroom came out with a big smile on his face and said, Now, Wes, take a gander at what we found here. He took a dog-eared five-by-seven photograph out of his suit pocket and showed it around, and I could see it was a garishly lit exposure of a young woman exhibiting her private parts.

The grim-faced one shook his head and said, Nice try, Trent, but no cigar. Nobody's going to buy him having shot that. The three of them turned their backs to me, and I must say I was now utterly confounded. I heard them whispering and the grim-faced one hissing, and I could see the shoulders of the one in charge going up and down. Finally they all turned around and just looked at me for a time, and then the grim-faced one looked at the other two and said to me, Mr. White, thank you for your time, we'll be in touch, and the three of them turned back around and filed out the door. And as he was closing the door, the grim-faced one looked back at me, right into my eyes, looking very sad, very disappointed, as though I'd let him down terribly, so terribly.

It had been O'Connor who'd called Wesley at home at ten o'clock the night before. He heard Welshinger and Trent discussing their plans with the dispatcher at seven-thirty. O'Connor had mulled the matter over at the bar at Alary's Club and decided at nine that he owed it to his boss to call him. Then it took him another hour to make the call, to numb himself to the fear of the reprisals Welshinger and Trent might prepare for him for snitching, if they found out. By the time he called Wesley, O'Connor's ears and eyes and mouth were nicely blunted by the Schenley's Canadian he'd been nursing, like they were stuffed with cotton batting.

In the morning, when he came to pick up Wesley, O'Connor fudged the question of exactly how or when he'd learned that Welshinger and Trent were going to call on Herbert White, and Wesley did not make an issue of it. He knew the kind of power they—and Welshinger in particular—wielded around the Public Safety Building. They had an intimate relationship with the captain, whose appetite for results that he could bring to the notice of the commissioner and the mayor they sated with a smorgasbord of crimes discovered and crimes solved in a perfect one-to-one ratio. Of course, Wesley knew things about Welshinger and Trent, as did anybody who was paying the slightest attention; things that, had Welshinger and Trent not been running it, the vice division itself would have taken great interest in. But then Welshinger and Trent knew things about Wesley, not to say about everybody; and what those things were nobody could say, and that was their real power. They knew things that you'd done, that you might have done, thought about doing, even things you didn't know you could do but might be capable of doing, and it was all the same to them: They could book you for any of it, bring you down for things you might have dreamed and forgotten—hell, for things somebody else had dreamed about *you* and forgotten. Welshinger and Trent had never forgotten anything; they didn't even need to remember. They just knew.

So Wesley wouldn't go to the captain. Anyone who complained about the Vice Boys—as they were called—just looked like a crybaby, like a loser whining about winners. The status of the Mortensen case would remain "Under Investigation," with no arrest pending. He wasn't going to get anywhere with White, not right now at least, but he had the satisfaction of knowing that now neither would Welshinger. Welshinger had figured to make White his fish and bring him in on both vice and murder charges, collect the glory, and leave Wesley looking like a chump. Now, thanks to Wesley's interference, that wouldn't happen. Welshinger would be very, very angry. White would get to go back to his scrapbooks, his nose picking in his darkroom, his vacuum cleaners, his Aragon girls. Wesley would send O'Connor over to the Mortensen girl's apartment for another look around, and Wesley would sit at his desk—it might be for months—and wait for Welshinger to come for him.

Friday, October 6, 1939

I was a long time falling asleep last night, and when I awoke I scarcely had time to dress and catch the streetcar to work. I filed invoices in the morning, and at one point Mr. Wright came over to me and for no reason at all set his hand upon my shoulder and said, "Herbert, you look a little peaked today," said why didn't I go fetch myself a cup of coffee or a seltzer, and it would be on him, and I thought I might have wept there and then.

After work, I walked all the way home, as I knew I could not face the apartment in the state it was in, and I could not face cooking either, so I stopped at the White Castle and had coffee and one hamburger. After I'd eaten, the waitress came and poured me an extra half cup of coffee, as she knows I like. She asked me if the policeman who had been looking for me to ask me some questions had found me, and I said, Oh, yes indeed, he had. I do not know the waitress's name, but she always has a lacy handkerchief pinned to her bodice.

It seemed to take a very long time to walk home, the hill that runs up to the cathedral very steep. The leaves are mostly fallen now, I notice, and they cover the sidewalks and one wades through them and they lap one's ankles like shallow water. I suppose it will be an early winter. I went inside the cathedral and sat in the back to catch my breath. I had no desire to go behind the altar and light any candles, a practice I admit to having grown rather fond of—assuming the Catholics do not try to recruit me should I be noticed—but which today seemed pointless. After all, these saints are nothing more than statues, and all the candles in the world shall never bring them to life, for they were never dead—they were stone all the while.

So I sat in the very back, not only because of that but because some sort of service was taking place, though there was only a priest and a boy. I did not pay much attention to what they were doing or what the priest was saying—that being in Latin, as I suppose—and I might almost have dozed off, but for the boy ringing a bell. He rang it once, and then the priest said a few more words, and the boy rang the bell again. It rather gave me a start, and perhaps it is indeed designed to get people's attention.

Either that, I suppose, or perhaps to call God down to attend the proceedings, to ring for him rather as Nanna used to ring for Molly to come out from the kitchen and fetch our plates away. I remember always thinking that Molly was quite lovely. She had green eyes and a band of freckles on her nose and, in her jumper and her pinafore, was rather fetching, not to say curvaceous.

I came home and opened the door with dread, for I knew the mess that awaited me. The one who ruined most of my darkroom supplies had ransacked my bedroom also. There were prints and negatives all over the floor, although he had left many boxes untouched, almost as if he had grown weary of the whole business himself. At some point he had gone in the bathroom as well, for this morning I found my toothbrush and razor and spectacles in the toilet bowl and the toilet itself used. I fished these items out with my developing tongs.

In truth, it did not take me more than an hour to set things straight, and although much has been forever damaged, nothing is utterly lost. Many negatives were crumpled or scratched, many of Nanna and the house we all lived in together, and many more of girls I have photographed and whose names I have forgotten. But I suppose one might say that now these negatives bear the impression not of one moment but of two—the time when I exposed them and also, in the fissures and crazings and folds, the imprint of last night. Someday, when all this is forgotten, I shall go to print one of them and remember it once again, or perhaps I shall only puzzle over it (the exact operation of my memory in any given situation is always a mystery). Perhaps I shall only say, However did these become so scratched? and wonder what possibly could have happened.

Now the apartment is really quite tidy, very much as it was before, although I cannot say that it *feels* the same, although I have done everything I can to set it to rights, to make it exactly as it was before. Until now, I had always felt that it was good, good in the way the world is good, but now I am not so sure; and perhaps, if I am going to be logical, that misgiving ought to extend to the world as well. But I have also thought that the creator of the world must be good, even if the world itself turns bad. Perhaps it is necessary for him to return periodically to straighten things out, or perhaps he never goes away. But right now I have difficulty imagining that. I feel he must have made us and left us alone with this file of scratched and battered negatives of all the time that shall ever be, and although it seems we must inexorably enact each one, in fact we are dreadfully free.

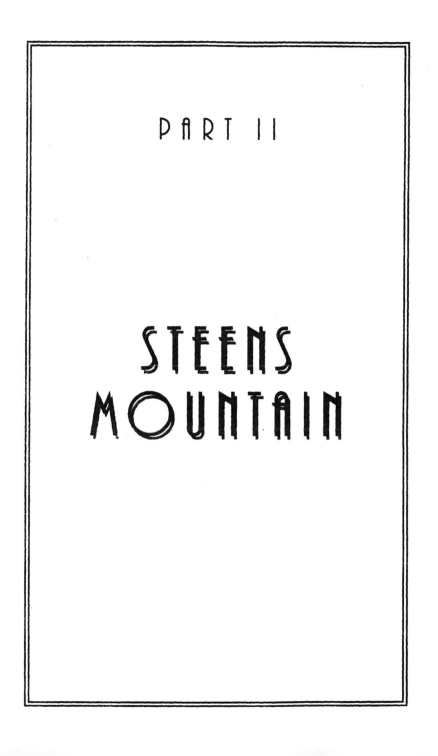

PART II

STEENS
MOUNTAIN

PANTHEON PICTURES CORPORATION
12985 WASHINGTON BOULEVARD
CULVER CITY, CALIFORNIA

October 9, 1939

Dear Friend,

Thank you ever so much for your kind letter. I am always delighted to hear from my fans.

I am enclosing a personally autographed photograph which I hope you will enjoy.

And remember to look for me this month at a theater near you in Pantheon Pictures' *Steens Mountain*! It's my most thrilling role yet—the story of a woman trapped in a desperate, ill-starred love affair with a man on the run, set in the towering desolation of the American West!

Yours very sincerely,
Veronica Galvin

FTER HE HAD SHOWN HER THE PRINTS, HE HELD OUT THE letter to her, cradling it in the giant cup of his hand as though it were very fragile. "I'm very excited about this, Ruby," he said. "I mean that she's coming. That she wants to see me."

Ruby took the letter and read it. "I'm not so sure, Herbert." She looked at the paper and the signature. The ink was blue, like the kind they used to stamp prices on cans at the grocery store. "I think maybe they send a letter out like this to everyone who writes her."

"Oh, I think you must be mistaken. You see, I've been corresponding with her for some time. Not just fan letters either. Serious letters about serious things." Herbert took the letter back from Ruby and pointed to the top. "You see—she even calls me 'Friend.' "

Ruby laid her palm on his other hand so softly he scarcely felt it. "I don't know, Herbert. I hope you're right. But maybe she only means that her new picture is coming here, not her herself."

"If she is coming and wants to see me, I could introduce you. And perhaps she could help you out when you get to Hollywood. It would be quite a coup to be acquainted with Veronica Galvin. It would open a few doors, I'd wager."

"I'm sure it would, Herbert," Ruby said. "And you're awfully kind to think of it. But then you're always thinking of other people," and she gave his hand a squeeze. He realized that she had been holding it all the while, and Herbert thought his heart might fall into the pit of his stomach, like a stone into the bottom of a very deep lake.

Saturday, October 14, 1939
I had Miss Ruby Fahey over this afternoon, and we had a de-

lightful visit. She seemed very pleased with the portfolio of her poses that I had printed for her, and of course I couldn't help but share with her the letter I received from Veronica Galvin in this morning's post. Ruby—I now feel perfectly comfortable in addressing her in the familiar—is not so sure that the letter means what it seems to mean, but then again she is not as acquainted as I with Miss Galvin's style, this being the *third* missive I have received from her (the third autographed portrait as well, I might add).

But be that as it may, I think Ruby and I are launched on a fine friendship. Even if that were not the case, I should of course be in her debt, given her sympathy toward me when I told her about the happenings of last week and her kindness in speaking to a police officer (who, it happens, sometimes frequents the Aragon Ballroom) on my behalf and her assurance to me that the matter was closed and they would trouble me no more.

She is, altogether, a genuinely kind and tender person, to say nothing of her bodily attractions. Just before she left I was nearly moved to invite her to join me at the pictures tomorrow, but I wondered if perhaps this might be construed as rather forward and thus said nothing of it. I certainly would not want to do anything to discommode her. Moreover, I suppose it is the case that I am habituated to attending the pictures by myself and perhaps I would not be very good company. And I would not want to be misunderstood: It is, after all, to my mind a very intimate thing.

Wesley had worked Sundays for the last three weeks, but this Sunday, with the Mortensen case stalled by a dearth of leads and the ministrations of the Vice Boys, he found himself with a day off. So he went to the pictures: a new release, in Technicolor, called *Hollywood Cavalcade*, with Alice Faye and Don Ameche. But he didn't even stay through the newsreel. He couldn't bear it, what with Hitler and Stalin and their friendship pact and then a preview of a new Western featuring Marlene Dietrich in a saloon brawl and then Lindbergh warning that America must stay out of the European war.

So he left, padding up the slope of the dark aisle with his back bent like he was lugging a sack of horseshoes. And among the faces and heads, he thought he saw Herbert White: Herbert White, for Christ's sake, sitting like an iceberg in the gray sea of newsreel light, with Hitler's tanks rolling into Warsaw on the screen.

The day blazed outside, clear as ice water, and Wesley thought he would walk home, all the way down West Seventh Street. It would kill time; it might clear his head. He tugged on the brim of his fedora and lit a cigarette, tried to make himself amble, make himself stroll. But he felt he ought to be working; and as he approached Seven Corners, it was as though he were puttering around his office on a holiday, conscious of what lay in the drawers of his desk needing to be done. The street, the buildings, and the empty parking places looked raw, wind battered and forlorn, and the sound of Wesley's shoes scraping on the pavement was wearing at him, the grit and the dirt and the filth of the city and the world grinding at his soles, sawing through his skull, drilling in his teeth. By the time he crossed Exchange Street, he was irritable as boiled coffee, and then he saw the girl.

She was wearing a polka-dot dress and brown shoes and anklets and an undersize jacket like the flying monkeys' in *The Wizard of Oz.* She had to be shivering, and she was standing as if waiting for a bus, only she wasn't at a bus stop. He thought he somehow knew her, and he pitched the burning nub of his cigarette into the gutter and started walking faster. Then she seemed to look at him, still a quarter of a block away, but with her eyes gaping wide as though she was scared and a foot from him. She spun away quickly and tried to turn the frayed red collar of the jacket up to cover her face, though it scarcely grazed her jaw. Wesley saw it was the girl he'd brought in from Shacktown two weeks before, the one with the boy in the locomotive boiler.

He stopped perhaps four feet behind her, and she was looking away at the auditorium building, standing with her shoulders squared like she knew he was there and wasn't going to talk to him on account of being angry. Wesley backed off a foot, and then he said, "You're going to get cold out here, dressed like that."

"You ain't wearing nothing but a suit coat," the girl said after a time, still turned away from him.

"It's wool. And I'm just walking home. You—you're standing here on the street."

"I ain't doing nothing," she said, and turned around to him. "Nothing for you to bother about."

He looked at her face, whiter in the daylight than it had seemed in the firelight of the Shacktown night, but still framed with limp brown hair pinioned by two red barrettes, her lips and eyes swollen, too big for her little face, just as her hands were too big and her arms too long for her body. "You told me you were going home," Wesley said finally. "Promised me, in fact."

The girl looked down at the pavement. "Had to make some money first, didn't I?" she said. "I got these clothes working at the Acme Steam Laundry. Saved up bus fare too."

Wesley jerked his thumb over his shoulder in the direction he'd just come from. "Bus depot's back that way. I could show you."

"I can find my own way. I ain't bothering anyone here."

"Maybe somebody will get a notion to bother you. This isn't the best place for a young girl to be standing around."

"You needn't concern yourself." The girl began to turn back toward the street.

"I have to concern myself," Wesley said. "Even if it's Sunday, even if it's my day off. I'm a police officer and you're a minor, loitering and whatever else."

The girl spun back and jutted her chin angrily. "I ain't no minor. Turned sixteen last week, didn't I?"

Wesley looked at her and he wanted to look down at her body, but he held his eyes on her face. "That's assuming you were fifteen the week before that. Seeing how good you keep your promises, that would be anybody's guess, wouldn't it?"

The girl's face softened. "I'm sixteen. Truly I am."

Wesley felt around in his jacket pocket for his cigarettes. "Well, Margie—"

"Maggie."

"Maggie, then." He shook a cigarette out of the pack. "There's things you can do when you're sixteen and things that you can't. Standing around here without adult say-so is one of the things you can't."

The girl smiled slightly, as though she were going to tease him. "But you could give me one of those smokes, couldn't you?"

"You really sixteen?"

"Born October 8, 1923."

"Okay then," Wesley said. "Happy birthday." He put the cigarette between his lips and fished another out of the pack and gave it to the girl, and the girl took it between her fingers and looked at it, as though examining a diamond ring. Wesley struck a match and lit his own cigarette and then cupped the match in his hands and held it under the girl's face, the flame a little amber drop in the cave of his palms, in the shadow of her hair. She drew in the smoke, and it streamed back out of her mouth like a flock of soaring birds, and for the first time Wesley noticed she was wearing lipstick.

He said, "Aren't you going to say thank you?"

"Sure. Thanks." She inhaled again and said, "It's swell."

Wesley looked down at his feet and then he looked up. "So assuming you've got any right to be out here at all, what exactly are you fixing to do with yourself?"

The girl sighed, "Oh, I'm going home. To Moline, like I told you." She looked down the street toward the bus depot. "But maybe not today."

"But this week maybe?"

"Sure. This week."

Wesley nodded. "That's good." He started to turn from her, to walk away, but he found himself turning back, and the girl was looking at him intently. Then she opened her mouth, and her lips were full and violet, as though they were blotting up the sky's stark aquamarine. "So what are you doing?" she said.

"Just walking home." Wesley shrugged.

"Mind if I walk with you? Just a little ways?"

"It's a free country. Suit yourself." Wesley pulled his shoulders in and began to walk, and the girl came up alongside him. Then they were standing, saying nothing, waiting for the light at the empty intersection of Seven Corners to change.

"I always think Sunday's sort of the saddest day," the girl began, and the light changed and they trudged across the street together. "Like the world's empty, like nobody's home."

"Folks seem to find things to occupy themselves," Wesley offered.

"Oh, I suppose you could ride a streetcar, if you had the nickel. Or go to the show if you had a quarter. But I ain't got a quarter, not to spare for a show."

"You got four bits for that lipstick somehow."

"I *had* that, from Billy. It was a gift. Gave me some toilet water too."

"You could go to church, on a Sunday," Wesley said. "Maybe it would do you some good."

"Never did for anyone I knew. Course, everyone I ever knew is sick or broke or dead or just wandering around lost somewhere," Maggie said. "I suppose you go to church all regular."

Wesley shook his head. "Not so you'd notice."

"So what are you telling me to go for?"

"It's not the same thing. You're young and still getting your character formed, still learning how to do right, how to live right." Wesley fingered his hat brim and gave it a pull. "Me, I'm old. Finished. Winding down. But you—you could get something out of it."

"Don't know what." Maggie pointed into a shop window set between a grocery store and a barbershop. "I mean, looky there. Pretty little Shirley Temple dolly in the window. Now, if some little girl wants it today, has her heart set on it, she can't have it on account of the store being closed on account of it being Sunday—all thanks to that church you think I ought to be sitting in."

"Well, I don't know about that. Seems to me folks are going to want a day off once a week, church or no church."

"Yeah, but those same folks are going to be needing stuff, wanting stuff, and that's just as important, maybe more important. You wait and see. Someday, in the future, you're going to be able to buy whatever you want when you want it, with nobody to stop you. And if I had a little girl and she said, 'Mama, pretty please, I sure would like that dolly,' we'd march right in there and buy it. Heck, we'd put it on account." Maggie looked at Wesley with an expression of triumph.

"Maybe so," he said, and turned his head away, as if talking to someone else. "But I just come from the newsreel at the Orpheum, and it was nothing but tanks and war over in Europe. And we'll get sucked into it, just like we did last time. So there's your future—Mr. Hitler or Mr. Stalin or the both of them as far as the eye can see."

Maggie looked at him quizzically. "You didn't stay for the feature?"

"Figured I couldn't stomach it. Alice Faye and that Don Ameche, with the slick little pencil mustache. Got better things to do."

"Waste of a quarter."

Wesley shrugged. "Didn't cost me anything. They let us in for free. Makes 'em feel more secure, having a cop in the audience."

"You kind of got it made, don't you? Being a policeman, go wherever you want to go, do whatever you want, and nobody can say nothing about it."

"Oh, yeah, it's swell. All the free ham sandwiches and weak coffee I want. Sitting parked in cars in the dark. Visiting the fine folks up in Shacktown. Meeting people from all walks of life, some of them rapists and killers, some of them just flat-out dead."

The girl stopped at the edge of the curb. They must have walked four blocks by now. She looked at him and said, "If it's so bad, why don't you do something else?"

Wesley got out his cigarettes. He didn't think to offer the girl another, nor did she ask, and he struck a match and lit one. "It's a little late now. I've been doing this for more years than you got birthdays. And I suppose now I'm what they'd say is an expert in my field. I got what they call expertise. I got a line in misery and wickedness like Carter's got pills."

They began to walk again, and Maggie said, "Kind of seems like the way you see it, it's too late for anything at all."

"Maybe. But I'd just as soon avoid surprises anyhow." Wesley didn't say any more, and they walked another block in silence. He wasn't going to tell her where the world was going. She must know. Her own life was proof, its mischance and cruelty like a stain on her dress.

He stopped at the curb. "Well, this is my street, so I'll say so long."

Maggie nodded, and then she looked down and away.

Wesley said, "So you're going to catch that bus, aren't you?"

"Sure."

"I don't want to have to worry about you, Maggie. You got to go home, no matter how bad it is. Because that's all any of us have got. So you go home, okay?"

"Sure," she said, and then she looked up at him and said, "I wonder if you could let me have another of those smokes."

Wesley dug in his pocket and shook his head. He found the pack and held it out to her. "There's only a couple left. Go ahead and take it."

The girl smiled. "Thanks. Appreciate it."

"You got matches?"

She shook her head.

Wesley searched himself again and handed her the box. "Here, then," he said, and he began to walk up the side street. He looked back and called out to her. "You go home now, Maggie. Don't make me worry about you." The girl nodded and waved to him, clutching the cigarette pack and matchbox in her other hand.

When Wesley got to the front of his house, a block and a half north, he looked back and he thought he could see her, smoking one of the cigarettes and gazing up the street in his direction. He walked up to his stoop and got out his key and began to open the door of his little house, and he stopped. He took six steps back down the walk and examined the house, and it was like a brittle brown leaf in the brilliant light and he thought he might cry, though for whose sake he could not say. He turned around and walked out to the sidewalk and looked back down to the corner where he'd left the girl, thinking he would call out to her, call her name, "Maggie." But when his eyes at last focused, the girl was gone and there was only a streetcar gliding by the place where they had stood together.

Sunday, October 15, 1939

I went to the pictures today at the Orpheum—*Hollywood Cavalcade,* with Don Ameche and Miss Alice Faye. It was not a drama but rather a sort of comedic history of the picture business from its origins, with contemporary stars re-creating the classics of twenty years ago alongside some of the original actors, but of course with sound and Technicolor. Thus did Miss Faye play a Mack Sennett bathing beauty and Don Ameche the director of a Keystone Cops picture, in what I suppose is a film of a film of a film being filmed. But then one has the real Buster Keaton and the real Ben Turpin walking through the midst of this diorama of the past, and so the past and the present are all quite *literally* mixed up together. The audience seemed to find this pleasant enough—save for a tall, rather bent man I saw leave at the end of the newsreel—but I believe I found it a little disconcerting. It makes me all too conscious of the failings of my memory.

For example, my recollection of the pictures released prior to, say, a few months ago and for a dozen or so years before that is, without recourse to my scrapbooks and memorabilia, very poor indeed; and that encompasses the whole of the time in which we have had talkies and some time before. Thus these pictures from fifteen or twenty years ago, re-created as though they were relics from the distant past—as I suppose *Buffalo Bill's Wild West Show* might have been for Father and Mother—are to me very fresh indeed: fresh in the sense not of depicting recent events but of seeming to have taken place in the only past I can recall living in. It is not that I somehow think I have just finished inhabiting 1916 or 1923 or what have you, for my recollections have the quality of something finished and done, of stories, so to speak, which I associate with memory. Rather, it is that they are for the most part the only stories—the only history—that I have inside my own self as opposed to in a scrapbook, and for that reason they are very bold and immediate, like dreams from which I am always just awakening.

I do not mean to say that I did not enjoy the picture. There was much in it about the making of moving pictures, which is something I am always curious about. Once, I persuaded the projectionist at the Tower Theater to let me come inside his little cell where the projectors are, and he showed me how the carbon rod burns inside the projector with a pure white light, like a Roman candle. Also, how the film runs off the spool and through the machine and passes through what he called the "gate" and is there illuminated and projected onto the screen and then moves past it and is gathered up again on the other spool. Of the screen, he explained how it is coated with something like glass to make it shiny—one might say it is almost gilded or bejeweled—and that is why the pictures on the movie screen have that glow.

I think it is that—the particular incandescence or luminosity—that I love about the pictures most, and I will watch almost

88

anything to see it. It is as though the world thus illuminated—as if from within itself—is more real than what we ordinarily see; as though it is the world as perhaps it truly is. And if a picture is in Technicolor, as of course the truly special ones now tend to be, so much the better. For it seems to me that those colors—whereby a girl's hair appears truly to be spun gold and her lips the hue of a plum and the sun that lights them is bright as an egg yolk—must be the world's "true colors" (if I may make a pun) and not the dull and murky shades our vision usually grants us. That is what the movies reveal to us—that and, I suppose, memories for those of us who have no memories—and I see no reason to believe that it is not so.

Wesley came into work on Monday morning, and there on his desk, like a vulture in a cottonwood tree, sat Farrell of the *Dispatch*. He wheeled around on the bony spoon of his hip and said, "Lieutenant, it's been too long. Thought I'd come in and catch up with you." He smiled at Wesley and eyed him. "So how's tricks?"

Wesley walked around to the back of his desk and set his newspaper down and put his hat on top of it. Then, on the other side of his blotter, he set down his cigarettes and his box of matches. He cradled his hands over the back of his chair and at last looked up at Farrell. "Tricks?" he said. "It ain't Halloween yet, not that I've heard."

Farrell ignored him and slid the newspaper out from Wesley's hat. "The *News*, eh? I should have guessed," he said. "You shouldn't read this crap. It'll give you a headache."

"Not as big a one as the likes of you." Wesley sat down and put his hand on his telephone, as though he needed to make a call. "So I'll keep my paper, thanks all the same."

Farrell handed him the newspaper. "Suit yourself. Guess you

just don't like genuine modern journalism, newspapering that keeps up with the times," Farrell said. "We got wire services, reporters with a little pep. At the *News*, they're still using smoke signals, Ouija boards, burning bushes."

"I get all the news I can take. I got a bellyful of news."

"So give me some."

Wesley lifted his hand off the telephone and extended his palms. "I just don't have a thing for you. Shelves are bare." He smiled archly. "You know if I had anything you'd be the first to know."

"Hey, I'm here to help, that's all."

Wesley put his hand back on the telephone and lifted the earpiece. "And I'm here to work. It's called police work, serving the public."

"The public doesn't like unsolved crime, particularly unsolved murders. Interferes with their digestion," Farrell said. "So let me reassure them for you."

Wesley pulled the mouthpiece toward him. "I told you I've got nothing."

"I hear you had a suspect maybe a week ago and then backed off him."

"Didn't pan out. Happens all the time."

"Couldn't have been somebody who resembled the ID you had by the Lawton Steps? Big guy, strange-looking, early in the morning?"

Wesley hung the earpiece back on the telephone. "So you know about that. Guess you been busy."

"You should have told me. It's only fair."

"You didn't ask."

"So you found him."

Wesley said, "I don't know what we found. Just some guy. Who was the wrong guy."

"What makes you so sure?"

"Interrogated him, even searched his place."

"Heard that too."

"You hear a lot. What do you need to talk to me for?"

"It's your case." Farrell grinned and dipped his shoulders.

"That's what I heard too."

"So how come your friends in Vice know so much about it?"

"It's a small place down here. We're all just one big happy family."

"But Vice is interested in this guy." Farrell leaned toward Wesley. "The word 'pervert' was used."

"Well, he might be, for all I know. But there's no evidence he ever murdered anybody, and that's where my interest in him ends."

"So who is he? Where's he live?"

"I've got no business telling you that. I figure your Vice friends could tell you if they cared to."

"They don't. Say it's a matter under current investigation," Farrell said. "They only give what they want—a crumb here, a crumb there."

"So they sent you to me?"

"Not in so many words. But it seemed to be . . . suggested."

Wesley leaned back in his chair and folded his hands. "I'd say they had you running in circles." He reached for his cigarettes. "It's a dead lead, Farrell. I mean, don't you think I'd like a suspect I could collar for this girl? Don't you think I'd like to take credit for that in the papers? But this isn't the guy. Believe me"— and Wesley struck a match and lit up—"when I find him, you'll be the first to know." He inhaled the smoke and let it out. "Right now, I'd say Welshinger and Trent—"

"Just Trent. Welshinger doesn't deign to talk to the press."

"Well, I have to give him credit for that. Anyhow, I'd say Trent's just having fun with you. Not that he's not a serious guy, a real serious guy, but maybe there's less to it than you think."

"I guess I'll have to find out," Farrell said.

"Please yourself."

"I always do," Farrell said, and left.

Wesley reached for the telephone again and then remembered that he had no one to call, that he had only been trying to get rid of Farrell by pantomiming that he was busy. In fact, he was dead in the water. He had been hoping he might get some breathing space during which to develop some new leads, maybe talk to all the Aragon girls again. Or maybe just figure out some way to convince himself that the murderer was a transient, somebody six states away by now, out of his reach and therefore out of sight, out of mind.

But now the Vice Boys had set Farrell on Wesley's scent again, just to punish him for getting in their way, for not letting them take down White—who for all Wesley knew was the murderer; who for all White himself knew was the murderer. Except now, after what had happened, Wesley didn't want him anymore, evidence or no evidence. Welshinger had Wesley pegged: It was like he had a broken heart. Where once he was totally fixed on White, captivated by him, now he didn't ever want to think about him or see him again. And the truth was, having been stung, he didn't want anyone else either. He had thought he wanted to do this thing for the dead girl, but he found the urge had left him, that he was too old or something. There was nothing left but weight, gravity pulling him down. Maybe he ought to retire and let Welshinger and Trent and Farrell claim the future, which was surely theirs and not his. He must already be the past, without the wit to see it. Not that he liked the past, but it didn't harry him like the present or intimidate him like the future. It just lay still, as if resting; retired, emptied out, and a little sad, like Maggie's Sundays.

Hyman Stein saw the big guy come in Monday night, crossing the room as though in his bedroom slippers. He'd asked the bartender for a ginger ale and sat staring at the counter for a while, churning his drink with the swizzle stick. Then he spoke to the bartender, and the bartender waved Hyman over, and the big guy asked if "Miss Fahey" was "in attendance this evening." Hyman told him she ought to be in around seven o'clock and mentioned that other girls were already there if he wanted a dance, but the big guy said he'd wait. Hyman went back to the office, and while he was walking through the green glass-bead curtain that led to the office and the girls' dressing rooms, he wondered if this could be the guy Lieutenant Welshinger had told him to look out for, the one who was supposed to be a regular and who might try to recruit his girls into vice activities.

In fact, the same night—perhaps a week before—Welshinger had spoken to Hyman Stein, he'd also talked to Ruby Fahey. He'd been sitting in the corner booth with Trent, drinking Seagram's and 7UP, and when the room quieted down, around eleven o'clock, he motioned Ruby over with one hand and waved Trent away with the other. Ruby knew who he was—Hyman pointed out all the cops who came in, saying they must under all circumstances be treated as what he liked to call "VIPs"—and knew that he was to be considered the biggest VIP of all, although for what reason Hyman never said.

So she had gone right over when he signaled her, and she could not even say if he had used his hand at all or perhaps had only set his still, azure-blue eyes on her and she had been drawn over to him like smoke up a chimney. Anyway, he patted the seat next to him, and once she sat down, he was very solicitous about ordering her a drink and listening to her as though he had all the time in the world. That was what she noticed about Welshinger, that and the cool draft she felt on her right shoulder, almost as though it were coming out of his mouth. Every cop she had ever met was in a hurry, itchy and tetchy, but Welshinger sat and smiled and nodded, as patient as your favorite spinster aunt; like he already knew everything you were going to say but since he liked you so much he was pleased as punch to hear it all over again.

So Ruby scarcely noticed that after a little while she was telling Welshinger about regular customers he seemed to be interested in, and she could not even say how the subject had come up or how—after she'd told him about Mr. Reeves, who wanted girls to come to his house and dress up in a nurse's uniform and give him enemas, and Jimmy, who smoked "tea" and procured abortions and was supposed to be a little arty—she'd begun to talk about Herbert White. Ruby had called Herbert just the other day about photographs he'd taken of her to use when she went to Hollywood, and he had told her some policemen had ransacked his place and threatened him and accused him of having something to do with Char Mortensen's death, which was the most ridiculous thing she had ever heard in her life seeing how Herbert was meeker than Cream of Wheat, even if he was big as Croesus—no, maybe not Croesus, maybe more like Humpty-Dumpty and, say, Paul Bunyan.

At that, Welshinger not only nodded, as he had been doing all along, but said yes, he understood, and wasn't it a shame. There'd been a terrible mix-up down at the department and it was a damn shame, but she ought to tell her friend that she had it on the best authority that he wouldn't have any further problems. Better not to say exactly on *whose* authority, if she wouldn't mind; in fact, if she could keep a secret—and he was sure she could—the whole sorry mess was on account of some bungling in the homicide division. There was a lack of professionalism, of expertise, among the officers there, sadly enough, which officially was none of Welshinger's business. But maybe if Ruby was willing to keep him apprised of her friend's movements and activities as best she could . . . well, maybe he could act as a sort of guardian angel for Herbert and at the same time persuade the Homicide people to back off him, seeing as how Welshinger would be keeping an eye on him. It wasn't much, Welshinger admitted, but would Ruby consider letting him do her that little favor? He put his hand over Ruby's hand, not touching her, but just sheltering her hand with his own, and he said he could see that Ruby was a nice girl, a very attractive girl, a girl that was going places, and Welshinger liked to do a favor where he could for a girl like that. Would Ruby permit him?

Ruby had agreed without a thought and, on Saturday, informed Herbert of this fortuitous intervention on his behalf, without mentioning the name of his benefactor, as she had promised. Now, on Monday, when she arrived at the Aragon at about seven-fifteen, she was a little surprised to find Herbert waiting for her at the bar, a bit preoccupied, perhaps even agitated, over what she could not imagine.

Monday, October 16, 1939

I write this evening having just returned from the Aragon Ballroom and having had a very exciting visit with Miss Ruby (I dub her thusly, thinking "Miss Fahey" too formal, given the new intimacy of our relation but "Ruby" insufficiently elevated to render justice to the esteem in which I hold her). In fact, it would be fair to say I can scarcely contain myself!

The purpose of my visit was to put a proposition to her, to wit, that I might photograph a further folio of poses of her. I must say I had every expectation of her declining, since she had already posed for me three times. In fact she said she would be delighted; that in fact she would consider it "swell" and that she would look forward to spending more time with me! Needless to say, I could not have been more delighted or surprised. She further allowed, to my even greater chagrin, that she had been meaning to "check up" on me by way of "looking out" for me, as though to say that she thinks of herself as a sort of guardian or protector! It is a curious and wonderful world indeed wherein an orphan such as myself, destitute of all family for well nigh twenty years, is at last in middle age thus befriended by a lovely young woman nearly a generation his junior!

I should, I suppose, explain what impelled me to go to see her in the first place. The thought stole upon me yesterday evening, as I was preparing for bed, that perhaps in Miss Ruby Fahey I had stumbled up on my ideal model: someone with whom I might make not just a few photographs or even a portfolio but, so to speak, an entire *oeuvre,* as they say in art circles—a series of photographs in which my camera might explore one physiognomy in great detail over time: a face and body in all its states and seasons, one might say, rather than piecemeal.

Now, when this idea struck—and I do mean *struck,* for it was like a thunderbolt—and I realized Miss Ruby's perfect suitability to be my model, it was all I could do not to dress myself there and then and seek her consent that very evening. But I was able to restrain myself, albeit with no little tossing and turning last night, for it was as though I had suddenly come to see my life's purpose, grandiose as perhaps that may sound.

I think some of the credit for this sea change must lie with Miss Ruby herself, for not only is she matchless in her beauty (not, admittedly, perhaps the equal of Miss Veronica Galvin, but this is not, after all, Hollywood) but our relationship is exceedingly companionable. We get on very amiably, and I genuinely believe we are friends: I am utterly in her debt with regard to clearing up the appalling events of the week before last and hope I may find some small way in which I might repay her. When I think of her face, her sweetness and prettiness, and her kindness, and with what cheer and want of self-regard she bestows these virtues on the likes of me, I believe I am the recipient of an utterly unexpected, unwarranted, and seemingly boundless blessing. It is as though I were standing on my doorstep on a winter's evening with my hat and gloves and scarf, preparing to set off on a journey, holding my hat before me absentmindedly, and into it, with a little sizzle like a firework, fell a shooting star.

The girl was sitting on Wesley's stoop on Tuesday evening. She had a coat now, a big brown man's coat, somebody's castoff.

Wesley said, "It's news to me if the bus to Moline stops here."

The girl looked up and smiled at him. "I just run out of smokes," she said.

Wesley nodded and took his pack from his pocket and gave her a cigarette. He took out another for himself, sat next to her on the stoop, and lighted their two cigarettes. He inhaled and then looked at her and said, "So you got a crime to report?"

This time she looked a little wounded. She gazed down at her feet or perhaps at the fractures in Wesley's sidewalk. She finally said, "I just come by to say hello," and added, "seeing how I was in the neighborhood."

"Looking for a handout, I suppose." Wesley had not had a good day.

The girl suddenly faced him, firm-lipped but with her eyes alight as he recalled them the first time he had seen her, with Billy in the steam boiler. "Not looking for nothing. Just come to say how d'y'do." Her face loosened. "But you're a sour one, ain't you. Suspicious too." She looked away again. "Even what with you being a policeman, there's no call to be treating everybody that way."

"Hard habit to break. World starts to seem like a quarry with something under every rock."

The girl smiled at him and shook her hair. "I ain't no snake. I thought we was friends. You done me a favor once. Remember?"

"So I did. Must have been feeling peculiar that day." Wesley stood. "But seeing how that's the case, I suppose I ought to at least give you a cup of coffee." He took out his key and motioned toward the door. The girl stood next to him, and the cylinders in the lock rasped and the door clicked open.

"Folks in this neighborhood all lock their doors?"

"Probably just me," Wesley said. "I'm suspicious, right?"

The girl stood just inside the doorway while Wesley went into the sitting room and opened the blinds. The house seemed to recoil before the light, and the girl thought every surface in the house looked orangy brown, like old newspaper spattered with tobacco juice. Dust spun over the faded rugs.

Wesley was walking back toward the kitchen, talking as he went. "I don't keep much in the way of groceries here, but I know I got some coffee somewhere, maybe some Uneeda biscuits too." He disappeared, and Maggie stood alone in the little dining room as though inside a beer bottle, the whole world silent and stale.

Wesley came back out of the kitchen looking chagrined. "Thought I had some. But I don't," he said. He shrugged. "I got a bottle of seltzer and a jar of strawberry conserve. And a box of baking soda. Other than that, the cupboard's kind of bare."

"That's okay," Maggie said, and she stood next to the table, waiting for him to tell her what to do. He was looking at her as though he were remembering something; his eyes swept up the length of her coat, and then he drew in his breath and licked his upper lip quickly and said, "Well, sit down for a minute at least. Take a load off of your feet." He led her into the sitting room and patted the cushion of a spindly-legged davenport. Maggie sat down without taking her coat off, and Wesley backed himself away from her, half bent, and settled into a chair across the room with an old doily slung over its back.

Maggie cradled her hands in her lap, and then she said, "So what do you eat here, seeing as there's no groceries." Her eyes scanned the room, following the hookless picture rail around its perimeter and at last coming to rest on Wesley.

"Well, I kind of told you—you know, how people are always giving me ham sandwiches and coffee and red hots and bags of peanuts and so forth. Chicken legs. Hamburgers. It kind of adds up over the day."

"Kind of the way I been eating."

"You been getting enough? You look kind of skinny," Wesley said.

"I tend that way. From my mama's people. But I get plenty. Girls at the laundry all share."

Wesley swallowed and then said, "Where you sleeping?"

"I'm flopping here and there."

"What? Outside? Up where I found you?"

"No, no," Maggie said. "Just around. With friends."

"What kind of friends?"

"Not men friends, if that's what you're thinking. Only man friend I ever had, your buddies run out of town, didn't they?" Maggie pressed her cigarette out in the ashtray on the bare table next to the davenport. "So don't worry." She jutted her chin in the direction of the kitchen. "*I* ought to worry about *you*. No food. Living in this dark old place like a mole in a hole. You're the one needs tending."

Wesley demurred. "Suits me well enough," he said, but he felt a little ashamed.

"Looky here," Maggie said. "You done me a favor. Let me do you one back." She stood and Wesley looked at her in the long coat, at the places where the threadbare hem lapped her ankle socks and where her nail-bitten hands hid in the furrows of the sleeves. She opened the coat and let it fall on the davenport like a veil from her face. It seemed to Wesley that she stood very erect, almost noble in her viscose polka-dot dress, as if she were the statue of Lady Justice or an angel. She said, "Let me at that kitchen of yours," and in her scuffed and cracked brown shoes strode into the heart of Wesley's little house.

Maggie found a rusted canister of Bon-Ami and a brush under the sink, and she set to work. She cleaned the stove and the drain board, and then she swept and mopped the floor, removing a huge tangle of dust bunnies from beneath the icebox and a scab of grease and crumbs that underlay the stove. She continued in this manner until seven o'clock, then announced she was going home.

Wesley began to ask where "home" might be, and Maggie interrupted, saying, "With a girlfriend." He had been standing in the kitchen doorway all this time, half amused but also half humiliated, as though she had been scrubbing the soil from the crotch of his underwear. Then he said quietly, "You know if I could I'd let you stay. But a young girl being seen to board with a police officer, it wouldn't do, would it?"

Maggie shook her head. "No, I don't suppose it would. Anyhow, I got somewhere to go, don't I?" She moved to fetch her coat, took it from the davenport, and turned back to face Wesley. "How about you just say, 'Thank you very kindly for the washing and scrubbing, miss,' and leave it at that? 'Cause you got no cause to worry about me or anybody else. You got your hands full with yourself. Seems to me you can scarcely wash behind your own ears."

She put on the coat, and now—he could not say through what moment or transformation—Wesley saw that she was a young woman, not so very different from his Rose when they'd first met; from his Louise in the last few years before she left. He could see the weight of her, the shape of her, the shadow she cast back across the davenport and the empty wall. He nodded and said, "Thank you very kindly, miss, for the washing and scrubbing."

Tuesday, October 17, 1939

Filed all morning, hard-boiled egg inside the station for lunch, straightened supply room and swept in the afternoon. Got off streetcar at the top of the hill and walked back to light a candle for luck. Then home, to begin preparations for tomorrow's initial session with Miss Ruby.

Have kept this brief, as I am beside myself with anticipation. As Nanna used to say, if I were a cat, I'd have kittens!

* * *

Wesley thought he could see Maggie's hair coming up the street, no longer dull brown but a luminous sienna. She stood when he came up the sidewalk, and Wesley saw she was holding a sack.

"So what you got there, young lady?" He was afraid it might contain her belongings. But then a minute before that, when he rounded the corner into his street, he'd been afraid she wouldn't be waiting for him, as he had pictured her doing all day—pictured her so many times, with such an ache of hoping, that it was more prayer than picturing.

"Food," she said. "For your empty larder. Bacon. Eggs. Crisco. Milk. Bisquick. And coffee."

"Where'd you get the money for all that?"

She smiled at him defiantly. "Had some saved. For a bus ticket."

"Christ, Maggie. I shouldn't cuss around you, but Christ." Wesley sighed.

He let them inside. Maggie went to the back and put her groceries on the drain board. She came out again and laid her coat on the davenport. Wesley saw she had a different dress, dull red like wine.

"Where'd you get that?"

"None of your beeswax. Always investigating, aren't you, Lieutenant? Always shellacking everything with vinegar. Try saying something nice. Then maybe you'll find yourself thinking something nice by the by, too."

Wesley said, "It's pretty."

"That's better."

Then Wesley was moved, as though the floor of his little house had thrown him off kilter, having yawed like the deck of a ship, to say more. "You're a pretty girl, Maggie," he said.

"And that's even better still," Maggie replied. "Now, we got coffee, hotcakes, bacon, and eggs. How d'you like your eggs?"

"Over easy."

"I had a feeling it weren't sunny side up."

She came to his house in this manner the next two days, and on Friday, after she had finished cooking and washing up, she fell asleep on the davenport, and without a thought he covered her with an old wool car robe he and Rose had gotten for a wedding present.

The next night, Saturday night, he showed her Louise's room. He jutted his chin in the direction of the bed and said, low and shyly, "You might as well sleep here." Maggie made her way to the bed hesitantly, on the balls of her feet, as though she were walking through a flower bed. She sat down, pressing her palms into the bed on either side of her, and crossed her ankles. Then she released her weight with a smile, settling into the mattress, and looked up at Wesley, smiling still more. Wesley cupped his hand over the precipitous slope of his face, shielding his weary eyes from her beauty, shielding her eyes from the sight of the tears he thought must now come, for joy's sake.

Wednesday, October 18, 1939

I write this at eight o'clock after a most eventful evening. Miss Ruby left an hour ago after a ninety-minute session, and now the negatives are washing and the radio is playing very low.

She arrived promptly at five-thirty, I having rushed home by streetcar in order to be here by five-fifteen. I had set up my lights and camera the night before and cleared a corner of the parlor to make, as it were, an atelier where we would have lots of room to work. I wanted everything to be just as it should be, not only for the sake of the work but in the interests of Miss Ruby's comfort. For these photographs I also for the first time decided to use two electric photolamps rather than a flash or a single Mazda lamp. I am keen to get the best technical results I can and also to use light more effectively as a means of "modeling" Miss Ruby's form through the judicious application of light and shade.

As I said, she arrived exactly as agreed, bringing a couple of dresses she thought might be suitable, as well as some scarves and a boa. She went back to my bedroom to change, and I must say I felt a huge sort of breathlessness at the idea that she was in my room shedding and then donning her garments, rather as if some mystery of great enormity were taking place right here in my humble quarters!

She looked "stunning" (as the magazines say) when she came out, wearing a dress of a medium-blue shade and with her legs bare, as I had requested. There is perhaps no point in my trying to say how it is her beauty strikes me—it is to that end that I take photographs after all—but I must aver that each time I see her, the force of it is both different and stronger: not so much something I see and wonder at, but a light that illuminates me, in whose intensity I bask. The dress served to accentuate the curve—I want to say the scroll, the arc—of the place where the base of her bust flares away from her midriff, and she had tied back her hair in the way she must know I like (falling in a wave over one shoulder), though I do not know that I have ever mentioned it. Her face was lightly rouged, her lips were scarcely tinted. She does know that I do not care for a lot of "face paint."

I led her, thusly attired, to the divan. I had already envisioned her posing seated with her knees bent and her bare feet exposed up on the divan, perhaps holding her head back so as to let her hair fall perpendicular. I took her shoes—I could feel a warm moistness inside them: not, heaven forbid, that she had sweated in them but rather as though she had merely breathed upon them for a moment—and instructed her as to the pose I was hoping for. As it transpired, she ended up leaning back onto her palms, her face turned up at the ceiling, her hair dangling free, and her torso erect skyward. It was, I believe, an exquisite pose, at once ecstatic and innocent.

I then turned my lights on. I had 150 watts to her left front and 75 to her right and a further 100 behind and above her, this being the classic arrangement the magazines suggest. As I turned them on, beginning with the rear one and finishing, as a sort of grand finale, with the 150-watt "key" light, I could not but think back to *Hollywood Cavalcade* and the banks of kliegs portrayed therein.

But scarcely had I got behind the ground glass of my camera, checked the diaphragm, and placed my finger on the shutter release, than the lights went out—not just my photo lamps but every light in the house, together with the radio, which I had tuned to NBC Red, hoping some music might help Miss Ruby relax.

Needless to say, it was an unexpected development, and one not a little awkward. Ruby cried, "Herbert," and I suspect I replied "Yes?" rather weakly, for the parlor was black as a cave and I had utterly lost my bearings. Then I added, "We appear to have blown a fuse." Miss Ruby said, "Do you know where the box is?" and though she sounded very far away, I could smell what I believe must have been her hair, or rather the shampoo she cleanses her hair with.

The fuse box is in fact in the basement, but I told Miss Ruby I had best secure a candle prior to going down. I could now discern some dim shapes in the room, and made my way in the direction of where I thought the fireplace lay, holding my hands out before me. Having taken some dozen steps forward, I found myself at the bookcase which holds my scrapbooks, and from there I successfully felt my way to the fireplace mantel and the candles and the box of Ohio Blue Tips I keep there. It took me but a few seconds to procure myself a lighted candle and another for Miss Ruby, who had now joined me next to the fireplace.

I said I would go down and replace the fuse, and Miss Ruby insisted on accompanying me, saying she found the dark "spooky." I readily agreed, for to tell the truth, I was not eager to make the descent alone, and our having been thrown together in this dilemma seemed to have established a special closeness between us just then. She was holding the candle with both hands, and I could see the light coloring her lips, and the flesh of her nostrils was rendered translucent and deep crimson by the flame.

We went out in the hallway and found no one was about. Presumably the other tenants were out, or their electricity supply had not been affected by our little accident. In fact, the light in the foyer was still on, and I suppose, had I thought of it, that must have meant the basement lights were functioning. However, in the event, we went down with only our candles for illumination. The stairs were rather steep, and when I opened the door, the cold came up out of the basement, together with the smell of coal and damp laundry soap I associate with Nanna's basement, albeit lacking its particular aroma of scorched linen. As I stepped over the threshold, I felt Miss Ruby's hand on my waist. If you don't mind, Herbert, she said, I think I'll hang on to you. I could feel the tips of her fingers through the fabric of my shirt, and I suspect I nearly tripped, head over heels, down the basement stairs.

But our descent passed without incident. We shuffled together across the basement floor like dancers or tightrope walkers and at last reached the fuse box, on top of which I was blessed to find a box of replacement Buss fuses. It took some time to locate my fuse—or rather fuses, for the apartment has two dedicated to it—and replace the old one. I must say I was mightily distracted by Miss Ruby, who clung to my side and whose breath I could feel come in little pulses. It occurs to me now that perhaps not since I was last dandled on Nanna's knee have I had such proximity to the body of a woman, however bizarre and unforeseen the circumstance.

Just as we reached the top of the stairs, we heard a pop from inside my apartment, and upon entering discovered that, although the lights were now functioning again, my 150-watt photo lamp had exploded, presumably overwhelmed by the surge of restored electricity. Now, Miss Ruby had been barefooted all this time, and in returning to her station on the divan, she stepped on a piece of the shattered photo lamp and gave a little yelp. I ran over to her and insisted that she sit while I inspected the wound, although she declared it was nothing. It was on the littlest toe of her right foot, and while she was correct in believing it was a small cut, it bled profusely; as I held her foot in my hand, the blood welled up out of the cut and fell in drops on the floor like the dripping of a faucet. I have never been able to fathom the color of blood, as it seems to be at once red and somehow blue—not violet or purple, mind you, but simultaneously red and blue, as though it were both hot and cold, or ice and flame. But I digress.

I found tincture of iodine and an adhesive bandage in the

bathroom and said I would dress her wound. She sat smiling, as though she were indulging me, and I felt her wince when I applied the iodine. I found myself saying, "There, there," to her, as someone once must have said to me, and patted her on the leg when I was done, and said, "All better." She smiled again, and in that moment I felt a great tenderness toward her, a feeling of wanting to enfold her within myself, as I suppose a parent must feel toward a child. Yet I could not but notice that this emotion seemed to be the shadow image of what I feel when I am, as it were, overwhelmed by beauty, by the need to merge with it, and the consuming physical sensations that accompany that urge. Or perhaps—and this seems more the case to me now—it is the feeling I had tending Miss Ruby's wound that is the original and the other that is the shadow. But that, too, is neither here nor there. In any case, in the midst of these twinned feelings, I thought it best to withdraw rather quickly from the divan and take my post behind the camera.

Having at last recovered from these various excitements, we worked for about an hour, and I exposed two rolls in all. As I had no spare 150-watt bulb, the smaller photolamps had to suffice, so my experiments with more lighting will have to wait until I can get down to Fisher's and obtain another. Miss Ruby resumed the pose she had struck when the mishap with the fuse occurred, and we staged some variations on it in prone and supine positions, in what I like to think were in a Greco-Roman vein. In all these, Miss Ruby took pains to conceal the bandage on her toe, which she felt would hardly be decorous, hiding it in her hand, tucking her foot beneath her, or entwining it with its unblemished mate. It will be interesting, in viewing the finished prints, to see whether these contortions suggest that she was in fact hiding something, or that they merely came about for their own purposes, for the mere sake of art and beauty. I, of course, shall know the true reasons for a while, and then I shall forget them and will see the photographs just as anyone else might.

When we were done, she went back to my bedroom to change, and I tried to occupy myself with straightening up the parlor. But I found myself unable to do anything but stand stock-still in the hallway with the light hanging over me, very stark, and the radio rather dim in the background, and, dimmer still, the faint sounds of Miss Ruby and her clothes, moving into one another.

She came out, and I straightened myself with rather a start. It is odd how when a woman leaves a room and then comes back, even if only for a moment, she seems to be someone else—or at least altered—when she returns. Now, perhaps this is simply because women replenish their makeup so frequently and also adjust their hair, as though they thought themselves perpetually decaying or unfinished. But perhaps they are merely in that constant state of becoming that I like to think we all are in, and somehow it is more evident in the female sex than the male. It may also be the case that this is a result of their special affinity to beauty. In contrast, it has always seemed to me that men alter very little, no matter how often they change their clothes, developing only very slowly the wrinklings and surface protuberances that come with age, rather like potatoes lardered somewhere cool and dark.

In any event, Miss Ruby bade me good night very warmly and agreed to a further session in a few days. She mentioned in parting that she was sure she had left a pair of shoes here last month.

I told her I did not recall her doing so and did not remember having come across any footwear other than my own, which being size fourteen, I joked, I should be likely to be able to differentiate from hers. But I shall have a look around before her next visit.

On Thursday night at the Aragon Ballroom, Ruby Fahey sat with Clare and Gwendolyn in the corner booth, the "VIP booth," Hyman liked to call it, and waited for customers—even one customer—to come in. The truth was that except for weekends, business was slow; to Hyman's way of thinking, it grew a little slower each day and had been doing so for years, and that was a view confirmed by the figures in his ledger, a book tall as a stovepipe hat, in which he recorded each night's receipts in green ink. He told the girls people just weren't "convivial" anymore, but secretly he thought they somehow just weren't as lonely; lonely enough, that is, to take solace in a dance with a pretty girl they didn't know, for the cost of a dollar and a drink.

Back five years, in 1934 or so, when things looked really bleak, people knew how to take their comfort where and when they could. A fellow came to the Aragon and he didn't want to leave, he wanted to stay all night. Tomorrow was a bill collector waiting at the bottom of the stairs. But now the future was like one of those new men's room vending machines a guy had tried to sell him last month, a treasure chest with a mirror on it so that same fellow could look at himself and think: So who's Mr. Lucky? Maybe me! And inside, for two bits, there were Bakelite combs, chrome nail clippers with key chain attached, Brylcreem to give your hair that radium-phosphorescent sheen, Sen-Sen to make your breath sweet while you sweet-talked your sweetie, DeLay cream to make loving last longer, last all night and into the morning, into a dawn that was nothing more or less than the rosy smile of the future herself. But the future was going to be the death of Hyman Stein, and the Aragon his headstone.

So the girls waited and talked and sipped soda pop out of highball glasses. Gwendolyn had had a date with a guy who sold Packards, and was hoping he'd call her back. Clare was thinking of learning ballet. Ruby told them about her session with Herbert White the night before, about the blown fuse and how sweet he was when he tended her foot, how it was what she imagined being rescued by a Saint Bernard dog must be like: the warm, slow-breathing bulk, hovering patiently, intently.

Clare said, "So did he lick your face?" and Gwendolyn tittered, and then they both slapped the tabletop and giggled together. Clare leaned into Ruby. "Seriously, doesn't he ever try anything?"

"He could have kissed me then, or before, in the basement. I wouldn't have minded. I'd have kind of liked it."

"Sister," Gwendolyn said, "I believe you're touched."

Clare shook her head in feigned disbelief. "Ruby, I bet you could have any man you wanted. But you don't care. You just want to spoon with Quasimodo and his Kodak."

"He's sweet," Ruby said.

"He ought to be," said Clare. "Goofy old thing getting the likes of you to pose for him. Does he drool like a Saint Bernard too?"

"He's a total gentleman. He's respectful. But I can tell he adores me."

"Then you ought to charge him at least," said Gwendolyn.

"He gives me copies of whatever he takes. That's fair enough. Besides, he's my friend."

"The kind of friend you'd like to have kiss you," Clare said.

Gwendolyn rolled her eyes and shuddered. "Imagine what the rest of him is like."

Ruby straightened herself as though to bring the matter to a close. "It's not like that," she said emphatically. "He's just kind. Like he thinks everything in the world is his responsibility to care for. Not like he's to blame or guilty for it. But like it's his to tend, like a garden."

Clare said, "Bet he'd like to plant some seeds—"

"Good evening, ladies." Welshinger stood next to the table as though he'd been there all the time, as though they'd lowered him out of the ceiling on wires.

"Evening," chirped Clare and Gwendolyn, almost in unison.

"You girls behaving yourselves?" Welshinger said, and slid his hand onto the table. He didn't wait for anyone to answer. "I bet you are. I don't even need to ask, do I?" He looked at Gwendolyn and Clare. "Girls, why don't you go keep my friend Lieutenant Trent company at the bar for a moment, while Ruby and I have a word?" Gwendolyn and Clare nodded and slipped out of the booth, and when they had crossed the room, Welshinger sat down next to Ruby. "So you got anything for me, Ruby?" he said. "What gives with your friend Mr. White?"

"Nothing, really. I was over there last night. He was taking my picture again."

"He say anything about what he's up to, who he's seeing?"

"I don't think he's up to anything. I don't think he does anything at all but go to work and take photos and go to the pictures."

"Going to see him again anytime soon?"

"He's going to take my picture again on Sunday. And Saturday we're going to the opening night of a movie he wants to see. With Veronica Galvin. She's his favorite star."

"Any other women he likes that you know of? That he's got a thing for?"

"No; nobody at all that he's mentioned to me."

"Good." Welshinger got up. "So you keep on keeping tabs on him for me, okay? That way I can help him out, help you out." Ruby nodded, and then she reached out and touched his sleeve as he began to move away. "I was just wondering if maybe when you needed to talk to me, maybe you wouldn't do it in front of the girls. I wouldn't want them to think that I was in any kind of trouble. . . ."

Welshinger's face suddenly hardened, and then it eased again in an instant. He bent down and spoke to her slowly, liltingly, as to a child. "Oh, but you could be in trouble, Ruby. You could be, you see. Without even knowing it." He stood erect again. "That's why it's good that I'm your friend. So I can help you."

Saturday, October 21, 1939

A day of great excitement and, I must admit, some disappointment. Miss Ruby was to accompany me to the opening of Veronica Galvin's new picture, *Steens Mountain*, and at work this morning I could scarcely keep my head about my business. After work ended at noon, I went to Husch Brothers and bought a new necktie for the occasion, and went home and bathed and dressed. Miss Ruby, who, it transpires, lives not far from me, was to come by at four o'clock, the show being scheduled for five o'clock at the Paramount.

She arrived promptly—I daresay a few minutes early—and looked as stunning as I have ever seen her. I insisted that I photograph her there and then, even if only a snapshot, and she agreed, provided I would join her in the photograph. Thus did I set up my camera before the fireplace with a flashbulb and used my long release cable to trip the shutter. I am not sure this produces a very elegant result, but it should nonetheless make for a jolly souvenir. When I took the picture, she put her arm around my waist, and after I had tripped the shutter and we were done, she did not pull her arm away but let it rest there a moment. I cannot really describe how this made me feel.

After that, we walked up to the stop and waited for the streetcar to come, and when it arrived we took seats in the very back. As we rode through the tunnel, Miss Ruby allowed as how the tunnel always gave her what she called the "heebie-jeebies"; she worried it might cave in, and the little glimpses that the lightbulbs hung on the walls gave as the streetcars passed suggested the tunnel was dank and full of spiders. I told her I thought it was engineered to a very high standard; in fact, my father had taken me to the opening of the tunnel when I was four years old—it is one of the earliest things I can remember—and he had told me what a fine achievement it was. Miss Ruby asked me to tell her about my parents, and I said there was not much to say, my having lost them both so early; or rather having lost my mother at birth and my father to his grief—lost him to his loss, I suppose—and then to the war. But I told her I had a letter he had sent me from the front, which I treasured very deeply, and that I would show it to her sometime.

We arrived at the Paramount in plenty of time, and as I bought our tickets, I inquired of the man in the ticket booth whether this was in fact the "premiere" of the new Veronica Galvin picture, *Steens Mountain*. He said he didn't know anything about any premiere but that it was the first showing, and there was a fresh newsreel too. Now, I thought that perhaps the nature of the occasion was not a matter of public knowledge—

that Miss Galvin preferred that it be a semiprivate function, limited to those with whom she had corresponded and perhaps a few civic dignitaries. But the ticket man denied knowing anything about this as well. Finally I told him that Miss Galvin had written to me about the matter, and he said, "That's nice for you, Mac," and dismissed me, as others were waiting to purchase tickets.

Well, I supposed there was no reason for him to know anything about it, not being the manager, whom I attempted to locate once Miss Ruby and I were inside the lobby. I was directed to his assistant, who was working behind the confectionery counter, and I introduced myself and said I was expecting to rendezvous here with a personage he might be familiar with, and winked broadly. This produced no response, and I asked if his superior was on the premises, and he said no, did I have a complaint? And I said, No, no complaint at all, though I was now deeply puzzled.

Miss Ruby then took my arm and said that perhaps the letter really had meant only that the picture and not Miss Galvin herself was coming. I admitted that this could be the case, but secretly entertained the idea that perhaps Miss Galvin was only late or had planned to appear after the movie, rather than before.

We went inside and took seats toward the back. This is not my custom, but I wanted to be able to reconnoiter the lobby doors should Miss Galvin and her party come and watch the movie from that location, this being the habit of Hollywood professionals. The previews and the newsreel were shown, and although a few latecomers arrived during this time—the theater was scarcely one-third full—there was no one I recognized. I do not remember anything much about the newsreel, save that apparently England is going to be in the war and this may in turn be a force for dragging our own country into the European conflagration.

Although I glanced from time to time at the doors behind me, I concentrated on the feature once it was under way. I noticed from the credits that the writer and director of this new Veronica Galvin movie are identical to those of most of her other pictures. I suppose this is Miss Galvin's doing and that they constitute a "company" of artists of the kind Mr. Orson Welles is head of. One cannot help but notice that there is a certain similarity in the plot and characters as well. In this picture, for example, Miss Galvin plays a waitress in a café at the site of an enormous dam being built in the Pacific Northwest. She becomes involved with one of the workers on the project, who unbeknownst to her has a criminal past and is trying to avoid capture by working under a "nom de plume" among the thousands of men employed at the site. Unhappily, a man is killed on the face of the dam—accidentally, as it happens—and Miss Galvin's amour is wrongly accused. He flees in a stolen car, accompanied by Miss Galvin, who is hopelessly in love with him, even after he at last tells her about his past. They are pursued and at last cornered by the authorities in a desolate spot called Steens Mountain in eastern Oregon. There, surrounded as they are by federal "G-men," state troopers, and the local sheriff, Miss Galvin convinces him that he must give himself up if they are to have a future together. He agrees and goes out into the open, where the authorities, misinterpreting his movement, shoot him dead. Miss Galvin is, needless to say, devastated and is comforted to a certain extent in the final scene by the wise old local sheriff. He tells her, Ma'am, some men is just made for wrong and bad luck, and no soul under heaven can help them be otherwise.

I was quite moved by the performances and, as ever, by Miss Galvin's beauty. She looked very becoming in her waitress uniform and also, in the later wilderness scenes, in a pair of tawny, high-waisted slacks and a plaid woolen shirt. I asked Miss Ruby if she had ever had occasion to wear a uniform, and she said no, not since school. I suspect she was quite charming to behold in those days!

In the lobby after the show, I insisted that we wait a while longer, but no one came, and when the audience for the seven o'clock performance began to file in, Miss Ruby suggested that we leave. I agreed, although doubtless she could read the disappointment on my face and tried to comfort me, saying it must be very sad for me, but Veronica Galvin was lucky indeed to have such devoted fans as I. Then she proposed that I come with her to the Aragon Ballroom. She didn't have to begin work until seven-thirty, and we could sit at the bar and enjoy each other's company until then. I said it was very kind of her to think of that, but I was not sure I would be very good company, as I was suddenly feeling a bit fatigued. The truth was that I now found the idea of seeing her—or really even imagining her—at work dancing with other men terribly disconcerting, although I have never given this a thought before.

Anyway, she patted my arm several times, saying she would see me tomorrow for our photographic session, and then she kissed me on my cheek and held her face next to mine for what seemed to me a very long time. Now that I am home by myself, I realize that once again, in that moment, I felt the two feelings I felt with her the other day: the tenderness and the desire. I am still wondering which feeling is the parent and which is the child; or as I put it at the time, which is the original and which the shadow. But now I perceive that it is even more complicated

117

than that, for I am assuming that the original is the cause of the shadow, when in fact it is only part of the cause. Perhaps it is because I have just returned from the pictures, and from looking back every few minutes to see if anyone was standing by the door and seeing only the dust and the cigarette smoke in the beam of the projector; but now I understand that the cause of the shadow is as much the light that illuminates the original as it is the original itself. In fact, perhaps the light, which I had not thought to think of before—had not seen or noticed before— is the true cause of both. I am inclined to think that the two feelings I felt may be species or varieties of love, but of the nature of the light I cannot yet speak.

On Sunday morning, Wesley awoke at six-thirty, and in passing down the hall past the door of Louise's old room he felt something was amiss; there was no daylight coming into the hall from her room, where there was always light at this time of year. Then he realized the shade must be pulled down and that the girl, Maggie, was asleep in Louise's bed. He could hear her breathing softly, and as his eyes adjusted to the sunlight that was leaching into the room through the window shade, he could make out her shape under the covers.

He went into the kitchen and filled the basket of the percolator with coffee and set it on the stove and sat down at the kitchen table. He wondered what he ought to do about the girl; he wondered how he could get rid of her. But he could not bend his mind in that direction. Instead he kept thinking of the old flannel robe in Louise's closet and how the girl might look in it. Around seven o'clock, he took a cup of coffee to the doorway of Louise's room and stood there, not sure what he was doing. All of a sudden the girl sat up, with a kind of start, and then she looked at him and smiled. She webbed her hands together and put them behind her head and stretched, and her chest arced up and toward Wesley's eyes. He saw she was wearing an old white undershirt, and he could see her nipples through the abraded fabric and they looked like raisins under cheesecloth, like brown eyes through a veil.

She spoke. "That coffee wouldn't have my name on it, I don't suppose."

"Sure does," Wesley said, and stepped across the room and handed her the cup. He went to the closet and found the robe hanging on a hook on the back of the door. He remembered putting those hooks up on a Sunday morning like this one, maybe a dozen years ago, when Louise had grown tall enough to want them up high, like a grown-up would have them.

"Cold morning," he said. "Put this on."

She nodded, and after Wesley handed the robe to her, she held it to her chest all bunched together, like a big hank of rope. She said, "My granny had one like this. Green plaid. Said it was a Royal Stuart plaid. I don't know if that was true or if she was making it up." She swung her legs out from under the covers. "She was always making things up for me. Just for fun."

Her feet were skimming the face of the floor, and Wesley saw her sitting there in her bone-yellow drawers as she threaded her arms into the robe. He wondered whether the shadow he'd seen for an instant down there near her thighs had been her pubic hair. He thought about having that thought, and the thought itself aroused him. Then he thought of how he was noticing everything he should not notice; and not merely noticing it in passing but pondering what he noticed and wanting to know more about it.

He contemplated the fact that that was what he was doing here on a Sunday morning, in his daughter's bedroom, looking at a half-dressed sixteen-year-old girl. Wesley tried to say to himself, Have you no shame? But he knew he had shame—that at whatever filling station they pumped shame at, his tank had been topped off—and guilt to go with it, and shame for the guilt that was left over that he hadn't yet taken on.

He looked away. That was the only way out he could see. Then he said, more to the doorframe than to the girl, "You get yourself dressed, and we'll have us some breakfast."

The girl stood up at the side of the bed and yawned and ran her fingers through her tangled hair. "Sounds good to me," she said, and looked over to the open door of the closet. "I ain't got much that's clean. You mind if I take something out of there, pull it on for the morning? Just till I get my stuff laundered."

Wesley said, "Sure. Be my guest. Don't know why I still got all that stuff anyhow." He shrugged and went down the hall.

The girl called after him. "I got us pork chops for breakfast. Take 'em out of the icebox if you want."

She came out a moment later in a blue and white dress of Louise's with a sailor-type collar. She stood by the kitchen table and tied the bow, and Wesley saw she was barefoot and that her feet were small, white, smooth but a little scraped up, a little dirty, like a child's. He made his eyes turn away from the rest of her, because he knew they wanted to follow the sight of her feet to her calves and then her thighs and so on, right up her body. She scooped a dollop of Crisco into the fry pan on the stove. She turned back and smiled at him and said, "Think I'll make us a little gravy to go along with the chops, if you got no objection."

"No objection at all," Wesley said. He watched her cook, and he looked at her short calves and her heart-shaped backside and her skinny shoulders, which had taken on all the labors of his little house, and he still felt what he had to admit was desire, but he also felt a kind of peace. He recognized it for the peace that comes with gratitude, with the acknowledgment of unearned grace; of good that tumbles into one's life like a ball from the other side of a high fence which conceals a child's game being played in a neighbor's yard. He could not recall the last time he had felt this way, but he knew it was very long ago.

So Wesley lit a cigarette and watched Maggie turn the pork chops in the pan, barefoot before the stove in his little house, and breathed in his contentment. He knew he would have to return to the problem he had posed himself when he first got up this morning—how to rid himself of this girl Maggie, how to lose what he had just come to love—but he could not do it right now.

Ruby Fahey came to Herbert's apartment shortly after two o'clock, at the time he would normally be sitting in the Orpheum or the Paramount or the Tower or the Strand, holding a roll of Necco wafers in his fist. Indeed, when he answered the door, he was dressed as if to go out, with a bow tie and a vest, albeit without his homburg. He looked at her shyly but happily; his eyes were like the tiny bulbs of flashlights, and he said, "I've made us some tea. To warm us up before we start."

Ruby sat on the sofa, and Herbert sat in an armchair next to it. He tapped his fingers on an envelope on the side table between them and said, "I remembered that I said I'd show you this—the letter from my father, from the front."

"Oh, how sweet of you," Ruby said, "but there's something I want to know." She paused, and Herbert handed her a cup of tea he'd poured and looked at her expectantly. She went on. "Now, what with your memory problem, how do you remember little things like that? I mean little things we just mentioned in passing, in the streetcar, riding through the tunnel."

"I don't know. I just do. Maybe because it was important to me," Herbert said. "Because it was for you."

Ruby reached out and patted his hand. "And you, you're too good," she said. "But I mean, you know some things and they must be from years ago and you still know them. For example, you know who the President is, right?"

Herbert's head bobbed. "Mr. Roosevelt." He took a sip of tea.

"And how long do you remember him being President?"

"Oh, forever, really."

"But you know he hasn't really been President forever."

Herbert smiled. "Oh, of course. But it seems that way. His name is in the newspaper every day, and so every day, more or less, I paste him into my scrapbook. And I suppose that's how I remember him. Because he's a constant presence, like the sun, like the way I think of Nanna, my grandmother."

"But you remember other people being President too."

"Of course. I remember Mr. Wilson and then Mr. Harding. After that, there was the one that didn't speak, but I can't put my finger on the name." Herbert set down his teacup. "But of course, if he didn't say anything, maybe there's nothing much to remember about him."

"I think you mean Coolidge," Ruby said. "Anyway, I just wanted to ask. It doesn't make you feel funny or queer, does it? That I ask about personal things?"

"I don't mind at all. I just wish that I could answer better, that I knew more. I never really thought to care about it before, but now I rather wish I remembered more, for your sake. So I could have more of a personality, more of a past."

"You have tons of personality, Herbert," Ruby said, and

brushed her fingers over the back of his hand. "And lots of people I know would love to not have a past." She giggled. "Us girls, for example. A girl isn't supposed to have a 'past.' "

"Why ever not?" Herbert looked befuddled.

"Well, not a past like a family or a hometown or whatever. I mean a romantic past. With men. You know, like a bad reputation. I suppose a man always wants a girl to be fresh, to be new—at least to him."

"And you always are. I was noticing that just the other day."

Ruby laughed. "You wouldn't try to snow a girl, would you, Herbert?" She laughed again. "Now read me that letter."

"All right," Herbert said, and took a last sip of his tea. "It's dated April 9, 1915, so I was eleven years old. And beneath that it says 'Somewhere in France.' All the letters were censored, you know, so even if he'd said where he was, they would have just cut it out or blanked it out. So when you think about it, since he's dead, no one will ever know where he was. It's just a blank, and always shall be."

Herbert drew himself up a little in his chair. "Anyway . . . ," he said, and began to read.

My dear Herbert,

I have been in France now for a little over a month and now am quite close to the line, where I shall be going shortly. The other men and I had an uneventful voyage from Montreal, although the sea can be stormy that time of year. I had never been to sea before, or even to the seashore, never mind to Europe, and now I have done all those things in one go. I hope you shall get to do them too, although under circumstances of peace.

As I said, I am now quite close to the line, and one can hear the sounds of battle, particularly the big guns, which have a very deep and magnificent rumble, not unlike the sound of the streetcars in the tunnel . . .

Herbert looked up at Ruby. "Imagine that," he said.

. . . not unlike the sound of the streetcars in the tunnel, but ever so much deeper. It is the deepest thing I have ever heard, deeper than thunder. But then everything here is so new and different, so altered, from anything most of us have experienced.

I shall write you again as soon as I can, and at the front I shall also try to find some souvenirs and mementos for you. I am told German articles are not difficult to come by, and of course there is much shrapnel and shell casings and so forth. That way, when I come home, you shall be able to have a picture of where I have been.

Please try not to be a trial to your grandmother, and send her my love. I miss you both very much, and I wish I could be at home with you. But to be here—to take a stand against the German aggression—is what must be done if all of us, if the world, in fact, is to have a future.

With all my love,

Papa

Ruby was pushing the back of her hand against the corner of her eye, and Herbert put the letter down. She sniffled and said, "So how soon after that . . . ?"

"Oh, only a few weeks. I remember Nanna telling me that it had happened. She was already all dressed in black, and she called me into the parlor, sitting very stiffly, and said, 'Now, Herbert,' as if I were going to get a big dressing-down for something naughty I'd done. But instead it was that."

"It must have been so, so hard. You were just a little boy."

"I don't know how it was. I don't remember. But I don't suppose I knew it could be any other way. That's the good thing about being a child. For that matter, I suppose that's the good thing about having a memory like mine too. It's a blessing, really. At times, at least."

Ruby took his hand. "You know, I think if your father were alive, he'd be very, very proud of you—of the fine person you've grown up to be."

"I hope you'd be right," Herbert said. "I don't know. I suppose he would be thinking about how the Germans are starting all over again and that all he'd done was for nothing, it hadn't done any good at all. He was a very serious, grave man anyway. Perhaps losing my mother did that to him, and every time he saw me, he thought of—" Herbert stopped and said, "Well, we're not here to worry the past, are we? We should take some pictures. You look awfully lovely today. I should think I could make some exposures just as you are."

Ruby picked up a paper sack she'd carried with her when she arrived. "Actually, I brought something along I thought we could try out, Herbert. A bathing costume, really. Like the Hollywood actresses pose in. If you wouldn't mind, I mean."

Herbert bit his lower lip. "Well, the apartment isn't very warm, and it's almost November, you know. Wouldn't you get cold?"

"The lights are really quite hot. Heavens, I could pose naked and be plenty warm."

Herbert looked away, and then his voice came out, soft and ragged. "You could?"

He raised his hand to his chin and covered his mouth with his fingers. Ruby craned her neck around to see him. "You mean you'd like me to?"

"Oh, no. I could never . . ."

"Because I would if you want. I wouldn't mind at all. Because I know you're an artist, Herbert."

Herbert's voice was soft and quaking. "I've always wanted to. And thought about it. With you, I mean . . ."

"I'd be happy to. I'd be honored, Herbert." Ruby stood. "So you go get your equipment ready, and I'll just go freshen myself up." She walked down the hall to his bedroom and shut the door.

Herbert rose unsteadily and moved over to the corner. He turned on one lamp and then another, and he reached for the third—a new 150-watt lamp—but thought better of using it. Letting his hand fall back to his side, he moved over to his camera and put his hand out and gripped one of the tripod legs to steady himself. He felt he was scarcely breathing—that he had no breath and at the very same time would burst. He checked his camera. He had ten exposures. Then he turned around and Ruby was there, standing in his huge flannel robe with her lips glistening, plumping up her hair. "So, here I am," she said.

"I see," Herbert said. "Rather, I see that you are . . . that you're very beautiful."

She smiled and looked at him. "You're kinder than I deserve. I'm just a girl, an average girl." And Herbert thought, but didn't say, for his voice was lost to him, You're almost like heaven.

Ruby moved on tiptoe to the divan, picking up the robe so it flopped around her ankles. She seated herself and looked at Herbert and said, "Well, I suppose . . . ," and began to pull the robe apart and down from her shoulders. But Herbert threw his hands up and shouted raspily, "Wait!"

He lowered his hands and moved around in front of his camera, perhaps five feet from her, and said, "I just thought we might want to give some thought to this—to how you should pose."

Ruby swung her legs onto the divan. "I suppose we could just do what we were doing last time. Like this." And she drew up her knees and laid her hands across her ankles.

Herbert glanced away and then back at her, and said, "Oh, that would be wonderful." He stopped and then he moved toward her, and Ruby could see that he was flushed and that his eyes were moist and red. Then he was standing next to the divan, and he let himself down onto it as though he were lowering himself with a rope. When he was seated next to her, in the little space in the bend of her waist where her hips flared under the robe, he put his hands out as though he was carrying a big book like one of his scrapbooks before him, and at last set his two hands on her shoulders. His voice rattled out of his huge chest. "I just never, ever thought . . ."

Ruby raised her arm and set her hand on the back of Herbert's neck. She said, "Do you want to kiss me, Herbert? I've always wanted you to kiss me," and she parted her lips and began to move her face toward him. But Herbert let out a sort of sob and pulled the front of the robe apart and laid his face between her breasts and kissed the slope of one breast and then the taut flesh of the nipple. Ruby felt him shudder and stiffen, as though he'd been pierced by a needle, and then his body loosened again. He wailed for an instant in the very top of his voice, as a pup might do, and sobbed and pulled his head away. He stood up quickly, his hair in a tangle of sweat and his rumpled vest and pants appearing three sizes too big for him, as if he'd collapsed from the inside.

Ruby looked at him for a long while and he looked back, and then she took the lapels of the robe in her hands and covered her breasts. Herbert stood there all the while, just in front of his camera, staring as though he'd just seen a dirigible fall burning out of the sky. Then Ruby saw the moisture blooming out in an oval on the front of his pants, spreading over either side of the pleat so it looked like a butterfly's wings.

She peered up at his face and said, "Oh, Herbert. It's all right, really it is."

Herbert looked down at his pants and quickly moved behind the camera, holding his hands cupped over the spot. He said, "I don't know what to say. I suppose you think I'm disgusting."

"I don't think anything of the kind."

"It was just that I saw you—" Herbert put his palm to his forehead. "No, it wasn't even that. I was thinking of seeing you, seeing you naked, seeing all your . . . beauty. Your beauty all at once. And I couldn't bear it. I mean, it was more than I could bear—than my eyes could fathom." He gazed at her.

Ruby said nothing. She turned on the divan and put her feet on the floor, and then she smiled at Herbert. "I'm glad you like me," she said. "Or at least, I think that's what you mean."

"Oh, yes. That's it. Exactly. I just wasn't accustomed . . . I have no experience . . ."

"I know. I understand."

"Well, I suppose, under the circumstances . . ." Herbert halted and began again. "Actually, I think I feel a bit faint. I think perhaps I should lie down."

Ruby stood quickly and began to move toward the hallway. "It won't take me but a minute to get my things together," she said softly.

"Wait," Herbert said. "I don't mean to send you away. Although I suppose you'll never want to see me again."

Ruby turned around and faced him. "No, that's not true. I do. These things happen, Herbert. Sometimes they happen too soon. Or too late, or not at all. But it doesn't mean anything or change anything. And I don't mind." She reached her hand out toward his left arm, which he was holding as though it were injured. She took his sleeve between her fingertips and rubbed the fabric between them. "But maybe we ought to stop, just for today." Herbert nodded.

When she came out, Herbert was standing by the door, eyes downcast, holding the sack she'd brought her swimsuit in. And she thought: Maybe this is all my fault. Maybe I've ruined everything, spoiled it, hurt him just by wanting to be good to him.

She took the sack, and turned her welling eyes away so he wouldn't see, and said, "Good-bye, Herbert. I'll see you soon." He said, "Good-bye," and then he repeated himself, adding something odd, which she'd never heard him say before. "Good-bye, good-bye, Miss Ruby."

Sunday, October 22, 1939

I shall not record exactly what happened today, as I have no desire to ever recall it. I have turned beauty into shame, and I cannot comprehend the thing I have committed.

After my foul deed was done, after Miss Ruby was dispatched, I cleaned myself up, as my clothing was soiled, and I dressed in my other suit. I went out into the afternoon and it was raining and I didn't bring a coat or a hat and I don't think I even noticed, being so much distracted. I don't know where I walked. I know I went by the little park on the corner of Western Avenue, where the fountain with the Indian is, and I saw that they had already covered it over with a kind of shed for the winter. Then I must have gone up along Western Avenue, because I remember seeing a row of cars like one sees in a wedding party, and I suppose that must have been in the hotel, that there must have been a reception taking place there.

When I found myself on Selby Avenue, that is when I must have known what I intended all along—that I should go to the cathedral and make a clean breast of the whole business, that I should find the priest that I spoke to before in his closet and tell him everything. I think it was then, too, that I noticed I was soaked to the skin, that my shoes were squeaking, full of rainwater as I walked. But I no longer cared.

I went into the cathedral. I suppose it was four or four-thirty in the afternoon, and it was very quiet, and I went along the row of chapels behind the altar and out into the side aisle where the priest had been before. I think I found the right closet, and I opened the door and went in, but no one was there. I went back out and tapped on the adjacent door as softly as I could, but no one answered, and after a time I stopped and went and sat in the pew just opposite that closet. I held my head in my hands and wept. I think this is what is called despair. It is how the Catholics believe the damned feel in hell.

After a time, I looked up. The cathedral still seemed to be empty. I think I could hear the rain beating down on the ceiling, although the ceiling is very, very high. I know I smelled what must have been the fragrance of incense. It was very floral, like the scent Nanna always wore, but brindled and deep. I tried to make myself feel better, to remember that eventually I would forget all this.

But I couldn't sit still. I thought I would try again to find the priest, or some other priest, who perhaps inhabited one of the other closets. I went along the row back toward the chapels, looking in the doors. They were all empty or locked, and then I came to a door near the place where the chapels begin, and I opened it. There was a dim lightbulb lit inside and a winding stairway going down, and I went in and closed the door after me. The stairs went down, more than one flight, I should think, and at the bottom there was a corridor with big pipes running along the sides and ceiling, big pipes padded with some kind of insulation. I went down along the corridor to the left, and I could hear a deep thrumming sound and what I realized was the sound of steam. At the end of the corridor, there was a metal door and a sort of window fitted with a screen of fine bars. I tried to open the door, but just as I turned the handle, I felt a kind of rumble in the earth and then I heard a much deeper rumble coming and I saw a row of lights flash by through the opening and the sound was very loud and very deep and then ebbed away. I realized this was an entrance to the streetcar tunnel, and another row of lights flashed by, going in the other direction, and I thought back to another time and pictured Miss Ruby, Miss Ruby in the tunnel amid the roaring and the lights.

Just then I heard a man's voice, and I whirled around and there was a fellow dressed in overalls coming down the corridor toward me. He stopped about fifteen feet away from me and said, Ain't nobody supposed to be down here. Then he looked at me and seemed to draw back, as if he were afraid, and said, You look like you went six rounds with the devil. I told him I had gotten caught in the rainstorm and had come down here by mistake and begged his pardon. He said that was all right, that he'd show me the way out, but that maybe I ought to come sit by the boiler for a minute and dry out—that even a big galoot like me could catch his death in this weather. I said no, though he was very kind, and he followed me back down the corridor and up the stairs and let me out. He said, God bless you now, and I heard him latch the door behind me.

I scarcely remember coming home. I do not think I even recall taking this book down and beginning to write in it. But I know now that I ought to take up Mr. Wright on the suggestion he made to me only last week: that I have more than a month's vacation time coming and I ought to use it, anytime I like, as business is slow. So I think I shall tell him I am going away tomorrow, and I shall not say where because I need to get away from everything that has befallen me and that I have done. I think I need to go see the places that I have only ever seen at the pictures, and I think it is time, too, that I see the ocean for myself.

Just before the rainstorm on Sunday afternoon, Wesley Horner and Maggie went walking uptown, up Pleasant Avenue, along the bottom of the bluff on whose crown the well-to-do people of the city lived. They stopped at a little park cradled in the wedge where two streets met, and Wesley pointed up and to the west, to where the sun was beginning to descend. "Up there, on that slope, that's where that girl was found," he said.

"What girl is that?" Maggie asked.

"The one that was murdered. The one I told you about. First time we met, way back when."

"Way back two weeks ago and some," Maggie said. "So did you catch the one that did it?"

"Not yet."

"You going to?"

"I doubt it," Wesley said. "Trail's pretty cold now."

"Do you usually catch 'em?"

"Maybe half the time. Thing is, what with your modern transportation—cars, express trains, and so on—anybody who doesn't want to be someplace can be some other place just like that. I mean, how am I supposed to catch somebody who's done a murder this morning if they can be in Chicago tonight, in New Orleans the next day? Can't be done. And unless it's a federal case or something, nobody's going to bother to try."

"So you figure whoever done it left town," Maggie said.

"That's my guess. Nobody who knew the girl could think of anyone she knew who might have done it—anyone who made any sense as a suspect—so it had to be a stranger. Of course, nowadays everybody's a stranger, nobody stays where they're from. Used to be a big deal if you'd ever been anyplace; used to be a big deal if you ever had a stranger come through your town. But now, especially for the last ten years or so, people just disappear, reappear God knows where, like they blew away with a dust storm or joined the circus." Wesley put his hands in his pockets and began to walk on. Maggie followed after, wearing a navy-blue coat of Louise's, which was a little too small. "Makes police work difficult, I'll tell you that," Wesley went on. "How you going to keep folks in line if they won't stay put?"

Maggie drew even with him, and they kept walking west. "But you're from here, right?"

"Nope. From North Dakota. Place near Dickinson called New Upsala. Came here in '12." Wesley smiled, or rather broadened his mouth into the grimace that with him passed for a grin. "Year the *Titanic* went down."

"So why'd you leave New Oopsda, or whatever it is."

"New Upsala. Named after a place in Sweden by a bunch of sucker immigrants who believed the railroad when they said you could farm there. Which you couldn't. Which my grandfather found out the hard way, and my father harder still. By the time I was your age, any fool could see it. So being any fool, I up and moved here."

"You ever go back, see your folks?"

"Both dead. After '34 and '5, I suspect the town is too."

"My folks is dead. So's Granny," Maggie said.

Wesley stopped. "You didn't tell me that."

"You didn't ask," Maggie said. "Hey, how about a cigarette? A girl's lungs get cold."

Wesley nodded, found his pack, and shook two out and lit them. He handed one to the girl. "So who were you planning to go home to in Moline?"

"Nobody. There's nobody I know there. Wasn't really going to go to Moline anyhow."

"That's not what you told me."

"I told you what you wanted to hear."

Wesley leaned in close to her face, and the smoke spun out of his nostrils and lapped her face. He smiled. "That's lying to a police officer."

"That ain't lying. That's just leaving out the parts you'd miss anyway, on account of being a bad listener," Maggie said, grinning back. "Fellow like you that knows it all and got it all figured out. I mean, what's the use? Girl can't be bothered."

"What else haven't you told me?"

"Nothing much. I got nothing to hide."

"So you won't mind saying what you were really doing in between the time I took you out of Shacktown and the time we met up at Seven Corners."

Maggie pulled on her cigarette. "Let's see now." She blew the smoke out. "Slept in the park one night. Under a holly bush— people don't bother you that way. Next night it got cold, so I went back out to Shacktown, slept there. You cops shouldn't be so ornery to folks out there. Mostly good people. Gave me a fire to sit by and half a can of pork and beans to eat, didn't they?"

"You promised me you weren't going back there," Wesley said.

"I don't recall no such promise. Maybe it ain't just that you don't listen so good. Maybe you got a broken-down memory too."

"Could be. So go on."

"After that, I got work at the laundry and they let me sleep there a couple of nights, sleeping on top of big piles of hotel sheets and towels, pretty as a princess. Then I flopped with some of the girls working there. Now I'm shacked up with a cop."

Wesley didn't laugh, didn't even smile. "Don't talk that way," he said, and began to walk away.

Maggie caught up with him, and she saw his eyes sink deep into his face as he drew hard on his cigarette. "Sorry," she said. "Didn't mean to get flip with you."

"It's okay," he said, turned away from her, and then he stopped and faced her. "So back then, when you were sleeping out and flopping, you weren't doing anything . . . you shouldn't have been."

"You mean stealing?"

"No, like with . . . men." Wesley's eyes were large, as though something were going to startle him. "Like what I saw you doing with your friend in Shacktown."

"I never did that with no one but Billy." Maggie was looking at the ground, holding her hands loosely together behind her back.

"You told me there was a railway cop."

Maggie was still looking down, and her voice was very small, more breath than voice. "He didn't do nothing but put his hand in my shirt while he was touching himself. Didn't take him but a second to finish his business."

"I suppose your friend, your Billy, put you up to that."

Maggie jerked her head up and looked straight at Wesley, her eyes awash with tears. "You lay off him. He's gone God knows where, all on your account."

Wesley stepped back from her. After a moment, he said, "If I hadn't done that, you'd have been in the county home. Or with Welshinger and Trent." He shook his head from side to side. "You think I'm a nosy, rotten, pushy cop? You ought to get to know the likes of them."

Maggie began to walk ahead of him, and the slope of the hill was beginning to steepen. She sniffled and then composed herself. "I don't mind so much that he's gone," she said. "He was going to go anyway. Said it was time for me to make my own way." Wesley was a yard behind her left shoulder, and although she didn't turn to look at him, she spoke as though he were there. "It's just that he looked after me when there wasn't anyone else. Granny raised me from when I was one, and then she passed on two years back. I didn't have anyone. I couldn't claim relief from the county— they'd have just stuck me in the orphanage. So there was Billy. I knew him from the neighborhood. He delivered groceries, and sometimes I'd bring bottles in to him at the store. Sometimes I'd go around picking up bottles just so I could go see him, looking so handsome in his apron, in his little white hat."

She stopped and faced Wesley, a bit out of breath. "So we was friends. And after Granny died he come by and said maybe I ought to come and stay at his place. So I did. He didn't try to love me up until way later, way after I'd started wanting him to."

"So how'd you end up here?"

"We was living under the grocery, and the owner died and no one bought it, so they closed it down. New landlord told us we had to go. So we left. Did stoop work and picking all through the summer, sleeping out. Fetched up here in September." She stopped and then pointed up to the brow of the hill. "Who lives up there?" she asked.

"The great and the worthy," Wesley said. "The people that had good liquor through prohibition, the people that had somebody to iron their sheets during the slump. Nobody we know."

"So they ain't going to up and disappear like you say everybody else been doing."

"No, they're here to stay. Got no reason to go anywhere. Not like the rest of us."

Maggie said, "Don't you . . . go nowhere, okay?"

"Got nowhere to go."

"And you got me now." Maggie smiled. "Sent Billy away, so you're stuck with me. Got me to mind. And me to mind you." She put out her hand, and he took it very slowly, not sure what it was she wanted him to do. She looked down the hill, back in the direction of his little house in the flats by the brewery, and she said, "Let's go home now."

Very early Tuesday, October 24, 1939

It is about four-thirty in the morning, and the train is stopped at a depot in a place called Dickinson, North Dakota. It is very dark, and I can just see pools of light here and there along the platform and steam coming up from under the train. I think a baggage cart went by, and now there is a whistle and the train is starting to move. I am awake because I cannot sleep, although it is a fine bedroom they have given me, with my own bed and sink and chair. I had not planned on such extravagant accommodations, but at the station they told me it was all they had left. And I suppose since this is to be "the trip of a lifetime," it is worth it.

I packed my bag Monday morning and went down to the

office and told Mr. Wright my plans—that I wanted to leave that very day if he would consent, as I was eager to get away. He said that would be fine, and I walked over to the station. I asked the man what trains left soon that would take me to the ocean, and he said which ocean, and I told him it didn't matter—I only wanted to get away right now and see the ocean. He said in that case he figured the Pacific would suit me well enough and told me the North Coast Limited left that evening at seven-thirty, but they only had drawing rooms. I told him I would have to go to the bank to get the money, and he said he would hold my reservation until six o'clock. I told him I would be back well before then.

Now, when I got to the First National Bank, I thought I might as well take out all the money I had in that account (the money Nanna left me being at the Trust Company), since I planned to be away two whole weeks. But the teller told me if I did that, they would have to close the account entirely, and I said I supposed that would be all right. I thought I would make a joke, so I went on to say I wasn't planning to come back anytime soon anyway and, as they say in the pictures, I was "heading for the coast," where I was going to "lie low." He didn't laugh, but then bankers are rather a grave bunch, all in all.

It was noon by then. I had lunch in the coffee shop in the bank building, and I thought I ought to get something to read. I went to the St. Paul Book & Stationery Company, and the man at the counter asked me if I had come for my usual Ideal No. 51, as he had them in stock again. I told him no; as a matter of fact, I would be letting my scrapbook go for a while, as I was leaving on a very long journey, and wondered if he might recommend a book to occupy me. He said he had just the thing. It was called *U.S.A.*, by a Mr. John Dos Passos, and is just now very highly thought of and must be a good thousand pages long. I said that sounded perfect, but I wondered if he could tell me what the plot was. He told me it was all about the U.S.A., just like the title said, and it was just the thing to take on a long journey. I said that I would take it, and he wrapped it up in paper for me and I went to the park on Kellogg Boulevard and sat on a bench, watching the barges on the river. I read a bit of the book while I sat, and I must say it is a very serendipitous choice, as Mr. Dos Passos is obviously a great fan of the pictures, just as I am. In fact, he calls some of his chapters "Newsreels," and they are meant to be more like a movie than a book. I am not sure I understand everything that is taking place or exactly what Mr. Dos Passos sometimes intends, but I have no doubt it shall keep me occupied for a long while.

At about four o'clock I started back to the station. As I was walking by the new post office, I thought perhaps I ought to get some stamps, as surely I would want to mail some picture postcards during my journey, but then I realized I could not think of anyone to whom I might send them. So I went on to the station and paid for my ticket and waited for the North Coast Limited to arrive from Chicago, which is its origin. At the station newsstand I bought this notebook (with "Rocky," the Great Northern Railway mascot, on the cover) to serve as a journal of my trip, having left my regular journal at home, as best I can tell. The train arrived about seven o'clock, and I got to my room about seven-fifteen. The North Coast Limited is indeed a very luxurious train: There is a barber and a hairstylist and a secretary to take dictation should a traveling captain of industry require it. You can get ice water right out of a tap in the corridor, and the porter polishes your shoes every night, or more often if you prefer!

I had dinner in the diner—Salisbury steak with one of the Railway's celebrated "Great Big Baked Potatoes," and tapioca for a sweet—and retired feeling quite grand. I read for a time, and then I slept. I woke up perhaps an hour ago with rather a start. I could not think where I was, and once I ascertained I was on a train, I could not for the life of me remember how I had gotten here. I rifled through my bag and found this journal, and once I began to write, the events of the day—or rather the previous day—came back. But it is still a somewhat alarming sensation, as usually I have no problem with recent events but now find I can scarcely remember what transpired yesterday, never mind the day before. Perhaps it is a form of travel sickness. In any case, I am quite sure about the future, as it is here before me in the timetable at my elbow, and it says we shall arrive in Seattle tomorrow morning at eight-fifteen.

As Wesley had dreaded, as Wesley had prayed, Maggie came to his bed late on Tuesday night. The door rasped open, rust on rust, and Wesley could see her standing, one hand resting on the knob and the light pouring under and through her legs, through the pilled, attenuated flannel of one of Louise's old nighties. She stood there a long time, not so much in hesitation as waiting to speak, and at last she said—as if she already knew he was wide awake—"It was cold in there. Figured I might as well come and get warm with you."

Wesley couldn't see her face on account of her being in the shadow, but he realized she must be able to see his by the hall light. He nodded and pulled back the covers next to him. She took two long strides as though she were stepping into water and slid beside him, facing him. She laid her head on the pillow next to his, and he felt her arm fall quietly onto his shoulder and her hand flutter down to his back. He knew she was smiling, and he knew she must feel his sex, the tip of which was just grazing her belly. It was hard and implacable as fired coal.

He pulled back his head from her head about a foot and propped himself on his elbow. He said, slowly, like the downstroke of a saw through green wood. "This is all wrong."

Maggie sat up in the bed, and the beam of light from the doorway fell across the left side of her face and her body. She shook her head. "No, it's right. Right as rain. That's what Granny always used to say: Right as rain." She reached down under herself and pulled the nightgown over her head. Wesley saw he'd been wrong about how her body would look. Her breasts were larger than he'd thought, ampler than Rose's, with bright little nipples, pink like a colored man's gums.

She lay down next to him again, and he croaked, dryly, weakly, "No, Maggie, honey, no."

She put her arms around him and drew him in. "Yes," she said, "yes," and he could feel her mons pressing against him like breath, like a sigh, and the hair soft, somnolent as felt. "You let me love you up, Wesley Horner. You let me love you," she said. "There's no one in this sorry world needs loving more than you."

Later, when she was sleeping, heeled over on her side with his arm spilled down the slope of her flank, his fingers curled around her hip bone, he lay awake, half content, half flayed with apprehension, like a condemned man after his last meal, before they come to lead him down. He knew now that this girl was his life, was his only life—because until now, for the last three years, he'd been without life entirely—and knew just as much, in a manner he could not describe, that on account of her he was as good as dead.

The telephone rang, and Maggie sat straight up in bed. "What the hell is that?"

"Telephone ringing," Wesley said, and he swung his legs out and set his feet on the floor.

"Didn't know you had one. Never heard it ring before."

"Scarcely ever does," Wesley said, and stood up. "Must be the station. Must be time to go to work."

Friday, October 27, 1939
Pacific Hotel
Tacoma, Washington

It has been a most eventful and thrilling two days since my arrival, and I have only now found the time and occasion to record them here. I am ensconced in a hotel in Tacoma, which is a city on the southern extremity of the Puget Sound, and I can see the harbor outside my window. I am told that part of the harbor is called the Saint Paul, after a timber concern called the Saint Paul and Tacoma Lumber Co., evidently founded by people of some sort from Saint Paul!

I arrived on time in Seattle Wednesday morning and made straight for the bus depot, for I had read a brochure on board the train describing a bus service that conveys tourists to the new Olympic National Park, which is very close to the sea. As it happened, the departure of the bus is designed to coincide with the arrival of the train, so I found myself on my way immediately, having seen none of Seattle, which I am told is a lovely, if somewhat harum-scarum, place.

The bus dropped me at a town called Port Angeles, the driver assuring me that this place was itself on the water and that I should find easy transport there to elsewhere on the Olympic Peninsula, should I desire. Now, when I got off the bus, I could indeed see a vast expanse of water before me, but also land faintly in the distance. I asked someone inside the depot if this water was indeed the ocean, and he said no, it was the strait that led out into the ocean. Accordingly, I went to the agent's window and told him I wanted to arrange transport to the seashore, and he told me the only thing going anytime soon was a little bus to a place called La Push, right on the Pacific Ocean, leaving in a few minutes, at three o'clock. I told him that would be fine, and he sold me a ticket, advising me that I ought to be sure to catch the bus back out of La Push when it left at six forty-five, as there wasn't anyplace a white man would want to sleep out there, the locals being entirely "smelly Indian salmon-suckers."

I had a very pleasant ride out—in fact, I was the only passenger, and the driver gave me a very informative commentary on the scenery and local history. He told me he had driven part of President Roosevelt's entourage during his visit here a few years back, which consequently resulted in the establishment of the new national park. He in turn asked me about myself, and repeating my little joke from the movies, I told him I had come west to "lie low" for a while. He asked me where else I was planning to visit. I told him my primary goal was to see the ocean, but I was also keen to take in Mount Rainier. He said that in that case I ought to take a room overnight in a town called Forks, on the main highway south before one gets to the La Push turnoff, and that in the morning I could thence get a bus to Tacoma, which is the closest city to Mount Rainier. He said he knew of a little inn with some nice rooms.

Now, I suppose I ought to say a little about the scenery. It is indeed very beautiful and very dramatic. There are mountains in the center of the peninsula, not so tall as Mount Rainier but very rugged, and snowbound for most of the year. But perhaps the most distinctive feature of the locale is the stupendous quantity of rainfall it receives—twenty feet a year in places, my driver told me—which results in an extraordinarily verdant growth of plant life, and in particular trees of enormous height and girth. Indeed, what with the ferns and moss and vines and dripping vegetation, the sense is of being in deepest jungle, save for the fact that the trees are mostly of the coniferous variety. My driver halted a few minutes in a grove of what he told me were the largest spruce trees in the world, and I must say the feeling was a little disconcerting, as though one has been swallowed by the proverbial whale and is sitting inside his enormous damp green gut, which imperceptibly seethes and drips and sighs.

We arrived at our destination about five o'clock. The driver parked at the top of a lane and told me if I followed it down I would find the beach. I did so, but before I saw the sea, I felt it and smelled it—a cold, clammy air that sheathed my hands and a scent of salt and what I must describe as fertilizer. I had read descriptions of these phenomena, of course, but I must say I felt as if I were coming into a place with which I was entirely familiar and which was utterly recognizable not as a memory but as a sensation in the body.

Then, before I saw it, I heard the sea, a little like wheels on rails mixed up with wind, and at last I came out of the forest and I saw it. There were some huge rocks out in the water, big as towers thrusting up, and beyond them nothing at all, and it was that, I realized, that I had really come to see—sheer emptiness all the way to the horizon and beyond; all the way to Asia, to where the sun disappears in the night.

The beach was not terribly sandy, being covered with pebbles and rocks and marine debris. There were also rocks, which must be submerged some of the time; and everywhere there were starfish—orange and yellow and purple—clinging to them. I sat on a big washed-up log, which was just as well, as I was still appareled in my traveling suit, and watched the boats come into the harbor, which is entered through a little slit in the rocks. Mostly, however, I watched the surface of the water. I had pictured the ocean somehow as being largely flat, but in fact the waves are enormous—no one can describe how enormous, I fear—and even the distant water is wrinkled like ruched-up muslin or like a furrowed field, stiff yet fluid, all entirely in motion.

After a time, I went down to the shoreline, to where the waves reached at their utmost extreme, and even let the water lap my shoes and knelt down and put my fingers into the sand. As I was doing this, I looked in front of me and saw a glass globe rolling toward me, right into my hands, as though someone were bowling it directly to me. I took it up and saw it was perhaps eight inches in diameter and a cloudy light bottle green color, with a stub at one end that suggested it was blown rather than cast. I stood and held it in front of me, in my hands, and I felt it was a gift from the sea and that it might even somehow have been intended to fall into my possession.

Now the sun was going down—it looked to be perhaps one hundred feet above the surface of the water (although I know that is an illusion)—and the light was becoming dim. Suddenly I saw there was a boy, perhaps twelve or so, coming toward me along the water's edge, and I could see by his black hair and tawny complexion that he was a genuine Indian. I wondered what I ought to say to him; indeed, I wondered if he could understand the English tongue; and I saw he was looking at the globe in my hands. I began to stammer a greeting, and he broke in: I see you got yourself a float. I said, Is that what it is? and he said, Ya, for holding the top of a net up on the water when you go fishing. I said I understood, but I had the sense that perhaps I had committed some faux pas in having it, so I asked, did it belong to his people and did he want it from me? He said it was from a Japanese boat and that he could find one of them every day if it suited him, so I should go right ahead and keep it.

Then he walked away, and I was alone with the sun going down—now nearly sinking into the waves—holding this floating globe that had come all the way from Japan, rather like the ball of the sun sitting in my hands, somehow come eastward here to me on this day now turning westward into night. I waited a while longer, until it was nearly dark, and then I walked back up the lane to the bus, with the ocean roaring behind me and the globe in my hands, still a little wet and sandy, and what I suppose was the salt of the sea drying on my fingers.

The driver left me in the town of Forks about a quarter after seven, at the door of what seemed to me to be a rather rustic tavern but which he assured me had excellent rooms. I went in and it was full of men, seemingly all wearing suspenders, and all big as me. I worked my way past them to the far end of the bar, trying to hold my bag—now with the glass globe inside it for safety's sake—above my head as I passed through the tumult. I asked the bartender if he had a room, and he gave me a key and said to pay him in the morning and pointed me up the stair. Once I got inside the little room with its metal bed and walls covered in unpainted wood batten board, I slept very deeply, although the noise from below was surely almost as loud as or louder than the sea at La Push.

Now I am in this altogether nicer room in Tacoma, where I arrived this afternoon after an uneventful bus ride through what seemed to be unending forest. As I said, I can see the ships in the harbor, and I have put the glass globe on top of the chest of drawers, where it looks very handsome. Tomorrow morning I am due to ride the bus out to Mount Rainier.

Sunday, October 29, 1939
On Board the Empire Builder

I am writing this inside the men's smoker on board the Great Northern Railway's Empire Builder. I did not plan to go home so soon, nor do I smoke, and I suppose I should recount the events that have led to my present situation before they become confused in my mind.

I arose very early to catch the bus to Mount Rainier. I was told I might go either to a place called Paradise or to one called Sunrise, and one might thus imagine that this is not an easy choice to make! In the end, I decided in favor of Sunrise, for it is the highest elevation on the mountain one can reach by road, and from there one can climb even higher by foot.

The bus circuited the northern side of the mountain, passing through the oddly named town of Enumclaw and thence along the east side and into the entrance of the national park. One ascends to Sunrise by a long series of hairpin turns, affording occasional glimpses of the mountain. At the top, the road straightens out onto a plateau, where there is a lodge. I was amazed to see snow here and there, for at this elevation winter has already begun.

I must of course speak of the mountain, although no words can be adequate to it. At Sunrise one is perhaps eight or nine miles as the crow flies from the summit, and yet the sensation is of the mountain's immediate, looming presence, so massive that one might reach out and touch its icy, glacier-mantled flanks. Perhaps due to the elevation, the air is thin here and plays tricks on the eyes; the mountain seems not merely to shimmer but to pulse, as though it were breathing, expanding and contracting. It is very cold at Sunrise, and sometimes a wind comes from the direction of the mountain, deep and chill and damp, and it is as the exhalation of a giant asleep in the snows.

I ate a ham sandwich in the lodge, which, I was informed, was to close for the season the next day, together with the road leading up here, for the snows would soon be too deep for it to be practicable to keep it open. In fact, although at that moment the sky was brilliantly clear, they expected more snow that very afternoon. I remarked to the woman who prepared my sandwich that the bleakness and austerity of the landscape around Sunrise—mostly devoid of trees and supporting only stunted vegetation adapted to the high elevation—reminded me of places I had seen in the pictures and wondered if any had been filmed here. She said she thought there might have been, and I asked her if any of them featured Miss Veronica Galvin. She said she didn't think so, being sure that if Veronica Galvin had been in these parts she would have heard about it.

I then set off in the direction of the mountain, on a trail that was supposed to afford a most spectacular view from a place called Burroughs Mountain. One walks on roughly level ground for perhaps two miles, through a small forest and past a charming little lake, and then the ascent begins in earnest, up a very steep slope covered in slides of rocks and boulders, among which hide gopher-like creatures that sit upright and periodically emit a sort of whistling call. I could not but think they were commenting on my presence, as there was no one else on the trail. At this point there was much more snow, so much so that at times it threatened to cover the trail entirely. I suppose I should have been cold, dressed as I was in my wool suit and vest, brown brogues, and homburg, but the labor of the ascent had if anything left me rather overheated. Fortunately, the trail again levels out and turns a corner near the top that offers a sudden and startling view of the mountain. I rested there awhile, and then I began to feel a little cold, as though an icy hand had stealthily settled itself upon my back, so I thought I ought to begin walking again.

I passed another mile or so, the mountain always before me. There was nothing around me but a few gnarled trees and bunches of heather and meadow grass, mostly covered by snow. For a long while the trail bisects the middle of a steep, rocky slope and must be only a little more than a foot wide, and at times this was entirely covered by what seemed to be permanent snowdrifts that had caked into heavy crystals of ice. The way was, as I said, very steep, and often left one with a vertiginous feeling, as though one might simply fall off the trail as from a precipice.

I must say that by the time I reached the place where the trail was completely blocked and obscured by the snow I was not a little afraid—not afraid for my safety but overawed by desolation and by the mountain, by the overwhelming presence of such a world that was so much greater, so much larger, than I: the world, I suppose, as it truly is, unseen by us. The illusion— I assume it is an illusion—of the mountain's palpitation was even more apparent, and I wanted to reach out my hand to steady myself, for fear of fainting, but it seemed there was nothing to take hold of save the mountain itself, and that was just beyond my reach.

About that time, around two-thirty by my pocket watch, it began to snow. I was looking at the mountain, around which the sky was clear, and the snow rather snuck up behind me. When

I felt it on my neck, I turned and looked over my left shoulder and saw that the sky was utterly black and that a huge bank of clouds was moving rapidly toward me like an enormous flight of ravens.

On the mountain, there is wind all the time, like the sound of an unseen, underground river. But now the wind came in earnest, and with it hard, icy gusts of snow, and I must say I truly became afraid, not in awe but in terror. I went back down the trail as fast as I could, but at times I could scarcely see, so thick was the snow flying in my face, buzzing and shrieking like an unfathomable swarm of insects. I felt as I imagined Miss Galvin's costar in *Steens Mountain* must have felt, pummeled by a hail of G-man bullets. And when I passed over the steep section—whose precipitousness I happily could not see now—I thought I might die: that surely I could not find my way forward and must remain fixed on this cliff in the cold. I wondered then what I could possibly do, where I might turn. I wanted someone to come and save me, but I could see that in fact I was utterly alone—that everything that there was in the world, I was already in the midst of. I cannot say how, but I found a kind of peace in this notion and was able to push on a little further, and at last the storm began to ease a little—although my feet were soaked and my cuffs and shoes full of snow and ice.

When at last I came to the place where I had rested earlier, I saw three men, and I was overjoyed, thinking they must be a rescue party, for two of them were in uniform. The one without a uniform moved toward me first, and I could see he was breathing deeply, winded from the climb, and his words came out in ragged bunches. He had a sad, long face, as though what once had been a broad smile had sagged and collapsed into his chin, and I thought I might have seen him before somewhere. He said, "Herbert W. White, I am placing you under arrest for the murder of Ruby Fahey in Saint Paul, Minnesota."

I don't know what I thought about what he said just then. I suppose having seen this kind of thing take place in so many pictures, I just waited to see what would happen next—whether I would submit, or flee, or pull out a gun and start shooting. So I waited to see what would happen—what I would do next— and I realized it was me I was waiting for, and I wasn't doing anything at all. The man went on, saying he was from the Saint Paul Police Department and that the man in the uniform with the Sergeant Preston–style hat was a park ranger and the other was from the sheriff of Pierce County, Washington. He added that he would have liked to have someone from the Federal Bureau of Investigation alóng too, since there was a question here of interstate flight, but in any case he was taking me into custody.

He took from his jacket pocket a pair of handcuffs, which were tangled up with a pack of Lucky Strike cigarettes, and the cigarettes fell out of the pack and into the snow. He said, G** d*** it, and I reached down to help pick them up, and he said, Don't make a move—they're all sopped now anyway. Then he tried to put the handcuffs on me, fumbling with them, and he said, Your wrists are too g**d*** big. He said, So I'll leave the bracelets off, but don't you try anything. I said of course I wouldn't, and he looked me right in the eye and said, You remember me, don't you? I said I wasn't sure I did, and he said, Suit yourself.

We walked the rest of the way down to the lodge together, through the thick clods of snow, and they drove me down the mountain to Tacoma. One of them kept me at the police station while the one from Saint Paul went to the Pacific Hotel and got the things from my room there. He showed me my bag and said, This everything? and I said I had a glass ball I'd found on the beach, by the ocean. He said, I'm sorry, I thought it was part of the hotel decorations. Then he said, Can't have nothing sharp like glass anyhow.

We got on the train yesterday evening, and we have sat up all this time in these seats in this room with the shoeshine man and the cigar smokers. I asked if I could write in my journal, and he said I might as well, as I wouldn't be allowed any writing materials where I was going. So to pass the time until we get home, I have been writing and rereading what I had written before. Mostly I think about having seen the sea at last and also the mountain, and I picture the snow and ice that caps the mountain and runs down the ridges. I see it as a starfish atop the mountain, and its arms are the glaciers, and that is how I keep the two things—the sea and the mountain—together in my mind, and by which I shall try to remember them.

PART III

GRAND CENTRAL TERMINAL

THEY FOUND RUBY IN THE NIGHT, A LITTLE AFTER ONE o'clock in the morning on Wednesday. A nervous, spindly little guy named Harold Olmstead was walking the tracks with his lantern, as he did every week, checking for broken joints in the rails and hazardous debris. He found her folded upon herself like a clothespin in the deepest part of the tunnel, maybe thirty feet from the hatch that went into the heating plant under the cathedral. He was making his way up the middle of the tunnel, between the two tracks, and he would not have seen her but for the skittering and squeaking of the rats. The tunnel was lit with blue lightbulbs interspersed with little twenty-five-watt lamps, so as not to create any glare for the streetcar drivers. It was when Olmstead turned in the direction of the noise of the rats that he saw her; or rather sensed the presence of something, like a shadow under water.

He ran back down to the call box at the Fourth Street entrance and called the night manager at the street railway, who called the police, and Olmstead waited, smoking furiously, for twenty minutes under the huge, hulking arch of the tunnel entrance. A patrolman came with a fellow sergeant named O'Connor, and they all went up the tunnel together and looked at the girl. Then Sergeant O'Connor said, "There's no trains through here this time of night?" and Olmstead said there weren't. "You call your boss and tell him no trains or anybody else in here until we say so, okay?" O'Connor said. They left the patrolman with the girl and walked back down to the entrance. Sergeant O'Connor said he was going to call the station and headed down toward the police call box on Pleasant Avenue. Olmstead called the night manager back and told him what O'Connor had said, and the night manager began to sputter and curse. Then he hung up, and Olmstead sat on the wall by the tunnel head and watched the clouds begin to drift in and swaddle the moon.

About a half hour later, another squad car arrived, and a detective, disheveled like balled-up linen and wearing a fedora, got out of the passenger side. He looked up at the tunnel head and then at O'Connor and Olmstead. He walked over to them and said to the sergeant, "So what do we got?"

"Dead girl halfway up the tunnel on the right. This guy was checking the tracks and found her about an hour ago."

Wesley looked at Olmstead and nodded, and then looked back at O'Connor. "She been there long, you think?"

"No smell that I could notice. But it's awful hard to see in there."

"Get us some flashlights out of the squad car," Wesley said. "You call the coroner?"

"The station was going to."

"You got a man inside there? Closed the tunnel to traffic?"

"Yes and yes," O'Connor said.

"Good. Let's just wait for the doctor." Wesley sat down on the wall next to Olmstead and lit a cigarette. He started asking Olmstead questions: how often and when he checked the tunnel; if he'd ever seen anybody in the tunnel before; if there was any way in except through the street.

Olmstead said he'd chased tramps out in the winter, and kids were always walking up it on a dare—it would be a hell of a thing if one of them got hit, but none ever had—and he'd been in there every Tuesday night for the last seven years. "There's a door—really just a half door, a hatch—into the cathedral heating plant," he added. "I suppose it's bolted from their side. Engineers put it in when they built the tunnel, I figure."

Wesley nodded and looked at O'Connor. "So there's three ways in—through here, through the Selby end, or through the cathedral." Wesley pitched his cigarette into the grate where the tracks left the street and went onto the ramp leading to the tunnel head. A car drove up and stopped. "Guess that'll be Nash," he said.

Wesley went over to Nash's car and told the coroner what he knew, and O'Connor got them each a flashlight. The three of them began to walk up the ramp into the tunnel, and Olmstead rose to go with them. "You wait here," Wesley called to him. "Take a load off your feet. But don't go anywhere, okay?" Olmstead nodded and sat back down on the wall. He looked at the sky and smelled the air. He thought snow might be coming.

It took Wesley, O'Connor, and Dr. Nash about two minutes to walk up the tunnel to where the girl was. The patrolman stood about fifteen feet from her, scanning the floor between himself and the girl with his flashlight. Wesley said, "Find anything?"

"No, sir. Just warning the rats away."

"They started in on her yet?"

"Not so I could see."

"Good. That's one little thing, isn't it, Doctor?" Wesley said. Nash was already kneeling next to the girl, and Wesley could scarcely see him. There was a blue lightbulb on the wall a few feet down from him, but it threw more of a shadow than a light, like a stain. All Wesley could see was the spot of Nash's flashlight beam moving over the girl. He hunched down next to Nash and aimed his own flashlight onto the body. It was a girl with brown hair, maybe twenty-five or thirty years old, in a sheer rayon dress. She was doubled over, almost coiled against herself, with her chin pressed down against her torso and her face nearly touching her knees, her ankles locked together beneath her, her arms and hands splayed, like a ballerina taking a bow. Her feet were bare.

Nash was feeling the girl's neck, and then he pushed his fingers underneath her armpit and tried to flex her arm. He looked up at Wesley. "I suppose you don't want her moved until you get some photos." Wesley nodded. "Can't see anything in here anyway," Nash said. "You have them be careful when they take her out. I don't see any blood, but I don't know what's underneath her. There's something in her hair too."

Nash stood up, and so did Wesley. They had been speaking in near whispers, and now Wesley spoke at his normal volume, and his voice clattered in the tunnel like falling rock. "So what do you know, Doctor?"

"Not much. I think it's another strangulation."

"Any idea when?"

"Oh, let's see." Nash tucked his flashlight under his arm and began to count on his fingers. "It's Tuesday night, Wednesday morning, so . . . I'd say she died no earlier than Sunday, no later than Tuesday morning early. Mind you, that's not to say she was *here* then."

"So probably between Sunday and Monday nights?"

"More or less." Nash took his flashlight in his hand again and looked at his wristwatch. "Quarter of three," he said. "I'm going back to bed, if you don't mind. You get her down to the morgue by ten o'clock, we can talk at the end of the day."

"Will do," Wesley said. He and Nash and O'Connor stepped over the track and began to walk down the center of the tunnel. There was a rivulet of water snaking down the concrete strip between the tracks, and it arced in and out of their path and then dropped into a grate at the tunnel head. When they emerged, the moon was gone, and Olmstead was now standing with his hands thrust in his pockets. Snow was floating around the streetlamp, hanging in the air like constellations and cobwebs of lace. Wesley thought of Maggie, of the hollow in his bed where her body must now be lying, of her breathing, of the damp and citric smell of her loins.

O'Connor said, "Strangled. No shoes. Seems familiar somehow."

"Yeah," said Wesley. "Love's old sweet song." He sighed and looked at O'Connor. "I'm going home till morning. This is your show for now. Get the photographer and the morgue guys out here. Then I suppose you ought to look into what our friend Mr. White's been up to."

Wesley went home and got back into bed, resting his palm on Maggie's hip and thinking of how he could tell her that what they'd done was all wrong and must never be done again. But all he could picture was her smiling at him and then mocking him, sputtering, "Oh, pshaw, Wesley!" and turning back to the stove, where the eggs and bacon would be frying in the morning.

As it turned out, he was overtaken by happenstance, and happenstance cleared his table like a pool shark on a streak: one in the corner, another in the side, a third banked and in the other pocket, with the cue ball left kissing the eight ball for the sinker. First, when O'Connor came to pick him up at eight-thirty, he said they'd had a missing persons report courtesy of the Jew at the Aragon, who'd called Welshinger in Vice to say that one of his girls had missed work for two days. Turned out she had a date with Herbert White for Saturday night and another on Sunday. That was the last anybody had seen of her. Then it turned out White had decided to go on vacation. By afternoon, Wesley and O'Connor knew where and when he'd gone and were on the phone with the authorities in Washington State. Wesley packed a satchel and stopped by the morgue on the way to the station to catch the North Coast Limited. Ruby Fahey had been struck on the left side of the head and throttled to death. There was semen in her hair. There were no other signs of assault or struggle. She might have been passing the time of day with her assailant before he laid her out flat.

Wesley tried to sleep as the train stole through the dried-up husks of crapped-out little towns in North Dakota, including the one he was born in, although it wasn't until the train was in Montana that he realized they must have passed through it. When the train stopped at Spokane around ten-thirty the next night, he called O'Connor from inside the station. The police in Washington State had found White. They'd pick Wesley up from the train in Seattle in the morning.

Wesley had never seen the likes of Mount Rainier, but the truth was it was lost on him. He was benumbed by thirty-six hours on the train and by the thought of Maggie and the memory of her, which poured down on him like rain. After they'd driven all the way to the ocean, just to talk to some Indian kid who told them, yeah, he'd seen a guy—"bigger than Joe Palooka"—on the beach; after they'd struck out in Forks and then Tacoma and driven up the mountain the next day in the gathering boil of the snowstorm, he wasn't weary: He was the walking dead. As he shuffled along behind the ranger up the trail, he was holding Maggie in his mind; or rather he was thinking she was holding what was left of him in her little soap-weathered hands, blowing on him like tinder she was trying to keep alight.

At the top, in the winding shroud of wind and snow, he looked at White, at this chump whose first thought was to help Wesley gather up his sodden Luckies out of the snow, and Wesley thought: There's no way this guy is a killer; or if he is, he's the devil himself, he's *that* evil.

On the train, White kept to himself. He wrote in a notebook and then read what he wrote, over and over again. Otherwise he had his nose stuck in the fattest book Wesley had ever seen, reading it very slowly, like he was going to make it last for the rest of his life. Only once did White really speak. He looked up from the fat book, straight at Wesley, who was smoking a cigarette and considering having the colored guy give him another shine, and said softly, "What's going to happen to me?" He sat limp but enormous, like a dehorned bull, with his hands hanging between his legs.

"First you go in county lockup," Wesley said. "Then the rest sort of depends on you."

"On me?"

"On how much you cooperate." Wesley didn't say anything more. He knew silence at this point would help soften a suspect up before the interrogation, help put the fear of God into him. But then Wesley wasn't sure this guy was disposed to be afraid of God in the first place or had much truck with him. But he was afraid of something, Wesley could tell; maybe just afraid of ceasing to be whatever he was, even if that was just evil. As for Wesley, he was afraid too: a thousand miles from his little house and afraid that somehow, when he got back, Maggie wouldn't be in it.

It was Monday morning when Wesley and White arrived in Saint Paul. O'Connor was waiting on the platform with two patrolmen. The first thing O'Connor saw was White's body filling the vestibule of the car, clutching his bag to his chest and coming through the door, Wesley appearing behind him. White stepped gingerly onto the platform and looked at O'Connor, and O'Connor nodded, and the patrolmen came up on either side of White, took his bag, and began to steer him toward the stairs up into the station.

O'Connor shook Wesley's hand and then said, "Jesus, Wes, you didn't cuff him?"

Wesley shrugged. "He wasn't going anywhere. So what gives?"

"I swear, it's like God's on our side. The evidence—it's like stealing candy from a baby." He and Wesley began to walk toward the exit, well behind White and the patrolmen. "Morning after you went to Seattle, the boilerman from the cathedral says he saw White by the door in the heating plant that connects to the tunnel. Saw him Sunday around suppertime, acting strange, he said."

"Christ," said Wesley.

"It gets better. We searched White's place. Lots of photos of the Fahey girl. But this is the pip: There's this diary he kept, and he practically confesses. Says he did something terrible to her, says he 'dispatched' her. He kept scrapbooks too. Had all the stories about the Mortensen girl."

"Did he say anything about her in the diary?"

"Not exactly. But there's possibilities. You gotta read between the lines."

"Christ, if we could nail him for both, it'd be like Christmas morning," Wesley said. "But let's not get ahead of ourselves. Frankly, after we book him in, I want to go home, get some sleep."

The Black Maria was parked in front of the station, and the patrolmen loaded White in the back and sealed the doors. Wesley and O'Connor followed them in O'Connor's car, and Wesley looked out the window at the city streets in the morning light and thought how it seemed he'd been away a very long time. They pulled in at the back of the Public Safety Building and waited while the patrolmen brought White out and shunted him into the station hall.

There was a crowd around the booking desk, Welshinger, Trent, and the captain among them. Farrell from the *Dispatch* was standing off to one side and tipped the brim of his hat to Wesley. There was a photographer holding a big Speed Graphic in front of him, and Farrell was whispering in his ear. When the booking officer seized White's big right hand to ink it up for printing, the photographer started shooting a volley of pictures, feeding fresh flashbulbs to the camera from his left coat pocket and depositing the spent, blistered ones in his right.

"Who put the reptiles onto this?" Wesley asked O'Connor.

"Don't know, but I'll give you three guesses."

"I'd only need one."

White stood before the desk, a head taller than the crowd around him. Sweat had broken out on his forehead, and his eyes fluttered and blinked as the flashbulbs pulsed and the photographer shuttled and snapped negative carriers in and out of the back of the camera. The booking officer, Sergeant Neuhaus, had his left hand now, and rolled his fingers roughly into the ink and onto the paper, and White watched, the sergeant's hand over his hand like a moth riding a turtle's back. Then he looked straight at Neuhaus and said, "What happened to Miss Ruby, to Miss Fahey?"

Neuhaus released his hand. "You ought to know, Mac," he said, and shook his head slowly back and forth.

White looked down at his hand, at the sooty fingertips, and Neuhaus handed him a rag. "I was very fond of her," White said. "I remember her well." Then he began to sob.

They took him into the cells, down to the tank, just the patrolmen and Wesley and O'Connor. The guard told White to take off his belt and suspenders and tie, and began to go through White's bag. "You want the book?" he said.

"I'm only just finishing the first part—*42nd Parallel,* it's called—so yes, if I could."

"Okay. Shirt, underwear, socks—that's okay too. But not the bag, or the writing pad and the pen. Don't want you passing notes to the other prisoners or poking out somebody's eye."

White turned to Wesley and spoke directly to him for the first time in nearly twelve hours. "Would you keep it for me, the journal?"

"Could be more evidence against you, what's in here," Wesley said. "If we needed any more."

"I don't have anything to hide, Lieutenant. It's just a memento of my journey. I wouldn't want it to get lost."

"Suit yourself," Wesley said, and took the notebook from the guard. It had a cartoon of a mountain goat on the cover.

Then the guard opened the gate, and he and the patrolmen took Herbert White inside, and White looked back at Wesley and said, "Thank you, Lieutenant."

"Sure," Wesley said.

Even before O'Connor dropped him off, even three blocks from his house, his breath was a little tight and there was a kind of heat rising up into his neck and his head like coffee through the stem pipe of a percolator, pushing and febrile. When O'Connor stopped, Wesley yanked his satchel off the back seat and opened the door in one motion. He said, "Come back for me at four. We'll have a little powwow, see what we've really got," and then he was gone.

At the door, Wesley got out his key, but when he put it in, he found the door was already unlocked, and before he could press it open the width of his body, Maggie was there. "You breaking and entering?" she said. "You ought to know there's a cop living here. Got a temper too."

"He's tired, mostly," Wesley said. "Wants some breakfast, I suspect." Then he looked at her, and she raised her arm and drew him into the house, and he whispered, "Wants his girl too."

Wesley pushed the door shut with his heel and held Maggie to him, pressed his face against her neck and shoulder, smelling the tang of her breath, the fetid duskiness of her hair. The radio was playing, and he thought it hadn't been played for years. There was new music coming out of it, layers of saxophones and clarinets alloyed with trombones. Maggie's voice came damp into the whorl of his ear. "I missed you so bad."

"I missed you too. Couldn't think straight. Couldn't hardly see where I was."

He put his mouth on her mouth, or perhaps he only met her lips as they were rising to his. They breathed each other's breaths, and then Wesley pulled away and said, not knowing why, "About what we did, the night before I left—"

"Is what we'll do tonight. Every night."

"I was thinking it was wrong, but when I was away it was all I could think of ever wanting. Not *it*, I mean. I mean you."

"Told you so. Right as rain, wasn't it?"

"Guess so. Guess you knew better, outsmarted me."

"Made a fool of you," Maggie said, and her arms tumbled like slack water down his sides to his waist. "So let me tuck you into your bed right now. Let me rain on you some more."

After he'd read the diary, Wesley pulled his feet down off his desk and laid four cigarettes in a line across the top of it. "So here's our ducks, all in a row: Eyewitness saw him at the crime scene around the time of the crime. No one else sees *her* between then and discovery of the body. The guy at the Paramount who White was asking about some starlet sees her leave with White about quarter of seven Saturday. Then her girlfriends at the Aragon. They say she says White's going to take her picture the next day." Wesley picked up the left-hand cigarette and lit it. "That's hearsay, but it doesn't matter because it's in the diary, dated, in his handwriting. And no one ever saw her alive after that."

Wesley lifted a second cigarette and set it down emphatically. "So there's the timetable. There's the opportunity." He set the cigarette down and picked up another, the one he was smoking still hanging from his lip. "Now, here's motive: Even if you don't take the diary to be an out-and-out confession, it shows he's upset with the girl and that he's done something terrible. Maybe we don't even need to know what it is." He put down the cigarette and took up the last one on the desk. "Because he leaves town suddenly. He flees after being seen where the girl's body is found. He leaves without explanation. But the body's the explanation. So there you are." Wesley laid down the last cigarette. "One, two, three."

O'Connor said, "Maybe you show him what we got, maybe he'll confess."

"Maybe. Or start in with that bad-memory malarkey. I'd love to see him pull that crap in front of a judge and a jury. If they don't think he's a fruitcake going in, they would after that. Anyhow, I'll go to the captain now. Then I guess we'll see the DA in the morning."

"Congratulations, Wes."

"Thanks. Thanks for everything you did too," Wesley said. "But it just kind of fell into our laps, didn't it. Like winning the Irish Sweepstakes. Like a gift from heaven."

On Tuesday morning, Herbert asked the guard if he could see his paper, and the guard said that although he wasn't supposed to give anything to the prisoners, he didn't see how it could do any harm.

Herbert sat on the little cot in his cell and spread the newspaper out on the thin gray blanket. It was like doing his scrapbook, except that he didn't have his scrapbook; and when he saw the picture on the front page—his picture—and what was written beneath it, it was like doing his journal, only somebody else had written the entry for him:

SUSPECT ARRESTED IN DIME-A-DANCE MURDER

SAYS OF VICTIM, "I WAS VERY FOND OF HER"

Exclusive to the Dispatch *by*
CHARLES FARRELL

October 30—Office clerk Herbert W. White, 35, of St. Paul, was arrested today in connection with the murder of dime-a-dance girl Ruby Fahey. The body of Fahey, age 23, was discovered last Wednesday in the Selby Avenue streetcar tunnel. Death was by strangulation.

Police brought White back to St. Paul from Washington State, where he had fled the day after the murder. White was taken into custody at his mountaintop hideout by Lieutenant Wesley Horner of the St. Paul Police Homicide Squad, assisted by Washington State and Federal authorities.

Visibly shaken as he was

booked and fingerprinted, the six-foot-plus White asked police officers what had happened to the woman he called "Miss Ruby," adding, "I was very fond of her. I remember her well." As the suspect was led away to the cells, he broke down.

Police also suspect White in the month-old unsolved murder of strangled dime-a-dance girl Charlene Mortensen, who worked under the name Carla Marie LaBreque with Fahey at the Aragon Ballroom in downtown St. Paul. An unnamed police lieutenant said higher-ups at the police department and the district attorney's office had expressed distress at the homicide squad's lack of progress in the Mortensen case.

White is expected to be arraigned in Ramsey County Superior Court later this week.

Herbert read the article, and then he read it again, trying to see himself in it and remember what had happened, but it was as though he had lost his glasses: Parts of what the newspaper said seemed clear to him, but other parts he could not quite see. It was not a question so much of remembering or forgetting what the newspaper story said had happened as of it being like an object that was too far away or too much in motion to get a fix on. He felt he was at a great remove from the things the newspaper described, and he could not get them in focus. He wondered who it was that had written the story and what it was they had seen.

Of course, Herbert might have said he was at a remove from himself as well, that the person he was accustomed to imagine himself to be was far away, hazy in the distance or altogether lost in darkness. Herbert could not see himself, he was estranged from himself, not just because he was reading about the person he was purported to be in the newspaper, but because he felt that in some way he had lost himself by his own actions, and this had something to do with Ruby Fahey. He did not believe he had done what the newspaper implied he had done, but he felt he had done something, something he regretted. He might have said that the regret filled him, except that it was not so much a presence as an absence, a sense of all-encompassing lack in which he was deprived not only of Ruby but of himself and of what made him at home in the world.

He tried not to think about that, but it was not much help, for the absence of the thought, however distressing, was just one more thing he lacked, was missing, and had lost. He turned his attention back to the newspaper, hoping to divert himself, but everything else on the front page only served to confirm his deprivation. He saw that in Britain and France they were waiting for the last vestiges of peace to flicker out and die, for the bombing and invasion to begin; and he saw that today was the last day of the New York World's Fair, which he had wanted so badly to attend. He thought of the Perisphere, the perfectly round geometric solid that served as the fair's emblem, and he thought of the glass globe he had found on the sea's edge, and how his anticipation of the one in the future and his possession of the other in the past were now equally lost to him.

Then the detective with the long, sad face came into his cell, the one he half remembered like a face he was seeing at the bottom of a well. Herbert folded the newspaper in half and laid it at the end of the cot. He looked at Wesley and said, "It says in the newspaper that today is the last day of the World's Fair."

Wesley faced White at a distance of perhaps five feet. He saw there was a chair but thought it would be better to remain standing. "It's Halloween too," he said. "Trick or treat."

White was crouched on the side of the bed, looking up at

Wesley with his mournful eyes, his body massive and plaintive. He was like King Kong in captivity with spectacles, in brogues with the shoelaces removed. He didn't say anything in response to Wesley, and Wesley thought he should proceed cautiously, gently, as if he was White's only friend in a world that was out to do him in. In fact, both the prosecutor from the district attorney's office and the captain had been very clear about what they expected from Wesley: They wanted to arraign and convict White for both murders, and they wanted to do it quickly. There was an election soon. Given the preponderance of evidence against him, White could surely be made to see that a confession was the only means by which he might obtain a measure of clemency from the court and the district attorney. If Wesley couldn't persuade him of that, others would be given the opportunity to do so. So here Wesley was, sitting with the pitiful, helpless giant in his cage.

Wesley began. "You know, Herbert—I suppose I can call you Herbert, what with us having crossed half the country together— I'd be a liar if I didn't tell you it doesn't look real good for you."

"I don't really understand how it looks," White said, not petulantly, Wesley thought, but in genuine befuddlement.

Wesley thought he ought to sit down. He lowered himself onto the little ladder-back chair and leaned forward, spreading his hands like he was showing how wide the horizon was. "The charge is first-degree murder, Herbert. Probably twice over. And the evidence—no matter what you say, no matter what you do—is what they call irrefutable."

"I didn't do it. I would never hurt Miss Ruby, not intentionally. Never."

"That's not what the evidence says. And you know you could have done it. You told me that when we talked about the

Mortensen girl—that you were capable, that you could have been the one."

"I don't know what I might have said then. I scarcely remember meeting you."

Wesley put his hands on his knees and sat straight up. "You don't remember that, huh? What about the two cops who tore up your place and then I came and saved your bacon? You remember that?"

"I'm not sure. I can picture it, but no more than that."

Wesley stood. He knew he was getting angry, and he thought it might help if he moved around. He thought it might put the fear of God into White, since the friendly approach wasn't getting him anywhere. He lit a cigarette and paced back and forth in front of White. "So you can sort of picture it, but not much more? Let me help you picture something else. You keep up this I-don't-know, I-don't-remember malarkey, and the court considers the evidence. The witnesses. Your going on the lam. Your diary where you say you 'dispatched' Ruby Fahey—"

"You read my journal? You have it?"

"We have everything, Herbert. We've got you and your whole life tied up in wrapping paper with a big pink bow on it."

"You had no right."

"We had every right. Two girls are dead. I don't give a shit about rights. And you haven't got any rights, not now, except maybe to throw yourself on the mercy of the court. Because, like I was saying, the court considers all this evidence, and you just sit there saying, 'I didn't do it' or 'I don't know' or 'I don't remember,' and that's just a goddamn slap in the face to these two dead girls. So you don't give the court any alternative: double first-degree murder, life without parole, the whole nine yards, Herbert."

White shook his head back and forth. He said, "That's all very well and good. But I can't do—I can't say what never happened, what never was—what I don't even know."

"Consider this, Herbert. Picture this. You admit what you did, at least to the Fahey girl. You plead guilty to second-degree murder. You tell the court you couldn't control yourself, that you've got these mental problems. The court respects your honesty and you throw yourself on the court's mercy. You get fifteen years, maybe only serve ten or twelve of them. Then you get out. You're a free man."

Wesley stopped pacing and bent down in front of White. He said, "Look at me, Herbert," and White raised his face up from his hands and looked at Wesley. "Those are your choices. You can be a chump and a moron and keep up this bullshit. Or you can fess up and take your medicine and have a future. So what's it going to be, Herbert? Your life's in your own hands, not in mine, not in anybody else's. You choose." Wesley pulled himself up and went around behind the chair, laying his hands on the top rail of its back, and waited.

White looked down and unfolded his hands and then said, "I suppose I'd really rather like to do what you say. But I can't. It's not even a matter of telling the truth. It's just a question of having something rather than nothing. I haven't got Miss Ruby or my camera or my job anymore, and I haven't had a family for fifteen years. So all I have is"—and White stretched his hands out, with his palms level with the jail cell's floor—"this. This, and what I remember, and what I know and what I don't know. If I say what you want me to say—that I did this thing that I don't remember or know that I did—I give that up. And it's all I have, so I want to keep it."

Wesley pulled himself erect and loosed a sigh. "Suit yourself,

Herbert. It's your funeral. I can't help you if you don't want to help yourself." He went to the door and called through the bars for the guard to come and let him out. Waiting, he took a last pull on the butt of his cigarette and dropped it on the floor and ground it out. The guard came and unlocked the door. Wesley stepped through it and paused for a moment. He said to White, "You think about what I said, Herbert. Because maybe all you've got left isn't this stuff that you talk about. Maybe all you've got left is this one choice, to save your own life or not. Maybe that's all you've got— the one or the other. So you pick, Herbert."

White rose up from the cot, slowly, massively, and Wesley passed the rest of the way through the door, and the guard closed and locked it as White moved toward the bars. He held his hands as though he were clutching his hat, although they were empty and his hat must have been somewhere up on Mount Rainier. He said, "I want to thank you, Lieutenant. But I don't really think I can do what you say. I really don't."

Wesley nodded and turned away. The guard walked him down to the end of the corridor and let him out through another barred door. Wesley said, "Poor screwy bastard, he wants to take the fall for this."

"Well, he did it, didn't he?" the guard said.

"You know, sometimes I feel just like him, and I think, hell, I don't know what he did or didn't do either," Wesley said. "But yeah, sure, he did it."

Later in the morning, Wesley argued with the captain. No, he hadn't gotten a confession, but just by the way White talked, it was clear he was going to hang himself in the courtroom—that his daffiness, his lack of remorse, were just as damning as a confession.

The captain wasn't buying it; or maybe he personally agreed

with Wesley but what the district attorney wanted was a confession in time for election day. The captain said he'd like to let Welshinger have a try.

"Jesus Christ," Wesley said.

"You got a problem with him?"

"Maybe I do, maybe I don't. But White will."

"You said he claimed he'd forgotten all that."

"Lock him in a cell with Welshinger, maybe it all comes back and he clams up even tighter."

"Or he gets religion," the captain said.

"I don't hold with Welshinger's religion sometimes. Too physical."

"I hold with results. So I want you to let him have at White."

"If it's got to be that way. But you let me put it to him, okay? Like it came from me."

The captain smiled. "Sure, Wes. That's fine. I want all you guys to get along, to cooperate."

Wesley went down the hall to the vice room. Trent was eating a sandwich and working a crossword puzzle.

"So where is he, the monsignor?" Wesley said.

Trent looked up and flicked the tip of his pencil across the butt of his thumb. "Out in the back lot. I think he's simonizing his car or something," he said, and looked back down at his puzzle.

Wesley found Welshinger at the very rear of the parking compound, where the officers who had their own cars parked. He was bent down, rubbing the back bumper of his Hudson with a wad of fine steel wool. The trunk lid was open. Welshinger straightened himself and said, "Top of the morning, Lieutenant."

"Same to you. I see you're working on your lunch hour."

"No rest for the wicked." Welshinger grinned and resumed rubbing the bumper.

Wesley looked into the trunk. In addition to the spare tire and the jack, the interior was crammed with cartons of cigarettes, packages of nylon stockings, pint bottles of liquor, and wrapped candy boxes from Fanny Farmer. "Quite a treasure chest you got here." He saw a crumpled bag stuffed into a corner, with a woman's bathing suit protruding from it. Wesley reached in and fingered the shoulder strap as Welshinger rose up from the bumper. Still touching the suit, Wesley smiled and said, "Going to try out for Miss America?"

Welshinger's lips were expressionless. Then he smiled and said, "Don't soil the merchandise. Just something for a lady friend." He lowered the lid of the trunk. "So how's tricks? Do something for you?"

"Well, you know White?"

"Whole city knows, Wes."

"Yeah. Well, the DA wants a confession. I tried, but the bastard's being stubborn, thick about it. Says he can't remember, same crap as before. I thought maybe a different approach might help. Thought you might try your hand, if you'd oblige me."

Welshinger smiled broadly. "Well, sure. Anything for a pal, Wes," he said. "Did you buddy up to him or just lay down the law?"

"Little of both, but he just says no, like he sees the writing on the wall but if he cops to it he'd be giving up his religion or something."

"Well, I suspect I could help him see things a little different. Bend his will a bit—"

"But no rough stuff, okay?"

"Of course. Hell, Wes, it's all psychology, like a headshrinker working with the unconscious mind."

This notion wasn't clear to Wesley, but he nodded. "Sure."

"I suppose the DA's got ants in his pants about this," Welshinger said.

Wesley nodded. "Election's coming up."

"So I'll go see your boy tonight. Don't you worry about a thing, Brother Wes."

Welshinger reached out to clasp Wesley by the shoulder, and Wesley found himself wanting to shrink back but let Welshinger's hand rest on him like a cold breeze. He said, "Hey, thanks," and added, "No hard feelings about that time you were going to bust him for the pictures, right?"

"No, Wes, nothing." Welshinger's fingers dug into the tendons of Wesley's collarbone. "Hey, we're buddies. Helping each other out, okay? What's done is done. I got no affection for the past."

Maggie had cooked Wesley pork chops, as was now their custom on Tuesdays. Later in the night, when Maggie was making love to Wesley in his bed—now their bed—as though she were winding him in bandages, salving his wounds, in what would later seem to be the golden age of his love for her, that was when Welshinger went down to see Herbert White in his cell.

Welshinger sent the guard away, handing him a quarter. "Go get yourself a cup of coffee. Get yourself a hamburger too. Lock the door. It's just me and Mr. White down here, and we'll be having a tay-to-tay for a half hour or so." The guard nodded and let Welshinger into White's cell. They regarded each other without words for some time, and then Welshinger heard the faraway slam of the guard leaving the block, the gate clunking like two boxcars coupling in the dark.

"You remember me, Herb?" Welshinger said.

"I think I might."

"Well, that's progress. I hear you got a bad memory." Welshinger bared his teeth in a tiny grin and suddenly stepped toward White, thrusting his face to within inches of White's pallid, moist forehead and huge eyes. "Sit down, Herb," Welshinger said through his teeth. "Makes me nervous when you're standing up and I'm trying to talk to you. Don't make me nervous. I get unpredictable when I'm nervous." White sat, slowly, gingerly, like a concert pianist settling into his bench, and then he looked up at Welshinger, as though to get his approval.

Welshinger took two steps back. "Comfortable, Herb?"

White nodded, bobbing his head deeply, like a trick pony.

"Good," Welshinger said. "You know, Herb, I read your diary or whatever it is. You got a way with words."

"You read it too?"

"Oh, I suppose lots of people around the station have. Hell, Herb, I suppose during the trial it'll end up in the papers."

"I never meant for it to be read, not by anyone but me. Does it have to be . . . circulated like that?"

"It's evidence now," Welshinger said. "Doesn't really belong to you anymore. Hell, *you* don't belong to you anymore. You belong to the state. Right now you belong to me." Welshinger chuckled.

"So perhaps you'd get it back for me—my journal, I mean."

"Hm. I suppose I could. I've got some pull around here. We'll see. All depends on you." Welshinger stopped for a moment and regarded the fingernails of his left hand. "So," he began again. "Where you learn all those words? Couldn't go to school like a normal kid, could you?"

"Nanna—my grandmother—taught me, and sometimes she hired tutors. Mostly we read together."

Welshinger cocked his head. "What kind of stuff?"

"Oh, poetry. Mostly Lord Tennyson. Emerson's essays as well. Sermons. Novels too, for pleasure—Dickens, Kipling. Sometimes I'd write little poems myself."

"Hm," Welshinger said. "That's real interesting." He sat down on the little ladder-back chair and scraped it forward until he was about a yard away from White. "You know, Herb, you probably think I don't know much, haven't read much, dumb cop and all. But I know a few things. I've done some reading. Psychology, for example. You know what that is?"

"Not in so many words."

"The science of the mind, Herb. The science of the mind. Comes out of Vienna, Austria."

White said, "Vienna is part of Germany now."

"Oh, the whole world's going to be part of Germany pretty soon, I guess. That's neither here or there. Anyway, what they discovered over there is that the mind is a lot more complicated, that what we see is just the top of the iceberg. It's like these cakes they got over there. Looks like a regular chocolate on the outside. Chocolate frosting. But inside, it's got layers. Not just cake. Also jam and marzipan and so forth. Stuff you never expected to be there. Hidden stuff." Welshinger halted. "You with me, Herb?"

White nodded.

"Good, 'cause this isn't easy. This is science. Anyway, there's hidden places in the mind, places that not only other people don't know about but that *you* don't know about, places in your very own mind. There's thoughts in there and lots of feelings and memories too, and this hidden stuff can make you do things—hell, control your whole life—and you don't even know it's there."

"Like a ghost haunting a house."

"Yeah. That's good, Herb. I can see you're following me. And the thing is, that's how we know this hidden stuff is there—that it's real. Because it's like that ghost. It's a lost soul, it's shackled and it wants to be free. So it does things—bangs on the pipes, monkeys with the electricity—to get your attention. And what it's saying is, 'Let me out. I want to be free.' You still with me?"

"I think so."

"Good. Okay, so it's exactly the same thing with these hidden thoughts and feelings and memories. They make noise because they want to get out. Because once they're out—once they're not hidden anymore—they can be free and they go away. The house—your mind—isn't haunted anymore."

"It's been exorcised, so to speak," White said.

"Right. You hit the nail right on the head. And that gets me to my point. See, I didn't come down here just to pass the time of day about this stuff. You're a smart guy. You could find out for yourself. It's all in the *Reader's Digest*, for anybody who wants to know." Welshinger shuffled his chair forward another six inches. "See, Herb, I think this has a bearing on your . . . situation. I think maybe it could even help you."

White was leaning forward now, his face a foot from Welshinger's. Welshinger's breath was cold and sweet, like air coming out from a fruit cellar door. White said, "Really?"

"Yeah, I really think so. See, I think if these doctors investigated your case, they'd have something to say about this bad memory of yours. I think they'd say there wasn't really anything wrong with your memory—that it's more that you don't want to remember."

"But I do, I would, more than anything sometimes."

"Wait a minute. I don't mean like that. Of course you want to remember, but there's things hidden in your mind that won't let you, because they're afraid of those memories. They don't want them to come out."

Herbert pulled back a little. "But I thought you said they wanted to come out."

"Well, they do. But they're scared to, to face those memories. That's what the psychology doctors do—they help them come out, when they don't want to. I know maybe that sounds like double-talk, like having it both ways. But it's not. It's science. Now, you with me?"

"I think so." White leaned forward again, his lips slightly parted.

"Good. Now, I think there's probably something hidden in your mind that you can't bear to face, can't bear to remember, so the way your mind *copes* with that is *to not remember anything at all.*" Welshinger smiled and put his palms on his knees. "What do you think, Herb? That make any sense?"

"I suppose it does. But I can't think of anything I've done that I wouldn't want to remember."

"Well, see, that's the beauty of it. Of course you can't think of anything like that, because it's already hidden away. It's too painful for your conscious mind to face."

"But if these things are buried, how does one know they exist at all until after they're uncovered?" White said. "And for that matter, how would one uncover them in the first place?"

"That's where the scientific technique comes in, the technique of psychoanalysis. See, you tell me your dreams or just whatever pops into your mind or stuff that happened when you were a kid, and I find clues about what's hidden," Welshinger said. He leaned toward White again and lowered his voice. "Let me give you an example, Herb. See, I know you were an orphan. Very sad story.

Your ma died giving birth to you and your pa went off to war and didn't come back. Very sad; terrible, in fact. Maybe more than you could bear when you were a child."

"But I remember my father going away and then being killed perfectly well," White said. "And of course I don't remember being born—I don't suppose anyone does—but I've always known and remembered what happened to my mother."

"Well, sure you do, Herb. You remember the events. But maybe there's *feelings* you have about those events that you've shut away. For example, the science of psychology tells us that a child whose parent dies is likely to feel that it caused its parent's death."

"How is it that psychology knows that?" Herbert asked.

"Because it's a science, Herb. Okay, you with me?"

"I suppose."

"Good. Now, what that means is this: that it would be very natural for you to feel that you killed your mother, and that you would cope with that by keeping yourself from remembering things. Same thing with your pa: Deep inside you felt he went away to get away from you, because you'd killed your ma. And when he did that, he died. So in a way, you killed him too. And you couldn't bear it. So you killed your own memory."

White colored and pulled his face back, straightening his back. "That's an awfully . . . cruel thing to say." He stopped. "Besides, I already told you: I remember, I know all about those things."

"But you don't know what you do or what you did on account of them, Herb. And you can't know, because they're buried in your mind," Welshinger said. "You can't argue with this stuff, Herb. It's a science. It's not mumbo jumbo. It's not your Lord Tennyson. And of course you're going to deny that it's true. That's part of the science too: that when you confront the person with what's hidden in their mind, they'll resist seeing it for what it truly is."

"I thought it wanted to come out."

"Well, it does. Or at least the healthy part of the personality wants it to. But the diseased part doesn't want it to. It *wants* it to remain hidden. And that's part of the disease. See, that's how we know when we're onto something—when you say we're *not* onto something."

"It's rather confusing."

"It's logical as hell, Herb. It's the scientific method."

"So if I remember about my parents' dying but I forget lots of other things, that's a way of forgetting about my parents' dying?"

"That's about it in a nutshell," Welshinger said. "I know it doesn't always make sense to you. You're obviously not up on this stuff. But trust me, Herb. Hell, if you don't trust me, trust the science. Science doesn't lie, Herb."

White rubbed his chin with his thumb, inscribing little circles around it. Then he said, "Suppose you're right. Suppose I thought, as a child anyway, that I was responsible for my parents' deaths. What does that have to do with me . . . being here. For this thing you say I did, that I don't know anything about or at least don't remember."

"Now, there you are, Herb," Welshinger said. "See, it's not just that you thought that as a child. Deep inside your mind you believe it *now*—that you killed your mother and then you drove away your father and killed him too."

"But if I thought that, if I was so repelled by it, wouldn't I be the last person in the world to want to kill anyone else? Isn't that logical?"

"It might seem that way to most people, but actually it's just the opposite. See, your illness gives you this hankering to repeat that first unbearable memory—"

"But if I remember it, how is it unbearable? And if I really didn't kill anyone in the first place, what is there to repeat—"

Welshinger's eyes flared. "You're not paying attention, Herb, and you're making me nervous. Now, to repeat myself, it's your unconscious mind that believes this stuff—that believes it killed—and because it's buried, because it wants to come out but can't come out, it doesn't know what else to do but kill again, kill young women like your mother would have been when you killed her—"

Herbert rose up and stood, shaking and knitting his fingers together, as though wishing he could extend them out to grasp something while knowing there was nothing at all upon which they might find purchase. He sputtered, "That's absurd; that's . . . appalling."

Welshinger stepped toward him and stopped two inches from White's face and, almost breathing up White's nose, said, "It's the truth. And the more you say it's not, the more I know it is." Welshinger's voice dropped to a whisper, the brush of a dry hand across silk. "Accept it, Herb. Accept it. Then I'll help you."

White said nothing, and then he exhaled heavily and sat down on the cot again. "I still don't . . . see it. It's like you want me to believe all this—the hidden mind, the unbearable memories, the wanting to kill—on faith, to say that what I can't see, can't even imagine, with my own eyes is right in front of my face."

"It's not faith, Herb. It's just the opposite. It's science. You can't get away from it. Just like you can't get away from what's buried in your mind. You can't escape it, Herb. It's there, whether you want it to be or not."

"So what do I do?"

"You admit that it's there, Herb. That way it can come out, like it needs to. Then it won't bother you anymore. You won't want to kill anybody anymore."

"But . . . I didn't kill anybody—not that I know about."

"Exactly: not that you know about. But everybody else does, Herb. We've got enough evidence to put you away a dozen times. We've got evidence we're not even going to use. It's unsavory, and we don't need it to convict you." Welshinger stopped for a moment and tipped his head to the side. "Hell, we've got your dirty laundry. I mean for real. Your BVDs and your pants. You creamed your trousers with this last girl, Herb. You remember that?"

White colored and locked his eyes on the floor, on his laceless shoes. "I suppose I do."

"You remember anything else?"

"Not really. Just that I was upset, that Miss Ruby left and I was upset."

"That's not quite how it happened, Herb. Your mind won't let you see it, but that's not the whole story. See, all these women are your mother, as far as your unconscious mind is concerned. But you get the hots for 'em and act on it, and what have you done? You screwed your mother. You can't bear it, so what do you do? You kill the girl, try to erase her just like you erase your own memory."

"But I think all that happened with Miss Ruby was—"

"It doesn't matter what you think happened. We're past that, Herb. You have to trust me now, have to let me help you see what really happened, because you can't help yourself." Welshinger stretched out his hand and laid it on White's forearm for a moment, and then he withdrew it. "See, Herb, this is how it was. With the Mortensen girl, you got so excited you could hardly get it in. Then, when you saw what you'd done, you hit her on the head and dumped her down the hill by the Lawton Steps. Mind you, you couldn't help it, Herb. Because it's a sickness."

"A sickness—so it's not anything I would have meant to do. Because I can't even imagine ever hurting anyone."

"You wouldn't know it, Herb. It's all buried. It's a sickness deep inside you, and just like a sickness, it gets worse. With the Fahey girl, it was the same deal as Mortensen, only worse. This time you couldn't even hold off long enough to get your tool out. That's part of how we know you're sick, Herb—because you can't control yourself a little, the way a normal guy can. So, again, you killed her, but this time you got hot afterward too. So you diddled yourself and came in her hair. Then you carried her up and dumped her in the tunnel, in the dark, with the rats. That's how deep this sickness goes, Herb."

White brought his hands up to his face and covered his eyes with the butts of his palms, harrowed the paltry strands of hair on his head with his fingertips. "Oh, God," he said. "Oh, God." He sobbed and said, "But I just can't see it."

"You don't need to see it. It's just there, plain as the nose on your face." Welshinger touched White's shoulder. "Last month you told Lieutenant Horner that you had to admit that you couldn't say you hadn't done it, because of your memory. You'd have to say the same thing now, wouldn't you?"

White looked up, his face mottled, blanched and crimson, like blood on snow. "I suppose I would."

"So that kind of settles it. You admit you could have done it. Add that to the preponderance of evidence, to the scientific proof."

White shook his head back and forth, balefully, as though all Welshinger's accumulated words hung on his shoulders like a shawl. "So what do I do?" he said. "To save myself?"

"Admit what you did. Let what's buried come out. You'll do some time, but you'll be a whole person again."

"You mean my memory might be normal?"

"I'd guess so. Because you would have removed what was burying it, holding it down." Welshinger sat. "So let it out, Herb. Put it behind you. See, this stuff from the past you can't face is dragging you down. So get it off your chest. Give yourself a future, Herb. To hell with the past."

"So what do I do?"

"You make a confession. In writing."

"I sort of made one of those once, to a priest at the cathedral."

"Well, this will be a real one, not a phony. This one will work."

"But I still don't really know exactly what happened. So what do I say?"

Welshinger took a sheet of paper and a pen from his coat pocket. "I'll help you, Herb. Don't worry."

"And you'll see about getting my journal back?"

"I'll see what I can do." Welshinger handed Herbert the paper and pen. "You do the writing, Herb. You have such a way with words, such a fine hand."

The telephone rang after they had fallen asleep. This time Maggie did not wake but only mewled softly and rolled over, as though it were just a clock striking in the night.

Wesley got up and answered on the third ring.

"Wes," the voice said. "I got him. Nailed him sure as Christ on the cross."

"He talked?"

"Talked? Hell, he wrote—chapter and verse, in his own writing, signed and dated and sworn."

"Said he killed the Fahey girl?"

"Jackpot time, Wes. Said he did 'em both."

"Welshinger, I told you no rough stuff—"

"Never touched him, Wes. Just sweet reason."

Wesley sighed. "Jesus, I owe you." He wanted to laugh, to wake up Maggie and waltz her around the house. "This is swell. Heck, this is a miracle. And hey, Welshinger, I don't mind giving credit where credit's due."

Wesley could hear Welshinger's breath on the other end of the phone. "Listen, Wes. As far as I'm concerned, you guys got this yourselves. Did all the legwork. There's no need for me to be involved. You guys go ahead and take a bow. You deserve it. Tonight'll be our little secret."

"Jesus, I can't thank you enough. I really owe you."

"Hey, it's nothing, Wes. Someday you'll do me a favor, okay?"

"Hey, you bet."

"Okay, Wes. Merry Christmas. Sleep tight," the voice said, and the line clicked off.

Wesley moved back to his bedroom through the dark of the little house, like a mallard gliding on water. He sat down on the bed and the springs rasped and sighed beneath him, and he thought to wake Maggie, to tell her the news. But he stopped himself. He held his face a little above her ear and rested his hand on the coverlet that hid her waist. He listened to her breath, tumbling forward and back, slow and deep, as if she was opening herself and taking everything in and then letting it go again, as if she were the heart and soul of the world.

And really, she was only this stringy-haired girl from Moline, who didn't know a thing and could scarcely read. Yet who could deny that she, here and now, was a miracle, that she had saved Wesley's life, saved his very soul? Not Wesley, and he thought of his luck this night—he who had never believed in luck—and saw that not only was he lucky but he was flat-out blessed.

Herbert White found out on Thursday what had happened to him.

DIME-A-DANCE SUSPECT TO STAND TRIAL NEXT WEEK

CONFUSION IN COURT AS ACCUSED CLERK CONFESSES, WAVERS, COPS PLEA

Exclusive to the Dispatch *by*
CHARLES FARRELL

November 1—Accused dime-a-dance suspect Herbert W. White led court officers on a dance of his own today during his double murder arraignment.

Opening the proceedings for the state, District Attorney Edward Berglund advised Judge Ignatius Kelly that White had made a full confession of both murders to homicide squad officers.

Addressing White, Judge Kelly said he assumed that this development meant that the defendant wished to enter a plea of guilty.

Sitting at the defense table, flanked by two guards, White replied that he did not know what to do and asked Judge Kelly to advise him. Clearly irritated, Kelly asked a chagrined District Attorney Berglund if the accused had counsel present. "Not unless Your Honor appointed him unbeknownst to me," replied Berglund.

Judge Kelly then asked White if he wanted a lawyer, and White said he was unsure. "I rather feel as if I'm lost in the train station," he said, and alluded to a movie featuring B-picture starlet Veronica Galvin.

Kelly advised White that normally a confession indicated a desire to plead guilty. The suspect had the right to recant the confession, although it would doubtless still be used against him. Kelly then asked if White in fact wished to do so, and White replied, "I don't suppose so. I just made it last night."

Silencing the laughter that erupted in the courtroom, Kelly told White that in that case, were he to enter a plea of not guilty and then be subsequently convicted, it would "go very hard" on him. "I would consider that you had been toying with the court over a very grave matter."

Judge Kelly again asked what plea White wished to enter. White replied, "I'm still not sure. What do you suggest?" An exasperated Kelly turned to Berglund and said, "I think I'm going to have to appoint counsel for this man, whether he wants it or not."

Berglund, who faces a closely fought reelection bid next week, rose to his feet and argued that that would not serve the public interest. "The people of this city and state are anxious for a trial and a verdict in this appalling crime. Any delay would be an infringement of the people's rights." Berglund then suggested that Kelly might advise the defendant of his choices "in the dispassionate manner for which you are well known."

Saying, "I don't like this, but we'll continue," Kelly once again turned to White. Telling him to listen carefully, the judge told the defendant that if he believed his confession was still true, a guilty plea would be "consistent with that belief." White replied that he "didn't know what else to believe." Kelly then asked if that meant he wished to plead guilty, and White said he supposed it did. "That is not an unequivocal and germane answer," Kelly said, adding once again that if White should "toy with the court in this manner," it would "go hard" on him.

White appeared distracted, apparently searching the courtroom for an acquaintance, although it is not believed White has any living family. Pausing once more, Kelly asked White, "Do you wish to plead guilty?" and White at last said, "Yes, I do."

Kelly said, "Good," and, expressing relief that "this palaver is concluded," set a trial date of next Monday, November 6, if that was acceptable to Mr. Berglund. The district attorney said that in light of the defendant's guilty plea it was, adding that his place at the prosecution table would be taken by an assistant, as Berglund himself would be "busy on the hustings." Judge Kelly wished Berglund well in the election and adjourned court.

White, 35, a clerk at a St. Paul wholesale grocery firm, is charged with the murders of taxi dancers Charlene

Mortensen, 24, also known as Carla Marie LaBreque, and Ruby Fahey, 23. Reportedly a recluse with a taste for "cheesecake" photography, he was arrested last month after fleeing to Washington State.

After he had given the newspaper back to the guard, Herbert White took a nap. The metal lampshade on the bulb hanging over his bed was enameled green on the outside and white on the inside, like the ones on the platform at Union Station, and he dreamed about Veronica Galvin. He dreamed that he was saving her from Randall Moore—the one with the big fedora and outsize lapels—in *Grand Central Terminal*.

Had the first snow already fallen? Maggie could not say. For the last two weeks, she had scarcely left Wesley's little house and the grasp of the heat pouring off the range and the scent of bacon entwined with Lucky Strikes. On Friday afternoon, she lay with her shoes off on Wesley's funny old davenport, and she tipped herself forward and went to the window and looked out onto the yard. The leaves were plastered to the sidewalk, glazed with frost, shiny and lurid-colored, like the scales of a tropical snake. Then she breathed out, imagining the cloud her breath would make were she outside, and she lay back down and dug around on the side table for something to look at. Wesley had some old magazines with pictures of girls in their skivvies on the covers and titles like *Pep* and *Snap* and *High Heels;* she'd bought herself one called *True Experiences,* but she hadn't really read it. Maggie wasn't much for reading.

Next to the magazines that lay atop a yellowing doily, there was a notebook Wesley had brought home from work. It had a picture of a mountain goat on the cover, and the pages were lined in green, the first dozen or so filled with writing in an immaculate hand. It looked like writing she'd seen in a bookkeeper's ledger once at the grocery store, with Billy it must have been. She moved to put it back down, to have another try at *True Experiences,* when a picture postcard fell from between the notebook's back pages, straight down into her lap like a pigeon lighting on the back of a park bench.

Maggie picked it up. It had a picture of a tall building with a pointed top, dressed in stone or tile as white as a wedding cake. The caption said "Smith Tower, Tallest in the West." Soaring forty-two stories, Seattle's mighty Smith Tower is the tallest edifice west of the Mississippi." There was also handwriting on the card, the same handwriting as in the notebook. The card wasn't addressed, but there was a message:

My dear Miss Ruby,

I have scarcely passed through Seattle, but thought I would send you this card to mark my passage here. I had a very fine trip on the North Coast Limited. Now I am on my way to the coast, to see the ocean. I wish you were going with me.

I hope you can find it in your heart to forgive me for any unpleasantness that passed between us before I left. You are very dear to me indeed, and I already miss you very, very much.

Fondly,
Herbert

Maggie read it again, and she thought how sweet the words were, how romantic. She decided she would read the notebook

191

after all, instead of *True Experiences*. She was sure whatever was in the notebook would be real, not made-up stories like the ones in *True Experiences*.

On Friday morning and again on Saturday, Herbert White had gotten the guard to let him see the newspaper, but there wasn't anything about him either day. Nor had he made much progress with Mr. Dos Passos's *U.S.A.* There were too many characters— he supposed there'd better be, given the book's putative scope— and he couldn't keep them straight, and sometimes the parts called "Newsreels" weren't really like a movie but were more like words and pictures all jumbled up; more and more, that it is to say, like Herbert's mind.

Herbert pressed his face up against the bars and called down the corridor. "Guard? Sir? Please."

The guard came to his cell, holding a mug of coffee. "What's your pleasure now, Mr. White?"

"I was wondering if you'd heard anything about me getting my journal back?"

"Haven't heard anything like that. Who was going to get it for you?"

"The officer, the lieutenant, who was with me Tuesday night."

The guard sipped from his mug. "He got a name?"

"I don't know. He was here for a long time," Herbert said.

"Hm. I'll go look at the log. Won't be a minute, Mr. White," the guard said.

Herbert waited, and he heard drawers opening and slamming closed. The guard returned after a minute and said, "Nothing like a journal in the duty desk. Actually, there's nothing in the log either. About anybody visiting you. You sure it was Tuesday? I suppose most folks would be going to parties or making trick-or-treat with their youngsters. 'Cept you, of course."

"Oh, I'm absolutely positive," Herbert said. "He heard—or rather he took—my confession. Actually, I wrote it for him."

"Well, I don't know anything about that. What'd he look like, this lieutenant?"

Herbert pulled his face back a little from the bars and scratched his chin. "It's really rather hard to say—he looked like they all do, I suppose. I mean, with the long, hard faces and the hat they never take off, even indoors, even in front of a lady. He seemed to be my height."

"Wouldn't run across that every day."

"Well, I'm not entirely sure. It might have just seemed that way. I remember thinking he was like someone I'd met before, not so much in a different time or place but in a different shape."

"I don't know about that. Sorry not to be able to oblige."

Herbert said, "Perhaps the lieutenant just forgot."

"What was you going to do with this journal?"

"Write in it, I suppose."

The guard raised his eyebrows. "I don't know that they'd allow that anyhow. Not supposed to have pencils and pens. You could stab somebody."

Herbert said, "That's ridiculous. I've never hurt a soul in all my life."

The guard smiled. "That's not what it says in the papers, Mr. White."

"No, it isn't, is it?" Herbert said. "And I suppose what they say must be true."

"Oh, sometimes I bet they just make stuff up to sell a few more copies," the guard said, and turned to go back to his desk.

"Anyhow, you get bored, I got some more magazines. I got *True Detective* and *Modern Detective,* and *Life* too." The guard swung back around to face Herbert and lowered his voice, and then he winked. "And I got one that's a little saucy, called *Spice*—if you like that kind of thing."

It took Maggie until Saturday afternoon to finish reading the murderer's diary. She hadn't known what it was until Wesley got home Friday afternoon, and he seemed a little taken aback that she'd been looking at it. Then he said he supposed it would be all right; that it didn't have any evidentiary value and that White's goose was as good as cooked anyhow.

After Wesley told her what it was, she had an irresistible urge to go back to reading it, but when she picked it up she thought of the hands that had written it; hands that took the body of a girl not so very different from her and broke it in two. She wondered if the hands were big and cold, wondered how they would feel, if they were anything like Billy's—little and warm—or Wesley's—broad and dry like butcher paper. She shuddered. Wesley went outside, to the little shed at the back of the house. He said he had a mind to get out the ladder and clean the gutters. Maggie began to read.

She read slowly, and the writing itself slowed her down more. Besides, the diary was full of words she didn't know, like "ensconced"—maybe something to do with being like a scone, she thought, snug as a scone maybe—and words that just kind of hobbled you or damped the other words down, like the left-hand pedal on Granny's piano: words like "rather," "perhaps," and "somewhat."

So Maggie read slowly, and a little timidly and furtively, as though White—who Wesley had told her was big as a shithouse and weird as toadstools—might pop up and catch her at it. But by the time she was done, by the time Wesley had come back in, saying the gutters were already full of ice and it wasn't going to rain anyhow until April or so, she couldn't quite picture White that way. The man who had written the postcard was the same man who'd written the diary, and she couldn't see him murdering anybody. She could only see him looking out the window of a train or a bus, bewondered—that was one of Granny's words—and befuddled, blinking at the world like a mole with his first pair of spectacles.

For a time, she didn't say anything to Wesley. Since last Wednesday, when White had pleaded guilty, Wesley had been about as happy as she'd ever seen him, and she didn't want to spoil it for him. She was waiting on his eggs on Sunday morning—waiting for the yolks to get cakey after they'd been turned, for the edges of the whites to brown up a bit the way he liked them, like lace gone russet—and he said, "This time tomorrow, old man Kelly'll be sending White up the river. This time Tuesday, maybe I talk to the captain about a raise." He turned to Maggie at the stove. "Maybe get you a pretty dress."

"You sure he done it?" Maggie said quietly, and scooped the eggs off the bottom of the fry pan.

"He confessed, pleaded guilty," Wesley said.

"Confessed to Welshinger. You told me about Welshinger."

"Well, maybe I changed my mind a little about him. He didn't pound it out of White—just persuaded him. And he sure didn't stand over him with a club when he pleaded. That was White, on his own."

"But do you think he really did it?" Maggie put his plate in front of Wesley and sat down opposite him.

"It really doesn't matter now."

Maggie laid her palms on the oilcloth that covered the little splay-legged table. "It ought to. To matter, I mean."

Wesley looked up from his eggs. "It's done and through. Don't spoil my breakfast, Maggie." He looked not so much angry as hurt.

"I know, I know, sugar. I was just being curious. Just wondering. Only because for a while there you thought he hadn't done nothing."

Wesley reached for a piece of toast and set it on his plate. "I was wrong," he said. "I guess you could say he fooled me."

"I guess I could see how that could happen. I mean, reading what he wrote, he doesn't come across like anybody that would hurt a girl."

"But he did, sure as heck did," Wesley said. "Hurt two of them. Girls like you. Maybe not so sweet, but not bad girls—not bad enough to die anyhow."

"You want more eggs?" Maggie asked.

"Don't think so."

"Then you taking me out walking like we always do?"

"Sure. I'll take you up the hill, show you White's place if you want," Wesley said. "Take you promenading on murderer's row."

Maggie and Wesley walked down to Seven Corners and caught the streetcar up the hill, Wesley flashing his badge at the conductor as they boarded. After a couple of blocks, the streetcar entered the tunnel. Just about halfway through it, Wesley said, "He dragged her up the track from the bottom entrance and dumped her right about . . . here," and he tapped the window frame. It seemed to Maggie she could scarcely hear him over the rumble of the wheels; or perhaps he had really only been talking to himself.

They got out beyond the cathedral and crossed to the south side of the street, walking toward Western Avenue. "So why did he . . . leave her in there?" Maggie asked.

"Beats me. I mean, why did he dump the other one on the hill?"

"What did he say in the confession?"

"Didn't say anything about it."

"So what did he say?"

"Just what he needed to say for our purposes—that he did it. Hell, I scarcely read it."

Maggie stopped walking and looked at Wesley. "Why not?"

"Didn't need to. I mean, I glanced at it. Saw that it had what we needed."

"What about that diary I read? You look at that?"

"Christ, Maggie. I was sitting on the train with him when he was writing it. It was all after the fact, just his little book of travel memories." They began to walk again.

"You didn't think there might be something in there you might want to know about?"

"He wouldn't have given it to me if there was anything incriminating in it, would he?" Wesley said.

Maggie thought he was talking down to her a little. She looked straight ahead and said, "Maybe if he was as weird as you say, he would have—just to spite himself. Besides, maybe it wouldn't be incriminating. Maybe just the opposite. You'd never know. 'Less you read it, of course."

Wesley tried not to sound as thoroughly irritated as he felt. "Look, Maggie, I know what I'm doing. Been doing it since before you were born," he muttered, and began to walk faster, tacking forward against the cold, solid air, with Maggie pulled along behind him, bouncing like a dinghy in his wake.

They crossed Western Avenue and turned left and then right

again and went down two blocks, under the shadows of the bare-limbed elms. Wesley stopped and pointed. "That was his place." He took out his pack and fetched two cigarettes, giving one to Maggie and lighting them both. They stood on the sidewalk in front of Herbert White's apartment house and smoked and stared. The building was stone, Lake Superior brownstone, cut rough and hulking, like blocks for an ice castle.

"He had the lower left one," Wesley said. "Sat in there and pasted clippings in his scrapbooks."

"That ain't so odd," Maggie said. "I had a scrapbook once. Pasted magazine pictures in it, advertisements for pretty things and such."

"There was a little more to it than that with him. He had dozens of 'em. Filled with stuff going back to 1914 or so, back to the assassination of the archduke or whatever. He had the whole *world* in those things."

"Sounds kind of interesting," Maggie said. "Not really so odd."

"Other hobby he had was taking pictures and murdering pretty girls like you. That odd enough for you?"

Maggie drew on her cigarette, not replying. Then she said, "So why'd he keep all them scrapbooks for?"

"To help him remember," Wesley said. "See, he always claimed he had some kind of memory sickness—that he could remember what had just happened and what had happened a long time ago, but nothing in between. So he kept the scrapbooks so he could recollect himself a little."

"He told you that?"

"Kind of. Wrote about it too, in the diary."

"I didn't see anything about that."

"Not the one you read. The other one, the one downtown, in evidence."

Maggie flicked her cigarette out of her hand with the nail of her index finger and watched it arc into the gutter and sink among the damp leaves. "I'd kind of like to read that one too."

"Can't now," Wesley said. "Sealed away. State's evidence."

"So did you believe him about this memory business?"

"I don't know. Maybe. But it sure was convenient for him, wasn't it. I mean, whenever he didn't want to answer something, he'd just say 'I forget.' Beats lying. Sounds better too."

"So you think he was lying?" Maggie said.

"I suppose he had to be, some of the time. But he didn't strike me as a liar. I guess, being a cop, half the folks you meet are lying to you, and after a while—maybe half, maybe two-thirds of the time—you know they're lying. It's like they're sitting there telling you something with a smile on their face, but you can sort of feel that there's really nobody there—that they're made of glass or air or something, or nothing at all. There's something missing, not just in the story they're telling but in the person. Now, with White, there was always somebody there, plain as day—like a lump." Wesley shook his head. "Didn't know what to make of that."

"You think he's lying in these diaries?" Maggie said. "Didn't have no cause to, did he? It's not as though he was thinking: I'm going to gussy this up for when Lieutenant Horner comes along to read it."

"I suppose not."

"So you kind of got to believe what he wrote was true," Maggie said. "And in what I read he never says nothing about having killed anybody or running from the police. He was just going out west to see the ocean. That's a pretty regular thing to want to do."

"He told a couple of people he was leaving town so he could 'lie low.' That's pretty much admitting he's a fugitive."

"In what I read, he says he meant it to be a joke, like in the gangster pictures."

Wesley looked at Maggie. "He wrote that?"

"Sure did."

"Got a funny sense of humor, doesn't he?" Wesley said. "But it doesn't change anything. It's just something he wrote. In the diary we got downtown, he pretty much admits he killed the second girl."

"So that's just something he wrote too."

"Not when you add in the other evidence."

"So what did he say?" Maggie asked.

"Said he'd done something terrible to her, didn't even want to say what it was. Then he said he 'dispatched' her."

"What's 'dispatch'? That like the newspaper?"

"It means 'send away.' It can also mean to kill somebody."

Maggie said, "So how do you know which he meant?"

"You don't know, not right off. But in the light of the other evidence, that's what makes sense. Hell, in light of what else he wrote in the diary: 'Miss Ruby' this, 'Miss Ruby' that."

"He called her 'Miss Ruby'?" Maggie said. "The one he killed?"

"Yeah, Ruby Fahey."

"Well, if he killed her, what's he doing sending her a postcard from Seattle?"

"What postcard's that?"

"There was one inside the diary I read. Hadn't been mailed. No stamp."

Wesley shook his head. "I'll be damned."

Maggie looked at him. "So now you think maybe he's innocent?"

Wesley looked up and back at her. "No; I'm just thinking how weird he must be."

Maggie's eyes narrowed. She wanted to growl at him. "Jesus, Wesley. Why would he send a postcard to somebody he's killed, to somebody he knows is dead?"

"Because he's silly in the head. Or because he's smart. Trying to make an alibi, so he can say, 'Oh, I didn't even know she was dead, did I. Sent her a postcard from my vacation.' "

"But he didn't send it, did he?"

"More's the pity for him, I guess," Wesley said. "He screwed up. If they didn't, we'd never catch 'em in the first place."

Maggie wanted to stamp her feet, and she thought to herself that this must be their very first quarrel. She was thinking how she would want to remember this. Then she said, "Jesus, Wesley, you make me so mad. Give me a cigarette." He gave her one and lit it, and she went on sputtering and talking, with the smoke pouring from her mouth like steam bleeding from locomotive brakes. "Sometimes I think you are thick as a plank," she said, and began to walk in the direction they had come from, not looking back, already knowing he was coming. "Maybe not thick as a plank. Maybe blind, blind as a bat. Can't see a thing. And couldn't see anything straight if he could see, on account of he's hanging upside down."

Wesley came up alongside her. He was trying to hold his tongue. He was trying very hard not to say what he was itching to say: that she was sixteen years old and he was forty-four and what she knew about life you could put in a salt shaker with room left over. But it wasn't a point he wanted to make just now to her, or to himself. Instead he steered her right at Arundel Street. "Go down here, we can walk straight home down the hill."

Maggie nodded and went on talking. "How can you believe this stuff, Wesley, never mind say it? I mean, it's plain as the nose on your face to anybody that this guy isn't a murderer. Anybody could see it, from what he wrote, from his writing the girl."

Wesley spoke slowly. "And that's all it is, Maggie—what he wrote, what he said. It doesn't make anything true. It's not evidence. It's just a bunch of words."

"Anybody can see from that what he's really like. And him doing what you say doesn't make any sense, not to me."

At the corner of the busy street with all the mansions, he reached out to hold her arm, to keep her from walking straight out into traffic, but she pulled away, jerked her arm free from his grasp. In the middle of the street, just behind her, Wesley said, "Christ, Maggie, he confessed. He made a goddamned confession."

"That's just a bunch of words too," Maggie said, not even looking at him, as they stepped up onto the curb on the other side.

Wesley strode alongside her, down a smaller street that bent to the right, back behind the garages and servants' entrances of the big houses. He put his hand on her arm again, and this time she didn't pull away. "I'm sorry," Wesley said. "I don't mean to be . . . to be going contrary to what you say, to what you see." Maggie slowed her pace a little but kept walking.

"I understand how it *seems* to you," Wesley continued. "And maybe that's reasonable. Maybe that's how it would seem to most folks. But I can't look at things that way. 'Cause I'm dealing with evil, Maggie. And evil's always hidden away where you can't see it, under what seems normal or maybe even good. That's its nature. It's real, as real as anything, but you can't see it—even though it *is* real."

Wesley steered Maggie to the left, along a still smaller, dead-

202

end street, which corkscrewed down the beginning of a hill and ended in a curl like a question mark. "That's what I know about. I'm like a trapper, looking for evil's sign, its tracks. So when I say maybe Herbert White is evil, maybe there's something to it. I don't say it to be contrary, Maggie. I say it because I think it's true, even if sometimes it doesn't seem that way to everybody."

They had reached the end of the street and the top of a long set of steps that went down the hill. Wesley pointed down into the trees and the brush to the left. "That's where we found the first one. I showed you before from below. Looks different from here, don't it? Kind of quiet, kind of pretty."

Maggie nodded and threaded her arm deeper inside Wesley's. He pulled on the brim of his hat with his free hand. "The morning we found her, it was real early, almost still dawn. And it was like me and O'Connor and the coroner were all standing under water with this girl that had drowned, that had settled on this slope under all this bright, clear water. Later on, I thought how I wished I could have saved her—how I *ought* to have saved her. Course I couldn't have, but I made a kind of vow to get the guy who did it."

Maggie turned her face to Wesley. "And now you think you have, with White."

Wesley said, "I think so. I hope so." He tugged at her gently, and they began to descend the steps. "Of course, nothing's what it seems. Not just evil. Everything." He chuckled. "See, I thought I was saving you—from Shacktown, from the tramps and the streets, from men wanting to take advantage. And looky what happened. Look who's saved now. It was me getting saved all along."

"You saved me too," Maggie said. "You just can't see it." On the landing halfway down the steps, she stopped and pulled him close. "You're a good man, Wesley. Maybe better than I got coming. You just can't see too good. Maybe that's why you think everything's hidden or disguised. I don't mind. I cook your breakfast. Might as well be your eyes too."

"Six of one, half dozen of the other. Not to say I'm not grateful."

"But maybe you could look into saving this Mr. White. Just to be sure. You two got things in common. You can't see too good. He can't recollect hisself. Seems to me neither of you know whether you're coming or going."

Monday was Herbert White's day to be condemned and Wesley Horner's to glory in. He said as much to Farrell from the *Dispatch*, who'd asked him for a quote, and Wesley had obliged him, saying, "This is the only reward a police officer desires: to see justice done and the public served." He had wanted to round it out with something about "and wrongdoers punished" or some such, but "punished" wasn't quite the word he wanted; he was looking for something like "defeated" or "laid low" or "brought to their knees," and it hadn't come to him when Farrell was talking to him.

Wesley thought it was pretty good as it stood. Farrell liked it too, and now, bent over his Underwood in his hat on the fourth floor of the Dispatch Tower at lunchtime, he was trying to figure out where to put it. Problem was, he had only until two o'clock, and the story had been getting bigger all morning; it was going to fill the whole right-hand column of the front page and maybe another twelve or fourteen inches inside—or at least that's what they were holding open for him. Wesley Horner would make it in, but probably at the bottom, just by the skin of his teeth. Farrell figured Horner was worth cultivating. He had delivered the goods earlier on, albeit when pressed. Maybe now he'd learn to do it with a smile on his face. Maybe he'd come to realize Farrell was his friend. Farrell loosened his already loosened tie—the one with the trombones on it—and set to work.

Exclusive to the Dispatch *by*
CHARLES FARRELL

November 6—Self-confessed dime-a-dance murderer Herbert W. White was sentenced to life in prison this morning after a surprise appearance before Judge Ignatius Kelly by District Attorney Edward Berglund.

Berglund, who had said at last Wednesday's arraignment that he would be absent because of tomorrow's closely fought election, arrived in court just as Judge Kelly opened the proceedings. Wearing both a campaign button and a boutonniere, Berglund said, "Your Honor, I know I had said I would be unable to attend today's session. However, it behooves me to take time away from my other activities to speak on behalf of the People in a matter of grave urgency." As the courtroom buzzed with speculation, Berglund then asked permission to continue.

"The decision I originally made to absent myself from today's proceedings was made in light of the accused's confession and subsequent guilty plea, a situation which removed the need for the state to present any evidence or argue its case. Now, I know that under such circumstances, Your Honor has only to proceed directly to sentencing and that normally Your Honor might recess the court this morning and pronounce his sentence several days hence."

Then, gesturing toward White, Berglund said that this was an "unusual and special case" that "warranted unusual and special action." Referring twice to White as a "monster" who had committed crimes "so heinous and blood-curdling as to beggar the imaginations of decent people," Berglund pleaded with Kelly to pass sentence immediately and to treat White "as pitilessly as he treated these poor, innocent young women.

"The People demand this on their behalf and on behalf of justice," Berglund declaimed. "Even a day's delay—nay, an hour's delay—in delivering this monster to his just deserts is, in the People's eyes, unconscionable."

Judge Kelly halted Berglund in mid-oratory, saying that he appreciated Berglund finding time on "what must be an especially hectic day" to address the court. He then told Berglund he was prepared to move straight to sentencing and asked Berglund if he had any further remarks on the People's behalf.

Daubing his forehead with a monogrammed handkerchief,

Farrell knew the city editor wouldn't let that stand—it showed up Berglund for the silk-stocking, pantywaist Top of the Bluff conniver that he was—but decided to leave it in anyway. He'd say that he was feeling ornery, that he had a hangover. Hell, he *did* have a hangover. That much was true.

Berglund said that he understood that Judge Kelly strove to be fair and in fact might, in light of White's confession and guilty plea, "incline himself to show some scintilla of mercy, however small, to the defendant." Indeed, it was possible, Berglund said, that White "might have received the mistaken impression while in custody that were he to make a confession, the court would be lenient with him." Moreover, Judge Kelly might himself believe that such "blandishments" were offered.

However, Berglund said, in an orotund and stirring conclusion, "This district attorney, both as the People's tribune and as a citizen himself, has no truck with bargains and accommodations with monsters of the accused's ilk.

"I would sooner burn in

hell than strike a deal with the devil," said Berglund, "and no assurances were given this accused that his confession would serve any other purpose than to exact the severe punishment he so richly deserves. On behalf of the People, this district attorney—*their* district attorney—implores Your Honor to show as little mercy to the accused as he showed to these two poor girls."

Judge Kelly again thanked Berglund and turned to White, who had been staring raptly at the district attorney during his remarks. Kelly asked White if he wished to make a statement prior to his sentencing, and White replied, "What sort of statement?" With some irritation, Kelly responded that White might wish to plea for the court's mercy or to express remorse for what he had done. At this, White shook his head, and Kelly asked him, "Are you sorry for what you have done?" White said, "If I did what everyone says I did, then I am sorry for it."

Kelly told White that "The court will take that remark to reveal a lack of remorse, and a further instance of the flip and smart-aleck demeanor the accused has continually evinced during these proceedings."

Kelly then instructed White to rise, which White did, dwarfing the guards on either side of him. "Herbert W. White," the judge began, "it is the opinion of this court that District Attorney Berglund was if anything too kind in his estimation of you and your crimes. Indeed, I regret being unable to impose a capital sentence upon you, but that avenue has been unfortunately closed to me by the legislature, around the time of the war, I believe."

"I am rather sure it was in 1911," White burst out, to the laughter of courtroom spectators. A furious Judge Kelly advised White to remain silent and pronounced his sentence: "I therefore impose the maximum sentence permitted me: life imprisonment to be served in solitary confinement at the state prison at Stillwater."

Kelly then dismissed an electrified court, and White,

his eyes darting around the chamber, was led away. White, 35, a clerk at a St. Paul wholesale grocery firm, had been charged with the murders of taxi dancers Charlene Mortensen, 24, also known as Carla Marie LaBreque, and Ruby Fahey, 23. Reportedly a recluse with a taste for "cheesecake" photography, he was arrested last month after fleeing to Washington State. The officer who arrested him, Lieutenant Wesley Horner of the St. Paul Police homicide squad, said he was gratified "to see justice done and the public served."

Farrell gave it to Schmidt, the city editor, at one-thirty, and Schmidt came back to Farrell's desk ten minutes later.

"Nice try with that 'monogram' crap."

"A guy can only try," Farrell said.

"Well, maybe another time."

"Maybe after tomorrow, after the landslide, when it won't make any difference."

Schmidt said, "Hey, I don't make the news—"

"You don't even write it."

"Don't distract me. Make nice. Now, you're maybe two inches too long, so I'm probably going to cut the last 'graph."

"I kind of owe that cop."

"Sorry. The publisher kind of owes the advertiser who's bought the bottom of that page." Schmidt stopped. "Now, what else? Oh, yeah. What the hell's a boutonniere?"

"It's what Berglund wears in his lapel hole when he goes out kissing babies, carrying around the stone tablets, and so forth."

"Well, if I don't know, nobody else does," Schmidt said. "So there you are. We'll put a banner headline over this. Deserves it. Put it in your scrapbook."

"I don't have one."

"You ought to get one."

"Once it's done, it's done, as far as I'm concerned," Farrell said. "Just paper over the dam."

"Suit yourself," said Schmidt. "So what do you think about 'Dime-a-Dance quote Monster unquote Gets Life Term in Solitary,' with the kicker 'D.A. Begs for quote Merciless unquote Sentence'?"

"I think it's exquisite, Schmidt. I think it's sweet as a goddamned boutonniere."

Herbert White did not have to wait until morning for the newspaper. The guard brought it to him just before dinner. "You're the big news today," the guard said, and went back to his desk.

Herbert had sat very still in his cell since lunchtime, since they'd brought him back from the courthouse. He sat on the blanket on the cot and looked at the shelf where his book, *U.S.A.*, sat, and the book seemed to look back at him, insulted, scolding him for leaving it unread for so long. The book was as real as Herbert was; more real, in fact, for it had a life—a multiplicity of lives— and Herbert was utterly impoverished, hollowed out and destitute of himself. What he could not remember of himself, of his past, was lost to him; and what little he could recall of what had been his life before, he could never return to. For lack of any other life, he was what the newspaper said he was. He looked down at the headline, at what was now for all purposes his name— "Dime-a-Dance 'Monster' "—and he felt the rough edges of the broadsheet paper feather their weight down into his huge empty hands.

* * *

Wesley brought the paper home at dinnertime like a trophy to show Maggie. He was slightly out of breath—he'd been drinking since four o'clock with O'Connor, and even Trent and Welshinger had come into Alary's and bought him a drink—and he might have been a little loose in the ankles as he came up the walk to the front door. Maggie was frying liver and onions, heaping up onions in the side of the fry pan, and he stuck the paper under her face and said, "Get a load of them apples."

Maggie looked up at him, her eyes not quite meeting his. "Ain't exactly a surprise."

Wesley pulled himself up onto his tiptoes, like he was stretching to change a lightbulb, and flung the paper open, saying, "No, not that. This," and folded the paper over and put his thumb at the bottom of a column of type. "This here."

Maggie read, and then she smiled and said, "Well, ain't you the blue-eyed boy."

Wesley put his hand on Maggie's left arm and spun her toward him. She let go of the spatula she was holding, and it clattered in the pan. Wesley was grinning, and his eyes were unfocused and a little damp. "So," he said, "you proud of your old man?"

"Course I am," she said. "You're my sugar, ain't you?"

"Last time I checked, I was." Wesley laid his palm on her hip and slid it down onto her buttock. He pulled her closer. "Supposing we were to have a little loving, just to make sure."

Maggie pulled back slightly. "Which way you want your dinner, then—cold or burnt?"

"I don't care. Don't have much appetite anyhow."

"I'd venture you're full of beans," Maggie said. "But suit yourself." She turned off the gas burner.

Later, when he was lying in bed and Maggie had gotten up and put on Louise's old robe and gone back into the kitchen to restart dinner, he thought how making love to Maggie just now had been kind of like he'd imagined it would be before he'd ever laid a hand on her: him on top, her all open to him, and him driving, plowing into her. Because in fact, until now, it hadn't been that way, but more like she was open to him but enfolding him, like hands or enormous wings, and he was lost in them and harbored in them all at once.

Then, as he half heard the ring of the fry pan against the drain board and the bottoms of the plates echoing on the tabletop as Maggie laid them down, he realized she hadn't made a sound while they were making love, and that she always had before: like she was pulling him up to her, calling down a well hole to him to rise, to come into her. And he knew, in the way that a man doesn't like to admit he knows, that she had something on her mind; and he knew what it was, even as he would deny to anybody, including himself, that he knew what it was. He got up slowly and pulled on his trousers, which lay on the floor, pulled his undershirt over his head, and shuffled toward his dinner, seeing what lay in Maggie's mind just as he saw the light coming around the corner at the end of the hall: What was he going to do to do right by Herbert White, and when and how was he going to do it? It made him a little mad, because here he was at the end of the day that ought to be about the best day of his life, fixing to sit down to his supper, and his woman and Herbert White wanted to take it all away from him.

Since it was election day and since he'd worked so hard and so successfully on the White trial, the captain told Wesley to take Tuesday afternoon off. His first thought was to amble home on no particular schedule and just sit on the davenport and loaf, but he thought instead that he ought to do something for Maggie.

He telephoned his house from the station about eleven o'clock. Maggie answered, her "hello" inflected as though she were opening her door to a suspicious stranger.

"Hey, it's me—Wesley."

"Oh, so it is," Maggie said, her voice brightening. "You know, I don't think you ever called me on this thing before."

"Can't say that I have."

"That's okay. I'm not so sure I like it, what with the bell scaring me half to death and then your voice sounding like you're talking at me down a culvert."

Wesley said, "I just wanted to tell you I was coming home. Thought I might take you out to lunch."

"Well, well. That'd be sweet."

"So I'll see you around noon, okay?"

"Okay, sugar."

Wesley put the earpiece back on the hook. He had his face right up against the mouthpiece so he could talk low, even though there was no one else in the room. Sometime in the last few days, maybe only yesterday, he began to wonder what people around the station and the captain in particular would make of Maggie and him. He knew that whatever it was, it would not be good, although as far as he could tell, nobody knew she even existed, still less that she was living in his house.

He was thinking that and preparing to dismiss the whole matter from his mind in order to contemplate the lazy afternoon ahead, when the whole thing got bigger rather than smaller, a fog of dread that all of a sudden overtook him and swallowed him up. He saw with great clarity the danger of what he was doing with Maggie and how he had been wandering blithely around the city strewing clues to their relationship that were visible to anyone who cared to look. Maybe it wasn't illegal, but it sure as hell was illicit. If there wasn't anything in the morals code about it, there might as well be. He could hear the captain saying, "It just goes without saying, for Christ's sake, Wes. . . ." He might conjure up some nonsense about Maggie being a niece visiting from New Upsala or wherever, and he could see every lip in the station curl, every pair of eyes go cool and amused, while everyone stopped whatever he was doing to picture Wesley Horner doing the monkey with a sixteen-year-old.

Wesley had left his desk, left the homicide room, and was stepping through the front door of the station and descending to the street, but he wasn't seeing any of it. He was inside that cloud, and all around him inside it, like a diorama of bum luck and humiliation, were images of what was going to go wrong: how he'd lose his job and work as a janitor or a night watchman or a boiler tender; how the streetcar wouldn't stop for him in the middle of the block anymore; and how the folks who used to give him free coffee would smile and whisper when he walked by—how he'd be nothing.

He thought all that on the streetcar going to West Seventh Street, and when he got off and began to walk the two blocks to his house, he pictured the lunch he was planning to take Maggie to. He'd been hungry. He'd had his mind set on the blue plate special, whatever it turned out to be, since they wouldn't charge him for it, and he was going to tell Maggie to go to town, have a hamburger with all the trimmings and coleslaw and cottage fries and a chocolate malt. But now, a block from his door, he pictured the waitress—that spinster Clara, the one whose brother lost a leg working in the Soo Line yards—coming by with her face screwed up like a sour, wrung-out washrag and saying, "Coffee for you and your daughter?"

When Wesley came in the door, he let out a long, loud

exhalation of breath, and when Maggie came to greet him, gussied up in her polka-dot dress, he muttered wearily, "Started feeling queasy on the streetcar. Think I better sit down." He lowered himself stiffly onto the davenport, and Maggie came over and put her hand on the side of his head and then stepped back and looked at him, as though she were deciding whether a picture was hanging straight.

"Guess I better just put some soup on the stove," she said, and Wesley nodded back to her. "Maybe all your drinking and funning yesterday got the best of you," Maggie added, and went back out toward the kitchen.

"Could be," Wesley said. He thought she might be right, for there was no doubt, now that he was sitting here, that he truly did feel unanchored and hollow, weary and restless, all at the same time. He heard Maggie out in the kitchen, and he felt ashamed of the things he'd been thinking. He might be nothing in this town if he stuck with her, but he couldn't picture himself without her, sending her away, sending himself back to where she'd found him. And then he picked up Herbert White's notebook with the mountain goat on the cover.

On Wednesday morning, the guard brought Herbert the newspaper, just as he now always did, around ten o'clock.

"Looks like the DA owes you one," the guard said.

Herbert scanned the headlines, among them one that blared BERGLUND IN LANDSLIDE. He looked up at the guard. "He's the one that said all those terrible things about me."

"Got him reelected pretty nicely, didn't it?"

"I suppose it did."

"You go down, a lot of other folks go up: Berglund, Horner—"

"Who's that?" Herbert asked.

"Horner, the homicide lieutenant. The one that brought you in."

"Oh. Yes. So he did."

"Well, he's kind of a champ around here these days," the guard said. "Before that—before you—word around the station was, Horner was kind of asleep at the switch."

"I gave him my travel notebook," said Herbert.

"You mean that diary you were after me about?"

"No, this was different. It was just something I wrote in on my trip west. I gave it to that lieutenant when they brought me here," Herbert said. "Do you imagine that now that this is all over and done, I could get it back from him?"

"I can ask him. Or tell him you want to see him," the guard said. "You know they're taking you up to Stillwater tomorrow?"

"Yes, I think I did," Herbert said. "You know, I shan't want to leave. You've been very kind to me. Letting me read your newspaper and so forth."

"Truth be told, Mr. White, I kind of enjoyed your company myself," the guard said. "In spite of everything."

"If it wouldn't be an imposition, perhaps you might tell this Lieutenant Horner that I'd like to see him before I go."

"Kind of a funny thing to do, but I guess it can't hurt to ask," the guard said. "I'll call up there and see if he's around."

"I'd be very grateful," Herbert said, and the guard nodded and said, "Sure," and walked down the hall. Herbert picked up the newspaper and read slowly, conscious of the need to make the reading last. So he read the accounts of the election, precinct by precinct: of the city councilmen and the municipal judges and the comptroller, and of District Attorney Berglund, who, if the guard was right, must not really think Herbert such a monster after all.

* * *

Wesley had read Herbert White's notebook Tuesday afternoon, and although Maggie had seen him at it, she hadn't said a word. They'd finished supper without her mentioning it, and he was on the verge of thinking he was in the clear, when she spoke to him as she washed dishes in the sink, her back to him. "So what do you think about him now?" she said, as if she were picking up the thread of a conversation they'd been having all along.

"Think about who?" Wesley said.

Maggie turned around and set her hands on her hips, hooking her thumbs into the waist of the apron she wore. "Nice try, sugar," she said. "About White."

"What do you think I ought to think?"

"Jesus, Wesley." She scowled at him and turned back to the sink.

"Okay, okay," Wesley said. "Wait a minute. I read it, and I guess I see how you could think the way you do."

Maggie looked around at him quizzically. "How I could think the way I do," she said softly. "What, like I'm nuts or something?"

"No, no. It's just that I didn't see anything in there that would change anything as far as the law's concerned. I mean, it's not evidence."

"I heard this line before," Maggie said. "Seems like evidence is whatever you say it is. Or isn't."

"No; I see how an ordinary person like you, not a professional—"

Maggie smirked. "What the hell's that? A doctor or a college professor or something. You don't look like no professor to me. You look like a cop from New Oopsda, North Dakota." She laughed.

Wesley didn't smile. "I mean like an expert, like somebody

who's been doing police work for fifteen or twenty years." Maggie didn't say anything back, and he went on. "So anyhow, I see how you could say, 'This guy couldn't have done it,' but to me it's still just his say-so. I got to say, though, if he's making it all up, it's some piece of playacting."

"Anybody with eyes to see would tell you it ain't," Maggie said, and seized Wesley's empty plate from his place and turned back around to the sink and opened the tap.

"Maybe so, but you don't know what these types get up to. You know how they call the devil the prince of lies. That's his stock-in-trade. Lies—all shapes and sizes."

Maggie shut off the tap and set the plate on the drain board. "How's he get that little hat of his over them horns, that's what I want to know," she said. "You checked his feet? He got toes like a nanny goat?"

Wesley still wasn't smiling. The part of him that wasn't feeling stung by her mockery was getting angry. "You go ahead and fun me. But he's a confessed murderer. And he pled guilty and had a trial, fair and square."

Maggie whooped and slapped her hands on her thighs, then rubbed them on the apron to dry them. "Fair and square. Don't *you* fun *me*. You told me what goes on. It's just the people who got everything, who know everybody, taking down the people who got nothing, who don't know a soul. People like me," Maggie said, nearly in a whisper, and looked up at Wesley. "People like you, if you had eyes to see it, Wesley."

"He confessed, Maggie."

"That confession—now, there's your playacting. Hell, you ain't even read it. Probably fried him in flaming lard to get it."

Wesley stood up, not sure if the urge he had to hit her was going to pass. He looked away, off at the icebox, at the corner where the water heater stood skinny and white, like a nun standing in the shadow. He felt tingling in the corners of his eyes, and he rubbed them and looked back at Maggie. "That ain't fair, Maggie. It's not right to think that about me. You got no business being here, being my . . . girl, if that's what you think about me."

Maggie looked up and into his eyes and stepped toward him. "I'm sorry," she said. "I didn't mean you'd ever do that. Just maybe some of the others, the ones you told me about."

"They—he—didn't do nothing bad to get it out of White. I believe that," Wesley said. "But if you want, I'll go look at it. At the confession. Just to keep you happy," and he knew that that, too, was the wrong thing to say, but he seemed to himself to have lost the capacity to say the right thing, still less to do it. Maggie just looked at him, and he realized she was going to let it pass, that she figured now they were even. They were taking turns hurting each other, because the love had gone so far they couldn't bear it, and now they were unraveling it together, strand by strand.

At the station in the morning, Wesley wasn't thinking about that or about the confession. He was smoking and drinking coffee and passing the time of day with O'Connor. He felt entitled to a little procrastination. He was going to take his time, his sweet time. The phone rang, and O'Connor picked it up. He listened, muttered a few words, and put it down, snickering. "Guess who wants to talk to you, boss."

Wesley just sat there at his desk and looked at O'Connor like they were doing knock-knock jokes. "Who?" he finally said.

"White. Herbert White. The Dime-a-Dance Monster himself." O'Connor fluttered his fingers in the air. "Woo woo," he keened. "Spooky Herb."

"Christ on a crutch," Wesley sighed. It was not that this never happened, although usually it was on the way out of the courtroom after the verdict or sentencing. Sometimes they made as if to pump his hand, to tell him it had been a worthy contest. More often they said they'd get him someday, although no one ever had done so.

"He's going up tomorrow, right?" Wesley said. O'Connor nodded. Wesley stood. "Might as well go down there now, pay him a call."

Wesley descended to the basement and rang the bell at the lockup door. He hadn't been here since he'd tried to get White's confession, and he hadn't laid eyes on White since the sentencing. The guard let him in and led him down the corridor to White's cell and asked him, "You want to go in or just stand out here?"

"Sure, let me in. We're old acquaintances."

The guard unlocked the door, and Wesley stepped inside. White stood up from where he was sitting on the cot. He still looked big, maybe even bigger, although his complexion was more pallid, his clothes yet more rumpled. He swung the paddle of his left hand toward the chair. "Please, sit," he said.

"Okay." Wesley sat down and took out his cigarettes. He looked at White. "You want one of—oh, you don't use these, do you?"

"No, I never learned the habit."

Still cocky as hell, or oblivious or whatever he was, Wesley thought, and he said, "Maybe you'll pick it up in Stillwater. It's a good way to pass the time."

White didn't react with anger or humiliation. Instead he simply said, "I was hoping I might write a little each day, like I used to. That's why I wanted to see you." White tipped his head to one side, a little bashfully. "You remember the notebook I gave you to keep? The one from the train, with the goat?"

219

"Yeah."

"I wondered if I might have it back. Before I go, if it's not too much trouble."

"I don't have it here. I took it home," Wesley said. "For safe-keeping."

"Perhaps you could bring it in in the morning."

"I guess I could. But I bet they wouldn't let you keep it anyhow. You're going to solitary, Herbert. No privileges. Just you and a slop bucket."

"Oh," White said. "I didn't know. You see, I haven't much experience of this kind of thing."

"Tell you what. I'll keep your book for you, but I'll give you some paper, okay?" Wesley wasn't sure why he was doing this. Maybe for Maggie's sake, to let her hang on to the notebook, so she could badger him with it; maybe for White, who Wesley knew would become completely unglued in solitary; hell, maybe for his own sake, if only to keep square with Maggie.

He dug into his coat pocket and took out a small newsprint pad of blank yellow sheets that he used to take crime scene notes. "Here," he said. "It's yours."

White said, "Thank you," and took the pad and looked at it. "I was rather hoping for something I could write a letter on."

"So write a small letter," Wesley said. "With lots of pages."

"They say brevity is the soul of wit," White said.

"I bet it is."

White looked at Wesley deeply, searchingly. "I'd still need . . . ," and he made writing motions in the air, dropped his hands to his sides sheepishly.

"What the hell," said Wesley. "Break one rule, might as well break 'em all." He reached into his pocket again and withdrew a pencil. "Hate these goddamned things anyhow. It's the hard-leaded kind. Makes a crummy gray line you can't even see. Of course, it stays sharp longer. Might be a help to you." He handed White the pencil.

"Thank you," White said, and he held the pencil loosely in his fist. "That's exceedingly kind of you."

"Sure. You bet," Wesley said. "I'll tell the guard you got it from me, that it's okay, seeing how you're leaving."

"That's awfully good of you."

"You hurt anybody with that, I don't know nothing about it, okay?" Wesley said.

White began, "I'd never hurt any—"

Wesley laughed. "Give me a break, Herbert." He moved to the door and called out to the guard, and then he turned back to White. "Before I go, just for the hell of it, answer me a question." White bobbed his head, and Wesley continued. "Back a month, month and a half ago, when we came to see you about the Mortensen girl, was you lying?"

"I don't remember," White said. "I mean, I don't remember your coming. But I'm sure I told the truth."

The guard's key scraped and clunked in the door, and Wesley backed toward it. "What about later?" he said. "When I brought you in. When you confessed to the other lieutenant."

"Oh, I'm sure that must have been the truth too."

Wesley nodded curtly and then turned around to the guard and wagged his chin from side to side. He said, "See you in the funny papers, Herbert," and went out.

Herbert White wrote his letter that night by the dirty glow of the bulb in his cell, which hung from the ceiling yellow and forlorn like a dead wasp wrapped in spider silk. He spoiled three sheets of paper before he was able to get his handwriting small enough to fit on the page in a seemly fashion, and then finally his capital letters were no bigger than an eyelash or the cuticle of his little finger.

Ramsey County Jail
Saint Paul, Minnesota

November 8, 1939

Dear Miss Galvin,

I suppose you will see by my address that I am not at my usual abode; that I am, in fact, in rather desperate straits. Indeed I wondered if I ought to write you at all, since my situation is so shameful. But you are now my only friend in all the world.

I am to be taken to the state penitentiary tomorrow morning and put into solitary confinement to serve a life sentence for murder. I shall try to tell you as best I can how this has come about.

I had a friend named Ruby Fahey, and now that I think of it, I realize that she was my best friend. She had modeled for me over several months, and she was very beautiful and kind. I think we became quite "close." At some point I came to feel that everything that had happened in my life before I knew her was of no account and that the only future I could imagine contained her and only her. At the same time I began to feel a great passion for her—as though I must be drawn through and into her as a thread through the eye of a needle—and I suppose I thus must have fallen in love with her. Although I could not imagine it at the time, I think she too entertained some affection toward me.

Last month, on one of the occasions when she came to pose for me, a deeply embarrassing and awkward incident occurred between us (the precise nature of which I do not entirely recall and would in any case refrain from describing in detail). I do not think it was a lovers' quarrel or "tiff," but afterward I was so disturbed and ashamed that I determined to leave home on a vacation I had long dreamed of taking, namely, a trip to see the ocean. Accordingly, I bought a train ticket to Seattle, Washington.

Once arrived, I did indeed see the ocean. How vast—I want to say how vast and how terrible—is the sea, although I suppose you must know this, since I gather Hollywood is not far from it. I also visited Mount Rainier, which is truly majestic (and, I must say, also vast and terrible). It was my first view of a mountain peak aside from photographs and, of course, your own cinematic oeuvre. (I think especially of *City of the World* and *Steens Mountain*. I want here and now to take the opportunity to tell you how impressed I was with your performance in the latter. I had hoped to see you at the Saint Paul premiere, but alas, it was not to be.)

Indeed, through a startling coincidence, my experience on Mount Rainier might have been straight out of one of these films. For as I descended the mountain in a fearful snowstorm, I was intercepted by three policemen, who placed me under arrest as a fugitive from the murder of my own dear Ruby! Not knowing what in heaven's name they could be talking about, I went with them quietly, although I now wish, had I possessed the means, that I could have fought them; that indeed I might have died in a blaze of gunfire on the mountain itself!

When they brought me back here, I explained to them that I was sure I would never do such a thing, but when pressed, I also admitted that I could not recollect *not* doing it. I have written you before, I believe, about my lapses of memory; that in fact much of my past is one great lapse of memory. At any rate, I was determined not to admit I had committed this crime, not only because I could not in the slightest *imagine* myself doing such a thing, but because I felt I must hang on to some notion of what I believed myself to be or be nothing at all, and what I felt for Miss Ruby (as I always called her) was now my entire past and future.

However, by a process and a logic that is now a little vague to me, I came to accept that, remembered or not, I must have committed this crime. I came, I suppose, to believe that I must have done so in the absence of anything else to believe, and that by believing I might somehow be healed. So I confessed to that murder and, for good measure, another one that they said I'd done.

I cannot say I feel healed, although perhaps prison will have that effect. So for now, I am no longer the man who loved Ruby Fahey but what they call the "Dime-a-Dance Monster," and I suppose if that is who I am, I must never have loved Miss Ruby at all. It is all as in a movie to me now—no, not a movie, for I believe what I see in the movies—or rather the images I used to see in my photographic darkroom, things inverted, light become dark, and everything just the opposite of what it seemed. But lately, people who apparently know better than I have been telling me that this is the way the world truly is, although I never ventured to believe it until now.

I miss Miss Ruby so much, although some might say I haven't the right. I miss her as I miss my father, and my grandmother Nanna, and my mother, whom I never knew, and whom I therefore suppose I haven't the right (or reason) to miss either.

Until now, I had always thought that memory must be about the past, and that some other act—wishing or dreaming—must constitute our relation to the future. I supposed, too, that missing someone, aching for that person's company and the loss of ever enjoying it again, must also be tied entirely to the past. But now, now that I find myself with no future save the four walls of a cell and no past save as a "monster" whose thoughts and deeds I cannot recall, I see that I have nothing but the things I miss: that missing will now be my whole life.

I always grieved because I did not think that I had memory like other people. But now I suppose I shall have memory, for what is memory if not the thought of what we once had and now lack? And I suppose I now have a future too, for what is the future if not the desire to fill those lacks, and with what can we fill them except what we have already known in memory? Perhaps that is really all the future and everything we entertain for it and desire of it: merely the memory searching ahead for what it once had, or thought it glimpsed.

The love I must somehow believe I felt for Miss Ruby was, I think, rather like this. For she was all I wished to see, and to that end, I took her picture again and again, in order that I could always have what I had had of her, and partake of it in her absence with my eyes, and with memory see what I would see when she returned.

That is what I believe, or rather what I believe when I am not believing the other thing, about how I shall be healed by my confession and by prison. I suppose it is neither here nor there. Perhaps I can even believe them both. In any case, I hope you can find it in your heart to write me back, and I am sure the jailer here would forward any reply you made to my new address. I know that as a public personage you must be careful about whom you associate with, but perhaps, given the roles you have played, you can find some sympathy for me. I think particularly of *Grand Central Terminal,* at the end, where you were being pursued through the platforms and passages under the great station of the great city and didn't even know by whom. That is how my life has seemed of late. Thus, it goes without saying that some of my most profound memories are of you and your pictures, and that my anticipation of your forthcoming work has always been among my greatest consolations. It seems to me that after a fashion we have spent many hours together and that, save for those moments of love and of beauty that were some time ago vouchsafed to me, they are what is most real and true to me.

Assuring you of my devoted best wishes,
Yours sincerely,
Herbert W. White

White found that when he was done, the letter consisted of fourteen little pages, and he had also found that he could keep his pencil sharp by rubbing it against the edge of a brick in the wall, that indeed he could in this way maintain an extremely well-honed point.

After he had finished, he called to the guard. He heard the guard's chair scrape and his footsteps come down the corridor.

"Yep?"

"I know this is asking a great deal, but as I'm leaving tomorrow, perhaps you'd consider it. I wanted to post this"—White held up the folded clutch of pages—"and it needs an envelope and a stamp. It's to . . . my closest friend. She doesn't know where I'm going, and I want her to know."

"I suppose I can oblige you with that," the guard said. "Let me see what I got in the desk."

While the guard went back down the hall, Herbert laid the letter on his pillow on the cot and then he went to the bars of the door and waited, still holding the pencil, its shank Kodak yellow, the point shining dully gray. The guard came back, licking a stamp and pressing it onto the envelope with his thumb. He said, "Here you go," and moved toward Herbert, and Herbert put his free arm out through the bars to take it. And Herbert saw suddenly and seamlessly, as though the dirty bulb in his cell had been replaced by a klieg light, how he could seize the guard around the neck with his free extended arm, pull his face close up against the bars, and thrust the pencil into the guard's left eye, up to the hilt, deep into the brain; then catch him as he began to fall and take the guard's neck into his hands and throttle him with his thumbs, resting his little fingers and knuckles in the wells that the guard's collarbone formed on either side of his neck, while Herbert pressed and finally stilled him. He saw it pass in a graceful arc of motion, like a magician drawing a silken scarf through a golden band.

Herbert said, "Thank you," in a shallow, soft bark, and moved backward to his cot and sat himself down heavily. He breathed deep. He knew that what he had pictured was not mere fancy but must be something that existed in his memory from somewhere, sometime, even in a time yet to be: perhaps in a movie, for it was that real to him.

In the morning, from the homicide office window, Wesley watched them load up Herbert White to take him to Stillwater. Two guards had come down from the prison, and if the transfer was done in the usual manner, they would be joined by two officers from the station, traffic or beat cops or others who weren't terribly essential. So Wesley was a little surprised when he saw that the party leading White in shackles out the back basement entrance consisted of two state penitentiary guards plus Welshinger and Trent;

he was even more surprised when they packed White into Welshinger's big Hudson, with Welshinger himself at the wheel. White was wearing the same suit he'd had on when Wesley brought him down from the mountain. It was cold, and his shirt collar flapped in the wind. He was the only one of the party without a tie and a hat. The Hudson sat in the parking lot for a moment, and then one of the windows rolled down and Wesley saw somebody—either one of the guards from Stillwater or Trent— toss a matchstick out onto the pavement. Then the other state guard pulled up alone in the state Chevrolet behind the Hudson, and the two cars drove away.

Wesley had told Maggie last night that he'd talked to White one last time and how he'd given him the paper and the pencil, and Maggie, who was heating a can of beans and frying some eggs in a little bacon fat, moved her head up and down like she thought that was pretty swell of him. Before she could say anything about it—start in and let it wick away all the juice of the evening ahead, in which Wesley was picturing some good loving—he also told her that he was going to look at the confession, at the whole evidence file, in fact, the next morning. At that, she looked at him appreciatively and said, "I just want you to do right by this, like I know you'd do for anybody." Later, when he lay atop her, his hips cradled and bucking between her legs, she kept pushing her breasts up to meet his chest, as if her body were a raft bearing him out to sea over big swells.

The file was in the basement, at the opposite end of the building from the lockup and the garage. There was a whole room full of filing cabinets, and the cabinets trailed out the door and down passages left and right, overhung with steam pipes wrapped in asbestos. O'Connor said he'd brought the file down on Wednesday, after it had come back from the district attorney's office, and had put it in the "Homicide, Completed, 1936–Present" drawer. Wesley drew the drawer open. It was three-quarters filled and ought to last them through 1940, maybe '41 if people didn't get too far out of hand.

The label on the file said "Mortensen-Fahey/White, Sept.–Oct. 1939." There was an outer slipcase made of a marbled, oxblood-colored card stock with cloth sides, and inside were several ordinary folders: one holding photos and Dr. Nash's two reports; another containing Wesley's notes and the witness interviews conducted by O'Connor; a third with White's journal and the photos he'd taken of Ruby Fahey as well as the unidentified photograph of Charlene Mortensen; and a fourth of paperwork that had passed between the station and the district attorney's office, among which Wesley found Herbert White's confession.

Wesley set the rest of the file on the back of the cabinet and put the confession down in front of him. He lit a cigarette, and then he read:

I, Herbert W. White, residing in this city, do make the following statement in the presence of witnesses of my own free will and declare it to be true.

That on September 30, 1939, at approximately twelve o'clock midnight, I did with malice aforethought kill Charlene Mortensen, also known as Carla Marie LaBreque, by battery to the head, and did deposit her corpse in the vicinity of Lawton Street and Grand Avenue in this city.

That on October 22, 1939, at approximately five o'clock in the afternoon, I did in a similar manner kill Ruby Fahey and did deposit her corpse inside the Selby Avenue street railway tunnel in this city, and did afterward flee this state for the purpose of avoiding prosecution for these acts.

I swear that this is my true and voluntary statement made this 31st day of October, 1939, at Saint Paul, Minnesota.

Herbert W. White

The writing, which Wesley quickly recognized as White's perfect copperplate hand, filled perhaps two-thirds of the sheet. Under White's signature, a further signature was scrawled in another hand, and beneath that, in block letters, was printed "Wesley Horner, Lt., SPPD, witness."

Wesley was at first flummoxed and then angry, and he drew on his cigarette so hard that the coal dropped off and fell onto the confession. He swiped the coal off the paper with the side of his hand and it burned like hell, like a wasp sting. He let his arms hang by his sides and breathed in and out, and then he took off his hat and set it on top of the confession, where now, just to the right of White's signature, there was a tiny scorch, like a fleck of butterscotch.

After a time, he saw that for all his gall, Welshinger had had to do what he had done; that there had to be a witness and it would cause the fewest problems, prompt the fewest questions, if that witness was Wesley. Of course, the captain had authorized Welshinger to take a shot at getting White to talk, so it wasn't as though there would be anything untoward about his witnessing the confession. But this way, it was, for better or worse, entirely Wesley's baby— his to take the credit for, or the fall—and it had after all turned out for the better. Maybe Welshinger had seen that and wanted to do Wesley a good turn. Maybe he was, after all, Wesley's buddy.

Wesley was calm now, and he put his hat back on and picked up the confession. He wasn't going to wave it around under anybody's nose, credit or no credit, of course. The captain, for one, knew who'd really pulled it; so did O'Connor and Trent, even if neither of them would ever say anything. He slid the paper back into its folder and grasped the slipcase. Then he stopped and lit himself another cigarette, and as if to pass the time of day, he took out the coroner's folder and laid it open. There was the Mortensen girl lying on the hill, and under that photo was another, a close-up of her shoulders and neck, with the marks like streaks of tarnish on either side of her windpipe. There were more photographs, and then there were pictures of Ruby Fahey, her skin white and ablaze against the black tunnel pavement, and her neck too and the twin shadows.

On the left flap of the folder, Nash had clipped copies of the death certificates. Wesley remembered being at the morgue with Nash after he had done the autopsy on the Mortensen girl, and how afterward he had sworn to save her, if only after a fashion, by finding her killer. And he had done that, and maybe, by virtue of his success, he'd saved himself too; that, and by virtue of Maggie, who had sent him down to look at this confession. Wesley glanced at the upper-right-hand corner of one death certificate, where Nash had written the cause of death, and then he looked again, harder, and flipped back to the same place on the other certificate. They were identical: "Asphyxiation by manual strangulation." That was what Nash had said, what was self-evident to anyone who saw the girls in the first place, and Wesley found himself thinking of White's big, soft hands. But then Wesley saw that the confession had said something else, and he wondered now if anyone had been saved at all, least of all him, Herbert White's sworn confessor.

Wesley waited all afternoon for Welshinger to return from Stillwater, and at five o'clock, when it was nearly dark, he telephoned

Maggie to say he'd be home later than usual; that he was sorry to be late and to be calling on the telephone, whose ring so frightened her, but he was looking into something about White, like he said he would, like she wanted him to.

The big Hudson rolled into the parking lot behind the station about six-thirty, after night had come and the damp on the pavement was congealing into a glaze of ice. He saw Trent get out and go to his own car, a Buick—how the Vice Boys managed to afford such cars was a mystery to Wesley, who didn't have a car at all— and then Welshinger pulled the Hudson into a stall and got out and checked to see if all the doors were locked. Wesley was going to run out and intercept him, but he saw that he was coming into the station.

Wesley went into the corridor and waited to hear Welshinger's footsteps. It was half dark, with most of the lights off and the offices empty, and then Welshinger's steps, light and hollow, rang on the terrazzo like the tap of rich man's walking stick. Even before Wesley saw his face, he heard him call out, as though he could see around corners, even dark corners. "Hey, Wes, working late?"

Wesley moved out into the center of the corridor and began to walk toward the voice, toward the tall, angular cluster of shadows that must be Welshinger's hat rack of a body. "I was just going to Alary's," he said. "Thought I'd stand you a drink if you wanted to come."

Welshinger said, "Well, I'd be pleased as punch. Been kind of a long day, actually. Took a little outing up to Stillwater, got your friend White all settled and tucked in for the night."

"Captain send you?"

"No, I just went. Somebody had to go. I figured you'd be too busy, and sometimes I like a day out of town." They pushed through the front doors of the station. "Hope you didn't mind."

"Oh, hell no. Glad you could do it."

"Didn't say a word going up there, our boy didn't. Just looked out at the river the whole time. Me and Trent stuck around while they processed him. Took 'em a while to find a striped suit big enough for him. I filled in the guards on his story." Welshinger chuckled. "I think they'll arrange a fine reception for him, make him feel right at home."

Wesley didn't say anything, and they walked in silence for the last half block to Alary's Club. Wesley motioned toward a booth at the back, where he knew it would be quiet, where the traffic and beat cops at the bar wouldn't see them. They sat down, and then Wesley said he'd go fetch them drinks, and Welshinger said he fancied scotch, if that was all the same to Wesley. Wesley went up to the window at the back end of the bar and ordered a double for Welshinger and a Schmidt's for himself.

He sat back down in the booth and pushed the scotch over to Welshinger.

"Much obliged, Wes," Welshinger said. "So how's tricks? Getting ready for the busy holiday homicide season? Always lots of business for both of us, eh?"

"Suppose so. Mind you, I wouldn't mind a little quiet spell, what with coming off the White thing and all."

Welshinger rapped his knuckles on the tabletop. "You sure deserve it. Worked out sweet for all concerned."

Wesley sipped his beer and said, "You know, I was looking at the case file today, taking it down to the file room after we got it back from the DA."

"Hope they stick a letter of commendation with your name on it in there, Wes," Welshinger said. "Matter of fact, I got it on pretty good authority that's in the works."

"Well, I appreciate that. I'm obliged to you more than I can say," Wesley said. "Now that you mention it, I meant to say I had a look at that confession you pulled. Hadn't really done that before. I was kind of surprised to see my name on it."

"That was all to your benefit, Wes—to give credit where credit was due and keep everything shipshape." Welshinger picked up his glass and drank. "Nice job on the signature, if I say so myself. Pretty close, eh?"

"Oh, yeah. First I saw it, I thought it was me. Took me a second to remember I hadn't been anywhere near it."

"Well, this way, you were as good as there, plucking White's strings."

"Anyhow, like you say, it's no big deal," Wesley said. "But you know what's funny? The confession says he beat the girls to death. And that ain't how it happened."

Welshinger's eyes widened slightly and then relaxed. He smiled. "Well, that's what he wrote. I just helped him out a little."

"I don't suppose he just happened to know all the boilerplate."

"Wes, you know how it's done. Got to be done right if it's going to be any good."

"Yeah, I know, I know. Don't get me wrong. I don't suppose he came up with 'battery' either. Not a word most folks use, 'less they're talking about flashlights." Wesley drank again and set his beer down. "So he told you he beat 'em to death?"

"I suppose he did, Wes. Doesn't make any difference, does it? Dead is dead, and White's convicted and upriver."

"It just doesn't sit right with me. I mean, it all ought to be square—the coroner's stuff and the evidence and the confession."

"It's nothing to sweat," Welshinger said, and raised his glass to his lips. It was already empty. "It's just a word, Wes. Doesn't change the fact that he was guilty as sin and we—you—put him away. Don't get stuck on a word. It's like the book says: The word killeth."

Wesley nodded, and Welshinger stood and picked up his glass. "I'm going to get myself another one of these. Can I get you something?"

"No; I'm fine."

When Welshinger came back, he sat down and smiled. "So," he said. "What else is cooking—"

Wesley cut in. "I still don't know about White, I just don't."

"Wes, for Christ's sake, it's ancient history. Anyway, you know he had a gimpy memory. So he got mixed up. Big deal."

"You never believed him about that memory crap. Neither did I. You thought it was a load of bullshit."

"Hell, maybe I rushed him. It was Halloween. There was parties I wanted to get to," Welshinger said. "So maybe he said 'I beat her over the head' and then he was going to say 'and then I strangled her,' but it just got left out. Anyhow," Welshinger said, "what's done is done, eh?" He lifted his glass again. "Cheers."

Wesley looked at his hands for a moment, and then he looked up. "I don't know, Welshinger. I think I want to look into this. Just for my peace of mind."

They were both silent for a time, and then Welshinger said, "Wes, I don't think that's a very good idea. You'd just be raining on your own parade."

"It's something I got to do."

Welshinger set his glass down on the table. "I really wouldn't monkey with it," he said, and then he picked up the glass again and tapped it on the table three times. "I really wouldn't." He shook his head. "Confession has your name on it, Wes. Far as the world knows, you took it, you swore it. And if it's fucked up, you fucked it up."

"Then I guess the real story would have to come out."

"Who'd believe you, Wes? It would seem awful self-serving. Awfully unbelievable too, you saying, 'Oh, yeah, I was running this whole case, but I got this guy from another division to pull my confession for me.' Who'd believe that?"

"The captain knows different."

"He. wouldn't say so. And I know his mind pretty good," Welshinger said. "I suppose you can go ahead and take yourself down. But I can't let you do that—not to the department. Makes us all look like shit. I'd say you're being a little self-centered here, Wes. What are you going to do after you slit your own gizzard? Get White turned loose?"

"If he didn't do it, that's what—"

"Christ, Wes. Listen to yourself. 'Me, me, me. Fuck the department. For that matter, fuck the community that wants to be protected from goons like White,' " Welshinger said in a high whine. "Not very public-spirited."

Wesley said nothing, and Welshinger began again, in a soft voice. "Listen to me, Wes. Let me help you out. Don't monkey with this thing. You pulled the confession. Your name's on the bottom of it. That's how it is, that's how it's going to stay. Enjoy your commendation. Probably get a raise too. I could just about guarantee that."

"Sorry. I got to do this. I got my reasons."

Welshinger's mouth broadened. "And I got you by the short and curlies, Wes."

"I got nothing you could want, nothing you could take," Wesley said. "So I got nothing to lose." He opened his hands and laid them palms up on the table.

Welshinger took up his glass and pressed it onto Wesley's palm.

He began to rotate it slowly and to press his weight into it. "Word is, Wes, you got a girlfriend. A *little* girlfriend. Hank Trent says you guys busted her boyfriend up at Shacktown last month. Says you got her socked away in your house. That right?"

Wesley said, "None of your goddamned business."

"I don't mind, Wes. Far be it from me to say a fellow shouldn't enjoy the spoils of our labors. Of course, you wouldn't want to be greedy, or stupid." Welshinger let up on the glass, removed it, and looked at Wesley's hand. The base had left a hexagonal furrow that was white and red. "Oh, Christ. I'm sorry. Guess I thought you was a coaster. Nasty mark. Looks like a fucking Star of David. Hey, you a Jew, Wes?"

Wesley sighed. "I'm whatever you say I am."

"Well, that could explain some stuff I wondered about. See, I hear this girl of yours is maybe fifteen years old. Guess she's not much to look at, but hell, that young flesh—all tight and kind of tangy smelling, like lemon drops."

"Go to hell, Welshinger."

"Don't talk that way, Wes. I'm trying to help you. See, I'm not one to judge my fellowman, but other people aren't so broad-minded. If it got out that a senior police officer was shacked up with a fifteen-year-old girl, it wouldn't sit well, it wouldn't be seemly. A fellow wouldn't just lose his commendation. He'd lose his job. His pension." Welshinger stopped and smiled, and then he tilted his head and made a quizzical face. "You think you'd like working as a night watchman, Wes?"

Wesley was feeling weary now. He didn't want this to go on. "I'm not aiming to try it. I suppose I could do whatever I needed to," he said without much conviction. "But I ain't aiming to find out."

"That's good. Because I want you to think about what I'm saying, really weigh it in your mind. Will you do that for me, just that?"

"Sure. I'll think about it."

"That's good, Wes," Welshinger said, and he leaned back and stretched his arms above his head. He yawned. "For a minute there, you were making me nervous. I hate getting nervous. Don't know if I'm coming or going. Of course, they say nerves is the sickness of our times. Or that it's going to be. You know, the whole world rushing ahead. Wheels turning, pistons thrusting, steam whistling, dynamos spinning around and around—faster and faster and faster. Makes people antsy, gives 'em the heebie-jeebies. No reason they can put their finger on—everything just kind of *feels* that way, know what I mean?"

"I guess."

"Me, I hate it. But it's the wave of the future, everybody going nuts like there's a bill collector following 'em around that they can't see." Welshinger stood up. "Well, guess I better move along," he said. "You want a ride? It's no problem. Fine automobile, the Hudson. Your chum Herb thought it rode swell."

Wesley said, "It's okay. I'll make my own way."

"Well, no rest for the weary, eh, Wes? You give my regards to your little lady friend too. You tell her Lieutenant Welshinger says hello."

PART IV

HELL'S CANYON

HERBERT WHITE HAD WATCHED WELSHINGER AND TRENT drive away, the big car, thrumming in the prison courtyard, throwing off vapor into the cold like a sweating horse, inscribing an arc on the gravel, and disappearing through the gate. Then they led him inside through an arch like the portico of a castle or a cathedral formed of sandstone blocks.

There were six guards, one on either arm, two in front of him, two behind. Just inside the arch, they took him into a room with two windows covered in chain link and a big wooden table like the one in Nanna's kitchen, the one the cook would set pies on to cool.

They told him to put his paper sack down and take off his clothes, all of them, and lay them on the table. None of them said anything. They watched him pull off his last sock and step out of his skivvies and begin to turn pink and white in the cold. Then one of them came forward carrying a hand pump with a canister fastened to its stem and began to spray him with a white powder, pumping until Herbert was shrouded in the stuff and began to cough. Then the one with the pump said, "That ought to do 'er."

Another one came forward with a pile of clothing and said, "Put 'em on." He made as though to hand the pile to Herbert, and

Herbert reached out to receive it, but the guard feinted to his left and set them down on the table. Herbert looked at him with puzzlement and the guard snarled, "I said put 'em on."

There were socks and undershorts of a coarse gray-brown cotton, denim trousers, and a denim tunic such as Herbert had seen railway engineers wear. He put them on. The trousers fit snug in the waist and the cuffs hung three inches above his ankles. The sleeves of the tunic reached perhaps halfway down his forearms, and he could scarcely flex his elbows. When he breathed in, the gaps between the buttons parted and revealed patches of his chest and gut.

The guard who had brought him the clothes looked him up and down and nodded. Then he said, "What size shoes you take?"

"Fourteen, I believe. Usually."

"Only got up to twelve."

"I imagine they'd be much too small," Herbert said. "Perhaps I could just wear the ones I brought with me."

"Can't wear civilian clothes in here," the guard said, and withdrew a box from a shelf behind him. He took out a pair of dull black work shoes.

"I suppose I could just go barefooted until you got some fourteens," Herbert said brightly.

"Don't be a smart-ass. Got to wear shoes," the guard said, handing him the shoes. Herbert began to settle himself down onto the floor in order to pull the shoes on. The guard shouted, "Hey, nobody said for you to sit down." Herbert jerked himself up, and he stood on one leg and then the other and pushed the shoes over his toes. His heels hung out perhaps an inch behind the backs of the shoes.

The guard said, "Ain't you going to tie 'em?"

"I don't see how I could."

The guard opened his mouth, to reveal a wad of chewing gum, upon which he closed his jaw with a snap. "Suit yourself." He tipped his head toward the door. Herbert picked up his sack and followed the guards forward, creeping, pushing his shoes along so they wouldn't slip off. They went back outside, across a courtyard. The sun had fallen beyond the wall, and Herbert saw ice crystals spinning under the lamp over the door they were leading him toward. Inside, there was a desk with another guard behind it. One of the men accompanying Herbert handed this guard an envelope, and he opened it and spread some papers out before him. He wrote something at the bottom of one page, then he looked up. "What the hell day is it?" he said.

"Thursday," somebody said.

The guard at the desk scowled. "Not the day of the week. The day of the month, of the year."

"It's 1939, Frank," someone else said. "Been 1939 all day. Will be tomorrow too."

"Can it, smarty-pants. The date, the fucking date."

"The ninth. November ninth."

"Thank *you,*" said the guard behind the desk, with mock courtesy. He wrote something else and said to himself, "Getting late. Getting dark. Getting cold." He looked up and said, "So this is Mr. White," and then he gazed at Herbert. "You look like a scarecrow leaking straw. But I read about you in the papers," he said, and put the documents he'd written on into a folder and set it down next to him. "I even heard your name on the radio."

"Heavens," Herbert said.

The guard smiled. "Heavens. Yes, heavens. Heavens to fucking Betsy," he said, and nodded to the other guards, who then led Herbert away. There was a barred gate and then another and stairs down to where the linoleum floor gave way to stone and the walls sweated and the breath of the six guards and Herbert made a bank of fog, translucent, which moved with Herbert's scraping shoes down the dim corridor like a ghost.

There was another barred door, and then they stopped before a metal door with two slits in it, one at the top and another at the very bottom. The guard who'd given Herbert the clothes and the shoes opened it and nodded, and Herbert nodded back and went inside. There was a clear lightbulb hanging from the ceiling, the filament like a worm aflame, and beyond it a tiny barred window near the ceiling, the glass reinforced with chicken wire. Beneath the window, fastened to the left-hand wall, was a metal cot frame and a mattress with a gray blanket on it.

The guard said, "This is it. Lights on from six in the morning till six at night. Don't monkey with the bulb. Don't go sticking your dick in the socket or nothing. Same with the window. You break it, you freeze your ass." He tapped a pail by the inside of the door with his foot. "Here's for your necessaries. Don't spill it. Ain't nobody going to mop up after you."

The guard stepped out into the corridor and began to swing the door shut. "Food comes in the slot down here. When it comes in, you keep your mitts away. You push it back out when you're told." The door closed the rest of the way, and then there was a sound like railroad cars coupling and footsteps and rustling voices down the hall; and then silence save for the breathing of the walls, rasping and moist and clotted.

It must have been later that night that they came back; after Herbert had taken off the denim trousers and tunic and lain down under the blanket, just after the first time he had woken up and comprehended the utter darkness beneath which he huddled and the cold that was insinuating itself all around him. He was about to see if he could feel the tunic down at the bottom of the cot, where he thought he had set it, and perhaps put it on, when he heard a sound like ice fracturing and the door opened and a parallelogram of light fell across him and then the shadows of four men.

"Get up," one of them said. "You always get up when an officer comes in." Herbert thought it might be the one who'd given him the clothes earlier, but he could not see his face, or the faces of any of them. "That's the rules. Takes a little time to get oriented, but we'll get you sorted out in no time." The voice moved closer, and its breath stank of stale tobacco and gravy. "Welshinger said you might take a little training, that we ought to make you right at home." Herbert had been rubbing the sleep from his eyes and was beginning to rise while the voice was talking, and then it was closer still and became a hiss. "So stand up. Stand up so's I can knock you down," and then a heavy, blunt blow struck the left side of his head as though the very ceiling had collapsed on him, and he could not tell if it was merely the guard's fist or the side of his arm or perhaps a piece of wood or a section of pipe.

Herbert had fallen to his knees while the ache rang up and out through his head like a struck bell tolling. He could see his bare knees and the guard's black shoes before him, and he looked up at the guard and began to say, "Please—" but there was another blow, this time to the other side of his head, and the voice said, "Yeah, on your knees. On your fucking knees." Then the other three shadows came into the cell and encircled him and began to kick him in the stomach and groin as they simultaneously laid down blows on his kidneys with what Herbert realized must be wooden truncheons.

Herbert was lying on his side on the floor, and after a time he no longer felt the smack of the blows on his skin but felt only the way they reverberated through him, deep into his viscera like he was a hole being emptied out with shovels and pickaxes and the hole was filling with nausea and starting to overflow. His only garment, the rough cotton drawers, were in shreds, and he could hear the men above him, breathing heavily, panting as if engaged in a great labor, and one by one they slacked off until the one who had begun it delivered a last, disconsolate kick and stepped back away from him.

Herbert lay as still as he could on the floor, thinking that if they believed he was unconscious or dead they would not begin again. But then he heard a crumpling sound, and somebody said, "Hey, what do we got here?" A big book thumped on the cot and then little leaves of paper fluttered to the floor, the last few sheets of the pad Lieutenant Horner had given him, which he had brought here with him in his paper sack.

"Got a pencil too," the same voice said. "Can a prisoner have a pencil? I don't know that he can."

The first voice Herbert had heard spoke. "I know he can't have paper. Pencil's not much good without paper."

"So you want he should keep it?"

"Is it sharp?" the other said. "I mean, could he conjure up a weapon out of it?"

"Pretty sharp. Sharp enough, I guess."

There was silence for a moment. Then the first guard spoke again: "Give me that," and Herbert heard somebody move forward, and the shadows of two arms fell across the floor in front of his face. "Yeah, we'll let him keep it. Keep it for a souvenir." Herbert thought he heard the guard flick his thumb against the pencil point. "Help him remember what he done to those girls, kind of like what they call a memory aid."

Herbert was still lying very quietly on the floor, wondering what the guard could mean and whether they were now going to leave the pencil behind and go away and let him be, let him lie there in the chill, welling pool of his blood and urine and vomit. But then he heard the shuffling of feet and felt the shadows close around him again, and hands were on his legs, turning him over and prizing them apart.

When Maggie had announced that she intended them to have a genuine Thanksgiving dinner, Wesley had gone looking for a turkey. He knew a butcher shop, Phelan's, on the east side that he figured would give him one cheap or maybe for free, and he had O'Connor drive him over and wait outside.

There was a woman in an old black coat standing next to the enameled meat case, gabbling away at the butcher, whose name Wesley couldn't quite remember. He wasn't sure if he'd been in here since before Rose died; wasn't sure if he'd ever bought himself any butcher cuts in all that time—just stew meat and chicken and a few pork chops.

The butcher looked up at Wesley and folded white paper around some meat and handed it to the woman. He said, "There you go, darling," and turned back to Wesley while the woman, still seemingly talking to him, wandered off. He said, "You're Officer . . ."

"Horner," Wesley said.

"Yeah, Horner. It was just coming to me," the butcher said. "Haven't seen you in a while. How's tricks? How's the missus?"

"Getting by. Missus passed on."

"Gee, I'm sorry."

"That's okay. It was a long time ago. Like you said."

The butcher looked at Wesley and didn't say anything. Then he tipped his head in the direction of the woman in the black coat,

247

who was out on the sidewalk now. "She's the neighborhood widow. Comes in here to pass the time of day, talks to whoever'll listen— me, folks on the street, herself. It's all the same to her, I guess." The butcher shrugged, and then he winked at Wesley. "Don't you go letting yourself get that lonesome." He laid his hand on a loin of beef and started to put it in the case. "No cause to—good-looking man of means like yourself." He laughed and then cocked his eyes at Wesley to inquire what he might want.

"I was thinking about having company for Thanksgiving. Thought I might have a turkey."

"I got some fine hen turkeys coming in beginning of the week. How many you having?"

"Oh, hell, I'm sure one would do me."

The butcher laughed. "Not turkeys—how many people you got coming to dinner?"

Wesley swallowed and then grinned as though he'd been joking all along. "Oh, two or three at most."

"Ten- or twelve-pound ought to do you, then. Plus leave something for hash and soup. You know how to cook it?"

"I got a lady friend knows how."

"That's the best way," the butcher said. "Leave it to the ladies."

"So I'll come in, say, Tuesday next week—day before the day before—and pick it up, okay?"

"You got it."

Wesley turned to leave, and then he turned back. "Say, what'll that run me, that turkey?"

The butcher scratched his chin and looked at Wesley. "Oh, there'll be no charge. On account of your . . ." The butcher halted and then said, "Just on account of old time's sake, okay?"

"You're a gent," Wesley said, and he tugged on the brim of his hat and went out.

He had O'Connor drive him home for lunch, told him he'd make his own way back to the station. It had been almost a week since he'd talked to Welshinger, and for all that time he hadn't felt quite right about leaving Maggie alone in the house. In fact, she wasn't there as much during the day lately, having decided she ought to take a shift at the steam laundry. Wesley told her there was no need for her to work—that he could look after the both of them—but she said she'd feel better making a "contribution." Wesley said she was making plenty contribution with the cooking and cleaning and such. Then Maggie told him that wasn't a contribution; that was just picking up after a soul who didn't have sense enough to pick up after himself, like tending the lame and the halt out of simple Christian charity.

Wesley didn't argue with her. He knew he wasn't going to sway her. He had never made her believe anything she was not already prepared to believe. She might scarcely be sixteen, but she was fully formed before he'd ever laid eyes on her, fashioned and tempered by things beyond his ken. Lately she hadn't said anything about Herbert White. When he'd got home from talking to Welshinger, he told her he'd consulted the powers that be and they'd said there was nothing to be done. He was sorry, but that was the world they were living in. Maggie nodded and thanked him for trying.

White seemed to have vacated Maggie's mind, only to take up residence in Wesley's. Or rather Wesley was preoccupied with Welshinger and what Welshinger might do to ensure Wesley's silence about White and White's confession. He figured Welshinger was watching his house, or having it watched; he was probably watching Maggie at the steam laundry too, maybe having a talk with her boss about how unfortunate it would be if the gas main to the laundry had to be shut down on account of getting ruptured.

Maybe he'd followed Maggie to and from work; and maybe one day he'd sit down next to her in the streetcar and take out a packet of Sen-Sen and offer her a palmful and start to pass the time of day with her, sweet-talk her and slip her a pair of nylons, breathing on her with that scent like smoke and dried lilacs. Maybe he already had.

Maggie wasn't at home. She was at work. He wondered if Welshinger already knew her schedule, or maybe he had the house watched all the time. Even if he wasn't getting anything on Maggie, he was making his presence felt. And now he'd know Wesley was spending a lot of time at home during working hours, and maybe, just by the by with the captain, he'd let drop how Wes Horner sure wasn't at his desk much these days, was he? Nothing was lost on Welshinger, nothing wasted. Truth be told, Wesley hadn't seen any sign of Welshinger or Trent. But that didn't mean a thing. Welshinger would find out whatever he needed to know. And Wesley couldn't win, no matter what.

He put his hat down on the little dining room table, on the edge of the lace doily in its center, and looked in the kitchen. It was dark. The shade was still pulled down and there was light bleeding orange around its edges, like rust beginning to spread. Wesley saw there was nothing to keep him here and wondered whether he ought to sit down for a minute or catch the streetcar back downtown. But he saw it made absolutely no difference what he did, that causes and effects about which Wesley had no say-so had been laid down like ties and rails and he was on a runaway train highballing down them. And he'd almost come to believe that Maggie—her pretty body, her care and kindness, her tending of everything his shabby life contained, all the words and motions that in sum he had come to see as love—had turned him around. But the truth was that Welshinger had punched his ticket;

he had the timetable in one hand and a shiny pocket watch in the other, and he knew when and where Wesley was getting off.

Back when his heart was sour, before Maggie had come along, he figured it all came down to fate, or maybe to original sin, to the world's inescapable rottenness. Things had all been arranged before you even arrived, the pins set up to fall a certain way, the clothes in which you'd play the chump all laid out on the bed. A guy like White could be standing in the right place at the wrong time and have a murder charge fall onto his head like bird shit into his hair; and a guy like Wesley could find his own name signed on the bottom of a piece of paper that made the shit stick. Who knew what really happened? It was the sequence of events that counted, that passed for truth and ruled people's lives: how x was followed by y and y was followed by z. It wasn't fate, it wasn't the fallen world. It was just time, rolling up the beach one wave at a time, one after another, row after row, grinding the world down to sand and dust. It undid beauty, it undid love, and it would undo life. Time was death—that was all it really was—and Welshinger was the guy with the watch, the timekeeper.

Wednesday night, Welshinger was sitting at the empty bar of the Cherokee at the south end of the High Bridge and he was drinking Manhattans, setting little whirlpools in motion with his swizzle stick and then staring down into the drink like he was reading a crystal ball or something. The bartender was pretty sure this one made four, not that Welshinger showed it. He never showed it. Nobody here had ever seen him drunk, although he always had a drink in his hand. The bartender might have tried to sell him a French Dip or a Coney Island but, after all the years, knew better. No one had ever seen Welshinger eat either, although he pissed by the gallon and farted like a thunderstorm.

The bartender looked over at Welshinger and said, "So what you got going for tomorrow?"

Welshinger looked up at him wearily. "For tomorrow?"

"For Thanksgiving. Thanksgiving dinner and all."

"I'm working, I guess."

"It's a holiday," the bartender said.

"Not for me it ain't."

"That's tough. They ought to give you a break."

"Evil don't take no days off. I guess if you don't know that, you don't take the job." Welshinger fished his wallet out of his back pants pocket. He looked at the bartender. "So what's on the meter?"

"A buck's close enough."

"Here's two. On account of you're taking a holiday and I won't be coming in."

"Well, don't be drinking alone."

"Oh, I'm never alone. I got friends all over." Welshinger pulled himself away from his stool, screwed up his shoulders, and stretched out his arms. "Always tired. Bone tired. No rest in this life."

"I know the feeling."

"See you around," Welshinger said, and he turned and went out the door into the night, into the snow that fell in stinging gusts and bursts as if the sky were sowing the earth with salt.

Thursday morning, Wesley sat at the kitchen table, smoking and drinking coffee, and watched Maggie get the turkey ready for the oven, patting it this way and that and rolling it around like it was a baby she was diapering. She had what he figured was the turkey's guts simmering in a saucepan, and after she'd stuffed its inside with damp bread, looking like a vet delivering a breeched

252

calf, she slapped the turkey on what Wesley imagined must be its fanny and said, "There. That ought to do her."

Wesley pulled another cigarette from the pack, the last one, although he didn't worry. Since Maggie had come, they kept a carton's worth of packs in the kitchen cupboard, stacked like bricks next to the salt and pepper and baking powder. "You done this before?" Wesley said, and lit his cigarette.

"Not on my own. Done it with Granny a bunch of times," Maggie said. "Not much to it, really. I reckon even a man could do it if he set his mind to."

"I'd just as soon leave it to you."

Maggie opened the oven door and pushed the turkey inside. Wesley watched her calves stretch taut and her backside jut toward him, and he stood and came up behind her and said, "But there's some things I like to take in hand myself, things I got to do 'cause I can't help doing 'em." He put his hands on Maggie's waist and slid his fingers around to her hip bones, slowly raising his palms up and over her belly until he was cupping her breasts. She spun around, the rayon of her dress rustling through his fingers, and put her face close to his. "Somebody's got to mind that turkey," she said.

"That turkey's way past caring. Somebody's got to tend me, 'fore I burst."

Maggie laid her mouth over his, and then, clasping each other, yoked in one another's arms, they shuffled slowly to the bedroom. They made love deliberately, and afterward Wesley dozed, and when he awoke, the house was abrim with the smell of roast turkey, like butter folded into smoking gold. He could hear a ringing, scratching sound from far away, of metal on metal, and he knew from all the years before when Rose was still with him that it was the sound of gravy being made, of supper's imminence. He pulled on his trousers and an old shirt soft as mattress batting and went out to the kitchen. Maggie was tipping the roasting pan up on one corner and emptying the gravy into a coffee cup. "You get some nice rest?" she said, and smiled at him.

"Eased in body and soul," Wesley said.

"That's good. You ain't resting like you should. I know. I can tell." Maggie picked up a can and latched the can opener down on it and began to turn the key.

"I've never been much for sleep," Wesley said, moving next to Maggie and setting his hand on her shoulder. "But I've slept a damn sight better since you came."

"Me too. Good soft bed with an old thing like you in it sure beats sleeping in a culvert." Maggie turned the can over and set it in a soup bowl and began to open the other end.

"What's this about?" Wesley said.

"This is a special Thanksgiving treat." Maggie picked the freed lid off the end of the can with a spoon and pushed against the contents. A cylinder of red jelly emerged from the other end and at last plopped into the soup bowl.

"What the hell's that?" Wesley said.

"That's your traditional cranberry jelly, just like the Pilgrim fathers ate."

"Give me a taste."

"You ain't getting nothing until the turkey's done and carved," Maggie said. She looked down at Wesley's feet. "You planning on coming to Thanksgiving dinner barefoot?"

"Sorry." Wesley went to the bedroom and put on a pair of brown socks and his duty brogues. When he came back, the turkey and the gravy and the cranberry jelly and the vegetables were on the dining table and Maggie was setting a butcher knife and a spare fork down at his place. She looked up at him and said, "You know how to carve one of these things?"

Wesley was going to say "I remember," but he stopped himself and said, "I know. Sure I do." Maggie went over to the table with the mirror above it by the front door in the living room and straightened her collar and tugged at the hem of her dress. Then she picked up a brush and ran it through her hair a couple of times. She came back to the table and rested her hands on the chair back and said, "There we are."

Wesley started to sit down, and Maggie said, "Ain't you going to say grace?"

"Say what?"

"A blessing. Seems to me you're the one that was telling me how I ought to be sitting in church on Sunday, and here you are fixing to sit down without a by-your-leave."

"I guess I'm not in the habit," Wesley said.

"Me neither. But seeing how we bothered to make a genuine Thanksgiving dinner and all . . ."

Wesley nodded. "I don't know any prayers, but I'll try going through the motions." He cleared his throat and then he said, "For these gifts that we are about to receive . . . ," but he couldn't remember what was supposed to come after that. He looked up at Maggie imploringly, and finally she looked back at him and said, "God bless us every one?"

"Right," Wesley said. "God bless us every one," and then he shrugged and said, "And deliver us from evil. Amen."

"Amen," said Maggie.

Wesley nodded and said, "Guess that about covers it," and he and Maggie sat down to eat.

Herbert was quite sure he had been at Stillwater nearly three weeks as of today, although he could not say whether it was Wednesday or Thursday, because he thought he might have misplaced a day somewhere. The morning after the night in which the guards had beat him up, there had been a tray on the floor next to him when he awoke, a bowl of corn mush and a cup of water, which he assumed must be breakfast. He scarcely moved that day. He could not raise himself to the cot, but he managed to tug down the denim tunic and the blanket and to cover himself with them. His legs were cold but, more to the point, largely without sensation, as though they had been broken at midthigh.

Herbert could feel a sting like nettles in his crotch where he had soiled himself, and after a long time he reached his hand down, and when he brought it back before his eyes he saw there was also blood on it. As the minutes passed—perhaps they were hours, who could say?—he detected another sensation, something blunt pressing into one of his thighs, and after a time he marshaled an intention to reach down and see what it was; and a little after that he pushed his hand along his back and backside and felt a piece of wood. He lifted it to his face and saw it was the pencil Lieutenant Horner had given him, the wood of the sharpened end now a similar tint to that of the eraser.

Herbert clutched the pencil for a long time, and then he reached out his arm aimlessly and made a mark on the plaster beneath the cot. That was how he came to mark the days that followed, a scratch for each one, and he left the pencil there against the wall, not by design but because he heard a voice at the door just at that moment and dropped it. The voice was muffled and congested, and Herbert thought it said, "Glimmer day," which he thought was very odd, and he said nothing back, thinking that he had imagined it or dreamed it. But then there was the thud of a fist on the door and a loud repetition: "Glimmer day!" A moment later, the voice came directly through the grille in the top of the door, and now it was distinct: "I said 'Dinner tray,' God damn it. Push out your breakfast tray, for Christ's sake."

Herbert felt the edge of the tray about a foot from his head, and it seemed to be part of the floor, rooted there like a stump. "I'm not sure I can," he said.

"What say? Speak the fuck up."

Herbert tried to raise his head, so as to make himself heard. He framed the words as distinctly as he could, like a set of nesting boxes. "I'm not sure I can . . . push it out," he enunciated, but the last few words came out tangled and watery.

"Suit yourself. No breakfast tray, no dinner tray. Haven't been here a day, and already a discipline problem. I heard they already had to give you some correction." The voice became a little quieter. "Give you a bit of friendly advice: A negative attitude is no way to win friends and influence people." Then it was gone.

Thereafter, Herbert made a mark each day. On the second day, although he had spent the night still lying on the floor, he was able to push the tray out through the slot in the base of the door, and another tray slid in, identical to the previous morning's. He rolled onto his back, and pressing his palms against the floor, he raised his back and leaned it against the side of the cot. He took a sip of water from the enameled metal cup, wincing as pressure from the cup's rim opened the scabs on his lips and then again as the raw flesh clung to the metal when he withdrew it. He took up a few curds of the corn mush with his fingers and pushed them into his mouth, and after some effort he was able to swallow them. That afternoon he lifted himself up onto the cot and sat there upright for a while, and then the lights went out, so he knew it was six in the evening. In the dark, he found the denim trousers, and he pulled them on. He could feel his legs now, but he did not think he could stand. He was still bleeding from his rectum, and he thought he had better not eat anything until it stopped.

On the following day, the day he made the third mark, and a little after he'd exchanged yesterday's dinner tray for today's breakfast tray, he heard a key in the door. The door opened out and Herbert saw two guards, gripping truncheons, and one of them barked, "Slop!"

"I beg your pardon?" Herbert said. He could not be sure if he had seen either of them before.

"Slop—your bucket," the guard said, indicating the pail in the corner.

"Oh, yes," Herbert said. He began to try to stand up.

"Back!" the other guard bellowed. "You stay against the back wall whenever an officer comes in here."

"I see," Herbert said, and added, "I'm afraid I disposed of my shorts in there. They became . . . soiled, and then I used them to mop up the floor."

"Those is state property," the first guard said, while the other guard picked up the pail and went out into the corridor with it. "You won't be getting another pair." He looked at Herbert, and the other guard came back and dropped the empty pail in the corner, where it spun on its base for a moment and settled with a clang. "Not that I suppose you'd care," the first guard continued. "Place smells like a shithouse. Damn shame. They just plastered and painted it before you come." The guard looked around and back at Herbert, who was standing against the rough limestone wall where the window was, flanked by two walls finished in smooth light gray. "You look like shit."

"I haven't a mirror—"

"Don't get smart. You think you can't have it any worse?" The guard sucked his cheeks together, pursed his lips, and spat into the pail. "Just try me."

Herbert looked at his hands. They were caked in a single shade of dusky brown, veined with black at his cuticles and in the lines of his fingers and palms. He looked up at the guard. "I was only agreeing with you. If I could just freshen up . . ."

"You get a shower and a change of clothes every other week. Rest of the time you ought to try and maintain a little dignity." The guard backed out the door into the hall, where his partner already stood. He shut the door part of the way, and then he stopped and said, "I'll tell you a little something. You probably think being in prison, being in the hole, is what lowers you—that that's your problem. But it ain't. It's all how you see things. It's all in your own mind. If you think you're a turd, that's what makes you a turd. It ain't me. It ain't this place. It's you. It's entirely up to you who you are. You think about that."

Herbert said, "It seems to me I've heard this before. I gather it's the latest thinking."

The guard shook his head from side to side. "Guess you haven't heard it enough for it to stick," he said, and then he shut the door.

On the day he made the tenth mark, three guards came and took him to the shower room and watched him as he scrubbed himself, daubing at his flesh, still stained with yellow and green patches of bruise, with the brush. The soap stung his scabs and scarcely lathered under the dribble of tepid hard water that issued from the showerhead. As he scrubbed his hair and the thickening beard on his face, a group of guards assembled in the door and watched him silently. Someone joked about "bath time at the elephant house," and then they cut off the water and handed him fresh denims, thin and brittle with starch, and marched him back to his cell.

The blood had stopped by the day of the fourteenth mark, and his appetite returned. At first, thwarted by the paltry servings and the unvarying menu of corn mush, boiled vegetables, bread, and gristly broth—or was it meant to be stew?—his stomach ached with hunger, sharply at first but then more dully, like a memory that guttered but was never entirely extinguished. By the day of the twentieth mark, he could have been said to be feeling almost himself, if by self was meant the capacity to sense his body as a single entity, more or less in one piece, located in this one place and not another.

Now, on the twenty-first day, which by various calculations he had determined must be a Wednesday or a Thursday, he decided to risk asking which one it might be. When his breakfast tray came, his voice rolled small and apologetic through the slot in the bottom of the door like a stray marble, asking, "I wonder if you know what day today might be?"

The tray slid through the slot, singing grittily against the floor. "Holiday. Thanksgiving."

"Oh. I see. Thank you."

Herbert looked at the tray, and on it a square of corn bread, furrowed and sunken on top, glowered back at him. So it was Thursday, and the thought that he knew this brightened him.

He knelt by the cot and lowered his head to look for the pencil under it, and when he had found it he made the mark for the day. Then, still holding the pencil, he stood up and looked around. He had already measured the dimensions of the cell with his body: perhaps six feet wide by nine feet long. In its center, the bulb glowed in its socket, and since the ceiling was low—perhaps seven and a half feet—he could reach out and hold it in his hand like an egg if he desired. But after what the guard had told him the first day, he didn't dare for fear of breaking it in his grip and never getting it replaced; for fear of having no light at all.

There was some light, Herbert supposed, that must find its way in through the window, although the window was blocked by dead leaves and the leaves themselves were covered in a drift of snow whose depth he could not guess. Perhaps in the summer, when they would switch the bulb in his cell off before dusk and the leaves would have decayed away, he would see the sun through the window.

His dinner tray came, and as he ate and licked his fingers clean, he held the pencil all the while. Afterward, sitting on the edge of the cot, he conceived the idea to write something. But he could not think what he might write upon, for the few sheets of paper that remained from the pad Lieutenant Horner had given him had gone into the pail after he had used them to clean himself. But then he glanced up at the wall opposite him, smooth and dull gray like a sheet of zinc, and he thought of writing on it. What would be the harm in it? The pencil lead was itself so hard that it scarcely left a detectable mark on white paper; on a light-gray wall, chances were no one would see any writing who was not looking for it. Herbert touched the tip of the pencil to his tongue and slowly, irresistibly as air rising through water, stood and went to the corner of the wall adjacent to the window and began to write.

Stillwater, Minnesota

Day 21

Today is Thanksgiving Day. I have already had my Thanksgiving dinner, such as it was: boiled yams and some poultry meat with thin gravy which I suppose is intended to be turkey, although for all I know it was chicken. It is a far sight from the other Thanksgiving dinners I have had in my life, but then everything here is a far sight—a far cry, indeed—from every other thing in my life before. Even alone on Laurel Avenue, I would make myself a nice piece of ham and bring a slice of pie back from the bakery the afternoon before and have it for dessert with a cup of Constant Comment tea. Nanna always had three pies, even though there were only three of us; even later, when there were only two of us. I would have a slice of each—pecan, pumpkin, and apple—and by the time I was eleven I could manage more, although there was always plenty to send home with the gardener or whoever else might want some.

Upon reflection, it seems to me that Thanksgiving is inevitably a somber day, if not a sad one. Even when Father was alive—and how I remember Thanksgiving 1915, the first time Nanna and I sat down for a formal dinner after he was gone and it seems we scarcely spoke or looked at each other—it was that way. Perhaps it is the time of year. It is supposed to be a harvest feast, but, at least in Minnesota, the harvest is long over, and there is generally snow on the ground, or a crusty, slippery mix of leaves and ice that makes for unpleasant walking. Father and I would always have what he called a "constitutional" after Thanksgiving dinner. He would stand in the pantry with his coat on and his muffler around his neck and take a glass of brandy, and then we would go out and walk on Summit Avenue, and it would always be right around the time the streetlights would come on. I do not think we talked of anything in particular, either at the table or afterward. I cannot recall our giving thanks, beyond saying the usual blessing.

Perhaps that is why we were somber. We were no more happy than usual to be eating—well, perhaps a little more happy, for the food was undoubtedly especially delicious—but we never had any expectation that we would not have food to eat; and so I suppose we were not particularly surprised or thankful when we did eat. That is not to say that we did not appreciate our advantages. I knew how many of the people below the hill lived, not to mention those in even less salubrious quarters of the city. But I do not recall thinking that I ought to be particularly thankful for what we had there and then, as though we might have easily enough been the recipients of some other fate.

I am not so sure this was a mark of ingratitude, although it may seem so. For if I had thanked God for sending us what we had in those good times—given him "credit" for it—would I not now have to charge him with responsibility for what I have in these times? For if he sent *that* then, surely he sent me *this* now; and if there is a rationale to this giving, I suppose he must have loved me then and now it seems he must hate me. If everything is in his power, to do and undo, he caused that then and he causes this now—and with good reason if I did the things they say I did. But then it seems to me that if everything is in his power, in some sense he made me and set my life in motion in order that—or at least knowing—I should do those very things. And he made Miss Ruby for beauty's sake, to show me what I might love but never possess and only lose, only destroy, not for want of love but on love's account.

I do not want to believe that. I could not love such a God as that, no more than he could have ever loved me or the Mortensen girl or Ruby.

I suppose that leaves me with only Ruby to love, or rather the memory of her, and I suppose I shall lose—he shall take—that too. I should have so much liked to have Thanksgiving dinner with her. But I would be happy merely

* * *

263

And there the light went out. Herbert had written two-thirds down the wall in a strip nearly exactly two feet wide. As he wrote, he had bent lower and lower and finally settled onto his knees, staying there until his legs had almost fallen asleep, as though weary with supplication or prayer.

Scarcely a week after Thanksgiving Day, Wesley came home to find a wreath of spruce boughs and holly hanging on his door, bound by a purple ribbon. He went inside and followed to the kitchen the trail made by Maggie's sounds and smells—the scratch of a steel spatula on cast iron, the seethe of Crisco, the scent of Luckies mingled with Wrigley's spearmint softly popping in her jaw like birdsong far away.

Wesley leaned into the doorframe. "Where'd we get that thingie on the door?"

"You don't like it?" Maggie looked up at him and then away just as quickly.

Wesley took a step toward her. "Oh, no, sugar. I like it fine. Pretty as can be. Smells good too."

Maggie looked up again and smiled. "Made it myself, if you want to know." She held up her right hand. "Pretty near wrecked my fingers on them holly prickers."

Wesley reached forward and cupped her hand in his, and at first jokingly, but then from a pity that stole up on him unawares out of a long unvisited room in his heart, he kissed her fingertips. As soon as he had done it, he pulled back, wanting to blush at his own tenderness.

Maggie looked at him as though she were trying to see something on his face that was very, very small. "That's about the sweetest thing you've ever done, Wes," she said. Still holding her hand, Wesley said, "Don't know what came over me," and he lowered their hands together and finally released hers, letting it hang still and limp at her side like the clapper of a silent bell.

"So where'd you get the pine and stuff?" Wesley finally asked.

"Out of the park, over by the laundry."

"That ain't legal, Maggie. There's an ordinance."

"Only took one little branch of each. Wasn't doing nobody any good. Now it's making us a genuine Christmas wreath."

"It's pretty as can be," Wesley said.

"Just used a little picture wire. Got the ribbon out of Louise's drawer—old hair ribbon like nobody wears anymore." Maggie looked at Wesley for a sign of assent.

He nodded and said, "It's fine. It's pretty. House has never looked so pretty, ever since you came, being so busy about it."

"I figure I'm just getting started." She smiled at Wesley, smiled a smile broader than Wesley thought her narrow chin could contain. "Figured I'd get us a Christmas tree and everything. Figured I'd give us the best Christmas ever, the best Christmas anybody's ever had."

Wesley said, "Where'd you figure you'd get the money for that Christmas tree?" He tried to speak gently, to not spoil it for her.

"I been saving up. There's a fellow selling 'em right down here on Seventh. I thought maybe I'd get us one this Saturday, then you could help me drag it home."

"I'd do that, except I'd say it was only right that I ought to buy it," Wesley said. "Seeing how . . ." He was going to say how it was his house or how he was the one that brought home the bacon, but that was not what he meant. "Seeing how . . . it's what I'd like to do," he said finally, and Maggie nodded.

It must have snowed all Friday night, for on Saturday morning, after they'd had their coffee and oatmeal porridge and Wesley had finished his second cup of coffee and his third cigarette, the snow was deep, the sidewalks were indistinguishable from the yards and verges on either side, the roads and curbs lost except by reference to the parked cars dotted here and there, and the street signs made unreadable by their flockings of snow. Up to their shins in it, Maggie and Wesley trudged down to West Seventh Street like boats plowing heavy seas. The whole neighborhood was silent and muffled in white, and the entire city seemed empty, as though harrowed by a plague that had passed through in the night, leaving only Maggie and Wesley among the living.

When they got onto Seventh, they walked another block and then saw a plume of smoke from a fire burning in a metal drum, and a man standing next to it, clutching his hands together over the smoke and the flames. He had a scarf wrapped two or three times around his head, and wool gloves that were stiff with pine pitch and had the fingertips cut off. Trees, bound up with twine and shrouded in snow, leaned against the wall of the building.

Wesley said, "We come for a tree. What do you got?"

"Starting early, I guess. Three weeks till Christmas. I scarcely got these unloaded," the man said.

Maggie said, "The quicker you start, the more you can have."

"Guess so," the man said. "Well, I got spruce and I got Norway pine. Some folks think the pine's more handsome. But your spruce is more aromatic. Anyhow, the spruce is two dollars. The pine'll run you four bits more."

Wesley looked at Maggie, and his mouth made a small *o*, and she put her hand on his arm to still him. She said, "I reckon we'll have a spruce. I'd sooner have that nice clean smell than be picking up them long needles laying like cat whiskers all over the parlor floor."

"That really what you want?" Wesley said.

"It truly is," Maggie replied, and Wesley peeled two dollar

266

bills from the roll deep in his pocket and handed them to the man. "I could bring it around for you in the truck," the man said, "if you was to wait till Monday."

Maggie and Wesley faced each other and Wesley shrugged, and Maggie said, "That's okay. We don't live but a few streets from here."

"Suit yourself," the man said, and turned to the row of trees leaning on the wall. He pulled one toward him. "This here's a nice one," he said, and Wesley took the weight of it into his hands and nodded. Hugging it to him, he began to pull it down the sidewalk in the direction of home, and Maggie came up alongside him. She looked back at the man and waved and said, "Merry Christmas," and the man waved with the bare, red tips of his fingers. Maggie turned to Wesley and shook her head. "You never figure out how to do things easy," she said. "Just lay it down and drag it, butt end first. I take one side, you take the other."

Wesley set the tree down, and Maggie and he threaded their hands through the twine, each clasping a bough at the base. They began to drag the tree along the snow-clogged pavement as if they were pulling a skiff out of the surf, onto the beach through the sea wrack and sand, and the tip of the spruce left a mark in the snow behind them, the keel's homeward trace.

All that week and into the next, Maggie was doing something, adding something to the house for Christmas's sake. She cleaned every room and every window, and then she stenciled rosy white stars on the window glass with Glass Wax. She hung ornaments among and on the boughs of the tree: garlands of milk-bottle tops strung on darning thread, and stars and angels' bodies fashioned from cigarette pack foil. She set acorns and holly berries and pine cones on the windowsills and door lintels in such quantity that a soul—in this case, Wesley—might wonder if squirrels had moved in. Then she commenced to bake, and by the fifteenth of December she'd cleaned the corner grocery out of cloves and powdered ginger and green and red sugar sparkles and silver balls and jimmies and hundreds-and-thousands.

Whenever Wesley came home there was something else, something new, and after a while he found himself feeling tingly each day when he got to the front door, almost eager to see what Maggie had done inside; and it took considerable effort for Wesley Horner to recollect the last time he'd been excited about much of anything. Growing up in North Dakota had not lent itself to much effervescence about future events, even if they were holidays; still less to sentimentality about snow and cold weather and red cheeks. Yet Wesley began to feel that his looking forward was akin to looking back, in the sense not of remembering anything in particular or of some generalized nostalgia, but of some better prior time which was nevertheless, somehow, to come: a sweeter past whose impending arrival was marked by the things, the signs, Maggie was laboring at just beyond his front door. It was as though she were lighting candles one at a time, and one by one, day by day, they were lighting the way to that place.

After a week of this, Wesley was not only ending the day but beginning it with a sort of itch, an itch of anticipation, as if he'd had just a little bit too much coffee and he was leaning forward into the world, his hair askew in the wind of its events, a half second ahead of everyone else. Every day he wanted to throw open the door and see what Maggie had conjured up in the house; and somehow in the morning that left him itching to throw open the door to see what was out there, feeling, against all his experience and against all reasonable odds, that it must be good. He trusted it, assumed and anticipated its goodness like a child; not the child he could actually recall being, skulking through Lutheran New Upsala, but the child he felt he must surely have been before that, in the time prior to his recollection, the child he now hungered to recall and the child he hungered to become, somehow the same, aborning in this very world right now.

It was driving him, moving him sweetly beyond himself, insisting that he be about its business. So he found himself thinking of ways to match and even raise the wagers Maggie was laying down, the bets that said Christmas would be everything she believed and promised it would. He thought of gifts that would please her, of how he could garland her raw limbs, her limp hair and narrow face, as she had garlanded the spruce they'd pulled through the snow and set up in their home. He was aflame with the anticipation of it, and the way it moved him was like the way lying with Maggie had first moved him, shifted him out of five years of inertia, dead as stone. Now he thought there was no difference between the anticipation and what he had come to know as love. It was moving Wesley to pour his love down on Maggie, and then it insisted he do something about Herbert White too; insisted that Wesley use his future to set the past right; that he let that perfect past whose presence now glimmered in his bones redeem the future.

Ten days before Christmas, on a Friday, Wesley asked O'Connor what he knew about buying clothes for a woman. O'Connor said he'd bought his wife a corsage once, but that was the limit of his experience. "I suppose you just go down to Bannon's or Husch Brothers and tell the salesgirl what you got in mind," he said, shrugging. "Or sometimes there's ads in the paper, with pictures and everything. Might see something you figure she'd fancy there." O'Connor handed Wesley the newspaper he'd been holding under his arm. "Take a look."

Wesley berthed his cigarette between his lips and began to turn the pages. Mannheimer's had some dresses, but he didn't see himself buying Maggie a dress. In the second section, back among the radio program listings and the recipes for lima bean casserole, he saw an article on the society page by Charles Farrell, now apparently off the crime beat and consigned to writing up receptions at the University Club, held for the likes of DA Edward Berglund and Judge Ignatius Kelly and their wives and retainers. Same cast, different picture, Wesley figured. Guess they finally fixed Farrell's wagon.

Then, a page after that, Wesley found it. There was a full-page ad for Schuneman's, with a drawing of a fashionable woman and the caption "Smart winter coats for the holidays." The woman wore a hat, and Wesley guessed her hair was shorter than Maggie's, but that didn't mean Maggie wouldn't look swell in the coat. Hell, the woman pictured in the ad didn't look like any woman Wesley had ever seen.

At lunchtime, Wesley walked down Wabasha Street until he got to Schuneman's. He doubted he'd ever been inside, even with Rose, who thought Schuneman's prices were too dear. He entered and saw the women's department off to one side and walked over to a glass case where two salesgirls stood talking. Neither of them acknowledged him, so he reached into his pocket and took out a two-bit piece and rapped it on the case. The girls looked at him, startled, and the one on his left said, "Yes?"

Wesley said, "I saw in the paper this morning where it said you've got some nice winter coats. For women. Smart winter coats for the holidays, it said."

"Oh, yes," said the salesgirl, and she moved out from behind the case and walked over to a long row of hanging garments. "They're over here. In lamb's wool. Brown or green." She rested her fingertips gingerly on the shoulder of a brown coat. "The brown's very smart, very popular in Chicago and New York and Hollywood."

Wesley looked at the coat she was fingering, and he reached out to touch the fabric for himself. It was very soft, almost like cotton balls, but denser. The color was like caramel or honey or maybe clean motor oil. "What about the green ones?" he said.

"They're just here," the girl said, stepping backward away from him and laying her hand on another coat. It was not a dull green but bright like Maggie's holly leaves, maybe even brighter: bright as the colored sugar she'd been sprinkling on the pecan sandies she baked on Saturday. "Now, there we are," Wesley said.

"What size would you require?" the girl said.

"Cripes, I don't know." Wesley looked at the girl. She was more or less Maggie's size, maybe smaller in the hips and more of a scarecrow in the chest, but close enough. "Pretty much the same as you, I guess."

"Well, that would make her a six," the girl said. "Of course, if it isn't right, your wife can bring it back for exchange."

"Yeah. I suppose she could," he said. "Anyhow, go ahead and wrap it up."

The girl carried the coat back to the glass case and folded it in thirds and wrapped it in tissue paper and set it in the bottom half of a slim brown box, over which she placed a matching lid. After she'd tied the box with white string, she said, "That will be twenty-four dollars and ninety-five cents."

"Chri—cripes," Wesley said. "Twenty-four ninety-five," he repeated, as though it were a question. He felt for his wallet, somehow feeling it might be missing. It was there, however, and he took it out. He wondered if he ought to flash his badge and see if she'd offer him a discount. But then he thought better of it. Nothing was going to get between Maggie and the gift of this coat. He scarcely had twenty-four dollars in his wallet, and he made up the last of the change with the quarter he'd rapped on the counter.

It was one o'clock by the time he'd eaten a Coney Island and walked back to the station. He was whistling, carrying the elegant department store box under his arm, when he came around the corner by the traffic division and nearly collided with Welshinger.

Welshinger smiled and said, "I guess at least one of the seven dwarfs is happy around here today. Been shopping?"

"Oh, just a little something . . ."

"For the little lady, I'll bet."

"Could be," Wesley said. He straightened himself and moved sideways toward the wall, gesturing for Welshinger to join him. "You know, there's something I've been meaning to talk to you about." He saw that Welshinger had made no effort to move in his direction, and rather than raise his voice, Wesley shuffled back toward Welshinger. He continued, "You know what we talked about at Alary's, about White?"

"Sheesh, Wes," Welshinger said wearily. "Enough."

"No," Wesley said, and he drew himself up close to Welshinger, so close he could feel the sighings of his breath. "No. I decided I have to do the right thing, follow the right procedure, if you like. I just want to tell the captain what happened with the confession, tell him I got doubts about White being the one." Welshinger tipped his head down and laid his fingertips across his eyes, and Wesley found himself wanting, somehow, to put his hand on Welshinger's shoulder, as though to comfort him. But he just said,

"That's all I want to do. Just to fess up. Anything beyond that is in the captain's hands."

Welshinger looked up at Wesley. "He's not going to do anything about nothing, Wes," he said, and sighed. "There's nothing for him *to* do, no reason to. Nobody gives a shit about White. So why is it so important for you to . . . fuck with this thing?" Welshinger looked away, still speaking. "Tell me, Wes. I really want to know."

"It just is. It's just something I got to do, that I can't rest easy with until I do. . . ."

"Talk to me about rest," Welshinger muttered. Then he looked deep into Wesley's eyes. "I told you what would have to happen if you did this, Wes. I told you what the future would be. Don't you believe me? Don't you care?"

"It's what I have to do."

"White's history, Wes. Done and gone. Put it behind you. What's past is past."

"It's not that simple," Wesley said. "I used to think it was, but now I don't."

"Suit yourself, Wes. I told you what would have to happen, clear as a crystal ball. I try to help, I try to be reasonable, but you're past reasoning, I guess." Welshinger looked at the package and then at Wesley. "It's a fucking shame, you going and spoiling Christmas for everybody like this," Welshinger said, and then he walked off, a little unsteadily, and Wesley stood watching. He could swear Welshinger was limping, dragging himself like a dog hit by a slow freight.

Tuesday, Day 40

I fancy we are well into the month of December now, quite close to Christmas, I should guess. I have overheard the guards speaking of the holiday to come, so I imagine it is quite soon. Also, I seem to recall that the shortest day of the year is around this time, although as I have noted before, it is hard to say, given the hours the lights are left on here. During the last few nights, however, I have detected some sort of light through the window, dull but discernible, rather like a streetlamp in fog, and each night it seems a little brighter. I suppose there are all sorts of explanations for this, chief among them the likelihood that we have had less snow lately, and as the bank against my window has receded, a light outside in the prison yard has become visible. But I have no notion of whether it has been snowing or not—although I can heartily attest to the cold!—nor can I explain why I should not have noticed this light when I first arrived, when the snow cover was still presumably small.

No, I believe it must be a star, one that has rotated into my view as the heavens turn through the seasons, some winter star, the apex of a constellation that becomes visible at this time of year. For all I know, it is the Christmas star of the Bible, though I believe that is strictly a matter of legend. If it were not, I'm afraid I would have to take it as another sign sent to mock me in my imprisonment and distress, for I never noticed it or even thought about it before.

It is odd that my thoughts turn to God so much of late. In the past I suppose I believed in creation, which rather suggests a creator, but I never said so, or thought so, "out loud," so to speak. I suppose I assumed God's existence rather as one standing in daylight assumes the sun, though one never looks at it—indeed one dares not look at it directly. But now, literally removed as I am from the light, from virtually every created thing and surely from every good thing, God is constantly in my thoughts,

thoughts that are bitter and despairing and angry. It is odd indeed that feeling this way—I should almost say hating God—and having every reason to disbelieve, I find myself believing most, finding him most apparent in what seems to be his utter absence.

Herbert White had reached the very bottom of the wall, and he knew he might go on writing in this fashion indefinitely, so he stopped. He put down his pencil and waited, waited for them to put the lights out so the star might heave into view. He had grown to expect that it would, and that each night it would be a little brighter and a little nearer than the night before.

When Wesley came home Monday night, he slipped the box from Schuneman's under the bed in Louise's room, and then he went to see what Maggie was doing. She sat at the dining table, holding a pair of shears, cutting fabric into strips. She looked up at Wesley excitedly.

"I got this at the laundry—stuff nobody ever claimed—rayon, I guess. Anyhow, I figured I could cut it up and make little bows, put 'em around the house." She held up what seemed to be an old dress. "I got this red one with a kind of candy stripe on it. Ought to be gay as ponies on the tree."

Wesley nodded. "Be swell." He cleared his throat. "I been busy about Christmas myself. Did a little shopping today. Got a little something for somebody I know." Wesley grinned.

"Anybody I know?"

"I suspect so. She looks just like you, matter of fact."

"Is that so?" Maggie said, and stood up, smiling and pressing her hands together in front of her.

"Want to see what I got her?"

"Wouldn't that kind of spoil it? I mean, ain't you supposed to wait till Christmas Day?"

"In New Upsala, it was Christmas Eve. But that don't matter," Wesley said. "We're having our own Christmas, not worrying about anybody else's rules. Besides, this is something a girl could use before Christmas, something a girl could use right away."

Maggie rose up momentarily on her tiptoes, and her shoulders gave a little shiver. "I don't suppose that girl could be me," she said, and settled onto her feet and sighed. "Oh, Jesus, Wesley, just show me. Show me right now."

Wesley ran back to Louise's room and returned with the box and set it on the table in front of Maggie. She looked at it a long while, standing back a ways. "All done up in a box with string," she said finally.

"Go ahead. It ain't a snake. Open it, sugar. I'm dying of suspense myself."

Maggie picked up the shears and snipped the string, put them down, grasped the sides of the lid, and shook it up and free of the box. She leaned the lid against one of the dining chairs and regarded the tissue. "Now, what could it be . . . ?" and she glanced up at Wesley.

"Damn it, don't dawdle over it, sugar. I can't take it."

"Okay." Maggie thrust her hands under the tissue and folded it slowly back. The tissue rustled where it touched her quaking hands and then fell away as she lifted the coat out by its shoulders. "Criminy, Wesley," she said, and exhaled deeply. "It's the most beautiful thing I've ever seen." And she turned and faced him, now holding the coat against her as though she were a paper doll. Her cheeks were wet with tears, and she moved toward him, still holding up the coat before her as if she were naked beneath it, as if it were a pair of folded angel's wings. She said, "I love you, Wesley," and Wesley gasped, his voice and breath both emptied out of him, and said, "I love you too, so much."

Welshinger had been following her for three afternoons, following her in that green coat that made her stick out like a lighthouse when she walked back from the steam laundry behind the German Catholic church or even stood inside the streetcar. And Welshinger wondered, Where the hell did she get that coat? and then he realized that it must have been in the box Horner was holding on Monday, the afternoon before Horner'd gone to the captain with his story and the captain had looked at him like he'd just dropped in from Mars.

He knew she left the laundry every day at four. Sometimes she started at six in the morning; other days, when she worked a half shift, she started at ten. It had been Welshinger's original plan to get the manager of the steam laundry to fire her, and then he would cruise up, pretty as you please, and commiserate with her. But there hadn't been time to fool with that. It was Friday, a little after four. Her girlfriends had peeled off on their various tracks, and the girl was coming up to the corner of Exchange Street alone. Welshinger pulled to the curb in front of her and rolled down the window on the passenger side, calling out merrily, "Hey, aren't you a buddy of Wes Horner?"

The girl looked at him, a little stunned, and finally nodded. She was wearing some sort of corsage pinned to her coat, something concocted of ribbon and pine cones and papier-mâché fruit and little brass bells.

"Well, heck, any friend of Wes is a friend of mine," Welshinger said, and he thrust his hand out the window. The girl stepped forward and took it warily. Welshinger was going to say he was O'Connor, but maybe the girl had met O'Connor. He thought fast, shook the girl's hand, and said, "I'm Lieutenant Gundersen. I work with Wes down at the station."

The girl nodded but didn't do anything that indicated she recognized the name. So far so good. Welshinger went on. "Hey, we all think the world of Wes after that big case he broke. He's a real hero."

The girl seemed to scowl, but then she smiled. "Yeah, he's quite a guy," she said.

"Now, you . . ." Welshinger stopped and tapped his chin with his finger, the way a department store Santa might scratch his beard. "Your name is . . . ?"

"Maggie," the girl said softly but with little hesitation.

"Maggie. Now, there's a pretty name for a pretty girl," Welshinger said. "Hey there, that's a pretty coat too. Just the thing for the season, eh?"

"Wesley gave it to me. Just the other day."

"Well, for the love of Mike," Welshinger said. "You know what? Wes and I were passing the time of day in the hall at the station a couple of days back, and he had a box under his arm, and I bet that was what was in there. Now, how about that?"

"Could be," Maggie said, now not so much guarded as matter-of-fact.

"Nice big box from Schuneman's. Must have cost a pretty penny."

"I don't know. He didn't say."

"Well, it stands to rights. He's a good man, a generous man." Welshinger shook his head a little as though marveling, and then he looked up again. "That's about the prettiest coat I've ever seen."

"You like it?" the girl said, her face opening, forming a smile in the expectation of something good.

"I think it's swell," Welshinger said. "And you know what? I've known a lot of actresses and models and showgirls, and I know any of 'em would say that you had the style to really 'carry it off.' That's what they say: 'carry it off'—that's the professional lingo for a real pretty girl wearing something smart to its best advantage."

"Well," the girl said slowly, as though catching her breath. "I thank you very kindly."

Welshinger smiled. "Just stating the facts," he said. "Hey, come in out of that cold. I'll give you a ride. No sense walking when you can ride, eh?"

"Guess not," the girl said, and pulled open the door. She slid onto the seat, rubbing her hands against the upholstery. "Nice car," she said. "Like one of them Hollywood limousines, all plush inside."

"Well, it suits me fine. Like to spend my spare time keeping her in trim, simonizing her and such. She's like a wife to me, the Hudson."

"Ain't you got a real wife?" the girl said, with a trace of mockery in her voice, not smarty-pants but only joshing.

Welshinger laughed. It didn't matter what he said now. "Oh, you bet. Louella's her name. Coming up on our twentieth anniversary. High school sweethearts and all." Welshinger smiled in a way that suggested fond wistfulness. "We got"—and he pondered momentarily—"three kids. Yeah, three kids." He relaxed now, drifting into the story. "There's Grace, who's graduating this year. And another girl, Faith. She's . . . she's learning the baton, that's what she's doing. And then there's Billy. He wants to be a cop, just like his dad." Welshinger stopped, wondering if this was getting away from him a little.

"I had a best friend named Billy," the girl said, as Welshinger pulled away from the curb, driving west.

"Hey, small world, ain't it?" The girl didn't say anything. Welshinger didn't want her to get uneasy, so he said, "Where can I take you?"

The girl hesitated, as though weighing her options, and said, "Oh, if you just kept going down Seventh here and dropped me off around Smith Avenue, that would do me real nice."

"No problem, Maggie." They drove along slowly, into the graying dusk, Welshinger steering with the palm of his left hand. He told the girl that Faith might want to become a nurse, that she was thinking of joining the WACs, figuring she could get nurses' training on the government's ticket. Of course, anybody could see a war was coming, and he, being her dad, didn't want her anywhere where anything bad could happen to her. But she was a headstrong girl, a little like her mom when he had been courting her when he was a patrolman. Or rather, he meant to say, when they were in school, when he was on the basketball squad.

Welshinger went on for some time in this manner, growing more and more easy in it, and he sensed the girl relaxing, letting her body settle deeply into the seat next to him. Then, when they'd pulled up to a red light that he realized too late was Smith Avenue, he heard her grasp the door handle. "Hey," she said, "this thing busted?"

"Oh, heck, Maggie. I'm sorry. It's just rigged up police style, to open from the outside, so's the suspects can't go wandering off on their own. I'll come around and open it. Just let me get across the intersection here, where I can pull over."

"Okay," the girl said.

When the light changed, Welshinger let out the clutch and angled the car toward the curb on the other side of Smith Avenue. He stopped and set the hand brake. "Well," he said, shifting in his seat toward Maggie, "it's sure been.grand making your acquaintance."

"Likewise."

Welshinger made to open his door and then halted. "You know, Maggie, I was thinking how I was kind of cold and thirsty, and I wonder if maybe you'd fancy a little drink, maybe go somewhere and show off that pretty coat of yours."

"I ought to be getting home," the girl said.

"Oh, heck, Wes ain't going to be getting back for at least an hour."

The girl looked at him. "How did you know I live at Wesley's?"

Welshinger smiled. "Oh, honey. Wes and me are like brothers. He tells me everything. Told me how fond he was of you too."

"He did?"

"Sure. I don't suppose he could help himself, head over heels with a pretty girl," Welshinger said. "Why, you went and just changed his whole life. He couldn't keep that from a friend, from his best friend."

"He hasn't said much about you." Then she quickly added, "Not that I don't believe you."

"Oh, heck. You know how Wes is. Keeps things to himself, kind of thoughtful. No reason he ought to mention little old me," Welshinger said. "But I guess I can honestly say I don't have a dearer friend. He's a fine, fine fellow."

"Surely is," the girl said, and paused. "Well, I'd love to have that drink with you, but I ain't exactly legal for taverns and such." She looked at him. "I suppose you know that."

"Oh, yeah." Welshinger smiled. The girl had just saved him at least half an hour. "But that's no problem." He reached over and patted the glove compartment door. "Got my own cocktail lounge right here."

"You do?"

"Sure. Rye, bourbon, Canadian, the works."

"Well, I'll just try one."

"Great," Welshinger said. "You smoke?" He opened the glove compartment. "I got Camels; Luckies too."

"A Lucky would suit me fine."

Welshinger depressed the cigarette lighter and handed her the cigarettes. "Here, keep the pack."

"Oh," she said. "You don't have to go and do that."

"Hell," Welshinger said. "It's Christmas." He paused. "You know, I'm sorry, but it ain't good form for a police officer to be seen . . . refreshing himself right out in public. I wonder if you'd mind if we got off the main highway here before we have that drink." The cigarette lighter snapped, and Welshinger pulled it out and held it up. She leaned into his hands, then sat back, exhaling. "Sure," she said.

"Okeydokey. I'll just drive us down by the river. There's kind of a view." Welshinger pulled away from the curb, drove down Seventh a few blocks, and turned left down a narrower street, past houses, and then farther, past where the streetlamps gave out. He made several more turns and pulled into a large, empty lot above the river, with enormous heaps of coal piled around it. Then he stopped the car, cut the engine, and set the brake. He looked out. "Well, it ain't the Rainbow Room, but it'll do."

Maggie looked out and said, "What's the Rainbow Room?"

"Fancy cocktail lounge on top of a skyscraper in New York City." Welshinger reached into the glove compartment and took out a bottle and a couple of Dixie cups.

"You been there?"

"Oh, sure. I been everywhere," Welshinger said, filling the cups. "Sometimes I feel like I *am* everywhere." He laughed. "Don't know if I'm coming or going." He handed the girl a cup. "Here. Bottoms up." The girl drank. Welshinger said, "But look out there, right here. This is all you need." The girl looked out into the dark, toward the distant lights and the copses of trees in the river bottom. She couldn't see much. The car windows were fogging up.

"See, Maggie," Welshinger said, "this is the world. It's the same here as anyplace else. A few stars, a lot of night, like the whole world's tired, so tired that the sun goes 'snap,' off like a light, and it seems like it will never come back on. Fucker's burnt out. And maybe, tomorrow morning, it really won't. That'd give folks a start, wouldn't it?"

"Guess so," the girl said.

"You done with that drink?" Welshinger said.

"Pretty near." Maggie's eyes were ever so slightly unfocused, and she felt she had to blink to see right.

Welshinger took up the bottle again. "Here. Have a little more."

"I don't know if—"

"Hell, Maggie, ease up. It's Christmas," he said, and poured. He grasped the bottom of the seat and pushed it back. "Let's get comfortable."

The girl set her cup down on the open glove compartment lid and said, "Well, you know I'm mighty grateful, but I really think I ought to get on home."

"Hey, nothing to worry about. Relax," Welshinger said. "Trust me. We're three, maybe four minutes from your house. Got all the time in the world. Now finish up that drink." The girl picked up the cup and sipped again. "Good," Welshinger said. "Now, Maggie, help me out here a minute." He shifted his body toward her, and she saw he had taken his penis out of his fly. He reached for her hand.

The girl shouted, "Now wait a goddamn second!"

"Hey, hey, Maggie, don't get upset. Just hold the phone. Stay calm." Welshinger reached under the seat with his other hand and brought up a revolver. He held it loose in his left hand while he took Maggie's hand in his other and drew it to his penis. "This is just to help you concentrate, to help you attend to the task at hand." He pressed her fingers against his penis, and it began to lengthen, until it was twice as long as the palm of her hand. "Go on, honey. You know what to do. Don't tell me you don't know what to do."

"You ain't no friend of Wesley's," the girl said, beginning with a hiss and ending with a sob.

He laid the barrel of the revolver against the side of her head. "Sure I am, honey. Why, you got no idea how close we are. No idea at all. Anyhow, that's neither here nor there." He unfastened his belt and the top of his trousers and leaned back, letting the length of his penis ride on the top of his belly. "Now, take a gander. Is Wes bigger than—" Welshinger broke off, then continued. "No, no way. Nobody is, nobody in the whole fucking world."

He sat up and took the girl's hand and cupped her fingers around the pendulous bulk of his scrotum. "Feel my nuts, honey. Feel how big, feel . . . the weight," he rasped, almost whispered. He put her hand back on the shaft of his penis. The girl began to sob again, and he pressed the gun barrel harder against her. "I don't want a lot of racket. I don't like that. You just stay calm. All we're going to do is what you do with Wes. Won't take but a

284

minute. I don't like to waste time. Hell, I'm not even sure if I like to do this anymore. Too fucking tired. But I sort of have to. Once it's done, I can rest, ease up."

Welshinger looked at the girl, and she averted her face as soon as her eyes met his. He said, "Hey, don't cry. This ain't nothing. This is just how it is, how the world has to be, Maggie." He brushed the tears from the side of her face with his free hand and rested it on her neck, and then he said, "Now, you take off that coat, lay it out on the seat, so I can get a good look at you, see how pretty you are."

Wesley had O'Connor drive him home that evening. In the wake of purchasing the green coat, he'd decided to buy a new radio and couldn't see carrying it home on the streetcar. He never listened to the radio himself, and when Rose had passed on, he'd let the little wooden box that was shaped like a Gothic arch, like a tabernacle, gather dust and let the tubes fizzle out one by one. When Maggie first switched it on, shortly after she'd moved in, it played okay for a week and then let out a yelp and a deep hum, before it finally died altogether. It had been for Maggie's sake that he'd bought the new radio, although he'd begun to imagine himself starting to follow the news programs and maybe some of the crime serials. More than that, he imagined there being music, and Maggie humming and singing along with it, her voice and her breath coursing soft through the house, sounding like a tree aquiver with wind and birds.

She wasn't home when he came in, and he thought so much the better—now he could hide the radio away in Louise's room. He really was going to wait until Christmas to bring it out, or maybe Christmas Eve. He sat in the kitchen and ate one of the meringues she'd baked last night. She'd gone on about how "dainty" they were, like little clouds and snowdrifts. He hadn't had the heart to tell her that to his mind they tasted like cotton candy that had set up like Portland cement, that they made him fear for his teeth.

At six-thirty, Wesley made himself a pot of coffee. He fiddled with the percolator—he wasn't sure how much coffee went in the basket or if the thing could somehow explode on the stove burner—and tried to pretend he hadn't begun to worry, that anxiety wasn't creeping up his back like a cold draft under his shirt. At first he thought something might have happened to her; later, around nine, when he'd finished the coffee and dug out the bottle of Four Roses from under the sink and peeled the cellophane from a fresh pack of cigarettes, he conjured her lighting out on him, although to where or for what reason he could not imagine, and he was not sure which was more terrifying, the fact that he might have been betrayed or his incapacity to have ever imagined the possibility before. To free himself from that thought, he returned to the other—that some mishap had befallen her—and so he passed the evening, embracing alternate varieties of apprehension, alternative scenarios of losing everything by virtue of losing her.

At some point in the night, he got up from the table, from the empty glass and the brimming ashtray, and went to the davenport. He must have slept, at least briefly, and then at four-thirty he got up and made coffee again. He'd slept in his suit and shoes, and now he bundled himself against the ice-water cold of the coldest hour of the night and went out. He waited for the streetcar, looking for one of the dim lights in the far distance that he thought might be its headlamp to move a little ways in his direction. But it never came, or perhaps he could not bear to wait any longer, and he began to walk. At about five-thirty he reached the steam laundry, and he stood outside, shuffling his feet, hunching his shoulders, feeling dread flood his stomach like the bilge of a torpedoed ship, feeling some hope or rationalization momentarily pump it out, and then, overwhelmed, its filling once again.

At five minutes before six, the girls and their boss arrived, and Wesley stood shivering by the door, his hands gesticulating, quaking, while he asked them, one by one, what they knew. They all knew the same thing: that she had left at her regular time, happy as a magpie in her new coat, and stated no intention to do anything other than go home and bake something or other.

By six-thirty, he was at the station, at his desk, telephoning the hospitals and the bus depot and the railway police. At midmorning, he had O'Connor drive him home and bring him back, and then at lunchtime he went home again on the streetcar, and after he'd had O'Connor drive him home yet again at three o'clock— to a still empty house—he began to despair. He wondered if he ought to say something, just by the by, to Missing Persons, and then he realized that since Stan Bauer's retirement in October, *he* was Missing Persons. The reason for that—other than the fact that Missing Persons couldn't justify a full-time officer—was that there was no better hunt-and-sniff detective in the department than Wesley, or so they said. That was rich, now that he was picking his brains up off the floor like pieces of broken mirror, a dumb cop with no more smarts than a cabbage.

At five-thirty, he had O'Connor get the car and drive him home again, and after he went in and came out, he asked O'Connor to wait outside the package store while he bought a carton of smokes and two ponies of Four Roses. He told O'Connor to drive him to Shacktown and had him wait in the car while he got out. There were three or four fires burning, and maybe five or six tramps cooking their supper, all of whom scampered back into the shadows when they saw him striding up the slope.

Wesley went to each fire and called into the apparently empty night, "This ain't a roust. Just looking for a friend." The tramps came out, their heads emerging into the firelight like gophers from their holes, and he asked them if they'd seen a girl who used to flop here, now probably dressed in a green overcoat, and all the tramps said no, nobody had come last night or today, that it was cold and too deep into winter for any woman with sense to come out here.

After repeating this procedure at each of the fires, Wesley went up the slope to the wrecked locomotive where he'd first found Maggie. Someone had built a fire, now dead, at the front of the cylinder, and someone else had dragged a mattress inside. Wesley stepped past it and aimed his flashlight up to the far end. A cascade of ice sheeted down like a frozen waterfall, almost covering the pallet he'd found Maggie and her Billy on. Even in the cold, utterly dark and half buried in the ground and in the snow, the cylinder smelled fetid, of urine and sour bodies. Wesley lit a cigarette and stood awhile, letting his smoke roll along the cylinder, luminous in the flashlight beam like clouds under the moon. Then he walked down the slope, got into the car, and told O'Connor to drop him back at the station and take himself on home for the night.

At his desk, Wesley dialed the number of the telephone in his house and let it ring. He let it go on ringing while he smoked an entire cigarette, maybe for four or five minutes, and he hung up. He felt tears on his face, and he lit another cigarette to keep himself from sobbing. After he collected himself, he stood up and strode down the hall to the vice office.

Trent looked up from his desk as though he'd been filing his nails or performing some other act with great fastidiousness, although in fact he'd only been working a crossword. Wesley said, "Where's the monsignor?"

"Don't know. Gone for the day, I guess."

Wesley moved to the desk and fanned out his fingers on it like he was setting down a hand of cards. "Don't shit me, Hank. You guys keep tabs on each other. If he was my partner, I'd be damned sure to know where he was, just to mind my own back. So where is he?"

"He doesn't like to be bothered when he's off duty."

"I said not to shit me. Don't . . . fuck me either."

"Look, Wes, he doesn't tell me where he goes. I got a telephone number where I can find him some nights. That's it."

"So maybe I could just give him a little telephone call."

"Probably make him mad. But suit yourself. Better have a good reason." Trent wrote a number on a pad and tore off a slip. "Here."

Wesley said, "Obliged," and went back to his desk. He put his finger on the phone and felt frightened. He decided to walk down the street, toward the depot, and call from a phone booth. Once inside, he pushed himself into the corner as if to warm himself, put a nickel in the slot, and dialed.

"Cherokee," a voice answered.

"Lieutenant Welshinger there?"

"Sure. Wait a minute."

Wesley heard voices and the sound of furniture sliding in an empty room, and then Welshinger came on. "Yeah?"

"It's Wes Horner," Wesley said, and then added, "Sorry to bother you out of duty hours. Trent gave me the number. Didn't want to, but I was persistent."

"Hell, Wes, that's okay. Always glad to talk to you," Welshinger said. "You know that. So what can I do for you?"

"My girl's gone missing, gone since she got off work yesterday."

"Your girl? I thought she tore off to Chicago or some such with a fellow a few years back."

"You know what I'm talking about," Wesley said. "Maggie, the girl that's been . . . with me the last two months."

"Oh, her?" Welshinger said. "Gone missing? Heavens, Wes, I'm really sorry to hear that."

"I thought you might know something about it."

"Me? I haven't heard a thing. Spent the day processing whores and pimps like usual. Just now I was having a nice little cocktail."

"You said things, threats," Wesley said. "So I figured I ought to start with you."

"Well, I'm glad you consider me a man of my word, but I'm sure I don't have anything to offer you. I mean, Wes, these girls like that one are awfully . . . fickle. Did you ever stop to think she might have just moved on?"

"Christ," Wesley said, clenching his jaw hard. "I know what you said. And if you did it, did anything to her, I'll kill you." He stopped and lowered his voice. "So talk to me, or I'll come down there. I'm past caring, Welshinger, I truly am."

There was no sound for a moment, and then Welshinger said, "I think it's best if I just forget that I heard that, Wes. Threatening a police officer, blackmailing a police officer, is a very serious matter."

"You threatened me, you threatened my girl."

"I don't know anything about that, Wes. I mean, maybe it sounded that way to you," Welshinger said. "You can be a little naive, Wes. I may have offered my opinion, and you may have mistook it for something else. Most of the time the future isn't really very mysterious, if you look at it carefully. People do stupid things, and then stupid or unpleasant things happen to them. It's about that simple. Now, most people might call that fate or happenstance, but to me—to somebody with a scientific bent—it's just cause and effect. And that's probably exactly the kind of thing I was saying, and you just went and misunderstood."

"I think I better come down there."

"I don't think that's wise, Wes. I'm just going to finish this cocktail, and then I'm going to pack it in," Welshinger said. "You come in and see me tomorrow, first thing if you like."

"Look, you've got to . . . help me."

"I will, Wes, I will. You come in and see me, and we'll talk all about it. Hell, maybe she'll come home before then. I mean, these girls know where their bread is buttered," Welshinger said. "So maybe there's a good chance she'll be back, maybe not. Anyhow, not exactly a looker, was she? I mean, I know she was special to you. Hey, bet she looked swell in that coat you were carrying in the box the other day."

Wesley said, "I never said what was in that box."

"Oh, I'm pretty sure you did, Wes, but who knows. I got a sixth sense, a knack for all this stuff. Anyhow, we'll have a nice chat about the whole business tomorrow," Welshinger said, and before Wesley could reply, Welshinger was gone.

They said he fell from the High Bridge like a shooting star, like something aflame, and then he hit and went through the river ice with a hiss and disappeared. That was what the two tramps drinking Tokay wine, huddled under a hedge on Prospect Boulevard, said—the two tramps Welshinger had rousted at Shacktown back in October. Maybe before he jumped he had lit a cigarette and smoked it, standing at the rail, and tossed it down, or fell still somehow clutching it. Of course, no one could recall if Welshinger smoked in the first place, and on the other hand, the tramps were adamant, even after they'd been in the tank for thirty-six hours.

In any case, after he came back from the telephone, he had drunk down the last of his Manhattan and picked up his hat and said, "Well, that about finishes me."

The bartender said, "You have a good holiday, Lieutenant."

"You bet," said Welshinger. "Going to take a good long rest, lay down these weary bones." Then he went out, and that was the last anyone saw of him, except for the tramps; and even the hole in the ice was half frozen, closing back up like a camera's iris, when the county sheriff's crew went down to look at it the next morning. They never found a body, not then, not in the spring breakup, not ever.

Hank Trent took care of Welshinger's car, which was sold, the proceeds put into the Police Officers' Widows and Orphans Fund. He simonized it one last time and, in the station house, passed out the booze and cigarettes and nylons that had been in the trunk. The rest of the stuff in the trunk, which nobody saw because it was of no consequence to anybody, he dropped off at the Saint Vincent de Paul store: Charlene Mortensen's shoes, Ruby Fahey's swimsuit, Maggie's coat.

Wesley did not quite know how he ought to connect up Welshinger's act with Maggie's disappearance, or whether he ought to bother at all. He supposed he ought to regard Welshinger's passing as good riddance, but then he would think back to that last phone conversation and wonder if the leap from the High Bridge wasn't just Welshinger having the last laugh, his final, insouciant fuck-you to Wesley. Whatever Welshinger knew about Maggie, Wesley would now never know.

He awoke Christmas morning to find the sky broad and clear, blue as ice, and by midmorning he had come to believe that Maggie was not going to return. It was not that he had thought the matter through and concluded that this must be the case, but that he had succeeded in adopting the belief as an expedience, to muffle the agony of the past three days into a mere ache that might be tolerable, even if it had to last the rest of his life.

By noon, he'd drunk all the coffee in the pot and eaten every cookie left in the house, and then he persuaded himself to get the fifth of Four Roses from under the sink and set to work on it. While he was at it, he got out the carton of cigarettes he'd bought the day before and removed all the packs. Then he put the bottle and the cigarettes on the doily on the dining table, and drank from the bottle and stacked the cigarette packs in different configurations: in green towers and bunkers and ships and ice palaces. After an hour, he took the notion to get out the radio he'd bought. When he stood, he found that one of his legs leaned akimbo of the other, like he was a schoolkid's compass set to inscribe a steep arc, and it took him a little while to sort himself out, to make his way to Louise's room.

Wesley carried the radio back to the dining table cradled in both arms, and he set it down. It was dark-brown Bakelite with ivory knobs and a strip of brass trim around the window where the needle moved over the frequency numbers. He plugged it in and turned the knob and waited. After a time, he heard a hum, and he could see a glow like embers through the radio's ventilator grille. He waited awhile, and then he realized he would have to tune in a station if he was going to listen to anything. He didn't know any of the numbers, exactly, but he thought there was something around 800, and sure enough, he found some music playing in that vicinity.

The music—Christmas carols, mostly—suited him for a while. But as he listened, the music began to grate on him and then to outright annoy him, to feel like bugs in his scalp, and after a time he was so mad he was ready to hurl the radio away or, as he conceived, to take it out to the kitchen, set it in the soup kettle, and boil it. But he couldn't bring himself to do either of those things, so he just snapped the cord out of the wall and shoved the damn thing under Louise's bed again.

Then he went back to the table, back to the half inch of whiskey left in the bottle, and he began to weep, not so much for Maggie and what he'd lost, but because he was spending this Christmas as he'd spent last Christmas, albeit less soberly. He couldn't recall being bothered by it last year, but this year it harrowed his heart, because he had had, for a moment, his heart's desire and could remember having it. Last Christmas he had expected nothing, received nothing, remembered nothing, and he had been, in his way, at peace.

Wesley sat at the table until four o'clock, and then, when it was full dark and he knew no neighbor could see, he picked up the Christmas tree like a spear, still bristling with balls, foil, yarn, ribbon, and garlands, and carried it hurriedly through the kitchen, shouldered open the back door, and flung it into the yard. By evening it began to snow, and the snow continued through the night while the lights burned in Wesley's little house, in his kitchen and over Louise's bed. By dawn, the tree was completely buried in snow yet still discernible in form, like a white dory pulled from the sea and inverted on white sand, asleep on its gunwales.

*   *   *

Monday, Day 46

December 25, 1939

When the guard slid the tray in this morning he wished me Merry Christmas, so now, at last, I know what date it is and may keep a more normal sort of calendar. As for the rest, I have been recalling Christmases past with Nanna and, strangely enough, more recent Christmases. For example, I seem to remember one Christmas at which the secretaries at Griggs-Cooper dressed me up as Humpty-Dumpty for the office party. I am quite sure this was around the time that the King abdicated and President Roosevelt was reelected, so I suppose that must have been three years ago, 1936. Now, that is in the part of time I believed I could not remember, but in fact I am sure that if I wanted to, I might recall every Christmas during the last ten or fifteen years. Oddly, I associate this somehow with the star, as though little by little its light has been illuminating all the past that has heretofore been invisible to me; and that is the gift of the star.

Now I try this a little more, and I think: 1937, and there it is—there was another party, but no costumes this time, and Mr. Wright got quite overwrought and began to sob during his little address. That was also around the time the stock market gave everyone such a fright, as though it might be '29 all over again. And I made myself a canned ham that year for Christmas dinner.

Now I shall try 1935, and I find myself saying, "Of course!" for in December *Rio Negro* with Veronica Galvin opened at the Paramount. I had spent a lot of time earlier in the year writing chain letters—it was rather a fad all over the country—and I wondered if I would get any Christmas cards on that account, but I did not. On the other hand, I saw *Rio Negro* twice. At the office, we got Christmas bonuses, the first since before the slump, and I spent part of mine at Holm & Olson on corsages for the secretaries and some of the girls at the Aragon.

I feel I could continue in this manner indefinitely, recollecting each year and month as though unwrapping Christmas parcels, but I suppose it would be silly to write it all down—as I remember I once did—for now that I have a memory, there is no cause to. But just as a record of an experiment, so to speak, I record the following, to wit:

CHARLES A. LINDBERGH

May 1927—flies alone across the Atlantic to Paris, France

June 1929—marries Anne Morrow

March 1932—Lindbergh baby kidnapped by Bruno Richard Hauptmann

September 1934—Hauptmann arrested

Christmas 1935—Lindbergh moves to England

April 1936—Hauptmann executed

1939—Lindbergh returns home to warn us of involvement in Europe's war

That is twelve years recollected, easy as pie. As I say, it is silly to write it down—particularly since I have a limited amount of "paper"—but rather fun nonetheless, like playing ticktacktoe. It is a marvelous toy I have been given this Christmas, indeed! It is everything I have ever wanted.

Tuesday, Day 47
December 26, 1939

One thousand, nine hundred and thirty-nine years ago today, King Herod orders the slaughter of the innocents in Palestine

1914—my last Christmas with Father

Wednesday, Day 48

December 27, 1939

A Brief History of 1938

January—*Grand Central Terminal* at the Orpheum

February—Chancellor Hitler takes command of German armed forces

March—Floods in California

April—Austria annexed to Germany

May—Griggs-Cooper office picnic, Como Park

June—Louis–Schmeling boxing match

July—Howard Hughes flies around the world

August—*To Marry and to Burn* at the Tower

September—Prime Minister Chamberlain visits Chancellor Hitler in Munich

October—*The War of the Worlds* broadcast, with Mr. Orson Welles

November—Harold Stassen of West St. Paul elected governor

December—I buy small spruce for Christmas tree and photograph it.

Thursday, Day 49

December 28, 1939

My Typical Day, circa 1930 to 1939

7 A.M.—Rise, wash, shave, toast and tea

7:30 A.M.—Walk to Selby Street, board streetcar

8 A.M.—Work at Griggs-Cooper & Co.

10:30 A.M.—Coffee break

12 noon—Lunchtime. Buy sandwich in Pioneer Building. Sometimes visit St. Paul Union Depot or run "errands" to Fisher Photo, St. Paul Book & Stationery Co.

1 P.M.—Work

2:30 P.M.—Coffee break

5 P.M.—Home and supper, walk if weather is fine, otherwise streetcar. Two or three nights eat at White Castle at Seven Corners, otherwise hash, stew, etc. at home, with Sanka

6:30 or 7 P.M.—Work in darkroom, listen to radio music program

8 P.M.—Work on scrapbook

9 P.M.—Read, usually Lord Tennyson, Whitman, George Eliot, Trollope, Conrad

10 P.M.—To bed

Saturday—work 8:00–12:00 noon, lunch at White Castle, photography sessions, visit Aragon Ballroom at early evening

Sunday—darkroom work; attend pictures; more darkroom work; scrapbook from Sunday paper

Friday, Day 50
December 29, 1939

I read the above, and I think of how little there is of the particular in it; that one day of my life might very well have been another, year after year. And what I remember in detail I can rarely put an exact date to. At the time, and even now, what was most vivid to me is the walk home on those days when I did not ride the streetcar. I remember trees, or not so much trees as the leaves climbing the hill up to the cathedral and along the avenue, and I feel myself moving through and among them. In summer, at the bottom of the hill, I cannot see the Wilder Mansion for the leaves, or sometimes even the sky. And between the leaves overhanging above and the grass on the hill below, I might be standing inside a brilliant green Christmas tree ball—inside it, with the light shining through onto me. Then, in the autumn, little by little, the leaves begin to color, to flare, and to shrink back, and there are patches of blue among them as they shrivel, and one day I notice they are utterly fallen and decaying in the streets and on the grass, and the limbs stand naked against the blue, the bones that were beneath the green. Sometimes I wade through the leaves on the ground, knee deep, and they rustle against my legs and shatter under my feet. It is rather the same in the winter, in the snow—the leaves are like water one wades through, and the snow the same but heavier and denser, like water driven by the wind, like I remember the waves being in the Pacific Ocean. That was only two months ago. I wonder what happened to the glass globe I found. I wonder what happened to the boy on the beach. But that is neither here nor there and has nothing to do with leaves, save that in the spring they come in surprise, in ambush. One day you notice the buds studding the branches, the tiny pricks of green among the brown and gray, and they are, I suppose, like tiny globes of green glass that appear out of nowhere, and then it seems there is nothing else in the world.

Saturday, Day 51
December 30, 1939

That green, and the green of Miss Ruby's eyes. But I do not want to see that, to recollect it. Although to have a memory like everybody else's has been my most fervent desire throughout my life, now, in this circumstance, it would be unbearable. I shall have to avert my eyes, to compel myself to forget.

Sunday, Day 52
December 31, 1939

Some Notes on the World's Fair Time Capsule

The time capsule is about seven feet long and shaped like a

bullet. It is made of a copper alloy designed to resist corrosion and is filled with a gas that will preserve the contents. It is buried fifty feet under the Westinghouse Pavilion and is to be unearthed in 5,000 years, that is, in 6939 A.D. A book detailing its location has been deposited in all the nation's great libraries. Among its contents are: a Bible; a grammar of the English language; cosmetics; small tools; a woman's hat; a library of seventy-five books on acetate film; newspapers and magazines of our day; motion picture film, together with instructions on how to construct a motion picture projector.

That is most of what I can recall about the time capsule. I remember that at the time of its burial, it struck me as the most striking event of the Fair, a truly fantastical notion. For merely to imagine the world existing five thousand years hence seems beyond anyone's powers, or at least beyond mine. Stranger still is to picture the people of that time picturing the people of ours, or to picture that long a passage of time. Five thousand years before our time is I suppose about the time of the biblical Noah, or perhaps earlier; perhaps when we were living in caves, or perhaps before there were people at all that any of us should recognize as human.

I suppose when those future people dig the capsule up— when they literally "delve into the past"—we shall seem very primitive and rather pathetic to them, unless of course they have themselves not advanced or have in fact reverted to some less civilized stage of development. In that case, I suppose we might seem as the mythic figures of a golden age, like Greek gods. I was pleased to see that motion picture films were placed inside the capsule, although I do not know if these are dramatic pictures or newsreels. I would like to think that they would put a popular movie in, as even though the story might not be "true," I should think it would offer tremendous insight into the state of the human heart in our time. It should certainly reveal something of the nature of a life like mine, for although I suppose it has been unremarkable in almost every respect, there have been moments in it—I think of being with Miss Ruby, and I think of being arrested—when I have felt that a movie was all it could possibly be, or all that could ever do the experience justice. Not that anyone five thousand years from now, or even fifty years from now, will remember me or so much as hear my name. Of course, perhaps something might survive—my scrapbooks, some of my photographs, the journal I started last autumn, or even perhaps this wall and what I have written on it, if it is not painted over. Perhaps someone will uncover it, half obscured by dirt and weeds or whatever, and think: Now, who was this chap? But they shall never really know, just as now, when at last it seems I am able to remember most everything, I see that all I ever really recover are fragments, the shadow, the husk of what was once the green leaf.

That is the sad thing about memory, I suppose. It goes without saying that search as we will, we cannot know the future; but it seems we cannot even know the past, however much we search it; and so we are always longing for it and seeing it beyond our reach, anticipating what is past as though it were to come. In that way, having a memory is terribly sad, like visiting a graveyard, where even at the loveliest of times one must finally confess that underneath the verdure there are only the dead and gone, that which is lost to us, the things we once loved, that we still love. Now that I have it, I suppose that is all memory really is, for the most part: the hunger for what we have loved.

Tomorrow we commence the new year 1940 and the new decade.

Wesley supposed that there might not be a body until spring, disgorged in the breakup of the river, revealed in the melting of the snow; and then he would catch himself and feel ashamed. He had no reason to believe she was dead—he only knew she was gone—but a part of him simply wanted the certitude of seeing her flesh, of knowing where she was: an end of the story, or rather, for him, a beginning, for then he could do the one thing he knew how to do, track her killer. It was the only thing he could do for her, but it depended on her being dead, and he did not wish her dead.

In the days after the first of the year, in his calmer moments, he accepted that she had simply lit out for reasons of her own or had been compelled to do so. When he looked at the latter explanation, it seemed reasonable to assume that Welshinger had gotten to her, had threatened her, and she had taken the threat seriously. That was the likeliest explanation. Sometimes Wesley had thought Welshinger was simply a bully who'd lucked onto the tools of intimidation reserved for the police, but at other times he had to admit there was something weirder than that about him, as though he were a Lazarus brought back from the dead with a terrible hangover. Wesley recollected their last telephone conversation again and again. Welshinger seemed to be prepared to gloat about something, but that was his way, the sour, spoilsport triumph of a man who's won all the prizes but believes the prizes are worthless.

Wesley supposed that if they had met the next morning, Welshinger would have admitted nothing, but with his eyes, with the corners of his mouth, he would have communicated that he'd made good on his threat. So why did he forgo rubbing Wesley's face in that? Did his killing himself mean that Welshinger had won or had lost? Wesley certainly hadn't won. The captain had treated him like a rookie who needed reminding that the department did not reopen cases the district attorney had closed, cases the district attorney would no more want to open than he would his fly before his crowd of election-night well-wishers. Then, to seal his humiliation, Wesley had lost Maggie too. Finally, he'd lost his only means to make any difference, because he couldn't do anything about Maggie's disappearance, not without her body or some sign, some trace of it. So he settled for what he could do, for an action that would to him seem at least the simulacrum of his still being a detective, of being Lieutenant Wesley Horner. He decided to go see Herbert White.

Wesley had a friend who was well placed at Stillwater, Frank McCarthy, the officer who ran the guardroom and the prisoner intake, the very officer who'd checked White in two months before.

"So you working on something White might know about?" McCarthy asked Wesley on the telephone when he'd called.

"Nothing in particular, nothing official. Just a hunch I'm playing," Wesley said, adding, "I don't need to see him in an interview room. Just in his cell."

"You don't want to go down there, Wes. It's depressing."

"It's okay."

"We can't help you much if he gets disagreeable."

"He won't," Wesley said. "He's a pussycat."

"That's not what the papers said."

"The papers don't know him like I do."

Four days later, on the fourteenth of January, McCarthy took him down through the main block into solitary, pointing out cells occupied by men Wesley had helped put away. As he was opening the door to the stairs that went down to White's cell, McCarthy asked, "So what was it with Welshinger?"

"I don't know." Wesley shrugged.

"Always seemed like the cock of the walk to me, like the cat who swallowed the canary."

"Guess the canary didn't agree with him," Wesley said.

They descended as if going down into the bilge of a ship, darker, colder, and more fetid with each step. When they got to White's cell, Wesley could smell the odors of the bucket, of motionless air, before McCarthy even opened the door.

"Give me fifteen minutes," Wesley said. McCarthy nodded and closed the door behind him.

"Lieutenant Horner," White said, lifting himself off the bed. As he stood, it seemed his head must brush the ceiling. At any rate, the lightbulb hung even with his eyes, glaring against the greasy curls of his beard and the limp strands of his hair. He wore a denim tunic like a railroad engineer's and his feet were bare, although Wesley saw there was a pair of shoes set under the head of the cot. White put out his hand, pallid as a fish's belly, the fingernails exceedingly long but, Wesley saw, nonetheless clean. Wesley took the hand. "Mr. White," he said.

"I don't get many visitors," White said. He laughed. "In fact, I haven't had any until now. So you're very kind to come. Have a seat."

Wesley looked at the cot and said, "That's okay. I'll stand." Eyeing the bucket, he moved to the opposite corner of the cell, next to a window whose outside was blocked by an impasto of rotting leaves and snow.

"How can I help you?" White said, standing at the foot of the cot.

"I had some questions, some follow-up to your case."

"It all seems rather cut-and-dried—rather a long time ago—to me these days, but please be my guest."

Wesley could not think exactly what it was he wanted to ask, or if in fact he wanted to ask anything at all. He finally said, "I've been thinking a lot about your case, about the trial and the confession. I can't quite get a handle on your confession, can't quite get it to sit right with me."

"I see," White said.

"Thing is, I keep wondering if it was all aboveboard—if you gave it or if maybe Lieutenant Welshinger leaned on you a bit."

"Leaned on me?"

"Pressured you, threatened you."

"Oh, I don't think so," White said. "He was quite friendly, actually. He just reasoned with me. We had a long talk, and when we were done, it seemed that confessing was the thing to do."

"But he told you what to write, didn't he?"

"I suppose he did, but it wasn't anything that wasn't true," White said.

"But you couldn't remember what you'd done, so really he was putting words into your mouth, wasn't he?"

"Well, I suppose that's right. But after we'd talked, what he said really did seem to be the only thing that could have *been* the truth. You might say he proved that it was the truth, even if I couldn't recall it at the time," White said.

"At the time?" Wesley said. "You recall it now?"

"I don't recall it, no. But I remember what I was doing at the time . . . of the murders."

"You do?" Wesley said. He blew out a shallow gust of breath. "Christ. So now you remember. I suppose you remember everything."

"Well, perhaps not everything." White looked down, as though embarrassed. "But I do appear to have a . . . normal memory now."

"Sheesh, you got timing, bub," Wesley said, feeling angry. He looked hard at White. "You trying to make a monkey out of me? Again?"

White looked up at Wesley. "Certainly not. It just came. At Christmas. I don't know why or how."

"And I suppose now you remember doing those girls," Wesley said. "Or not doing them. Being at the pictures, a million miles away from the Lawton Steps, from the tunnel."

"There's no need for you to become . . . inflamed." White gestured around the cell. "After all, it's me in here, with this. Not you."

"Sorry. Beg your pardon," Wesley said. "So do you?"

"Do I remember? No, I don't. I believe I met Carla Marie LaBreque—"

"The Mortensen girl?"

"Yes. At the Aragon Ballroom. Just in passing, though. I'm sure I never photographed her."

"And the Fahey girl?" Wesley asked.

"Miss Ruby. Yes, of course. I remember being with her that day, the day they say I . . . hurt her. And we did have a tiff, and I did go down under the cathedral, but that was only because I was upset."

"You visit boiler rooms when you're upset?" Wesley found himself irritated. "Guess you take your comfort where you find it."

"No. I was looking for the priest. But he wasn't in his little house, his box."

"You were going to make a confession?"

"Well, I wanted to talk with him. I was very upset."

"But he wasn't there," Wesley said. "So why'd you go down below, down by the tunnel."

"I didn't know the tunnel connected with the basement. That

was neither here nor there. I was looking for the priest's box, and I opened the door. I suppose I'd already forgotten where it was. That's the way it was for me then. I was already forgetting where he was," White said. "It's funny. Now I remember. It's the third one on the left, as you stand looking at the back of the church."

"So you remember. So you also remember that you didn't kill those girls."

"I don't remember *not* killing them," White said. "And what the lieutenant said, the one who took my confession, was that even with a normal memory I might have done it and blanked it out."

Wesley extracted a cigarette, lit it, and drew on it furiously. "This is the same old crap, Herbert. I mean, you like it in here? What the hell do you want me to do for you anyhow?"

"Actually, it was you who came to see me," White said quietly. "But you *could* do something for me."

"And what's that?"

"Ask that priest to come and see me."

"You want to confess to him?"

"Well, talk to him. Confess, if you like, I suppose."

"Confess what?" Wesley said.

"I'm not sure," White said. "I'll know when I confess it."

"Going to keep me guessing, huh," Wesley said. "But that's okay. I play the fool for lots of people." He drew again on the cigarette. "I'll see what I can do. Third box on the left, right?"

"Facing the back, yes," White said. "You know, I don't believe I hurt Miss Ruby."

"So if you know that, why don't you just say so?"

"I didn't say I knew it. I said I believed. It's not the same thing."

"Suit yourself," said Wesley. "Sounds like hairsplitting to me. Anyhow, why do you believe that?"

"Because I loved her."

"People do some pretty sick, evil stuff on account of love."

White said, "I don't know about that. Maybe love just loses its way. Maybe it just forgets itself. So it's not love anymore. Not until it finds itself. Until it remembers itself."

"Beats me," Wesley said, thinking of Maggie on the highway somewhere, maybe on Highway 2, thumbing a ride right through—right past—New Upsala, North Dakota. "Beats me."

Wesley found the priest just where White said he would be, in a box on the north side. It had been in the early afternoon, two days later, and it was still light outside. In fact, it was still light inside the cathedral, even if to Wesley the cathedral felt dark, its air heavy, lousy with incense and the flickering and spitting of a thousand candles. It was not an atmosphere Wesley found comfortable. It was not quite American. It was like an immigrant kitchen where they cooked and ate the parts of the pig normal people threw away.

Wesley didn't know if he should knock on the door of the box, or just go in. He watched an old lady enter another box, clutching a small book that trailed colored ribbons in one hand and a string of beads in the other, and he followed her example. Inside, there was a little wooden seat, and he sat on it and then he said, "Hello?"

A grille slid open, and the shadowy head behind it said, "Yes?"

Wesley said, "You're the priest?"

"Yes."

"The one that's always here, in this box?"

"Yes. Always here. Did you want me to hear your confession?"

Wesley said, "Ah . . . no. I'm a police officer. I'm a Lutheran."

"That's quite a combination," the priest said. "Actually, perhaps a rather natural one—"

"It's my folks that was Lutheran."

"Well, be that as it may, did you want to make a confession? Or to talk to me?"

"It's sort of police business, really," Wesley said.

"Oh, have I done something?" The priest snorted quietly. "Usually it's the other way around in here, you see."

"Oh, no, no. Not at all," Wesley said. His nervousness was not abating. "There's a prisoner in Stillwater that wants to see you, and I told him I'd try to arrange it."

"Well, you know they have their own mission up there for the prisoners."

"He wanted to see you. Said he'd confessed to you before."

"So he's a member of this parish."

"I don't know," Wesley said. "I guess so. Maybe you read about him in the paper. His name's Herbert—"

"You mustn't tell me anything like that. It's not important," the priest said. "But I'll go. It would have to be next week, I'm afraid. And I'd have to find transport. I haven't a motorcar."

"I could drive you, me and my partner," Wesley said. "Wouldn't be no trouble."

"Very well. What about next Monday?"

"That would be swell."

"You can pick me up at the rectory behind the cathedral, where the tunnel comes up. Say, at nine o'clock."

"Sure. That's great."

"Very well," the priest said. "I shall see you then." The grille slid closed, and Wesley emerged into the church. When he got outside, past the door, he breathed deeply, as though he had been

309

holding his breath to protect his senses against some overpowering smell, or as though he had been underwater.

January 3, 1940

Dear Friend,

Thank you ever so much for your kind letter. I am always delighted to hear from my fans.

I am enclosing a personally autographed photograph which I hope you will enjoy.

And remember to look for me next month at a theater near you in Pantheon Pictures' *Hell's Canyon*! It's my most thrilling role yet—the story of a woman trapped in a desperate, ill-starred love affair with a man on the run, set in the towering desolation of the American West!

Yours very sincerely,

Veronica Galvin

The following Monday, Wesley and O'Connor picked up the priest by the tunnel head. He was corpulent and wore a black gown and a three-cornered hat with a little pompom on top. In fact, he looked a little like Herbert White costumed in something akin to a Shriner's getup.

O'Connor drove and chatted with the priest in his professional Irishman's mode, calling the priest "Monsignor" and talking about what a sweet soul his mother was. Wesley turned around in his seat and saw that the priest was in fact immersed in a fat little book not unlike the one the old lady in the cathedral had carried into the box. Once in a while his lips moved, and sometimes a tiny sigh escaped.

At Stillwater, Wesley and O'Connor turned the priest over to Frank McCarthy. Then the three of them waited in the guardroom, smoking and passing the time of day for over an hour. Wesley asked how White was getting along.

"He ain't in the population. Nobody to get along with," said McCarthy.

"No, I mean is he going nuts or anything?"

"Not that I heard. Slop patrol caught him writing on the wall. I suppose he ought to get some discipline for that," McCarthy said. "Of course, when he came in he got a pretty good boot massage. Didn't stand up for pretty near a week."

"Whose idea was that?"

"Oh, it's pretty standard for new recruits, especially if they've messed with women or children. And I suspect Welshinger put the word out to give it to him with all the trimmings."

Wesley frowned. "Well, Welshinger's dead. I ain't. So maybe you could put the word out to back off him. As a favor to me."

"I could try. But solitary is solitary."

"Okay, but let him do his scribbling," Wesley said. "I might want to see it, for official reasons. That's a good enough excuse. I think I'll even get him some paper. It ain't going to do anyone any harm."

"I got no problem with that," said McCarthy.

When the priest came out and they got back into the car, they rode for a while in silence, the priest reimmersed in his book. But after ten minutes Wesley could no longer contain himself. He turned around and leaned over the back seat. "So what did he tell you?" Wesley asked.

The priest looked straight at Wesley and said, "You know I can't tell you that, Lieutenant."

"I don't know nothing. I'm a Lutheran. Or at least my folks were."

"I suspect that even a Lutheran police officer knows I can't break the seal of the confessional."

"The seal?" Wesley said.

O'Connor inserted himself into the conversation. "Not the kind that balances a ball on its nose, Wes, the kind you throw a fish to." He laughed. O'Connor called over his shoulder, "Hey, Monsignor, that ain't a blasphemy, saying that, is it?"

"No. Callow, inane, perhaps. But not a mortal sin." The priest turned back to Wesley. "I can't divulge what is said to me during confession. Period."

Wesley exhaled and turned to the front of the car. After a time, he said, "It's just that I think maybe this guy shouldn't be in prison—that maybe he didn't do what he was convicted of."

"I see."

"I mean, he confessed to us—well, to another cop—but I'm not sure it was the truth. You know, he had this flaky memory, and he couldn't even say what he'd done or not done at the time." Wesley stopped and took out his cigarettes. "Smoke?" he said to the priest.

"Please."

Wesley handed the priest a cigarette and continued. "Now he says his memory's come back. So I was wondering . . ." Wesley stopped to hold the lighter up to the priest's face. "I was wondering if he might have said something to you, something to establish his innocence."

The priest blew out smoke and said, "I'm sorry. I really can't say."

Wesley's face colored, and he was aware of clenching his teeth. "Look. I'm trying to set this out straight for you. This could be an innocent man rotting in jail, in solitary. You smelled it. It's hell." Wesley tried to lower his voice. "I'd think if your church had a heart, it would want to do something about that."

The priest said nothing, and then he drew on his cigarette. "I like to think it has a heart, although I suppose some might say that's debatable." He stopped again, and then he said, "I will tell you something, and I suppose under the circumstances it would be correct to do so. But it is strictly confidential, all right?"

"Sure, of course," Wesley said. "So tell me. Please."

The priest began. "I will tell you that he didn't say anything to me that was . . . germane to what you mentioned, to his guilt or innocence."

"Christ on a crutch," Wesley sputtered.

"Wes, you can't talk like that in front of a priest," O'Connor interjected.

"Or, really, anyone at all," the priest said.

"I told you I was a Lutheran!" Wesley said.

The priest smiled. "That's the worst excuse I've ever heard."

"Look, I'm sorry. I got carried away." Wesley said, and turned away, biting the tip of his thumb, then tried again. "So there's nothing else you can tell me that he said? Or just that you said to him?"

"Only what I would say to anyone in his position. Or even to you."

"So shoot," Wesley said.

"I told him today was the feast of Saint Thomas Aquinas and that he ought to pray to him, to the angelic doctor—"

"A doctor for angels? The ones with broken wings, I bet."

"Watch it, Wes," O'Connor cut in.

"Saint Thomas is called that because of the majesty of his theology. He proved that God not only exists, but that He is good and that His creation must also be good," the priest continued. "Even men, men at their worst."

"I bet White liked that," Wesley said.

"I think he did. I think perhaps he already knew it."

"So he's a believer, a Catholic?"

"Not formally. But a believer, yes. It might have just been another one of those things he'd forgotten he knew."

"Like what else?" Wesley said quickly. "Like something about those girls—"

The priest silenced him with a smile. "I won't be drawn, Lieutenant. A valiant effort, but no cigar, I'm afraid."

Wesley faced forward and shook his head back and forth. "I really lucked out with this crew, O'Connor. Everybody's either got no memory or might as well not." He turned back to the priest. "Okay, I give up. So what else did you say to him? That it's . . . kosher to say to me?"

"I gave him a quotation from Pascal," the priest said as he ground out his cigarette in the ashtray mounted on the back of the seat. It says, 'If I had not known you, I would not have found you.' "

Wesley looked at the priest quizzically. "So?"

"It's about looking for God—that it's not that we stumble across Him somehow, having never known Him, but that even though it might not be apparent, we knew Him all along; that our seeking Him, our searching, is really a kind of remembering."

"I guess he liked that too. Sounds just like him."

"I suppose anyone might take comfort in it."

Wesley said, "Seems like kind of a brain twister to me."

"Oh, it's pretty straightforward, if you ponder it, perhaps pray on it awhile."

"I'm not much used to straightforward in my line of work. Everything's at angles, upside down and backward."

"Everything's a mystery, then," the priest said. "So much the better. I should think in that case a police officer would have no problem taking that on board. Even a Lutheran one."

Afterward, back at the cathedral rectory, Wesley told O'Connor he'd make his own way home, and he followed the priest to his door. "So what do I do?" Wesley said.

"About what?" the priest asked.

"About White."

"I should remind you that formally speaking I don't know any 'White.' "

"Sheesh. You sound just like him when he's doing his bad-memory routine." Wesley scowled. "This is serious. I don't know if he ought to be in prison, and he can't say. Or won't say. So what do I do?"

The priest said, "You must do what you think is right."

"Christ," Wesley spat. "Yeah, you heard me. Christ, Christ, Christ. Put that in your pipe and smoke it, padre. Christ . . ." Wesley stopped. His fists were clenched at his sides, and after a moment he loosened them as he stared at his feet. Then he looked up at the priest. "This world's full of suffering—people lost, people just up and gone. And all you've got to offer is a lot of smoke and bells and malarkey."

The priest said, "I suppose it must seem that way to you. I'm sorry." Then the priest vanished inside, and Wesley went and waited at the streetcar stop by the tunnel head.

After the letter from Veronica Galvin, after Lieutenant Horner and the priest had visited him, Herbert White was the recipient of more mail. The priest sent him a calendar with a note that he ought to meditate on the saints on their respective feast days. Then a few days after that, the guard who had been in charge of the paperwork when he'd first come to the prison brought him a pad of paper and a new pencil, saying that Lieutenant Horner had sent it. White thought that a fine thing, for he'd nearly filled the wall above the cot with writing, and he'd been warned to stop.

But he could not stop. He wrote every day, not a journal of what he had done, as he had compiled at home, for in Stillwater he never did anything that bore recording. Every day was like every other day, save for the saint whose name was on the calendar. Sometimes he transcribed what the calendar said about that day's saint, his or her particular virtues and tribulations, but mostly he wrote down whatever of the past came to mind: the details of every Saint Paul Winter Carnival he could recall; the way they'd taken inventory at Griggs-Cooper & Co.; the formulas for the chemicals he'd used in his darkroom; the names of the girls he'd been introduced to at the Aragon Ballroom; a chronology of the governors of Minnesota; a list of hats he had owned; the names of Nanna's cooks and maids; the complete text of Lord Tennyson's "Ulysses," which he was quite sure he'd gotten right, for the most part. He also sketched and mapped: the routes of the Saint Paul streetcar system; the floor plan of his apartment on Laurel Avenue; the trench lines of the Ypres salient. Herbert White did this every day, methodically, using both sides of every sheet in the pad. He did it not to pass the time but of necessity, for he saw that if his memory had come back all of a sudden, it might just as easily flee again at any time, and he wanted to get everything it contained down on paper.

Herbert White was also anxious lest he run out of paper, but he soon discovered that a fresh pad came every three weeks or so, courtesy, he was told, of Lieutenant Horner. Once he had assured himself that this would remain the case for the foreseeable future, he felt he could be more generous in allotting himself paper for purposes other than recording his memories. Sometimes he mused on various matters that seemed to him to be of importance; sometimes he thought he would write about Ruby Fahey, but then he would wonder what there was to say about her, for it was never the memory of her that had mattered to him but her presence, the fact that she was real and that he might be with her; that she was not merely Ruby but a palpable sign of an incomprehensible beauty, of a love he had no choice but to love.

Herbert had set the calendar upright on the floor under the window, next to the photograph of Veronica Galvin, as there were no nails or thumbtacks to put them on the wall. In addition to noting the various saints' days—together with brief biographies on the back of the page—the calendar marked the phases of the moon, and in this way Herbert White followed, or rather imagined, the conditions outside the window, which was now blocked by snow and debris. He could no longer see the star that had come at Christmas, but he could picture the moon, whether as utterly dark, as a sliver of silver ice, or as full, pouring down its light on the cloud tops.

In certain places the priest had marked the calendar, and he had done so at the box marking March 25, and White felt this ought to prompt some comment in his writing pad:

Today is the Feast of the Annunciation, according to my calendar, and the priest has written: "Pray especially to Mary on this day, and ask her to pray for you." I have not got this prayer business entirely clear—whether it is merely a kind of pondering or a kind of request or a sort of thanking. I suppose if my writing, which is to say my thinking made into memory, renders its subject its due, then it is indeed a sort of thanking, and I shall consider it such—it is my way of praying, however inadequate.

Having said that, I should remark that the upper page of the calendar for this month contains an illustration pertaining to this very day. It shows the Virgin Mary seated, with an angel addressing her. Mary looks to have been at some darning or embroidery, and there is a sort of ribbon issuing from the angel's mouth, with words written on it, the words, I suppose, that the angel is speaking, to wit, of course, that Mary has been chosen to give birth to God's son. (I knew some of this already; other information I have gleaned from the calendar.)

Speaking as an amateur photographer, I would say that Mary's expression and pose are quite striking. She does not seem taken aback or resigned to a fate imposed on her. Rather, it is a kind of obedient forbearance, as though she has determined that she will take this task not because her will has been dominated by His will but because it has become one with His will through a kind of strength that Mary herself already possesses. I think she must have been very strong and, at least in this picture, very beautiful, as beautiful as Veronica Galvin or, indeed, Miss Ruby. I wonder if it is somehow impious or untoward to notice that. It is at such times that I feel very mixed up about the difference between love and beauty—whether one loves on account of beauty or comes to see beauty on account of love. In any case, it seems impossible not to love this Mary as she is pictured here, at once daughter and mother, sister and beloved, perfectly serene and strong and compassionate.

I suppose one is meant to love her, that it is impossible not to love her. Perhaps that love, which the beauty makes inevitable, is what this prayer business is all about. Of course, that rather begs the question of whether one believes any of it, but then it seems that the question is itself beside the point. For the believing, the beauty of holding it in one's heart, is too beautiful to forgo.

Herbert White did not thereafter write often in this manner, for it still seemed to him important to get other things down. But he did often think of the angel with the ribbon issuing from its mouth, scrolled and curling as though it might be music, and sometimes he pictured his writing, his recording, in this way.

Shortly after that, about the middle of April, after the snow was melted, a spring work crew came through the yard outside his window, and in the course of its work cleared the leaves and debris from in front of it. Herbert White spent all that day and the next marveling at his view, although it consisted of nothing more than the high stone-walled quadrangle and the crew working within it. Sometime in the afternoon, he watched a ladder being set up against a very tall telephone pole. A man then scurried up the ladder and removed a large glass bulb from the fixture atop the pole, climbed down, and returned with another bulb, which he at last installed in the fixture.

That night, after the illumination in the cells was cut off, Herbert White saw his Christmas star again. Now he realized that it had been nothing more than the prison yard lamp all the time. But this did not deject him. He was glad to have it back—to see it bright against the glow of the moon, which rose and waxed just as his calendar said it would—for it was, after all, no less a light for not being a star.

Sometime later in April, when the last spindly icicle had fallen from the eaves of the roof outside the dining room of Wesley

Horner's little house, Wesley went outside, out the kitchen door and into his backyard. The first weeds and grasses were coming up amid the mud, thin and straggly like the wisps of a baby's hair. There was still some snow around the edges of the yard, huddled in pocked and dirty clots against the fence. Toward the center of the yard, twelve or fourteen feet from the kitchen door, lay the Christmas tree, its needles now a scabrous orange, like a bruise turning color, midway from yellow to violet. Its branches were draped with what seemed to be moldering seaweed and filthy tissue paper but were in fact strands of ribbon and yarn, odd shapes of colored paper and foil, threads of rotted or desiccated food, now bloated, drowned, and bled of color and form. Wesley had been following missing and unidentified persons reports from stations from Saint Paul to Spokane for some sign of Maggie, but this was all that had emerged of her from out of the winter, from beneath the snow.

The tree lay in the yard like a marker of a shameful deed: one that said he could deceive himself all he liked with notions that she had run off or been killed, but in truth he knew very well he had sent her—driven her—away, even if he could not precisely name the means by which he had done it. But he had neither the strength nor the will to get rid of the tree, no more than he could touch the full moon he saw rising, caged in the branches of the elm in the neighbor's yard. He imagined how cold it must be, how if he could hold it in his hands it would be like a ball of dry ice, searing his fingertips even as their own sweat locked him unalterably fast to it, so he could not let go.

When he went back inside, back to the kitchen table and his Luckies and his pony of Four Roses, he decided to call Frank McCarthy, to tell him he wanted to come up and see Herbert White.

The bucket smelled less noxious, more like humus than outright shit, and some kind of weed had grown up around the window, so that its edges seemed to glow with a green light. White himself was still pallid and had lost weight, and he rose and shambled toward Wesley like a polar bear after a very long and lean winter.

"How kind of you to come," White said softly, and cleared his throat, as if he was unused to speaking.

"Nothing to it," said Wesley. "Just thought I'd come and see how's tricks."

White's eyes widened, and he smiled. "Oh, I manage to keep busy, quite busy, really. And of course I must thank you for the writing materials."

"Think nothing of it. Ain't much else to do in here, is there?" Wesley said. "I mean, nothing much but think your thoughts. Might as well write 'em down."

"Indeed," said White.

"Actually, I wondered if I could, say, take a look. At what you been writing. Just for the heck of it. I thought there might be something that I could use to help you out, something maybe you remembered. That had a bearing on your . . . situation."

"Oh, indeed, it all does," said White. "And I'm happy for you to look." He reached under the cot and extracted two writing pads, their pages swollen with inscription, with the weight of White's pencil on their flimsy pulp paper. "These are the most recent," he said. "Please, go ahead."

Wesley set them on his knee and lit a cigarette, and then he began to flip through them, reading aloud now and then: "Griggs-Cooper & Co.—Our Part in the National Recovery Administration, 1933"; "Nanna's Weekly Menus, circa 1915"; "Winter

Carnival Ice Palace Memories, various"; "The Prettiest Girls I Have Known"; "Speed Records—Saint Paul to Chicago, Milwaukee Road, Burlington Route, et alia"; "Notes on the Leading Men of Miss Veronica Galvin"; "Photographic Papers—Velox versus Kodabromide"; "A 'Well-Turned' Leg: Toward a Definition"; "Thoughts on Saint John Bosco's Day"; "Plants Found in Nanna's Garden, with particular attention to roses."

Wesley continued to leaf through the first pad and then, stopping now and again to puff on his cigarette, the second. After a time, he looked up and said, "Herbert, what is this crap?"

"Well . . . it's what I write, isn't it?" White said, a little surprised. "What else could it be? There are two other pads, if you want to see. Plus this," he said, waving his arm toward the wall. Wesley leaned back a little on the cot and regarded the wall behind him more closely. It was swimming with tiny gray lines, like cracks in a pottery glaze, which Wesley recognized as White's writing. He looked back at White. "I just thought maybe you might remember something about those girls, something that might settle what really happened."

"Well, I do mention Miss Ruby in several places. As you must have plainly seen."

"I don't mean this stuff about her figure, or whatever it is. I mean about how she died."

"I've told you everything I know. Really I have."

"Suit yourself," Wesley muttered. "You've got a hell of a future, rotting in here."

"I never wanted a future," White said, and his eyes met Wesley's. "I wanted a past."

"You got a future whether you want one or not. Like the man says, time marches on."

"You sound rather like the officer who took down my confession," White said.

"Like Welshinger? That's a kick in the pants." Wesley threw his cigarette into the bucket, where it made a tiny sizzle.

White took the writing pads off the cot where Wesley had set them down. He smiled diffidently and said, "You see, these are my future, so to speak—recording the past, the things in my memory while I still have them."

"Some crummy pages nobody cares about, and this cell. That's quite a life, Herbert. Take a look around. This is nothing but a stinking shithouse with a bed in it. And you're locked inside."

White said, "It's not so very different from my darkroom at home. And I spent many happy hours there, happier than I knew."

"But you could leave it, Herbert. You could open the door and leave—go and be part of life, part of the world. You were in it. Now you're shut away."

White knitted his fingers together and examined them. "I'm not so sure about that," he said, and looked up again. "Maybe I was only looking at the world. It was just a photograph. But maybe now, in my . . . poverty, in my solitude, perhaps I'm in the world, truly, at last. I can feel it in my flesh, I can see it and smell it, and I have no other course but to love it."

"I'd say it smelled like shit, Herbert," Wesley said. "I don't want to insult you, but I think what you think you see isn't what's really there." He stood up to go. "Look, Herbert, I've just been trying to help, and there's a limit to what I can do."

"I know, though you must rest assured that I appreciate everything. I truly do."

"I'm sure you do. But I got to go now." Wesley banged on the door for the guard. "I got my own problems."

,

"Of course. I understand," White said. "I want to thank you for coming."

"Sure."

"And for the writing paper. I wonder if I might go on having it, if it's not too much trouble."

"Sure," Wesley said. "Whenever you want." The guard opened the door, and Wesley went out. In the guardroom, he stopped at Frank McCarthy's desk.

"So?" McCarthy said.

"Nothing," Wesley said. "Stark, raving nuts. Stir crazy. You should have told me, Frank."

"You didn't ask. Half of 'em down there is, sooner or later, at least for a while. If he gets too strange, hurts himself or anybody, we'll pull him out and put him in the hospital. If you want, I can kind of speed things up."

"Don't bother. Hell, he says he loves it. Leave him be," said Wesley. "It's the only thing I can do for him. That and keep the paper coming. Make sure he gets all he wants, okay?"

"Sure."

"Tell him it's me that sends it," Wesley said. "That I say hello, that I remember him."

When Wesley came home that night, he took out a pad identical to the ones Herbert White had been writing in and began to draft a letter. He put his ashtray at his right hand and his bottle and his glass at his left and set to work. He spoiled four sheets with mistakes and changes, and then, on the fifth, he was satisfied.

Dear Governor,

I was the arresting officer in the case that went to docket as *People* v. *Herbert W. White* in November last year. As you might have heard, the suspect pleaded guilty and was sentenced to life at Stillwater by Judge Kelly.

Except for circumstantial evidence collected by myself and my fellow officers, the state's case rested on White's confession. I was the officer who took down this confession, and after reflection, I believe the confession is false. I believe I applied undue pressure to White to confess and that he admitted to the charges against him under duress. I also think he was mentally ill at the time and has gotten more mentally sick in prison.

I therefore ask that you consider pardoning Herbert White, as all the other evidence against him was circumstantial. If you do not think he can be released, perhaps he could be confined in the state hospital instead.

I thank you for your consideration of this matter.

Yours very sincerely,

Lt. Wesley Horner

Wesley folded the letter in three and put it in the drawer with Rose's spools and bobbins, with the last of Maggie's pine cones and holly sprigs, now so dry that the tips of their leaves were as sharp as Rose's needles.

Wesley wasn't going to send the letter, not yet. It would be the end of his career, of any future he might have. But he wanted to make a clean breast of what had happened, even if only on a crummy pulp pad like Herbert White's. As for sending it, getting White out of his cell, out of prison—that wasn't what White wanted anyway, not anymore.

It was near the crest of summer, when the days were like boiling fog and the nights were sticky as tar, that Louise came home. She was sitting on the doorstep of Wesley's little house, with the same suitcase she'd left with five years before. Wesley saw her as he was coming up the street, home from the station, and he thought it was Maggie come back to him, and never in his whole life had hope so sung out in him as in that instant before he saw it was somebody else.

He wasn't sure who it was, once he had realized it was not Maggie, once his heart had fallen into his gut like a ball of cold iron. It almost could have been Rose, and then he thought it almost could be Maggie, but Maggie had never looked like this: Her hair was never quite that color, she had never held her legs bent beneath her, the calves angled from the thighs like legs that had held men fast between them, that had walked the world.

"Daddy?" she said, and then Wesley knew, and he stopped crumbling inside for want of her not being Maggie. He held himself very still, as if his heart were an egg he might crush in his hand. He just looked at her and nodded his head.

"I had . . . to come home," she said. "I couldn't take it— Chicago, him." Then she stood up, her hands folded together, and began to weep, looking at the ground. Wesley moved toward her, and he put his hand on her shoulder tentatively, like maybe he was touching something he wasn't quite sure he should touch. She drew herself into him, now sobbing, and Wesley said, "Weather couldn't be any worse down there than here," and laughed. Then he put his arms around her and held her, the sweat on his chin getting mixed with her tears.

Louise looked up at her father. She said, "I just want to come home for a while." She looked at him a bit longer, her mouth in an *o* of puzzlement. "Is that okay?" she said. "Will you take me in?"

"Like you never left, sugar," Wesley said. "Like you hadn't been gone a day. Hell, you got your room, just like you left it, clothes and all."

"It's okay? I'd cook and clean, pay room and board too. I figure I could get a job pretty easy, what with having worked in Chicago, at Marshall Field's and all."

"Bet that would impress the hell out of 'em at Schuneman's," Wesley said. "But don't you worry about that for now. You just keep me company. Living alone doesn't suit me." He held the screen door open and waited for Louise to go in. But she only went as far as the threshold, standing on her tiptoes and looking in as though over a high wall into the dark. Then she turned around and said with a look that made Wesley want to duck, "Daddy, where's Mama?"

Wesley's eyes fell to his feet, and then he looked up and said, "We better go in." He sucked air in between his teeth. "Lots happened while you were away. Your mama's gone, gone almost four years now."

He took Louise's arm under the elbow and steered her into the parlor where no one had sat for the better part of a year. She perched on the edge of the sofa and sobbed, holding her arms around herself, and shook as though her body was a tin roof shuddering in a windstorm.

He told her how Rose had sickened and faded and died. He walked her through it so it seemed as immobile as a house, so that the place where it all finished up seemed inevitable.

Then he said, "Didn't have anything to do with you. Cancer's cancer. Nothing to do with you at all." He said much the same thing again and again over the next half-hour until Louise's keening turned to snuffles. He knew it was a lie each time he said it— for he knew a soul could pretty much die purely for loss of another soul—but he kept saying it, tightening and loosening it like a tourniquet to her grief. And as her wracking eased, he felt no compunction about it. It was one of the soothing lies that fathers tell daughters, that parents of necessity tell children, the debts and afflictions they bear in secret, for love's sake.

After a time Louise stood up. She said, "You wouldn't mind if I looked around? For old times' sake?"

" 'Course not, sugar." He went ahead of her and turned on every light he could find. Louise looked down the hall and put her head around the door of her room, as if somebody might be hiding behind it. "Looks the same. Maybe smaller somehow. But just the same. Nice and clean. You do all this cleaning?"

Wesley said nothing for a moment. "Got nothing much else to do," he said. "Actually, I got me a girl to come in for a while. Guess she got me a little house proud. Even thought of taking the storm windows down this spring. Didn't do it, mind you. And hell, now it's nearly August, so what's the point?" Wesley laughed and Louise joined him, at first with tightness in her throat and then, at last, heartily.

Wesley had two pork chops in the icebox and a pony of Four Roses on the drain board. He'd figured to have both all to himself tonight, but he cooked Louise one of the chops and poured her a drink. She smoked her own Pall Malls and told him about Chicago, about life with the vacuum cleaner door-to-door man. It didn't take all that long to cover five years. They'd had fun for a while, and then he'd started to drink and cheat on her, while all the while she was bringing home three-quarters of their rent and groceries.

"He just wasn't a decent sort of man, when I got right down to it," Louise said. "Yelled at me. Hit me more than once."

"That ain't nice," Wesley said. He didn't ask her anything more about it. He'd left off being a detective all the time; maybe any of the time recently.

In the next few days, Louise settled into her room. She found the radio under her bed and wanted to know what the heck a nice new radio was doing hidden away like that. Wesley said he'd bought it and then decided he'd like the old one— "The one your mom liked to listen to while she ironed"—better. Truth be told, he said, he didn't much care for most of the radio programs these days.

Louise set up the radio on her bedside table, and in the evenings she played it, sitting on top of the bedspread, her legs still in nylon stockings from work at Schuneman's, smoking her Pall Malls. Sometimes she whistled along with the music. By the autumn, she wasn't home so much. She was going out with a young man she had sold a tie to, and by winter it was pretty serious. Then the door to the room sat open and the room was empty, pretty much as it had been for the last five years.

Not long after she'd first come back, Louise said some of her clothes were missing: nothing much—a blue and white dress, and a sweater, some socks.

"Must have given it to the Salvation Army," Wesley said. "You know how they come knocking, and you got to give 'em something to get rid of 'em. Wasn't anything that was a favorite of yours, a keepsake or something?"

"Oh, no. Just wondering."

"Truth be told, I didn't know that you were ever coming back. Figured you might hate me or something. So I guess I was keeping faith by leaving everything just the way it was," Wesley said. "Or I wanted something to remember you by."

"I never hated you. Or Mom, or anybody. I just got sort of swept up and swept away," Louise said. "Young love, dumb love, I guess. No hard feelings, though, okay? Everything all right?"

"Right as rain, sugar."

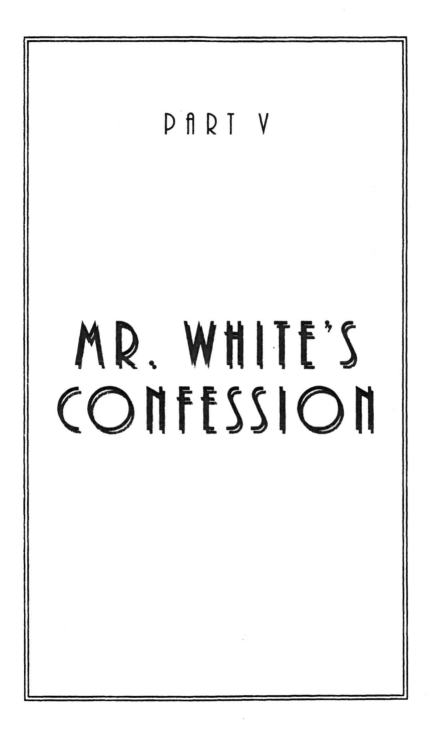

PART V

MR. WHITE'S CONFESSION

Tuesday, Day 243

July 9, 1940

Today is Saint Veronica's Day. I suppose she must be the namesake of Miss Veronica Galvin, and a very apt one it is! For it was Saint Veronica who offered Jesus a cloth to wipe his face when he was carrying his cross up to the place of crucifixion, and when he handed it back, it bore the exact likeness of his face, as though it were projected on a movie screen.

Now, I suppose anyone would say that it is at best a rather tenuous connection—indeed, perhaps, an altogether laughable one—but it has made me think not only of Miss Galvin and her motion pictures but of the photographs I used to make, for they too were projected images, albeit on paper and without motion. And I suppose one might say that what I am doing now with this writing is but another form of recording images, which is to say memories.

Having said that, perhaps I am saying that if all these things are images, then such images are all necessarily memories, and there is a kind of logic to that. For it seems to me that perhaps at bottom all our knowing, all our seeing, is limited to what we have remembered: What is to come is, after all, beyond our ken;

and what is happening at this moment, precisely now, we apprehend only after the moment is past, after it has become a memory. So memory is more than a souvenir of what was and is no more: It is in this sense everything we know and everything we have.

No wonder then that we cling so to memory and the images of memory—to photographs, to written recollections, and even to the movies, which are not only recordings, after all, but so often seem to me to be retellings of stories we in fact already know. Without memory and its images, we might forget not just our own past, our place in the world, but our very selves—that which gives us the sense of being. Yet we depend for that "reality" on representations and symbols of what, strictly speaking, is no more. Odd indeed.

Now, I wonder if Saint Veronica needed the image on that cloth to know that she had met Jesus, or if her recollection of that event in her mind would be sufficient. But I cannot imagine that she could ever have forgotten it, and perhaps the event made an ineradicable mark on her, such that it would always be with her, second nature to her, a memory deeper than memory. Perhaps thereafter, when she thought of Jesus, he was not so much a memory as a presence that took her ever unawares, like a bird that she might glance up and see on a branch, which has been there all the while. It would be not a representation or a symbol, like a photograph, but a sign, as smoke is a sign of fire and not a memory or an image of fire.

Perhaps all our striving and hunger in this world is for such signs, for that which is beyond memory, which is eternally present. And where we see it mostly, where it lays its finger upon us, is in beauty, which we know without prompting or recollection is as the smoke of the fire of creation, the word that immemorially recalls the memory of God.

It occurs to me that I have not written to Miss Galvin in some time, and I realize this is perhaps because, since my memory is working, I now know that she always sends the same letter in reply. But that is no excuse for being remiss. For I see that the words of the letter are only symbols and that the letter itself is a sign of a more important fact—that we know we are in each other's thoughts or, at the very least, that we are here in the world together.

Genl. Delivery

Port Angeles, Wash.

November 2, 1940

Dear Wesley,

I figure you must be wondering whatever became of me. To tell the truth, I was hoping you might forget about me. I have been aiming myself to forget about everything that happened last Xmas. In fact, the one that ran me out of town told me if I didn't forget it, he'd as soon kill me. That, and that he'd see you good as dead too. But I could not forget you so easy, not in my heart, not for true. I am sorry if I broke your heart. It broke mine to have to be going. But that is all I better say about it.

I am out here in Washington State. Matter of fact, I am living about as far west as you can go in the whole U.S.A. I come out here on the Northern Pacific, and that was quite a tale to tell. I knew Billy had people out here, and sure enough I found them and I found Billy too. He is working at fishing here and we are living in a little shack near the water, on the side of the big woods.

That brings me to the main part of my story here. I had a baby this last September, and Billy and me are raising him. I named him Wesley on account of you. I think of you all the time, but this way it will be like you are there when I see my boy. It will be like it was when I was cooking at the stove and I'd know you was behind me all the while without never having to turn around and look.

You know how you told me about that glass ball that White had when you took him in? Well, we got those here. They wash up on the beach, and I got two of them set up on top of the Franklin stove. When I see them I think of you and White. Not that you was two peas in a pod or anything, but that is what comes to mind. Also, those balls come all the way from Japan. I didn't know that, and when I picture it, it might as well be the other side of the moon.

Well, that's all for now. I got to go tend Baby Wesley. I will write you again, and don't you be shy either.

Your friend,
Maggie

Saturday, Day 367
November 9, 1940

Today is the first anniversary of my arrival at this place. I have been here one year, and as though in commemoration of that fact, I finished Mr. Dos Passos's *U.S.A.* yesterday—for the second time, in fact.

It is a very long book, long enough that one's memory of the beginning has grown rather hazy by the time one reaches the end. But that seems to me rather an advantage, for I shall shortly thus be able to begin to read it again with, as it were, a "clean slate": And as I am unlikely to be able to obtain any other books in this place, it is a fine thing to have one that suffices so nicely.

Moreover, when I begin to read again it will be like meeting all the characters for the first time, but also, as my memory of them crystallizes once more—develops, really, like a print in the tray—it will be like the return of old friends from long ago, come back like souls raised from the dead. For I have often felt in Mr. Dos Passos's book that the people in it are rather at the mercy of the great events transpiring around them; that they are lost in and overwhelmed by history, as if they were but leaves on its trees, blooms that flower, blow away, and are forgotten as others bud and take their places. And that strikes me as terribly sad, for it seems to me that even the worst of them are ultimately innocent. At one point, the book says of the character Eveline, "Maybe she'd been wrong from the start to want everything so justright and beautiful." But I don't think so, and that is why I write this and shall read and remember her story again—that is why I did everything I have done here. I suppose I thought that by remembering them, I could save them all, that they would be souls raised from the dead; not just Eveline but Nanna and Father, and even Miss Ruby.

For imagine that she might come back as Eveline will come back when I pick up Mr. Dos Passos's book again. Suppose she were to come back and it turned out she was not dead at all but had merely run away, having been threatened or intimidated as Veronica Galvin was in *Grand Central Terminal*. And suppose we then could at last be together, at least for a while. I suppose that then we might have been a family, as Father and Mother and I might have been a family, and then I suppose we might have had a child, a son, although this is nothing I have ever imagined before. But I suppose I would pick him up and set him upon my lap and tell him all about myself and about Father and Nanna. I would even tell him about Eveline and how they said of her, "Maybe she'd been wrong from the start to want everything so justright and beautiful." And I would tell him not ever to be afraid to want things exactly that way.

I imagine him years later with his own son, perhaps when I am long gone, and him taking the boy up into his own lap and saying, "Now, when I was your age, Father used to hold me just like this and tell me about his father and grandmother and the things he'd read and everything he remembered. But to tell you the truth, what I remember most were his big hands and his bow ties. He had a big neck too, and the ties they sold were always too short for him, so the wings of the bow were always rather tiny. Also, he had a big round head and not much hair, and what hair he did have he combed down very flat so his head looked like a globe with egg noodles pasted across the top. Did I tell you he'd been in prison? Mind you, he hadn't done anything. He was utterly innocent."

I see them going on in that way, and I don't even mind if he never gets around to telling the boy the tales I had told him when he was little. For perhaps the point of stories and of all remembering is not in the stories themselves but in the telling; in keeping faith with everyone who has come before us in this world, in marking the fact that we are here only on their account, that our presence, our life, is entirely the gift of their past. So it is with me, and so it would be with my son and my son's son: We are but memory enfleshed by love, the living sign by which all of us shall be known long after we are each forgotten, save by God, save in that sign. And that is all remembering remembers, it is all any tale can tell. It is enough.

WESLEY HORNER, 76, OFFICER WITH SPPD

By Charles Farrell

Wesley Horner, a former head of the homicide division of the St. Paul Police Department, died yesterday at St. Paul–Ramsey Hospital at the age of 76. The cause of death was cancer, according to family members.

Horner, who took early retirement from the department in 1941, was the investigating officer in many noteworthy murder cases of the late 1920s and 1930s, including gangland killings in the city's "wide-open" era during prohibition as well as the "dime-a-dance" slayings of 1939.

Horner was born in New Upsala, North Dakota. After his retirement from the police department, he worked in real estate sales for some years. He is survived by a daughter, Louise Baker of St. Paul, three grandchildren, and a nephew, Wesley Benoit of Port Angeles, Washington.

Mr. Horner is to be buried at Wittenburg Memorial Cemetery in Roseville.

HERBERT WHITE DID NOT FILL SCRAPBOOKS WITH CLIPpings anymore, but he saved this one. He would put it in his newest book, the one he'd started last year, in 1970, of which he'd scarcely filled four pages. He would put it in with that new kind of Scotch tape that you could write on, that looked like frosted glass and was supposed to last forever.

White did not know that Wesley Horner was still alive, or rather had been alive. White had been released from Stillwater in 1967, just shy of age sixty-three, just shy of twenty-eight years spent in prison. He'd been paroled mostly on account of his age, his self-evident harmlessness to society, and the expense of continuing to imprison him. There were also twenty-six letters from Wesley

Horner in his prisoner's file, forwarded from the governor's office, one written every year from 1941 onward, although White knew nothing of them.

When White came out of prison, his parole officer had a job for him as a box boy at the Red Owl Super Market on Grand Avenue. But he discovered by the by that the trust department at the bank had put half his money from Nanna into something called International Business Machines in 1942. He wouldn't really need to work at all, as it turned out.

He found an apartment on Holly Avenue, a block from his old place on Laurel. He went over to talk to the caretaker about whether anything might have been saved or put in storage from his former apartment, but the caretaker couldn't recollect hearing anything about it, not that he'd been there in 1939 and '40. But even with all his old prints, negatives, and scrapbooks lost and gone, Herbert White took up photography again. He bought a thirty-five-millimeter camera such as the photojournalists now used, and he set up a darkroom in his new apartment. He took photographs only outside now, landscapes or shots of patterns he'd see among the trees or buildings or in the clouds, but sometimes when he saw a particularly pretty girl he'd ask her if he might take her picture. And the girl would always say yes, for what could be the harm in indulging this large old man who somehow seemed small, a bald-headed infant in a homburg hat?

He walked in the places where he had always walked, the places he had walked in when he was a child, and he watched what he remembered of them wear away like flaking paint on the doorsill of the old earth. They'd closed the tunnel while he'd been in prison, when they'd gotten rid of the streetcars; they backfilled and paved over the tunnel head on Selby Avenue and gated up the tunnel mouth at the bottom of the hill. The last time he saw it, in the autumn of 1995, when Herbert White was older than anyone perhaps has a right to be, they'd blocked off the tunnel mouth entirely, replacing the fence with a wall. Curiously, the old paving remained, as did the rails, and he could picture them running into what was now utterly sealed away, to all intents and purposes a void. He found himself thinking of Ruby Fahey, trying to remember her face and the turn and the hollow in the back of her legs, but try as he might, he could not picture her but could only feel the ache of his emptied memory, the loss of what had recorded the loss of her.

He had been our recording angel all that while, all those years, but now Herbert White was no different from anyone else. His mind leveled itself as the world leveled what had been his habitations. Behind his right shoulder lay a barren field where Seven Corners used to be. Behind his left shoulder were the ribbons of the freeway, under which lay like fallow corn the dust of Wesley Horner's little house and the russet needles of Maggie's Christmas spruce. Herbert White himself was left alone with only the love of Ruby and without the clear memory of her; and that love was indistinguishable from all the other love and beauty that might be, from what glimmered in the trees, from the light shaking down out of the coloring leaves.

Discussion Questions

1. Because of his faulty memory, Herbert White can only recollect the formative experiences of his distant past—his father leaving to serve in World War I and Nanna's death—and the events of the immediate past, incidents that happened a few hours ago or perhaps the day before. Can what Herbert remembers be trusted? Is your memory any more trustworthy than this?

2. *Mr. White's Confession* is in many respects an examination of good and evil. In Herbert's world, what form does evil take? How does his understanding of it differ from Wesley's? From Maggie's? On page 22, Farrell, the newspaper reporter, says to Wesley, "Like the book says, none of us is without stain." Does that statement hold true even for Herbert, or is his character purely innocent?

3. Both Herbert and Wesley have unconventional relationships with women. What role does Maggie play in Wesley's life? How does Ruby affect Herbert? What is the importance of Herbert's "relationships" with film starlets like Veronica Galvin?

4. On page 122, Herbert says to Ruby, "I rather wish I remembered more, for your sake. So I could have more of a personality, more of a past." In what ways has Herbert's perception of his past formed him? How does Herbert's imperfect memory speak to the ways in which our own pasts, and our ability to remember them, shape who we are?

5. Most would agree that Herbert White's written confession to the murders of the two dancers was coerced and therefore not altogether true. Why do you think Herbert confessed?

6. On page 24, Herbert writes, "When I am making a print, when I am dodging or burning an exposure, I am gilding [places of beauty], illuminating them, or protecting the tenderest places from the scald of light, burnishing them with shadow. It is as close as I ever come to touching them, but I am helping them be—or rather become, for a photograph is only a moment of becoming." What do you make of Herbert White's hobby—what is the importance of his photography in relation to the novel as a whole? How does it relate to his problems with memory?

7. Robert Clark wrote Wesley Horner's sections of the novel using the conventions of hard-boiled pulp fiction. How does this technique fit with Wesley's character? How does this kind of writing differ from the journal entries of Mr. White? What kind of effect does this contrast have?

8. As the novel progresses, Herbert White comes to think about God more and more as his own circumstances steadily deteriorate. What do we learn from Herbert about faith? How does he come to his understanding of God? How does his relationship with God change throughout the course of the novel? What about Wesley? Although he doesn't think about God as intensely as Herbert does, he does experience a rebirth of faith. How does that come about?